Ashling

Isobelle Carmody

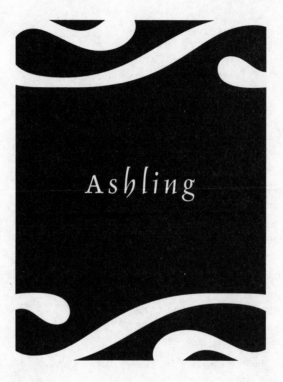

Ashling

Book Three of the Obernewtyn Chronicles

TOR®

A Tom Doherty Associates Book

New York

ASHLING

Copyright © 1995 by Isobelle Carmody

Map by Ellisa Mitchell

A Tor Book
Published by Tom Doherty Associates, LLC
175 Fifth Avenue
New York, NY 10010

Tor® is a registered trademark of Tom Doherty Associates, LLC.

ISBN 0-312-86956-8

Printed in the United States of America

For Shane

Acknowledgments

I would like to thank my editors, Kaye Ronai, Erica Irving, and Jenna Felice, for their enthusiasm and gentle precision, and Donato, for the enchanting mystery of his covers.

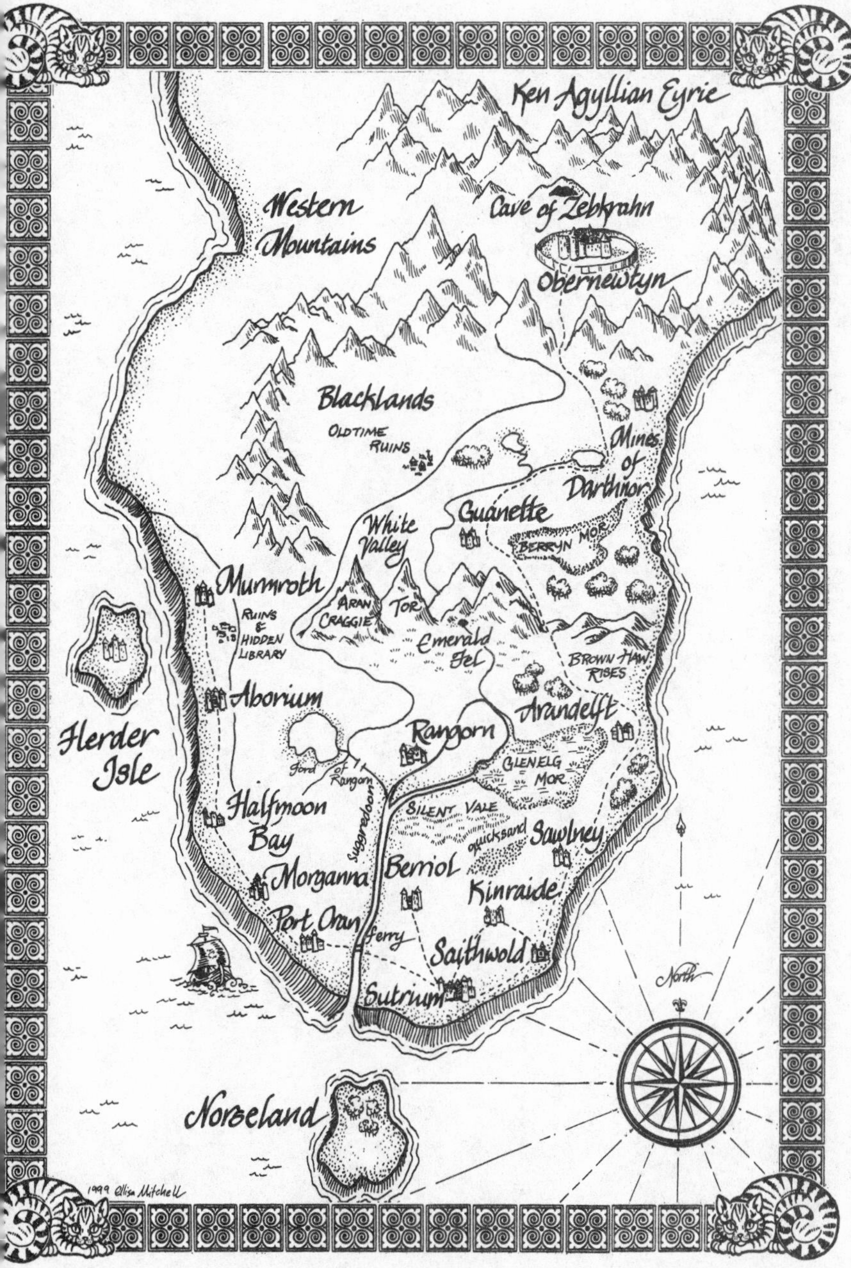
Ken Agyllian Eyrie
Western Mountains
Cave of Zebkrahn
Obernewtyn
Blacklands
OLDTIME RUINS
Mines of Darthnor
Guanette
White Valley
BERRYN MOR
Murmroth
ARAN CRAGGIE
TOR
RUINS & HIDDEN LIBRARY
Emerald Fel
BROWN HAW RISES
Aborium
Arandelft
Herder Isle
Rangorn
Ford of Rangorn
GLENELG MOR
Halfmoon Bay
SILENT VALE
Suggredoon
quicksand
Sawlney
Morganna
Beriol
Kinraide
Port Oran
ferry
Saithwold
North
Sutrium
Norseland
1999 Ellisa Mitchell

Ashling

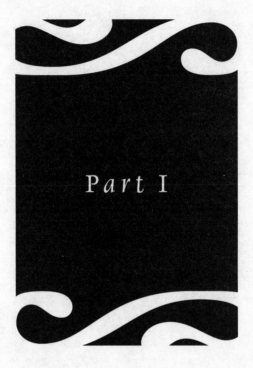

Part I

The Days of Rain

I

At *first sight, the gypsy woman appeared to be embracing the stake.* Her languid pose and mocking smile made it seem impossible that she was about to be burned. Blood dripped steadily out of slits from elbow to wrist, yet she showed neither pain nor fear.

The gray-gowned Herder lifted his palms to the sky as he chanted the purification prayer. The band sewn on the left sleeve of his gown showed he was a fifth-level priest. Not one of the inner cadre, but powerful nonetheless. He was old, bald-scalped and toothless, but his eyes glowed like live coals as he made the warding-off signs.

"Beware, demon," he hissed. "You have found an easy vessel in this foul gypsy's body. Yet I will drive you out."

Shockingly, the woman laughed aloud.

"You know I am not possessed, Herder. Say the truth and be done with it. Tell them that you burn me because I tried to heal a baby when your own worthless treatments failed."

The villagers, standing in a cluster about the stake, rustled like leaves with the wind passing through them, but no one spoke in the woman's defense, and none met her eyes.

"You used herb lore," the Herder said, with hissing emphasis. "It was such dabbling in forbidden lore that brought Lud's wrath onto the Beforetimers for their conceit. The Herder Faction heals with humility, trusting to Lud's guidance instead of sinful pride. The plagues were Lud's warning that the Landfolk tread the same dangerous and prideful path when they close their ears to the Faction, for Herders are the voices of Lud." He blinked and seemed to rein in his religious fervor. "The woman who allowed you to defile her child will also be burned for heresy."

A woman screamed and fainted, but no one moved to her aid.

"You are a fool," the gypsy's voice rang out. "You will not be allowed to burn her when the Council can have her sweating her life out in one of their stinking farms."

"I am a Herder. Lud and the Faction rules me, not the Council," the priest snapped. There was a sullen mutter from the crowd, but the Herder glared them to silence. "She invoked the black arts. Council lore grants me the right to burn her and any who treat with her."

"What black arts?" the gypsy demanded contemptuously.

The Herder turned back to her. "You told the woman her child would die and one day later it died. You cursed it and thereby revealed the demon within."

"I treated the babe, but saw quickly by its symptoms that it was too late to save it," the woman said. "It could not tolerate the potions you fed it. I told the parents it would die on the morrow, so that they might say their farewells and not waste the child's final hours."

"Do not waste your own final moments with lies," the Herder jeered, pushing a gloating smile into the woman's face.

Her hand snaked out suddenly and the priest wrenched back with a strangled cry. She gave a throaty laugh of triumph. "What are you afraid of, old goat? Do you think my gypsy skin might be catching?"

"Beg, demon! Proclaim your guilt, and the cleansing will be swift," he screamed, almost hysterical with fury.

She laughed again, a humorless bark. "Cease your ranting, old man. Kill me so that I don't have to see your ugly face anymore."

Even from the back of the crowd, I could see the Herder's face mottle with outrage. Then his lips folded into a vindictive smile. "Evil must not be permitted to think itself triumphant," he said silkily, and turned to speak a word to his acolyte, eyes glittering with malice.

The boy proffered a selection of long-handled metal tools.

"Th' bastard's goin' to brand her before he burns her," Matthew hissed into my ear, his highland accent thickened with anger.

"Am I blind?" I snapped. The amount of blood pooled about the woman's feet told me she would be lucky to live long enough to feel the flames of purification, let alone to be rescued, even if we could manage it. In spite of her defiance, her face was as white as smoke.

"We mun do somethin'," Matthew whispered urgently. He gestured to our gypsy disguise, as if it made some point of its own.

"Be silent and let me think." I sent the thought direct to his mind.

The sensible thing to do would be to accept that it was too late to save her, and withdraw before anyone noticed us. I looked at the gypsy again. Her chin lifted in defiance as the Herder approached with the brands.

I cursed under my breath and slid down from Zade's back, mentally asking the horse to stand quiet until I called. I told Matthew to turn the carriage and take himself back to the main road, not trusting his instinct for drama.

"Wait for me out of sight."

"What will you do? An' what about th' wheel rim?" he asked eagerly.

"It will hold," I said shortly. "If not, we'll free the horses and leave the carriage."

As soon as he was gone, I pushed my way through the crowd, at the same time extending a delicate coercive probe. Fortunately the Herder was not mind sensitive, so he was not aware of my intrusion.

"Where is her wagon?" I demanded aloud.

He swung to face me, eyes slitting at the sight of my gypsy attire. "By what right do you question a voice of Lud?" he snarled.

"By right of blood," I said.

It was Council lore that blood kin might speak in defense of their own. In the past, this had not stopped Herders doing what they wished and later making excuses to the Council for excessive zeal. But with the rift between Faction and Council, the priests' power had waned and they were less wont to openly flout Council lore. In any case it was only a stalling tactic, since I had no proof of kinship to the gypsy.

"Her wagon has been burned, as have all her Luddamned utensils and potions," the Herder said grudgingly, but his memory showed him rifling through the wagon and removing this and that piece before the thing was flamed. My probe slid sideways into a memory in which he had tortured to death the gypsy's bondmate and I shuddered inwardly.

"You have proof that you are related?" he demanded.

"All gypsies are brothers and sisters," I answered, not wanting to be caught openly in a lie.

"Do not taint my ears with the practices of your foul breed," he hissed. "I asked for proof of kinship—you have shown me none, therefore be silent."

I saw his mind form a plan to report me to the soldier-guards for

Sedition, thereby ridding himself of me in case I was related by blood. He turned back to the gypsy and snorted in annoyance at finding her hanging limply from her bindings.

Alarmed, I reached out a probe, but her body still pulsed with life. She had only fainted.

The Herder cast down the brand and reached for a torch to fire the woodpile at the foot of the stake. A great rage seared me. Throwing off caution, I reached into the bottom of my mind for the darkest of my Misfit Talents to stun him.

But before I could summon it, an arrow hurtled through the air to bed itself in the center of the Herder's sunken chest. He sucked in an agonized breath and clawed at the wooden stave, trying vainly to withdraw it. Then his eyes clouded and he collapsed, blood bubbling obscenely from his lips.

I disengaged my probe with a scream, almost dragged to my own doom by his swift spiral into death. Panting, I stared down at him in astonishment and, for a moment, silence reigned in the village clearing.

"The Herders will kill us all for this," a woman wailed, shattering the stillness, her eyes searching the trees for the archer.

"Not if we kill these gypsies and throw the bodies in the White Valley. We can say we saw nothing of what happened," a man began, but before he could outline his strategy, another arrow whistled through the air, piercing his neck.

He crumpled to the ground with a rattling gurgle.

That was enough for the rest. It was one thing to watch someone else die, and quite another to risk your own life. People scattered in all directions, crying out in terror.

I did not know who had loosed the arrows and there was no time to find out. Situated on the border of the high and lowlands, Guanette was visited regularly by off-duty soldierguards seeking amusement. At any minute a number might ride in and be drawn by the screams to investigate.

I rushed forward to the stake, ripping at the hem of my skirts. Fortunately the cuts on the gypsy's arms were shallow, since the aim of bloodpurging was to exact a full confession, not to kill. Still, the cuts were deep enough to drain her blood slowly. I bound the torn strips around her arms, automatically setting up a barrier to repel the chaotic wave of unconscious thought that flowed from the gypsy as our flesh met, then I cut through her bonds with shaking fingers, staggering as she fell heavily into my arms. A thick pot-metal band around her upper arm grazed my cheek.

All at once my hair was wrenched savagely from behind and I was pulled over backward, dragging the unconscious gypsy on top of me. For a second I lay still, winded, then the acolyte launched himself at me, renewing his attack, raining blows on my head, his eyes alight with fanatical rage.

"Demon gypsy! Holocaust scum! Halfbreed!" he screamed in a reedy voice. "They've killed my master! Soldierguards!"

Fighting free of the gypsy's dead weight, I shoved the boy hard, toppling him to the ground. He glared up at me, a handprint of the gypsy's blood on his chest.

"You will die for this," he hissed. "Lud has granted my masters great power to kill their enemies. One day we will destroy all of your kind, even the stinking Twenty-families."

I turned from him in disgust and hauled the woman to her feet. This was no easy task for she was tall and full bodied, her arms and upper body slicked with blood. By the time I had her upright, Zade had responded to my mental summons. From the corner of my eye I saw the acolyte's eyes bulge in astonishment as the horse knelt to receive the woman's body.

I groaned aloud as two soldierguards burst through the trees, wielding short-swords.

One dropped like a stone, pierced by another deadly arrow from my mysterious helper. The other soldierguard gave the dead man a sick look and flung himself behind a cart, scanning the treetops fearfully.

"Quickly, climb/get on my back," Zade sent, rising to stand upright. "Gahltha will be angered if you are harmed in my care."

Obediently, I vaulted onto him and wound my fingers in his mane, clamping my knees around the unconscious gypsy.

"Go!" I shouted and he leapt forward.

Using coercion, I locked my muscles in place, then turned my head, sending a second coercive bolt at the acolyte to erase all that he had seen. The block slammed into the boy's stunned mind, but not swiftly enough to prevent him throwing the bloodpurge knife.

It pinwheeled toward me with uncanny accuracy: blade, hilt, blade . . .

There was no time to summon the mental energy to deflect it but, instinctively, I threw my head backward.

A split second later the knife hammered into my temple.

I'm dead, I thought, and the world exploded into painful pieces, sending me into the abyss.

II

I was standing on a high plateau at the beginning of a path which led down into the terrible seared deadness of the Blacklands. It was night, and darkly quiet. The distant noise of liquid dripping slowly into liquid was the sound of seconds dissolving and falling away into the sea of time.

Far across the Blacklands I saw a flash of dull, yellowish light. I blinked and suddenly I was down in the valley, the bleary gleam I had seen from afar shining from the gaping maw of a tunnel cut into a rocky outcrop.

Entering, I walked until I reached the source of the light: two great carved doors set deep in a granite arch in the tunnel wall. Incredibly, though made of stone, the doors were ablaze. Opposite them, illuminated by the flame glow was a small grotto. I felt a surge of terror, for within it, dead and stuffed, was the Agyllian Elder, Atthis.

Then a voice spoke inside my mind; Atthis' voice from the past.

"Long ago I dreamed one would be born among the funaga—a seeker to cross the Blacklands in search of the deathmachines. One who possessed the power to destroy them . . . You are that Seeker. . . . Do not forget your promise to come without question when I call. . . . Speak of this quest to no one."

The voice had grown steadily softer and now it faded altogether.

"Atthis?" I whispered, but the bird in the grotto was as cold and silent as the rock, its clouded eyes gleaming with reflected flame.

I turned to face the doors again, for there was something about them that tugged at me. Before I could grasp at the elusive memory, they swung open. Standing in their fiery embrace was a radiantly beautiful boy with gleaming white hair.

"Ariel . . ." I whispered disbelievingly.

He gave a prim, cruel little smile. "Of course it is I. Did you really think we had done with one another?" His voice was as I remembered: high-pitched and taunting. "You cannot hide from me. But my revenge will wait, because there is a thing you must do for me."

"I won't do anything for you," I hissed.

"Do as you wish and you shall still do my bidding," he said with an angelic smile. "And when you have served my purpose I will kill you. Until then, let me give you a gift of pain to remember me by."

I backed away from him, but before he could do anything, Maruman leapt from the darkness into the tunnel. The old cat was huge—the size of a wild wolf—and he positioned himself between Ariel and me, tail twitching back and forth. Tattered ears flat to the skull, he gave a yowling cry. The sound lifted the hair on my neck.

Ariel's eyes widened with terror. He made a warding-off shape with his fingers and all at once, as if by moon fair conjury, it was not Ariel on the threshold of the burning doors, but another blond boy—Jik.

The sight of the empath filled me with sorrow and I barely noticed that Maruman had vanished.

"Promise," Jik murmured, the words barely audible against the crack of flame.

"Jik..." I began.

"Promise!" His voice drove into my mind, his eyes bright with dread.

Before I could summon the wit to answer, he lifted a hand to me. Instantly fire licked at his sleeve and leapt into his hair.

At last I found my voice.

I screamed, but the noise that came from my mouth was a slow, rumbling growl that shook the world.

∾

I opened my eyes and squinted in the dim light, my heart pounding sluggishly. The stone walls and tapestry hangings told me I was in the Healer hall at Obernewtyn.

I frowned. I had dreamed a long, oddly chaotic dream. And before that? The effort of trying to remember made my head throb.

Thunder rumbled ominously, and I looked out the window. Storm-clouds darkened the horizon, and distant flashes of lightning threw the edges of the high mountains into sharp relief. Closer, in the gardens, the tops of trees whirled in a dervish dance in the rising wind.

As if my waking had been a cue, it began to rain heavily. I started as someone moved to the window, blocking my view.

"So the Days of Rain begin," Rushton murmured.

The sadness in his voice startled me, for the Master of Obernewtyn rarely displayed emotion. I felt immediately uncomfortable at his presence. What was he doing here?

"It is as well this season is brief for, in truth, it casts a shadow on my spirits." Dameon's voice rose out of the darkness, with the slightly stilted formality of the high-born, for so he had been before being charged Misfit. The blind empath was the only one of us for whom the light made no difference. But what were they doing at my bedside? For that matter, what was I doing in the Healer hall?

"They feared for you, ElspethInnle," Maruman's voice whispered into my mind.

The old cat was curled by my head in his usual position. "You were in my dream!" I beastspoke him with a remembering astonishment. "But you were much bigger."

"Things are not always what they seem on the dreamtrails," he sent composedly.

"I wish it were summerdays all th' time." Matthew's voice came from a chair alongside the window.

"Softly," Rushton murmured. "You will waken her."

"I'm awake," I rasped. My mouth felt dry and furry.

Rushton turned on his heel to face the bed, and I could not see his face at all. After a momentary stillness, he crossed to a table, poured water into a mug and brought it to me. I was careful not to let our hands touch as I took it from him. Lifting my head slightly, I drank a mouthful, then froze at a sudden vision of a knife spinning through the air toward me.

"What happened in Guanette?" he asked.

I reached up to touch my temple. There was a slight lump on my head but no broken skin. Odd. I explained the sequence of events in Guanette after Matthew's departure, assuming he had told the rest. "The Herder's acolyte threw a knife at me just as I mounted Zade," I said at last. "I hadn't time to deflect it. The hilt must have hit me."

I had thought the blade struck me. I even seemed to recall the feel of it cutting into me. Or had that been part of the dream? I shuddered, remembering that in it Ariel had promised to kill me.

"Who would've thought that weedy acolyte would have had such a throw in him," Matthew marveled, with what seemed to me tasteless relish. "It's just lucky ye'd locked yer muscles in place. Zade brought ye to th' wagon absolutely frantic. I near died meself when I saw ye covered in blood. I thought ye were mortal wounded and raced back to Obernewtyn. Thank Lud th' wheel held. It were only when I got ye here that I realized it were th' gypsy's blood on ye, fer ye'd nowt a scrape."

Something in his description bothered me but I could not pinpoint it. I sat up, wincing as a bolt of pain struck my temples. Instinctively, I set a mental net to capture any hurt. It was a useful measure which enabled me to put off enduring pain. It was dangerous, however, if too much were allowed to build up.

"Is the gypsy all right?" I asked as the Healer guildmaster entered the chamber.

"It is difficult to tell," Roland answered gravely. "Because she lost so much blood she is weak, but the problem is more that her body appears resistant to healing."

I frowned. "How long have I been asleep?"

"Only a night. But you slept like the dead, if you will forgive the expression," the Healer guildmaster added dryly. "Obviously the blow concussed you, for there is only a slight abrasion at your temple. But you always did heal fast." He let a little pointed silence form, reminding me that he still believed there was more to the healing of my scarred legs the previous year than I had told.

"Fortunately it was not a serious wound," he went on, "since your mind will not allow healing access. But I suppose you know that well enough."

I hadn't known. It must be some sort of instinctive reflex. Roland shrugged. "Speaking of healing, you should be resting now." He looked around at the others.

"I'm goin'," the Farseeker ward said, rising. He looked down at me. "I'll tell Alad yer awake. Gahltha is madder'n hell that he was nowt with ye. He's convinced ye'd nowt have been hurt if he were."

"I hope he hasn't blamed Zade for what happened," I worried as the farseeker departed.

Dameon came to the bedside and as he bent to touch my hand I kept a tight hold on my emotional shield, wary of the empath's phenomenal Talent.

"I am glad you are safe, Elspeth," he said in his soft tones.

I nodded, forgetting he could not see, but he did not wait for an answer, gliding from the room with the slow grace that was caution, but which sometimes appeared to be instinct guiding him in compensation for his blindness.

Roland glared at Rushton.

"A moment," the Master of Obernewtyn said.

The Healer guildmaster shook his head in exasperation and moved away.

"You seem to go out of your way to try to get yourself killed," Rushton admonished gently, pulling a chair to sit by the bed.

From this angle, a lantern on the far wall cast enough light to show me the craggy plains of his face, but it was not possible to make out his expression. Nevertheless there was an intimacy in the moment that filled me with discomfort.

Maruman snorted derisively and curled back to sleep, for human emotions irritated his senses.

"I had no choice," I told Rushton awkwardly, wishing Roland had not left us alone.

Rushton's feelings for me had been distorted during a partial mind-bond we had undergone during the battle for Obernewtyn. Once, injured and delirious, he had called me his love. To my relief, he had not spoken of it since. Rushton had Misfit Talent but it was latent, and I reasoned that his feelings for me were the same. Nearly suffocated already by his solicitude, I had no desire to face the restrictions I felt sure would arise from waking his overt affections. Besides, there was no room in my life for such things.

"You know you talked in your sleep," Rushton said unexpectedly.

My heart beat faster at the thought of what I might have said. "I dreamed. It made no sense."

"You called out Ariel's name."

I heard again the dream—Ariel's promise to kill me—and felt chilled. "He can't hurt us while he is locked up in the Herder cloisters as an acolyte," Rushton said, guessing accurately at my thoughts.

If he is in a cloister, I thought. That was what we had heard, but I could not believe that Ariel would have tied himself up to an organization weakened by its estrangement from the Council. Ariel had always sought power, and a Herder acolyte would be little more than a lowly servitor for his masters.

"You said Jik's name too," Rushton went on.

I felt abruptly depressed. "I dream of Jik often. I wonder what it means."

"Too much death is all it means," Rushton said sharply. "That is the way of the world and you have to accept it. What happened to Jik was not your fault, Elspeth. No one could stop a firestorm. You should not judge yourself so harshly."

"I don't," I snapped. "My dreams judge me."

"Well, what are dreams but tricks of the mind?"

"Are they?" I asked coolly. I was less convinced of that. Sometimes dreams were gateways through which messages might come. Beasts called them ashlings: dreams that called.

Thunder rumbled again and Rushton glanced back over his shoulder at the sky, just as a distant flash of lightning illuminated the clouds, and the slanting gush of the rain. "The storm is getting closer," he murmured.

I took advantage of his inattention to think of a subject that would turn the conversation to less personal matters. "Did Matthew make sure he wasn't followed when he brought me back here from Guanette?"

Rushton turned back from the window. "The only person he saw leave was an older gypsy who rode hell for leather toward the lowlands. He is almost certainly the one who shot the arrows. I suppose he took you both for true gypsies and for some reason expected you to have gone that way. Fortunately, he did not take it into his head to track the wagon. By the time he realizes his mistake, the trail will be too old even for a gypsy. Just the same, I will ask Garth to have his coercers keep their eyes open so they can turn him aside if he does appear."

"I'm surprised the other soldierguard didn't come after me."

"I expect the gypsy put an end to him and to the acolyte. The villagers are probably still arguing about who should report the whole thing. It wouldn't surprise me if they had not even removed the corpses."

"The queerest thing was how frightened the villagers were of the

Herder. I thought the Faction had lost influence, but you would not have thought so to see them cowering."

"The plague has restored their power," Rushton said.

I frowned, remembering that the Herder in Guanette had spoken of the plague. It had erupted the previous year in Aborium or Morganna, spreading rapidly to all the populous coastal cities, and killing one in three who contracted it. Those who survived bore hideous scarring.

In the aftermath of the disease, there had been almost no one to work the farms and this had resulted in terrible shortages which had seen hundreds starve, and the shortages continued as many of the farms still lay abandoned and unproductive. We had seen little of its impact in the highlands, because it had barely touched the more remote parts of the Land.

"They claim it was a punishment on the Land for the treatment of the Herders," Rushton said, "and they keep the fear alive by saying that it will happen again unless they are obeyed."

I nodded, then wished I hadn't for the movement set up a dull throbbing ache in my head. "The Herder's acolyte said Lud had given his masters great power to smite their enemies."

"I must send word to the safe house in Sutrium, and ask Domick to look into the relationship between the Herders and the Council. At his last report, they were still at odds and I will be happier if that is still so," Rushton murmured.

To my relief he rose, his thoughts absorbed by these larger concerns. "I am thinking of sending someone down to make contact with the safe house. Domick's reports have been scant of late, and he has sent no word yet about how our offer of alliance was received by the rebels. I will speak of it at the next guildmerge if I have no word from them by then."

Briefly his eyes returned to me. "We will also have to decide, too, what to do with your gypsy when she wakes."

"If she wakes," Roland said, coming over determinedly.

Rushton nodded distractedly and allowed himself to be ushered out.

I lay back, weary and curiously depressed. Rushton had been right about one thing—there had been too much death. Grieving for it had drained the heart and soul out from me, and sometimes I felt as if all that was left of me was a pale, shadowish wraith. And now the gypsy might die too. Well, I had known that even as I strove to save her.

I looked out to the mountains almost lost in the blackness of the stormy evening, and wished for the thousandth time that Atthis would call, and that I might begin to live and act, instead of waiting.

III

Lantern light glimmered on patches of wet, black stone, dulling the pallid glow emanating from a thick phosphorescent crust on the rock wall.

Fian reached out and prodded gently at one of the scabbed mounds and a cloud of glowing insects rose, exposing uneven patches of bare rock as they flitted away into the echoing darkness.

"Do ye know these little beggars eat th' holocaust poisons but are nowt poisonous themselves?" he murmured.

I was startled at that, but did not comment. There was no reason to be silent, yet the thought of the mountain of stone pressing down on top of the subterranean cave network seemed to compact the darkness and thicken it, leaving no room for words.

I looked back, searching in vain for a glimpse of daylight but even the rock shelf we were walking along vanished into the shadows a few steps behind. The ledge had been laboriously cut out of the cave walls by the teknoguilders, and was designed to run from the White Valley entrance, shaped by the flow of the upper Suggredoon River, around the cavern walls just above the level of the subterranean lake. In spite of the constant flow of water from the Suggredoon, the lake remained at the same level because a steep channel offered an outlet through the other side of the mountain to the lowlands.

The only other way to move about the caverns was by raft, poling along the straight, narrow waterways between buildings that, leagues below, were streets. Clusters of the strange, glowing insects that were the cave's sole inhabitants lit segments of the stone walls and crumbling buildings, reflecting them in pale disconnected shimmers on the dark water, but the majority of the dead city and the caves that contained it were sunk in eternal night.

As ever, I could not help wondering how the city had survived the shifts in the earth, that had buried it under a mountain. How had not the enormous stone dwellings, hundreds of floors high, been crushed in the geological upheavals of the Great White? Was it yet another impossible feat of technology on the part of the Beforetimers that kept the city intact?

Or had fate saved the ancient city for some purpose of its own?

I shivered.

"This way," Garth panted, an undercurrent of excitement in his tone. He waved the tattered map vaguely ahead and moved through the labyrinth of broken stone with an energy and agility that belied his enormous bulk.

Behind him came the Teknoguild ward, Fian, with Rushton and myself at the rear. We were moving in single file, because the ledge path was too narrow to walk two abreast. I stared at Rushton's back wondering what had possessed him to permit an expedition of guild leaders into the least accessible water caves. Ordinarily he was violently opposed to our taking part in anything dangerous, considering us too valuable to be risked. His admonition to me in the Healer hall after the rescue of the gypsy in Guanette showed that this attitude had not changed.

For a moment my thoughts slipped back to the gypsy woman, pale and fading, baffling the Healerguild with her refusal to heal or waken.

I had been returning from a visit to the Healer guildmaster to check on her, when Rushton had summoned me to say that Garth had requested our presence on a journey into the caves under Tor the following day. I had been genuinely astounded at his apparent willingness to acquiesce. The fat Teknoguildmaster must have presented a compelling case.

It would have been nice if either of them had thought to tell *me* what we were supposed to be going to see, I thought with a flicker of irritation.

I glared up at the broad space between Rushton's shoulders thinking he was as high-handed as ever, ordering me to come without giving me a reason. As if he felt my gaze, he glanced back, but I let my eyes fall quickly.

"Damn!" he muttered, as he stumbled in the darkness. "Garth, how much further is this?"

Garth grunted something unintelligible from ahead and Rushton stumbled and cursed explosively again.

"Nowt far," Fian assured us, holding his lantern higher. His eyes met mine fleetingly over Rushton's bowed head, gleaming with amusement.

In spite of my mood, I found myself smiling in response. There was something irrepressible about the highlander. His eyes sparked with intelligence and a wry humor that stopped him being as painfully earnest as so many of his guild, though, if anything, it was rumored he was more foolhardy than the rest in his quest for knowledge. He was one of the few at Obernewtyn who did not treat me with stultified awe.

We came to a place where a brief murky stretch of water separated the ledgeway from a sloping island of rubble formed by the collapse of one of the towering Beforetime monoliths. Dark water lapped sluggishly on the makeshift landfall. Garth leapt across the intervening space with a grunt, and on the other side made his way to the foot of an intact building. The light from the lanterns reached no further than the row of square windows on the second level, before black shadows obscured the floors above. Most of the buildings in the underground city were submerged, excepting a few top floors. This had meant the only way to enter them was via a window, or by making a door. But at this end of the caverns, the ground sloped up so that almost all of the towering buildings were exposed. What made the area so dangerous was the possibility of a hundred-floor, stone building collapsing without warning.

As we approached the building, I saw that a hole had been knocked in its immense wall.

"This is it," Garth wheezed, flapping his hand in a flourish at the construction before us. "All five-hundred floors. Oh, you needn't worry," he added, seeing my look of horror. "It's quite stable because a good deal of it is buried in the rock above and behind. Including what would have been the front door. The astonishing thing is that we discovered this at all, especially with so much of the city under water. Of course, the very fact that so many buildings are still standing is incredible in the first place. We are becoming convinced that this city was one of the last built before the holocaust. The degree of technology here is far superior to that of other ruin sites and may well explain how this city survived when so many others did not. But there are certain strange facets to the architecture..."

"Garth, get on with it," Rushton said brusquely.

The Teknoguildmaster frowned at him. "I was simply making the point that the chance of us just happening on this was so unlikely, that one might be forgiven for thinking it was ordained."

"Happening on what?" I asked.

Garth ignored this. Giving Rushton an offended look, he turned to enter the building. I glanced up and the row of empty windows seemed to look down like eyes.

"Elspeth, are you all right?" Rushton asked, glancing back at me.

I flinched, as if his hand instead of his voice had reached out to me, the note of concern in his tone quashing a momentary surge of apprehension.

"I'm fine," I said tersely, and stepped through the gap and into a smooth, straight hallway. The last thing I wanted was him fussing over me.

"It took an age to knock th' hole in the wall," Fian said, coming through after us with the second lantern. "Them Beforetimers built solid."

"Our main fear was that we might destroy something irreplaceable by knocking a hole in the wall," Garth explained.

The building was cast along the lines of all Beforetime constructions, walls and floors bare, squared and uniform with no ornamentation. The Beforetimers were admittedly inspired at construction, but they lacked imagination.

Garth led us along the hall and up three featureless gray flights of stairs. Stepping out of the stairwell onto a small landing, the Teknoguild-master lifted his lantern to reveal that the wall facing us had words carved into it. They read: Reichler Clinic Reception.

I stopped dead.

My mind rushed back to the moment when I had found the book in a Beforetime library called *Powers of the Mind*. Standing in another ancient darkness I had read enough to understand that there had been Talented Misfits *before* the holocaust. The book had spoken of tests performed at the Reichler Clinic which proved conclusively that human beings in the Beforetime had possessed Misfit Talents, though these had been largely latent. It concluded forcefully that, in time, more and more people would be born with such powers, though it would take a great catalyst to release them into the conscious mind. We had taken this as proof that we were not mutated freaks, as the Herder Faction and Council claimed, but a natural progression in human evolution. And what greater catalyst could have occurred than the Great White?

The teknoguilders had regarded the book with skepticism after the initial euphoria, however, fearing it might merely be one of the fictions the

Beforetimers had produced in such number. But the discovery of the actual Reichler Clinic must resolve all doubt.

"Worth a bit of a walk through the dark, eh?" Garth sounded pleased by our reactions. "Of course, we knew from the book Elspeth found that the Reichler Clinic was somewhere in the mountains, if it existed. I must admit I had thought it would be located in the high mountains—perhaps even in our own valley." He poked at my arm. "I thought since you discovered the book and argued so strongly that it was true, you should see this, my dear," he added.

"Strange to think of Beforetimers comin' here to be tested to see if they was Misfits," Fian said dreamily.

I felt a strange chill at the thought that, a thousand years before, a girl like me might have come to the clinic, wondering if she was a freak because she could use her mind to speak to animals or to other people.

Garth led the way through the door alongside the sign and we found ourselves in a large room with metal benches. Windows along one wall opened to the darkness of the caves while along the other walls were a line of the unmistakable box-like metal structures that were Beforetime machines. These were smaller than the ones in the Teknoguild cave network.

"We know the Reichler Clinic was a paranormal research center," Garth said, in a lecturing tone of voice. "Paranormal was a Beforetime word for Talented Misfit. As Fian said, people would come here to be tested. We had no expectation of finding the clinic and, once it was found, it never occurred to me that we would find much in the way of information because damp has destroyed all but the most impervious materials in the city, and even they will not resist it forever."

"Garth..." Rushton began.

"Patience," Garth said, as if Rushton were an importunate novice. "As I was about to say, I did not expect to find anything here, but I was wrong. It appears that the people who ran the Reichler Clinic were forward thinking, and they sealed much of their information in a slippery, waterproof transparent material they called plast." He bent down with a grunt and opened a cupboard, lifting out a sheaf of what first appeared to be pieces of paper. On closer examination, they proved to be made of some sort of pliable material. There were words on the sheets, but I could make nothing of them.

"The plast-covered paper is absolutely impervious to water, although it is not resistant to heat. As you see, a good deal of the matter contained on the sheets is in one of the peculiar linguistic codes the Beforetimers were so fond of using. Hiding their information in this way always seemed to me a paranoid and pointless business but, as it transpired, they had cause to be careful and secretive. My guild is beginning to fathom the codes and these sheets are in one which the Beforetimers called Jerman. Fian has specialized in this code and he was able to translate enough to come up with some very odd intelligence—not about the Reichler Clinic, but about another Beforetime organization." He nodded regally at Fian, who took up the narrative.

"I believe th' code was used to store information that th' folk who ran th' Reichler Clinic wanted to keep secret," the highlander said. "I've only just begun decodin' th' plasts but it's clear from what I've read so far that they wanted to conceal th' fact that some of th' Misfits they tested were not latent."

"Conceal it from whom?" I wondered, and was startled to realize I had spoken aloud when Fian nodded.

"That's what got to me too. Why would they want to hide what was basically proof of th' things they wrote in that book ye found? Th' answer was in th' plast sheets. Th' Reichler Clinic were bein' investigated by a powerful organization called Govamen, which was connected to huge weapon tradin' houses that made a profit out of sellin' weaponmachines. Govamen was supposed to be stoppin' wars an' findin' other ways to resolve conflict between Beforetime Factions, but in reality it promoted war and reaped coin from people who wanted th' wars to go on—namely th' weaponmakers. Of course, th' connection between Govamen an' th' weapon tradin' houses was illicit. Th' Reichler Clinic folk learned of it by chance when they was tryin' to find out why they were bein' investigated."

"You mean, this organization conspired to promote war for profit?" Rushton demanded.

"I would not go that far," Garth said. "However it does seem to offer a solution as to why the Beforetimers had so many wars. It is a thing that has always troubled me about them."

"I still don't understand what this had to do with the Reichler Clinic hiding things," I said. "It wasn't forbidden to be a Misfit then, was it?"

"No. But th' Reichler Clinic people learned that th' part of Govamen investigatin' them was devoted to research an' development of paranormal abilities as *weapons*," Fian said. "This was th' symbol of th' research cell from Govamen."

He interrupted himself to point to a tiny picture denoting three minuscule birds flying in an endless spiral around a word I could not interpret.

"Look closely," Garth invited.

I did, and my eyes widened at the realization that the birds pictured were Agyllians—Guanette birds, as Landfolk called them.

"Fascinating, eh?" he demanded.

"Yes," I agreed faintly, thinking he had no idea how fascinating!

The Land resonated with myths about the red birds, and they were considered to be virtually extinct. But I knew that they dwelt in nests on high citadels of stone in the tallest mountains, because they had once brought me there and saved my life. The Elder of the birds, Atthis, had told me that they had existed since before the holocaust. I wondered if it could possibly be a coincidence that their image adorned material produced by the mysterious organization called Govamen, with its sinister connections to weaponmachine makers.

"Th' section in Govamen that used this as their mark," Fian tapped the triple bird design, "had apparently gone a lot further in its paranormal research than simply testin' th' minds of volunteers. It had actually tried to alter th' brains of animals to produce artificial Misfit Talents. Seems they had some spectacular initial results that came to nowt, before movin' onto experimentin' on humans. From what I have translated, th' Reichler Clinic people feared Govamen's interest in th' clinic meant they had th' idea of usin' th' people that they had tested as latent Misfit Talents. An' by usin,' I mean, kidnappin' an' usin' against their will."

I felt sick. That meant Misfits had been no more safe in the Beforetime than we were now. Perhaps it would always be so.

"This is all very interesting," Rushton interrupted. "But you could have told it to us safely and simply back at Obernewtyn. I presume there is some reason you have dragged us into this miserable place?"

Garth sighed. "All right. I could have told you what I am about to show you too, but it is so momentous I felt you would wish to see it. Perhaps I was wrong."

The fat teknoguilder moved to the other end of the room and as the light from the lantern he carried touched it, I could see a mural had been carved into the far wall depicting a mountain scene in perfect relief and intricate detail. It was a magnificent work, yet it seemed vaguely familiar.

"It's Obernewtyn," Rushton said in a stunned voice. "Or at least, it is where Obernewtyn is sited. The same spot. The trees are different but you can tell by the positioning of the mountains. But why on earth would its image be carved here?"

"I think ye'll find th' answer to that when ye read th' inscription on th' wee plaque," Fian said in an excited voice, pointing to a small metal square with raised lettering on the wall beside the mural.

Rushton leaned closer, and I heard him suck in a startled breath of air.

"What is it?" I demanded.

He gave me an unseeing look and I slipped past him to see for myself. The words read: Presented to the Founder of the Reichler Clinic, Hannah Seraphim, by her devoted admirer, Jacob Obernewtyn.

"Seraphim," I whispered, staring at Rushton. "That's *your* name, and Obernewtyn... What can it mean?"

He opened his mouth to speak, but abruptly the dazed look of amazement faded into a frown. "Listen," he said, tilting his head.

Then we all heard it. Someone was calling out.

"It's Matthew." I recognized the farseeker's voice.

I crossed to a window and peered out. From above, the watery caverns looked even more eerie. I spotted the ward by his lantern light bobbing along the ledge path, and shouted to him that I would come down. My voice echoed weirdly, reverberating between water and rock.

"I told him to do a routine scan of the villages for new Misfits," I explained to the others. "Maybe he's found someone."

"Be careful," Rushton cautioned.

I nodded impatiently and hurried back downstairs, wondering why after so many rescues he felt the need to warn me to take care.

Matthew looked so relieved when I joined him on the ledge, that I realized he had something more than a wild Misfit Talent to report.

"What is it?" I demanded, panting slightly.

"Ceirwan farsought me," the farseeker said. "He says ye mun all come back at once. Maryon's had a futuretellin' vision about th' gypsy woman we rescued."

IV

We *rushed back to Obernewtyn, only to discover that soon after her request* that we be sent for, Maryon had fallen into a second futuretelling trance from which she had yet to emerge. The Futuretell guilden had been unable to tell us anything more about his guildmistress's futuretelling, other than that it concerned the gypsy I had rescued and the future of Obernewtyn.

There had been nothing for it, but to go on with other matters until Maryon awoke. The whole affair completely overtook the excitement of finding the Reichler Clinic, and as we made our way to the kitchens for a late nightmeal Rushton asked me not to speak of the finding, until the Teknoguild had prepared a presentation.

"It seems strange to think of your being related to the very people who were interested in Misfit powers in the Beforetime," I murmured. "Do you suppose Jacob Obernewtyn built this place?"

Rushton shook his head. "Lukas Seraphim built Obernewtyn as it is now, but I remember Louis Larkin once telling me that my great-great-grandfather had built it on the ruins of an older building. It's my guess this Jacob built the original house that stood here."

"I wonder why Hannah Seraphim started the Reichler Clinic in the first place."

Rushton gave me a look. "It is a long time past and her world is dead. The teknoguilders' discovery of the Reichler Clinic is useful only in that it confirms absolutely that there were Misfits like us in the Beforetime. We have the present to deal with and that is quite enough without wasting time on historical puzzles. I am far more concerned to find out what a nameless gypsy could possibly have to do with Obernewtyn."

The Teknoguild discovery meant he could trace the line of his descent back to the Beforetime—he must surely be the only person alive who could do that, yet it was nothing to him because he was only concerned with the present. But he was wrong about the past being irrelevant. Past, present and future were linked by a thousand invisible threads. I existed in the present and yet my life was bound up in waiting for the future, to fulfil a deed whose seeds were sowed long ago in the Beforetime.

I did not sleep that night for wondering what had been so important it had necessitated our immediate return.

The following day, Maryon had still not wakened and I was distracted from my own guild's affairs by a growing apprehension that her untimely unconciousness was delaying the transmission of some vital news. Like Rushton, I could not begin to imagine what the gypsy had to do with Obernewtyn's fate, yet I felt it was somehow my responsibility because I had brought her among us.

∾

"Guildmistress?" Ceirwan's voice broke into my thoughts.

I blinked and became conscious of the room about me filled with the gray daylight that characterized the Days of Rain, and of the two farseekers sitting opposite staring at me.

My mind had drifted yet again and I shook my head in annoyance.

"I am sorry." I looked at the young farseeker novice beside the blond guilden. "Go on, Aras, you were saying you have thought of a new method of linking up farseeking minds."

The girl nodded eagerly. "Guildmistress, this new method is not like the old one, where a group of farseekers focused all of their energy through one mind."

She drew a star on the paper before her to represent the traditional mindmeld.

"The old way is limited because the central mind that focuses the whole thing can only hold so much energy." She drew a single beam radiating out from the star. "This merge enabled us to farseek maybe five times further than a single mind—no more. The new way of linking will enable any number of farseekers to contribute power to the overall merge. That means the distance over which we could farseek would be virtually limitless."

"Go on," I prompted. "How does it work?"

Aras drew a long line beside the star, with conjunctions at regular intervals.

"Like this. In a line rather than in a star shape. There is no need for a central mind to focus. All it requires is a single linear link between three people. That's the basic unit, but you can have as many units in it as you want."

"I don't see the point," I said. "The whole aim of a mindlink is to increase farseeking distance and power. As far as I can see, each of the farseekers linked into this sort of string would be locked into a small triple mindmeld. That will not increase the power of a single unit by more than a few times. And without a focusing mind, even linked, these triple melds could not combine their power into a larger pool of energy."

Aras looked disappointed at my reaction. "But you would not need any more energy. The merge can be used as a conduit. Each triple unit can link with another and then a single farseeker not connected into it could slide along the whole length—right from one end to the other, directing the line ahead wherever they wanted to go. To increase the distance would only require more farseekers joining the link."

I took a deep breath, seeing what she meant at last. Ceirwan was right. The idea was revolutionary. It could eventually offer us a way of reaching from one end of the Land to the other in a single farseeking leap.

"Have you tried any of this out?" I asked.

Aras shook her head, tossing her dark curls. "I'm not so good at doing things as I am at thinking them up," she said, looking a little crestfallen.

"You've done a wonderful job," I said firmly. "You just go on thinking up new ways to do things. There are plenty of us who don't think so well, to test out your theories."

Aras beamed. "Thank you, guildmistress."

I repressed a sigh at her reverent tone.

My dramatic return from the high mountains the previous year on Gahltha and the seeming miraculous healing of my burn-scarred legs had turned me into an object of reverence among many of the Misfits. My appearance had been greeted with astonishment and almost superstitious awe because everyone had believed me dead. Refusing to speak of where I had been and how I had been healed had bestowed an air of mystery on the whole matter that only made it worse.

In a way, the reaction of those at Obernewtyn had made me a Misfit all over again; a privileged outcast with too many secrets.

"All right, Aras, you can go now," Ceirwan told the girl.

She bobbed her head and hurried out as the guilden turned to me. "Do you think it will work?"

I recalled my mind to the possibilities inherent in Aras's mindlink with some effort. "I don't see why not, though it will take some practice. Remember how long it took us to perfect the old mindmeld, and how few minds could act as a focus?"

Curiously, Rushton's mind had the greatest storage capacity.

As if reading my thoughts, Ceirwan said, "Funny to think that Rushton has the biggest capacity for holding mental energy of us all, but that he can't use the power because his Talents are latent."

"I doubt he finds it funny," I said, knowing Rushton regretted his inability to use the Misfit power locked in his mind. He could be used as a focusing agent only if someone with coercive ability tapped his mind. He had no conscious access to it at all.

Ceirwan sobered. "You are very gloomy today."

I sighed, knowing it was true. "It's probably this endless rain," I said. "Let's go and see if Maryon has woken yet."

He nodded and we rose and went out of the farseeking chambers into the gardens. It was raining only very lightly, but dark clouds suggested there was more to come.

"What do you think of Garth's theory that normal people are developing natural and unconscious shields to stop Talented Misfits reading them?" Ceirwan asked, as we walked.

I shrugged. "There have always been unTalented people with natural mental shields, or mind sensitivity. Since most people have no idea there are Misfits like us, how could they develop defensive shields because of us?"

"Garth says it doesn't matter if they know about us or not. He said the unTalents are developing the ability to shield in response to *our* development of the power to enter their minds."

"It's true that there are a lot more people with natural shields than there were, but I doubt we are the cause. If so, that would put paid to the theory that we are the next step in human evolution. It would mean we are simply *one* strand in human evolution and the unTalents another. That practically brings us back to the Herder theory that we are mutations from true humanity."

I noticed Maruman sitting on a dry step under a broad eave and told Ceirwan to go on ahead to the Healer hall.

"Greetings, ElspethInnle," Maruman sent, as I approached him.

I lowered myself to sit beside the bedraggled cat, resisting the urge to gather him onto my lap and stroke the rough fur and misshapen head of my first and dearest friend. Every time Maruman disappeared, I worried, knowing he wandered far from Obernewtyn in the throes of his occasional strange fey fits. This time he had only been gone several days, disappearing soon after Roland had allowed me out of the Healer hall but on the previous occasion he had been gone for almost a full cycle of the moon, and when he returned his already damaged right eye had been so severely infected that Roland had no alternative but to remove it.

"Where have you been?" I asked calmly, knowing he did not approve of overt emotional displays.

He gave me a haughty look with his remaining yellow eye. "I am not a funaga slave," he sent coolly. "Maruman goes where he wills."

"Of course," I said. "I am merely curious about what you/Maruman saw in your journeying."

Maruman's eye narrowed, for he hated to be questioned and would tell exactly what he wished, when he wished it and not before. There would be no coaxing the contrary beast now. On impulse, I asked casually if the oldOne had spoken to him. The Agyllian Elder, Atthis, had first communicated to me through the cat's mind. I had no idea why the bird had used Maruman instead of approaching me directly, but the cat had since claimed the bird spoke often to him. I did not know if that was true.

I half expected him to snub me, but instead he gave me a queer look. "The oldOne tells Maruman: guard the dreampaths that lead to ElspethInnle," he sent. "Guard the innle when she journeys from the barud. Donot/never let her gojourney without you/Maruman yellow-eyes. One day ElspethInnle will lead the beasts to freedom from the funaga."

An icy surge of fear mingled with excitement replaced the lethargy that had settled such a weight on me over recent months. Barud meant home in beastspeak. Did this mean Atthis had at last decided it was time for me to leave Obernewtyn?

I chewed my lip, mulling it over. If Maruman had been contacted by Atthis, what did it mean that he was to guard the dreampaths leading to me? And, again, why hadn't Atthis sent a dream directly to *me*?

I felt a surge of frustration knowing the cat delighted in making up elaborate lies, and that this might as easily be a complete fabrication, or part of the queer garbled beast mythology, which Maruman had convinced himself referred to me.

"Elspeth!" Matthew called.

Maruman hissed in fright and vanished into the bushes and I bit back an unreasonable urge to lose my temper with the approaching far-seeker.

"What is it?" I called, standing up.

"Rushton wants to see ye right now. Maryon has woken up," he said earnestly.

Rushton's face was stony as he opened the door of his chamber and stepped back to let me enter.

The other guildleaders were seated about the small room, their faces grave. My eyes flew to the Futuretell guildmistress standing in a shadowed corner. Her dark eyes glinted enigmatically across the room at me and my heart began to beat unevenly.

"What has happened?"

"All in good time," Rushton said tightly, gesturing to an empty seat. I flushed, for he did not normally speak so sharply to me.

He opened his mouth, then shook his head as if thinking better of whatever he would have said. Instead he turned to the Healer guildmaster. "You'd better begin, Roland," he growled, flinging himself in a chair.

"Elspeth, as you know, the gypsy you rescued is resisting healing," Roland said. "We cannot work against her body to force her to heal, and it is impossible to enter her mind to see why she will not heal since she has a natural mental barrier."

"Are you saying she is dying?" I asked.

"Right now, we are keeping her stable. However, if this goes on for much longer, she will die."

"Maryon?" I said, turning to the tall woman. "What did you see in your futuretelling yesterday? What has the gypsy to do with Obernewtyn?"

Rushton rose and began to pace about the room.

The futureteller made a graceful gesture with her long fingers. "I saw many things. A journey over th' great water; a gray stone fortress wi' a Guanette bird flying o'er it." These words were spoken in a high oratory voice, but now Maryon dropped into a more normal voice, and its very flatness gave her words greater power. "I saw yon gypsy woman mun be returned safe to her people within a sevenday fer th' sake of Obernewtyn."

"Seven days!" I cried, still groping to understand the undercurrents of tension in the room. Futuretellers often came up with obscure deeds they said must be performed for this reason or that, or for no reason at all that they would divulge. But this was the most dramatic I could remember since Maryon's insistence that we take the newly rescued Herder acolyte, Jik, on the expedition that had ended in his death.

"Futuretellin' is nowt an exact study," Maryon said. "There is much to see which defies understandin'. But I did see that th' gypsy's people may be found in Sutrium."

"Sutrium!" That was almost worse than not knowing. Sutrium was the biggest town in the Land, and the most dangerous, being the base of the main Councilcourt.

Belatedly, I realized no one else had reacted to the mention of it and wondered why Rushton had not waited for me before telling what was to be told. It was not as if I had delayed coming, or had been difficult to find.

"Given that they *are* gypsies, I dinna know how long her people will bide there," Maryon was saying. She shrugged. "All I can tell ye is that they are there now." She broke off suddenly and there was an awkward little silence.

"Are we voting on whom to send with the gypsy?"

"There will be no voting on this matter. *You* will take her," Rushton said tersely.

I was genuinely astonished. Rushton had managed to convince the guildmerge to ban guildleaders from trips to the lowlands because there was too much risk. Now he commanded me like a novice to make a journey to the most oppressive city in the Land, with an unconscious gypsy fugitive!

"I will impose a deepsleep seal on her," the Healer guildmaster said, in such a way that let me understand this had been discussed too. "It will slow down her heartbeat and her dying. Kella can remove the seal in Sutrium, just before you hand her over."

"Why am *I* to take her?" I asked slowly.

Rushton's green eyes stared into mine for a moment, then he turned to Maryon. "Tell her."

The futureteller drew herself up to her considerable height. "Fer Obernewtyn's sake, Elspeth, th' gypsy mun be returned to her people. This was the futuretellin' fer which I sent to recall ye from the city under Tor. But yesterday when I fell into a second an' deeper trance, I learned another thing: *You* mun be th' one to take her back. Nowt fer Obernewtyn's sake, but fer yer own."

"Mine?" I echoed.

Maryon went on, her face grave. "Th' gypsy mun be delivered within a sevenday, Elspeth, fer th' sake of us all. But ye mun take her there fer yer own sake, fer by doin' so, you an' only you, will have th' chance to learn what the word *swallow* means. If ye fail, I have foreseen that *ye'll die afore th' next Days of Rain.*"

V

On the side of the road were patches of scrub and a few of the immense white-trunked Ur trees that characterized lowland terrain, and which had grown in great profusion around my childhood home in Rangorn.

I thought fleetingly of picking berries in their shade with my mother. Then I sighed and shook myself.

"Elspeth, are ye still mad at me fer volunteerin' to come with ye?" Matthew asked in a low voice.

I shook my head.

I had wanted to go alone and had argued against a second expeditioner. Rushton had simply lifted his black brows in a mocking way to ask if I did not think four eyes would see more than two, even if those two were so very gifted. Enraged by his implication that I was motivated by conceit to want to go alone, I had been unable to think of a sensible counter-argument, and so the vote had gone against me. Of course he had deliberately goaded me to produce exactly that result.

In spite of that, we had parted without anger. He had come to my chamber only hours before the dawn departure. I had seen from his eyes that he had not slept well, if at all.

"Since you must go to Sutrium, I need to know how Brydda's allies have taken our offer of alliance," he had begun. "I had thought to hear from them sooner than this, so perhaps something is wrong. I wish I could deal with this myself, but it is not possible."

Still bristling from having Matthew forced on me, I had felt he was hinting that I was incapable of doing what he asked, and my tone had been waspish.

"I will make sure I find out."

He had nodded absently, oblivious of my irritation. Without invitation, he sank into one of the chairs by my small fire. He looked fed up, as well he might at the knowledge that all of his planning and careful thought these long years past might fall awry, for the sake of a nameless gypsy in the wrong place at the wrong time.

Yet he had not bemoaned the unfairness of fate or cursed the gypsy when he spoke. His mind had been on other things.

"Of late, I have heard a number of rumors which suggest the rebels may be planning their rebellion against the Council for next year. Perhaps organizing that has simply taken precedence over our offer."

I had been surprised enough to forget my anger. "Surely Brydda would tell us if his people were on the verge of open rebellion!"

"He might keep bad news from us if they had rejected us as allies."

Well, that was true enough. The anger had drained out of me. "You think they have decided against an alliance with us?"

"I don't know and that is the problem," Rushton said. "I cannot plan without knowledge, and Domick has not supplied me with it."

"Does it matter so much if they don't want us?" I had asked. "After all, the Council may never build a soldier-guard camp up here. Or, not for years anyway. There has been talk about it before, that came to nothing. And even if they really mean it this time, maybe we can coerce them against the idea."

Rushton had given me a somber look. "The Council must find us and it may be sooner than later. We do not yet have the strength to fight them alone, even less so if they are recruiting as heavily as reports would have it. But there is more at stake in this than keeping Obernewtyn safe from the Council. If we are to survive after this rebellion, we must ally ourselves with the rebels."

There had been a touch of desperation in his tone.

"But if they want to fight the Council without us, what does it matter?" I had asked. "If they fight and win, it would solve all of our problems, and if they fail, well . . . we would be no worse off than we are now."

"If they fail, the Council will learn of us from them. If the rebels fight and win without us, we will have done nothing more than change oppressors. Worse, these oppressors will have intimate knowledge of us."

I had stared blankly at him.

He had looked across at me with haunted eyes. "I have told no one . . .

When I met Brydda's allies, they were very civil, but I did not need to be either empath or farseeker to recognize that they are not disposed to tolerate Misfits. They might not have shown their feelings so clearly had they realized I was a Misfit. I do not think they would make much distinction between us and ordinary Misfits," he added, with an emphasis that I had not understood. "But regardless of their attitude to Misfits, if we fight alongside them, we will have the protection of being their allies. They will not turn on us so easily then."

"But what if you are right and they won't have us?" I had asked, frightened as much by the dejection in his manner as by his words. I had been surprised to discover how much his determined will and belief that we would succeed gave me hope and confidence for the future. If he doubted . . .

I had forced myself to speak when he made no response. "We can't make them accept us as allies."

"We can and we will," Rushton had said, his voice suddenly harsh. "If they will not let us join them to fight the Council, then we will wait until they are on the verge of moving, and strike the first blow, forcing them to join us. That is why I need to know what they are up to. . . ."

∾

Rushton, Dameon and Ceirwan had seen us off, the gravity of the expedition at the last minute diverted by an hysterical tantrum on the part of the young empath-coercer, Dragon, whom we had rescued on a previous expedition. She had suddenly realized she would not be going with us and it had taken all of Dameon's empathy to prevent her flinging herself after us as the gypsy wagon pulled away in the gray mountain dawn.

My last sight of Rushton had been of him frowning after me, arms folded across his chest.

∾

Thunder rumbled and I looked up at the lowering sky, wondering if we would reach Sutrium before the storm broke. We had not long passed Glenelg Mor with its sodden earth invisible beneath a veil of mist, fed by steam hissing endlessly from some subterranean source.

I sent a brief command for Matthew to take up the reins, rather than letting them hang down loosely. "It will look odd if someone comes along and sees no one is steering the wagon."

"Gypsy horses are trained to stay on the road while their owners sleep. Besides, who in their right minds would be out so late with a storm brewin'?" Matthew grumbled, but he did as I bade.

A few minutes later a horse galloped around a bend behind us. I gave Matthew a pointed look, though in truth he was right about seldom meeting anyone on the road. He did not notice, because he was all agog at the sight of the exotic-looking, gold-skinned rider, wrapped in a purple cloak and bent low over the horse's neck.

"That were one of them Sador tribesfolk," Matthew said excitedly, when the rider had thundered from sight around a bend in the road ahead. "I'm goin' to visit Sador someday." His eyes glowed at the thought.

The road to the remote region with its nomadic inhabitants had been opened up in the last year, as the Blacklands taint along the western shore of the Land faded, allowing a slender, and some said dangerous, passage along the coast to the plain country.

I sent a mental enquiry to the equine, Jaygar, who had volunteered to pull the wagon. The big roan gave the mental equivalent of a shrug. "Gahltha rides to see what is ahead/before us on the road. He thinks of yoursafety, ElspethInnle."

I sighed a little, knowing that everything Gahltha did these days was governed by concern for my safety. I had told him and Maruman of Maryon's prediction, half expecting them to deride it, but they had simply said that they would go with me and no amount of argument would shift them. They were determined to watch over me until the moment when, somehow, I was supposed to lead the beasts to freedom. Maruman was curled up by the gypsy inside the wagon.

I asked Matthew how long Gahltha had been absent.

"Nowt long. He won't go too far with you here."

I ignored the questions implicit in his tone. There was no way of explaining Gahltha's transformation from a vicious human-hating fury into my devoted guardian, without relating the whole fantastic story of my deliverance from death by the Agyllian birds. It was Atthis who had called the black horse to carry me down from the high mountains, and whatever the ancient bird had said to keep him waiting through the long months of my convalescence had altered Gahltha completely. He had never spoken of it to me, but I guessed Atthis had played on the beasts' beliefs and legends to keep him there. Gahltha now believed utterly that I was to rescue beasts from their long slavery to humans. There had been endless whispered speculation among the younger Misfits since my return, as to what I had done to so change him.

I sighed. Everything that had happened at the Agyllian ken was so long ago, it seemed dreamlike in my memory. If not for Gahltha, I would have thought it so. Maruman's talk of Atthis and a journey had made me think the old bird would call at long last. Instead, I had been caught up in yet another expedition and another futuretelling—this time Maryon's. What would have happened if I had left the gypsy to die on the stake? Would Obernewtyn now be doomed, or would some other set of events have arisen from it?

I shook my head, sick of living my life at the directive of the vague whims of fate and futuretellers.

In the dream I had experienced while concussed from the knife blow, Atthis had been dead. Perhaps the old bird really had died. She had been very frail. She might never call to me again. I might, in truth, spend my whole life waiting for a signal that would not come.

Rushton had ended our dawn Council suggesting I say nothing of Maryon's prediction concerning myself to the general population of Obernewtyn. I had been only too glad to agree. Success would simply add to the myth surrounding me and, if I failed, it would not matter what had been predicted. Matthew had been told that the purpose of the journey was to return the gypsy to her people, so that we could learn more about them, and while in Sutrium, that we would inspect the safe house. But since the journey began, the farseeker had several times intimated that he suspected there was more to it than that. He was no fool.

I glanced back over my shoulder to where the gypsy lay on one of the wooden pallet beds. Maruman was now curled fast asleep at her feet. He disliked wagon travel and had slept continuously since our early morning departure. Leaving very early and traveling without a break would bring us to Sutrium within a single day, leaving five complete days in which to track down the gypsy's people, perhaps six if we did not count the day on which Maryon had announced her futuretelling. She had said the time limit might simply imply urgency and the need for speed, rather than being literally seven days, but Rushton said we must take it as seven days, just in case it was exact.

I turned my eyes to the gypsy's face. I judged her to be about forty years of age. Her features were too strong for beauty, but she was handsome and her hair was as black as my own. One sleeve had ridden up to reveal the pot-metal bracelet she wore pushed above her elbow. Since the rescue, I had scarcely thought of her as human. Unconscious, she had no personality. Remembering her courage on the stake, I hoped she would not die, for her sake as much as Obernewtyn's.

Yet her stubborn resistance to healing had begun to take its toll. Despite Roland's sleepseal, there was an unhealthy pall to her skin.

"She's nowt dead yet," Matthew said defiantly.

I frowned at him. "Let's hope she lives until we get to Sutrium, and that we have no trouble getting her through the gates." I did not say: And let us return her safely to her people before the seven days stipulated by Maryon have passed.

"We have papers," Matthew said.

"Yes. False ones. But, Lud willing, the soldierguards will not have a description of her or me yet."

The farseeker paled. As usual he had given no thought to the realities of the situation in his dreams of heroic deeds.

"I wonder where th' gypsy that shot them arrows in Guanette rode to in such a rush. It's odd he nivver came back at all, dinna ye think?"

I shrugged. "When we didn't appear, he probably thought we had been caught and killed. It's a pity we don't know where he went. That might help us return the gypsy more swiftly."

"I dinna see him very well through the trees, but he were tall and well muscled. He had gray hair in a gypsy plait an' he were wearin' a blue shirt," Matthew said dreamily. Beyond his sloppy shielding I caught a glimpse of a vision in which a tall gypsy hero thanked us regally for the return of his companion.

"There's no question of us chasing after this gypsy and just handing the woman over as if it were a public play," I said sharply.

Matthew flushed and his shield slammed into place. "Ye said ye'd give her to her people, an he mun be one of them."

"And so I will, but discreetly." If she lives, I thought. And if I can find them.

"How far have we to go to Sutrium?" the farseeker asked.

I shrugged. "Your guess is as good as mine. I've only been along this road the once, when I was sent from Sutrium to Obernewtyn. I can remember vividly how frightened I was of what I would find at Obernewtyn, but I hardly remember the journey at all."

It was little wonder I had been afraid. Rumors about Obernewtyn ranging from torture and gruesome experimentation to outright murder had abounded in the orphan home system and it had been common knowledge that the Obernewtyn Keeper, Madam Vega, paid over coin for newly charged young Misfits with unusual deviations. My sole desire had been to hide the true nature of my Misfit abilities from her. Ironic that, in the end, it was Madam Vega, in trying to murder Rushton, who had led me to discover the most fearsome of my Talents—the power to use my mind to kill.

I shivered at the memory of the wild, storm-ravaged night we had taken over Obernewtyn. Since then, I had learned to use the murderous ability that lay coiled in the depths of my mind as a weapon. But not to kill. Never again to kill.

As if he sensed the tenor of my thoughts, Matthew said, "If we hadn't stopped them, they would have gone on killing an' maimin' Misfits. It were us or them. I only wish Ariel had not escaped. . . ."

His voice trailed off and I knew he was blaming himself again for having failed to follow Alexi's malevolent assistant into the storm the night we took over Obernewtyn.

Matthew let out a formless exclamation of surprise, dragging me back to the present. We had reached the top of a long rise and Sutrium lay before us in the blighted light of the gathering storm.

It had grown much bigger than I remembered, spreading farther west until it joined up with settlements along the side of the Suggredoon River, and stretching east and north into straggling outlying districts and farmlands.

Behind the city lay the ocean and somewhere out there were Norse and Herder Isles. Beyond them, a poisoned world lay across vast and little-known seas.

In some ways, Sutrium was not unlike the coastal town of Aborium. We had journeyed there on the very expedition that had rescued the empath-coercer, Dragon. Whether it was my imagination or the knowledge that Sutrium was the home of the main Councilcourt, it seemed a dark and menacing place in the stormy afternoon.

Unlike Aborium, there were no watch towers. It was too big for such things to be of any use. But in any case there was no need, since there were three huge soldierguard camps on the city outskirts. One lay slightly inland on the banks of the Suggredoon, another on the other side near the ferry port, and the third to the east, among the farmlands.

How would the very first Councilmen, who had sworn not to follow in the sinful steps of the Beforetimers, view the sprawling city? I wondered. Surely all their fears that humans might tread the same doomed path of progress would be realized at the sight of it. In my mind's eye, I saw for a moment the shadowy, half-drowned city under Tor.

Thunder sounded again and, as if it were some heavenly signal, Gahltha emerged like a shadow from a thick copse of Ara trees a little down the slope. He waited, a dark shape against the pale speckled trunks and tremulous clouds of foliage, until Jaygar drew level with the wagon.

"The way to the funaga-li barud is not watched by danger," the black equine sent in his stringent mental voice. Funaga was the closest rendering of the beast thought-symbol for human. The form used by Gahltha was subtly derogatory, for though the old acid bitterness had vanished from his nature since his encounter with the Agyllians, he could never truly like humans or their works.

"It would be wise for ElspethInnle to ride thisequine," Gahltha sent. "Only the funaga walk without shackles/burdens in thisplace."

"Wait a moment," I said, and climbed in the back to change my skirt for trews. Coming out again, I stood up on the wagon's bench seat and the black horse came alongside, allowing me to transfer smoothly to his bare back. Sensing his approval at the ease of my mounting, I felt smug. Gahltha had taught me to ride as gypsies did. There had been many times during his painful lessons that I had felt certain they were simply a sadistic way to murder me! Yet I had survived, and there were few now at Obernewtyn who could match my skill. In fairness, that was because few rode as frequently. None among us rode a horse except at its invitation, since all thinking beasts were regarded as equal to humanfolk. I would as soon ask Matthew to carry me as ask one of the equines. Horses took part in expeditions at their own choosing, as beasts of burden, but only in pretense. They never carried humans otherwise, except at great need.

Gahltha was the exception.

After bringing me from the high mountains he had insisted on going back into them often; whether out of nostalgia or to remind himself of his promises, I never knew. Each time he went, he asked that I ride on his back. At first I had refused, disliking the way it increased the mystique my activities had already woven about me, but his determination had worn me down. And like him, I had come to love the headlong gallops over the whispering grasses, flattened to his back and feeling the two of us were, in those moments, a single wild spirit.

Oddly, this had caused the proud Obernewtyn equines to wonder if carrying humans must always be a sign of slavery. More than one of the beasts had suggested that a time might come when it would be useful to have Misfits who rode well. The matter was still under discussion among their kind.

"We must be nearin' th' outer gate," Matthew sent, as we reached the first shingled dwellings at the outer edge of the sprawling city. "Stay close."

Immediately I felt angry. Did he think he had been sent along as my guardian? "I do not expect any trouble," I said coldly.

"Who ever expects it?" Matthew responded, with a significant glance at the wagon where the gypsy woman slept. "A bit of care nivver hurt anyone."

He got into the back to cover the woman's face and I bit my lip to stifle a sharp retort, summoning the mental focus I would need to coerce the soldierguards at the city gates if there was any difficulty.

I reached out to take Gahltha's reins in my fingers as Matthew returned to his seat. My hands and body, like his, were stained a light gypsy tan. Brydda Llewellyn's mother, Katlyn, who had come to live at Obernewtyn, was a skilled herb lorist and she had perfected a dye that simulated gypsy skin tone, and which would not wash off easily, to aid our most common disguise. It was far safer to move about the Land as homeless gypsies than to pretend to be normal Landfolk, for they rarely traveled.

With a mental apology to Gahltha, I pulled the reins tight. They did not drag at his mouth, being a modified bridle that only looked as if it would control and direct a horse. The old bit and bridle were anathema to human and beast alike at Obernewtyn but, even so, I wondered if it would not have been wiser to use it on expeditions that would take us into the heart of Council territory, where spies would be watching for any deviations.

Well, it was too late now.

I concentrated on my attire, enhancing it slightly with coercion so that people would see a boy in the clothes. I had played the gypsy role so often I actually felt braver and more capable in my disguise than when I was myself. Gypsies had never pledged allegiance to the ruling Council. Forbidden to settle, they traveled constantly in small family troops, which was what made their guise so useful to us, but they were not liked, particularly the lighter-skinned halfbreeds. One saw very little of the darker, full-blood gypsies, for they preferred to travel away from cities and to keep their distance from Landfolk. Like the modified bridle, it was a risk to disguise ourselves as gypsies of any kind, given the prevailing attitude to them, but we had no alternative.

To my relief, despite the looming storm, or perhaps because of it, there was an early crowd at the gate; traders and farmers and the odd green-clad jack returning after a day's work trading outside the city. The number of people lined up to show papers would mean a longish wait, but less individual attention.

Approaching the end of the line, we fell in quietly behind the rest, ignoring cheeky signals from a cluster of children. Such a reception was so common for gypsies, that we would have stood out if we had reacted to it.

For the most part, the people about us were grim-faced and sour looking, and many bore the ugly marks of plague survivors. There was no chatter or end-of-day banter, only a brooding silence. People did not look into one another's eyes and the few words spoken were punctuated with wary, sliding glances.

It was a timely reminder that Sutrium was a subtle and dangerous city, filled with a treachery that must not be underestimated. The main thing was to get past the gate without any sort of fuss that would draw attention to us.

I looked up at the dark clouds, willing the storm to break. The soldierguards would scarcely glance at us if it was pouring rain on their heads.

"I will kill/trample funaga-li!" Jaygar's mental voice speared into my mind without warning. He began to push his way through people in front of us, dragging in his wake the wagon containing the unconscious gypsy, Maruman and a helpless Matthew.

VI

I sent out a coercive mental bolt, forcing Jaygar to a halt. Then I looked around frantically, trying to see what had provoked the normally placid equine to such a dangerous outburst.

I did not need to look far.

My own fury swelled at the sight of a small pony ahead of us trembling under the weight of a load of wood. But what made my blood boil, and what had surely incensed Jaygar, was the sight of a fat youth sitting on top of the load unconcernedly eating a bun.

Even as I watched, the mare staggered sideways under the weight of her burden, and the lout cursed her unsteadiness, whacking her with casual cruelty over the head.

"Release me!" Jaygar raged. "You have no right."

I did not loosen my mental hold. "I have the right to restrain any beast/funaga who endangers the rest," I sent, quoting from the expedition charter Rushton had made us draw up over long guildmerge sessions. Jaygar knew as well as I did that Avra had approved it on behalf of the Beastguild.

"Now will you obey/calm?"

The horse snorted angrily. "You would risk us/all for an unknown funaga, but not for thisbeast?"

"Risk comes from acting in stupid haste," I gritted. "Now will you obey, or must I waste more time in arguing with you?"

Chastened, Jaygar agreed, and I asked Gahltha to come up beside the mare. To my astonishment, he refused.

"I willnot let you endanger yourself," he sent. "This equine is one alone and yourlife's purpose will save/help many more than onelife."

"She is yourkind," I sent. "Surely you don't set mylife above hers?"

"ProtectInnle before/above all," Gahltha sent.

"Is that what Atthis told you?" I fumed. "Well, I am not Atthis's servant/slave. I won't spend my whole life waiting to perform a single deed, Gahltha. Not for you nor for Atthis. I will do what I can now, because tomorrow might never come. Now take me up beside the mare or I will get down and walk!"

After a long moment Gahltha moved forward, but there was an offended stiffness in his bearing. I wished I had the empathy to show him what I felt. So often words said only half of what you wanted to say, even words sent direct from mind to mind. But empathy was the one power I lacked utterly.

As we drew level with the mare, I made myself calm down. I did not want to show an interest that would be remembered later. From the corner of my eye I noted the exhausted sag of her head, and the scars on her knees and fetlocks from previous falls. Taking a deep breath to quieten my outrage, I reached out a probe to examine the bindings on her load. When I detected a weakness, I began to work at it with my mind, backward and forward.

This was exhausting, because the probe had to be densely focused to produce even the slightest physical force, but anger gave me additional determination, and in a short time the tie snapped with an audible twang.

The lout on top of the load gave a bellow, as he and the wood crashed to the ground.

A second after, a streak of lightning split the sky and people looked up fearfully, ever mindful that this might be a firestorm. At the same time it began to rain.

The lout got to his feet, red-faced with embarrassment and began to flay the mare viciously. She was so exhausted that she barely flinched under the onslaught.

"Get out of my way," I said insolently, pushing Gahltha forward to distract him. I blinked to clear the rain from my lashes.

"Halfbreed trash!" he yelled. "Don't tell me what to do."

"Then do something of your own will," I rejoined promptly. "Show us you can move your fat bum as fast as you flap your lips."

He stepped forward, lifting his stick to strike me, but Gahltha snorted and reared back, pawing the air. The youth cried out in fright and cowered back.

Thunder cracked again and lightning slashed above, shedding an eerie light on the motley crowd as the rain gathered force, creating a mental static that interfered with my Talent. I concentrated hard and prayed it would not get any worse.

"What's going on back here?" demanded the gate soldierguard, striding back along the line.

"The stupid horse lost its load," the lout blustered. "Then that gypsy tried to set his horse on me. Savage brute of a thing."

"T'was the lightning affrighted him," I said, lowering my voice.

"He overloaded the mare and the ropes broke," a woman said, spurred by a coercive prompt. I did not want the soldierguard to focus his attention too specifically on me. Sooner or later, if it had not done so already, news of the incident in Guanette would reach Sutrium and I did not want anyone remembering a gypsy who came through the gate soon after, even if I was now clad as a boy.

"Look at the poor thing," another woman shouted, after a mental prod. Then she blinked and looked startled at herself.

"It's a wonder it didn't keel over in the very path," someone else growled of their own accord.

"And what if it did?" the lout demanded truculently. "It's my property. I'll kill it right now if I feel like it."

I felt Jaygar's anger like the sun on my back.

"Do that and you'll be fined," the soldierguard snapped.

"Fined?" he squawked. "I've a right to do what I want to my own horse."

"I don't give a damn what you do to the beast. Just so long as its corpse don't clutter up the way. Now get this mess out of the road. Load it to one side and be quick about it."

Muttering and cursing, the lout dragged on the mare's bridle to shift her onto the grass verge and began to move the wood. She stared out unseeingly, eyes like dusty pebbles.

"Greetings, little sistermind," I sent.

She blinked and turned her dull gaze to me.

"This funaga is cruel to you."

"All yourkind are so. Your blood is curdled with cruelty." Her mental voice was infused with a dreamy kind of hopelessness. She didn't seem surprised to have a human talking to her. Perhaps she thought she was hallucinating.

"Not all funaga are thisway," I sent, but the mare was silent with disbelief or lethargy. I sighed, thinking this was not the moment to convert her. "If you hate this funaga, why not runfree?"

"Funaga are everywhere. The wind spawns them. If not this one, another would own me," she sent without bitterness. "When I take the longsleep, I will runfree."

Beastspeaking was often difficult to understand, because sometimes animals used words differently than we did. Equines called sleep the short-sleep and death the longsleep, believing the two states to be related. I shook the wetness from my face and licked my lips. The rain tasted sweet and cold.

"If there were a barud for freerunning in thiswaking, would you dare to run? Could you escape?"

"There is no such place," the mare sent flatly.

"Littlesistermind, I tell you such a place does exist, and if you go there you may runfree and nevermore wear the coldmetal in your lips."

"A barud with no funaga? That is as likely as skyfire without its roar." The flash of cynicism told me all of the spirit had not been beaten out of her.

"There are funaga," I admitted. "But these have the power to speak with beastminds, as I do. And none of them thinks of owning or making or hurting. They think of equines as brother/sisterminds."

She showed her disbelief again. I asked Gahltha and Jaygar to speak to her mind and convince her. Only when the black horse came close and showed her the false bit, did she believe and then she listened carefully as he described a route which would bring her to Obernewtyn.

The lout glared at me. "Get that black demon away from my horse, halfbreed."

I shrugged and drew Gahltha away at once, resigned to the knowledge that he would remember me when the mare disappeared. I sent to her, warning her to be careful she was not followed when she escaped from her human masters. "Runsafe, little sistermind and perhaps we will meet again in thiswaking."

"I am called Faraf," the mare sent. "And I swear this will be so. Nevermore shall I curse the funaga as one, for I know now that some burn with the heartfire."

My eyes pricked with sudden startled tears, for the mare had paid me a great compliment. Beastlegend told of a heart which burns eternally with the souls of all beasts who die and are yet to be born. This shared heart symbolizes the harmony between beasts, no matter what their physical form, nor how they prey on one another, and included Talented and unTalented beasts. Life and death are seen as part of an infinite cycle.

Beasts exclude humanity from this cycle of harmony, for they believe humans are not born of the heartfire, and therefore have no true soul. Some beasts claimed this was the reason for humankind's terror of death and their desire to dominate.

In implying that I shared the heartfire of beasts, the little mare was naming me her equal, and the bearer of a true soul.

I felt my spirits lift, for the rescue of the gypsy and the exchange with the mare reminded me that no matter what Atthis or Maryon or Gahltha thought, I was the mistress of my own life.

"Are you?" mocked an inner voice. "What of the prophecies?"

We had drawn almost level with the gate now. In front of us, the soldierguards were checking the soggy papers of a jack.

"Ye'll be lucky to find buyers for that lot," one of the soldierguards told the green-clad trader. "No one's got much coin these days, an' them that has wants exotics from Sador or lavish trinkets from the Twentyfamilies. Even with the Herders sayin' it's all Lud-curst."

I was surprised at the accent, for most soldierguards came from lowlander stock. It suggested that the Coercer guildmaster had been right in saying there had been an increase in recruitment. I wondered what sort of trader a Twentyfamilies was. I did not know what the word meant, but I was sure I had heard it before, and recently.

"We're away next," Matthew sent.

I saw that he was nervous. "Remember, don't be apologetic or humble. It isn't the gypsy way and it will seem odd."

The Farseeker ward had been on plenty of expeditions, but this was his first visit to the lowlands. It was one thing to fool an ignorant highlander, and another entirely to lie barefaced to hardened soldierguards.

"There may nowt be humble gypsies, but there's plenty of silent, surly ones," he said. "I'll be one of them, an' you can do th' talkin', same as ye did when we was caught by Henry Druid that time."

Henry Druid was a rebel Herder, who had disappeared after being driven from the Faction for refusing to destroy his collection of Beforetime books. On a previous expedition we had stumbled onto his secret camp, but it had since been destroyed, the Druid and his people killed or scattered. "My talking didn't stop them taking us prisoners," I pointed out, trying to distract Matthew from dwelling on his fears.

"They nivver guessed we weren't gypsies," he retorted. "If they had, they'd have burned us fer sure."

I thought, fleetingly, of the fanatical and charismatic Henry Druid and knew that was true enough. He retained the Faction's loathing of imperfection, and his followers would have torn us apart if he had commanded it. Oddly, even among his people, we had discovered Misfits concealing their Talents.

Gahltha twitched, as if reproaching my inattention.

The soldierguards had finished with the jack and were waving him through the gates. I noticed a man staring at Gahltha and realized the rain had washed away the dirt I had rubbed into his coat. Even at his most unkempt, the black horse had always been magnificent to look at. More than once, there had been trouble on expeditions because someone had coveted him. I had got into the habit of daubing his coat with filth as a safeguard.

I sent a swift message to him as the soldierguard gestured for us to come forward. Gahltha's smooth gait became an uneven lopsided lurch, his head drooped low and I was amused to hear him wheezing loudly as if his wind were gone.

My amusement faded as the soldierguard reached up for my papers, for the other with the highland accent had gestured at the wagon and Matthew pulled the curtains open. We had decided to pretend there were only two of us, just in case the Guanette incident had been reported and they were looking for an injured gypsy. If either moved to examine the rig, I would have to coerce them.

My heart leapt into my throat as the highland soldierguard climbed up onto the running board and peered inside the cabin.

"Nothing to trade?" the other soldierguard asked me.

"Some beads and braiding," I said, trying to pay attention.

The soldierguard sneered. "No market for low-quality halfbreed work."

I shrugged, riveted to the wagon. One step further and the other soldierguard could not help but see the gypsy. There was a loud hiss and the man fell back in fright.

"What's that? Some sort of fangcat?" he demanded of Matthew.

"It . . . It's injured," the farseeker stammered.

"Looks like it needs knockin' on th' head," the highlander growled, drawing out a short-sword.

"Perhaps, but it is said Lud curses them who hurt cats," Matthew said, in a desperately sinister voice.

He had gauged it well. The soldierguard was a highlander and, fortunately, as superstitious as the best of them. He backed away hastily, letting his sword drop.

At that moment the light rain became a drenching torrent and, with a curse, the soldierguard examining my papers thrust them unceremoniously into my hand and reminded me that gypsies had to report to the Council-court for an extension of permit if we stayed more than a sevenday.

"We won't be here more," I said, hoping that was true.

∽

"You did well," I told Matthew, when we had been passed through the gate. "Maruman says to thank you for preventing the man from knocking him on the head."

"Thank Lud for Maruman," he said fervently. "Another step an' that soldierguard would've seen th' gypsy."

In a few minutes, we had reached the outer rim of the labyrinth of narrow streets that was the city center of Sutrium. Dwellings here were built right up against one another, often with no more than a single dividing wall to separate them and with steeply thatched roofs that hung in shaggy fringes over doors and windows. Most were several floors high, which meant the streets weaving through them were shadowy and cold, seldom touched by the sun's rays. But there were gaps, too, where nothing stood. I saw several before their significance struck me: they had been burned. In some places a whole row of houses had been burned, while in others a single house had been razed, and those either side left untouched.

" 'Tis ice cold," Matthew shivered, distracting me from the burnt houses. "Feels like wintertime rather than Days of Rain."

"Better to be cold here," I said, turning my attention back to the road. "Stops us getting comfortable and careless."

"I dinna think there's much danger of that," Matthew said. He jerked his head toward the wagon's cabin. "Besides I was nowt thinkin' of myself."

"Look there," I interrupted, pointing to a striped awning. "Just as Domick described it."

"Were we supposed to turn left or right now?"

"West toward the Suggredoon. That would make it right." I hope, I thought.

Responding to my mental directive, Jaygar veered away from the main road down the next right-turning side street. It proved to be a narrow lane lined with workshops and frowsy dilapidated apartments. Even in the rain it stank of urine and refuse.

Without warning, a window opened and a bucket of swill was hurled across the stones.

A little further on, a man opened a door and stared out at us.

Uneasily I remembered that since the plagues and crop failures, there was little to sell in cities other than information. The sooner we located the safe house and got off the street the better.

We came around the corner and groaned at the sight of the sea. Rain had turned it into a seething gray mass. I was surprised when my senses detected powerful static from the direction of the water. There must be something nearby tainted with holocaust poisons.

"We should have turned left back there," I said. "See if you can turn around. We'll get behind you."

Gahltha edged obediently past the wagon, coming out behind it, his hoofs slipping on the greasy cobbles.

I opened my mouth to tell Matthew he might just manage it, and I almost bit my tongue off when Gahltha leapt forward and galloped at a breakneck pace back along the lane. I had no trouble keeping my seat thanks to our mountain rides, but I almost flew straight over his head onto the cobbles when he came to an abrupt halt and swung sideways, facing into a short dead-end street.

"What the hell are you doing?" I demanded, then I faltered, feeling the panicky shift in my mind that meant *someone was tampering with my thoughts!*

The alien probe sensed my awareness of it and fled from my mind. At once, I could see what I had been prevented from seeing sooner.

Crouched in the middle of the lane was Dragon, dripping wet and staring up at me with mingled defiance and fear!

VII

"What do ye mean ye followed us?" Matthew shouted.

Dragon backed away from his fury into the corner of the wagon, bumping the bedshelves. The gypsy stirred and the blankets fell from her face; I was startled by her pallor.

"Have ye any idea how worried they'll be at Obernewtyn when they find ye missin'?" Matthew raged for Dragon's formidable and instinctive mindshield made farseeking her nearly impossible.

"Keep your voice down," I snapped.

We had climbed inside the wagon out of the rain. It was hardly the safest place for a screaming argument.

"Did ye hear . . ." Matthew began wildly.

"I would have to be deaf not to," I interrupted in a cold, quiet voice. "Whatever Dragon did or didn't do is not going to matter a damn if someone calls the soldierguards on us for causing a disturbance."

The empath gave me a mutinous look. "Dragon come too," she said.

Even dirty and wet, her glorious mop of curls dangling in rat's tails, she was still incredibly lovely in the wagon lantern light. I could only pray we were not the only ones she coerced out of seeing her. Once seen, Dragon would not be easily forgotten. What puzzled me was how she had followed us. It was true that we had not made the trip at breakneck pace, but she could not have kept up on foot. She must have got some sort of ride. I hoped she had kept out of sight, but decided to pursue the matter later.

"Won't go back," she added mulishly, as if she feared she had not been clear enough.

Since there was no question of simply sending her back, I might have reassured her, but she must not be allowed to think she had won.

"This is a bad thing you have done, Dragon," I said sternly. "I am very angry. Dameon will be terribly worried about you."

Dragon adored the gentle Empath guildmaster who had taken her under his wing. With a stricken look, she burst into noisy tears and choked out that she had left a message with Louis Larkin to say she had gone to visit some of her animal friends. That mollified me slightly, for no one would worry overmuch to begin with. At least she had not gone away completely heedless of the trouble it would cause. Everyone would assume she was sulking over our departure for a little while, and since she had fended for herself alone for most of her life, no one would think of finding her and forcing her back to Obernewtyn. But we had to send a message back as soon as possible.

Dragon was staring at me with a woebegone expression. I put my arms around her thin shoulders with a sigh, knowing there was no use in trying to treat her as if she were any other disobedient novice. Despite her beauty and incredible illusion-making Talent, only the thinnest veneer of ordinary human behavior lay over the wild, half-starved waif I had coaxed from the Beforetime ruins outside Aborium. It had been foolish of us to expect her to accept our joint departure. After all Matthew had been her mentor, and I had brought her to Obernewtyn. No doubt she had felt we were abandoning her.

And the truth was, had I not been so preoccupied with my own thoughts, I would have felt her clumsy coercive manipulations and sent her back long before we reached Sutrium.

"Surely yer nowt goin' to let her gan away wi' this?" Matthew demanded.

"No. I'm going to turn her over to the soldierguards to teach her a lesson," I said sarcastically, wondering at the extent of his reaction. Did he think I would blame him for her presence? "What's done is done. Now let's move."

Dragon promptly turned her head and stuck her tongue out at him.

"Enough," I said firmly. "Lud knows how many tales will be told tomorrow about a gypsy wagon lurking in a side street. I think we have done enough to get ourselves noticed. Now let's find the safe house. Get the wagon turned around, Matthew."

The farseeker obeyed, his back stiff with outrage.

Dragon's eyes were huge with apprehension when I turned to face her. "Not go back," she begged.

"I won't send you back," I promised. "We're going to the safe house now to see Kella. You remember Kella?" Dragon's eyes warmed and she nodded eagerly. "Good. Now you must be very quiet or else the soldier-guards will stop us. Can you do that?"

Dragon nodded solemnly. "Quieter than Maruman stalking a squeaker," she vowed.

Hearing his name, the cat stretched luxuriously and peered down at us, his good eye glowing in the darkness.

"Maruman will you keep her/mornir quiet?" I sent. Mornir was the name the animals at Obernewtyn had given Dragon. It meant brightmane.

The old cat assented and began to wash himself industriously. I glanced at the gypsy. Her breathing was labored, her eyes sunk back in their sockets. If she did not get help soon, she would die in spite of Roland's seal.

Well, I could do no more than I was doing.

Cautioning Dragon again to stay quiet, I climbed out of the wagon, pulling the curtain to the cabin shut behind me. The lane ahead was empty and it was still raining hard, but it was too much to hope we had not been noticed. I remounted Gahltha and we retraced our steps as swiftly as we could, but it was full dark before we reached the small, oddly shaped trading market that Domick had described as the nearest landmark to the safe house. In the daylight, on a good day, it would doubtless be a pleasant spot to linger, but tonight it was a wet and windy pool of darkness, and completely deserted.

We crossed the square to a street leading off, abutted by a trader office on one side and a huge wagon-repair shed on the other. A sign glistening wetly in the wagon light told us the entrance to the repair yard was from the side street.

The gates were standing ajar, creaking slightly in the wind when we came to them. Beyond, the place was sunk in darkness. The shapes of half-dismantled wagons were standing about in the open, and the shed was nothing more than a square of shadow.

"Are ye sure this is it?" Matthew sent. "It dinna look as if anyone is here."

"They wouldn't advertize their presence," I said, though in fact it did look deserted. Jaygar pulled the wagon into the yard.

"There's a light in there," Matthew shouted over the racket made by the drumming rain on the shed roof. I looked where he was pointing and sure enough there was a dim glow from inside the shed.

"I'll go," I sent, and slid off Gahltha.

Inside, the shed smelled of damp metal and sawdust, but at least it was dry. The light we had seen was coming from a small room constructed down the very end of the enormous shed. Through a doorway, I could see a youth sitting at a table poring over something, the light from a lantern glancing off his cheeks.

He jumped to his feet when he spotted me. "What do you want, halfbreed?"

"I . . . I have a wheel rim that needs some attention," I stalled, startled by his aggressive tone.

"You'll have to go somewhere else. We don't fix halfbreed wagons," he said.

Before I could think how to respond to that, a door opened beside him and Kella stepped out. Seeing me, the healer's mouth fell open.

"Elspeth! By all the heavens! How did you get here?" Without waiting for an answer, she rushed across and flung her arms around me.

Instinctively, I stiffened. At Obernewtyn people treated me with such distant reverence, I could not remember the last time anyone had even touched me.

Misunderstanding, the healer let her arms fall to her sides and stepped away awkwardly. "I'm sorry," she stammered.

"No, I'm sorry," I said contritely. "I'd forgotten how it feels to be treated like an ordinary human being."

She looked bewildered. "But you mean . . ."

I laughed dismissively. "I don't mean anything, except that I am glad to see you." I looked pointedly at the strange youth.

"This is Balder," Kella said lightly. "He is one of Brydda's people lent to us as a watchman. Balder, this is a friend of mine and of Brydda's."

The boy nodded politely but his eyes were cold, and I could not help but recall Rushton's words about the intolerance of the rebel leaders. Obviously, the leaders were not the only ones we had to worry about.

I drew Kella out into the great shed on the pretext of seeing the wagon. "Why is he here?"

"I told you, he is guarding the safe house. It's all right," Kella said.

"He doesn't know anything except that we are friends of Brydda's, and that I am a healer. Brydda always sends someone when Domick goes out of the city on errands for the Councilcourt."

There were a dozen questions I wanted to ask her, but now was not the time. "We'll talk about this later. Matthew and Dragon are in the wagon...."

"Dragon!"

"There is also a woman who needs healing," I went on quickly.

Kella stiffened. "Take me to her," she commanded, imperious in her healer role.

Dragon was sitting wide-eyed in the corner of the wagon with Maruman, who had solved the problem of keeping her put by sitting on her lap. With barely a glance at them, Kella climbed into the cabin and pulled the blankets back from the pallet bed. Her eyes widened at the sight of the unconscious gypsy, but she composed herself swiftly, and lay her fingers lightly on the woman's neck. A moment later, she shook her head.

"It's impossible to treat her here. Wait, I'll send Balder away and then you can bring her in."

She was gone and a few minutes later the rebel came out of the shed wrapped up in a dark, oiled coat. When I was sure he had gone, I jumped down into the rainy dark and, between us, Matthew and I carried the gypsy inside.

"On th' floor?" the farseeker asked, as we reached the smaller room within the shed.

"Through here," Kella directed, opening the door she had come through. Beyond was a rickety set of steps going up into the darkness. Seeing the expression on my face, she gave a faint smile. "Things are rarely what they seem. You, of all people, should know that."

At the top of the steps was a dark landing and a door with blistered whitewash. Kella opened it with a flourish and bright light and warmth flowed out.

"The safe house," she said proudly. "The reason you can't see any light is that all the windows face the sky. There is only one ordinary window and it is blacked out with heavy cloth. You can't tell from below but the whole top of the shed is another floor."

She stepped into a short hall and opened a door. "This is our healing chamber. Bring her in."

The room was long and narrow with a row of straw mattresses made up as beds. The healer drew back the blankets on the nearest and we lay the gypsy on it.

"I'll unharness Jaygar and take the bit off Gahltha," Matthew said, turning to the door.

"Do that, then bring Maruman and Dragon up." I crossed to the door and closed it behind him. When I returned, Kella was kneeling by the mattress bed holding the gypsy's hand.

"These are not fresh wounds," she said, a question in the tone.

In as few words as I could manage, I explained my rescue of the gypsy, Roland's diagnosis and the sleepseal he had imposed. I said nothing yet of Maryon's predictions. I had half made up my mind to tell them at least part of it when we were all together.

"I don't understand why you brought her here," Kella said, beginning to unravel the stained bandages. "If Roland couldn't help her, I doubt I will be able to do better. I daren't take the seal off yet, but at least I can bathe her wounds and change the bandages." She moved to a small cooling cupboard, took out a stone jug of whitish fluid, and returned to bathe the gypsy's flaccid flesh.

"Maryon said her own people will be able to treat her."

"Gypsies know a great deal about healing," Kella agreed. "You mean to return her to them then?"

"That's one of the reasons we've come," I said truthfully.

Kella rebandaged the arms deftly, pulled the blankets up and rinsed her fingers in a bowl. "That is all I can do for now. At least it will stop any infection from setting in. You will have to move swiftly if you are to return her alive to her people though. An injury drains life energies, and she does not have much left to lose, even with a sleepseal to slow everything down. Come, we will go into the kitchen. You are soaked to the bone. I felt it when I touched you downstairs."

We went back into the hall and she indicated another door. "That is one of the sleeping chambers, and there is another closer to the kitchen." She opened the door alongside. "The bath house. There are three bathing barrels and we even have water piped in. The fire over there heats the water in the pipes and then it comes out of tubes to the barrels once you remove the stoppers. Unfortunately, it takes ages to heat. I'll light it if you like?"

I shook my head and gestured for her to go on.

The kitchen was, in spite of its considerable size, cozy and welcoming. It had been whitewashed so that even without windows, it seemed light. The air was warm and redolent with the odor of hundreds of tiny bunches of drying herbs hung in neat rows along all of the walls. There were shelves of foodstuffs and in the center of the room, on a woven rug, a thick scrub-wood table and some stools. A fire blazing on a narrow hearth completed the picture. As I crossed at once to warm myself, Kella filled a kettle and bent to hang it on a hook suspended over the flames.

"It's like a breath straight from Obernewtyn to see you here," she said with sudden fervency, her eyes bright. "I miss you all so much. I dream of the fields and mountains, and then I wake and I am still here."

The depth of longing in her eyes made me feel ashamed. In spite of Maryon's doom-filled predictions, I had been glad to get away from my cloistered existence at Obernewtyn, while poor Kella lived in constant danger to keep it that way.

"Sutrium is awful," she went on. "I never imagined people could be dragged so low. Even before Rushton took over there were times for laughter at Obernewtyn. Here no one laughs and if they do, people stare at them as if they have gone mad. And it is a hundred times worse since the plague. I pity these people their gray lives."

"Don't pity them too much," I said dryly. "Those same pitiable souls would stand by and watch us burn without lifting a finger."

"It's true enough. We're nowt but freaks to them," Matthew said, coming through the door carrying Maruman. The cat leapt to the ground and began to prowl about the room, smelling it. Kella knew better than to react to his presence, and pretended not to see him. Instead, she beamed at the ward.

"Lud, but you've grown now that I see you properly, Matthew. Has Brydda's mother been using herb lore on you instead of her garden?"

Matthew laughed. "Seems to me it's yerself who's shrinkin'!"

I thought his jest curiously apt, but Kella only slapped playfully at his arm and urged him to dry himself in front of the fire. Catching sight of Dragon hovering in the hall behind him, shoulders hunched in misery, the healer gave an exclamation and held out her arms. Dragon rushed at her and it was some minutes before she could pry herself loose from the girl's impassioned embrace.

"What a grub you are, love," Kella laughed. "It's a miracle you manage to stay dirty in so much rain. Will you let me wash your face?"

Dragon froze, blue eyes livid with fear. "No bath."

"No bath," the healer assured her, knowing as well as anyone Dragon's inexplicable terror of water. "Just a bit of a damp cloth."

As Kella ushered her from the kitchen, I wondered if Brydda had ever managed to find out anything more about Dragon's past.

Matthew scowled after them and I lost my temper with him.

"What it is that you want done about her, Matthew?" I snapped. He was as bad as Dragon, with less excuse for it. He had grown much from the thin, sharp-eyed boy I had first met at Obernewtyn, but sometimes he seemed less wise nowadays. I had said so once to Maryon in a fit of irritation, and she had said that perhaps I, too, had changed.

"They've done a good job here," Matthew said, after an awkward pause. "There is even a special yard where th' horses can graze without bein' seen."

I drew off my soaked boots and poured some of the boiling fement into two mugs, handing him one as a peace offering. "They've had quite a bit of help from Brydda Llewellyn by the sound of it."

"Of course," Matthew said easily, then he gave me a sharp look. "And why not? Surely ye dinna worry he'd betray us?"

I shook my head. His father, Grufydd, and his mother, the herb lorist, Katlyn, had come to live at Obernewtyn after the Council learned their son was the notorious rebel, the Black Dog, so betrayal on Brydda's part was completely out of the question. "It's not Brydda. It's the others. That rebel boy that was downstairs, for instance. Did you see the way he looked at us? If he feels that way about gypsies, how is he going to react when he discovers we're Misfits? There's no point in us pretending we're all allies until it has been agreed to officially by the rebels. In spite of what Brydda says, we don't really know where we stand with them."

"Is that why we're here?" Matthew demanded.

I was glad when Kella's return prevented my answering.

"I've put her into bed," Kella said. "The poor little mite was asleep before her head brushed the pillow. But why on earth did you bring her here?"

I explained, and the healer shook her head in wonder. "She must be very attached to follow you all this way, Elspeth."

Matthew rose explosively, pulled on his coat in one ferocious motion and went out, saying he was going to unpack the wagon.

Kella stared after him in astonishment. "Whatever is the matter with him?"

I laughed and, even to my own ears, it sounded a sour note. "I am beginning to suspect it wasn't me Dragon followed, but Matthew. I think he volunteered for this expedition specifically to get away from her."

"Oh, poor Dragon," Kella said compassionately. "I remember she followed him everywhere when I saw them together last, but I thought it was just an infatuation."

"More's the pity it isn't," I said, suddenly emptied of ill-humor. I stood up. "I am going to wash and put on some dry things."

"There are clothes in a trunk in the bathing room," Kella said.

A lantern was lit in the bathing room from Dragon's wash, and as I peeled off my soaking clothes, I caught sight of myself in a mirror hanging on the wall, a long, lean girl with thick, black hair falling past her waist and irritated moss-green eyes. I glared at myself, and realized abruptly that I felt less pity for Dragon's love, than exasperation at the inconvenience of it.

What a terrible business loving was. It was a troublesome and tiresome emotion destined more often to enrage the recipient, than to please them. Rushton's love for me, if that was what it could be called, had him determined to shut me up like a bird in a gilded cage, while Dragon's love for Matthew had driven him out of his home. What right had people to love you when you had not wanted it or asked for it?

Of course, in Dragon's case, the only wonder was that no one had foreseen the outcome of throwing together a volatile girl, who had spent most of her life in wretched loneliness, with a boy of Matthew's easy charm. Yet Dragon had ultimately saved Obernewtyn with his help. Her heartache and his irritation must be considered a small price to pay for that.

It seemed there was always a price to pay for loving.

I had a sudden vivid memory of a time when, taken in by Dragon's illusions, I had thought Obernewtyn destroyed. From my hiding place I had spotted a haggard Rushton with burning eyes, and imagined him despairing over the loss of Obernewtyn. Only later had I understood that this sorrow arose from his belief I was dead.

I shook my head and turned to rummage for dry clothing, not liking the tenor of my thoughts nor the way Rushton's face haunted me.

I fled from the accusation in my face to the kitchen, bringing the lamp with me. Matthew had come back inside and he and Kella were seated in front of the fire. I pulled up a stool and joined them. Maruman came over and leapt up onto my lap. His mind was closed and I did not try to force entry to it.

"How long before Domick comes home?" I asked Kella, wincing as claws penetrated cloth and flesh. "I presume he is at the Councilcourt?"

The healer nodded, the smile fading on her lips.

I guessed she was wondering if our arrival would put Domick in danger and, for the first time, I was aware of the strain in her face. There were lines around her eyes and her hands fidgeted constantly in swift, nervy gestures. I had been surprised at the strength of the longing in her voice as she talked of Obernewtyn, but now I thought of what her life in the safe house must be like. Every day she would watch her bondmate leave, knowing he went to work under the very noses of the Councilmen. If discovered, he would be killed.

It seemed far easier to take action, than to sit and wait. People like Kella had the worst of it—the waiting and wondering, and being helpless. In asking when Domick would return, I had surely voiced a question she never dared permit herself to ask.

Hearing the stair door bang in the wind, and heavy footsteps in the hall, I felt an echo of the profound relief I saw on Kella's face.

But when the door opened, a dark-clad stranger stepped inside.

VIII

It wasn't until Kella crossed the room to embrace the stranger that I realized it was Domick.

The last time I had seen the coercer was at Obernewtyn just before he and Kella left with Brydda to establish the safe house. Then, Domick had been on the edge of manhood, brown as a gypsy with shoulder-length dark hair and bold, serious eyes. There was no sign of that youth in the man that now stood before me.

His skin was milk pale and his long hair had been cropped very short. But most of all it was his expression that made him a stranger; or the lack of it. His face was a gaunt mask, the eyes two hooded slits. If he felt any surprise at seeing us in the safe house, it was not evident.

As a coercer, Domick had possessed that guild's characteristic dominating aspect, but his love for Kella had seemed to soften and temper his intensity. I could not begin to imagine what had happened to turn him into this hard-faced man.

"Has something gone wrong at Obernewtyn?" he asked, in a voice as even and emotionless as his expression.

"That is a harsh greeting for old friends," Kella scolded him gaily, and I saw that she had not mentioned his transformation because she did not perceive it. It seemed that love was truly blind.

Domick exerted himself to produce a semblance of liveliness. "Kella is right. Forgive my abruptness. It has been a bad night, but it is good to see you both." He smiled, but his eyes remained remote, and again I found myself wishing for empathy; this time to tell me what seethed under the stoniness of his face.

The coercer removed his oiled cloak, and I saw the tension in his movements as he crossed to hang it on a peg beside the fire. Sitting down, he reminded me of a spring coiling tight for a hard recoil. Maruman watched him, then hissed and sprang from my lap to prowl about the room.

"You have chosen a bad time to visit," Domick said, glancing up to indicate the rain thundering down on the roof.

"Needs must," I said.

He gave me a swift look. "Need?"

For the second time that night, I told the story of the rescue of the gypsy, and of our decision to return her to her people when Roland could not heal her. Despite my previous decision to tell them everything when we were all together, I said nothing of Maryon's predictions. Some instinct kept me silent in the face of Domick's queerness. At the same time, I realized there was no real need to speak of it at all. Either I would succeed or not. Telling them would change nothing.

"It was a risky thing for you to have gone in alone to face the Herder," Domick reproved. "Those villagers might have killed you at once."

"Not with th' gypsy shootin' arrows at them from th' trees," Matthew said gleefully. "Besides we could hardly leave her to burn now, could we?"

An odd expression flitted over the coercer's face. "Sometimes you have to put up with a lesser evil in dealing with a greater one."

Kella stared fixedly into the fire, as if disengaging herself from the conversation, but Matthew was openly indignant.

"Ye mean, we should have left her? I doubt she'd call that a lesser evil!"

Domick shrugged. "If you had been caught it would not have helped her and it may well have done great, even irreparable damage to our cause. Which, then, would be the greater evil? To let an unknown woman die, or to save her and see your friends perish for it?"

"We got her free didn't we, an' we weren't caught?" Matthew returned stubbornly. "If we thought like you, we'd nowt even have tried. There's evil fer ye. Nowt even tryin' to fix somethin' that's wrong."

"You are naive," Domick said dismissively. "If the woman is as sick as you say, there is every likelihood she will die despite your help."

Matthew flushed. "Meybbe I am naive, but rather that than bein' someone with ice fer blood an' a clever tongue an' shifty brain instead of a heart!"

They stared at one another for a moment, then Domick relaxed back into his seat. "And is that the reason you have come to Sutrium, Elspeth? To pay a social visit and to take an irrelevant gypsy back to her people?"

I suppressed a surge of anger at his callousness, and the temptation to tell him what Maryon had futuretold about this *irrelevant* gypsy. "I would like to see Brydda Llewellyn," I said mildly. "He might be able to suggest some safe way to locate her people."

"I am not sure there will be any way that could be called safe," Domick said. "Is she a halfbreed? I suppose she must be," he answered himself.

"I think so. Yes," I added more positively, remembering the Herder had called her that. "Does it make a difference?"

Both Kella and the coercer nodded.

"A Twentyfamilies gypsy would not break the Council lore forbidding healing," Domick explained.

"Twentyfamilies?" I echoed, startled to hear the odd word again. "What does that mean?"

"It is the name pureblood gypsies give to themselves," the coercer said. "It was not a name any but traders of expensive trinkets knew until the Herders started bandying it about. They hate gypsies and Twentyfamilies most of all, because it was they who negotiated the safe passage agreement with the Council that exempts gypsies from Herder lore. Herders preach that gypsies ought to be made to settle. They claim the plague was spread by their wanderings."

"The Herder in Guanette said the plagues were a punishment from Lud because of people ignoring the Faction," I said.

Domick shrugged. "Same thing. There is a lot of talk to that effect encouraged by the Herders, but it will not give them power to force the Council to make the Twentyfamilies settle. The halfbreeds are not so lucky for the safe passage agreement no longer includes them, yet nor are they allowed to settle. They are persecuted by Landfolk and Herders alike, as you know. But it is worse since the plague."

I began to see that returning the gypsy within the days remaining of Maryon's futuretold deadline would be even harder than I had anticipated.

Hitherto, I had imagined I understood something of gypsy society, but in truth what I knew arose solely from memories of a friendly troop of gypsies, who had come through Rangorn every few seasons when I was a child. I did not even know if they had been pure or halfbreed, because skin color among gypsies varied so much.

"You talk about Twentyfamilies gypsies and halfbreeds as if they were two separate races," I said.

"That is very nearly what they are," he answered. "The division between them has its origins in the days when gypsies first came to the Land. Some say they walked here, others say they came by sea. Either way, they didn't want to be ruled by Council or Herder lore so they came to an agreement with the Council to remain as visitors, never settling or farming the Land, never owning any of it."

"I know all of that," I said, faintly impatient.

"I suppose you know, too, how they got the Council to agree to let them remain as visitors?" Domick snapped.

Abashed, I shook my head. "I'm sorry. Tell it your own way."

He went on. "In exchange for safe passage status as visitors, the gypsies offered a yearly tithe: a percentage of the craftwares their people produced. Their works are rare and beautiful and none but Twentyfamilies artisans know the secrets of crafting them."

I remembered the soldierguard at the gate saying halfbreed trinkets were worthless while Twentyfamilies wares were much coveted, and felt a sudden curiosity to see them. Without warning, it came to me where I had first heard the term Twentyfamilies. The acolyte in Guanette had shouted something about them. "Even Twentyfamilies . . ." he had said venomously, but I could not remember the rest of his words.

"The craft skills are what separate pureblood from halfbreed. In the early days, there were some gypsies who mated with Landfolk, and so halfbreeds were born. In those first days, there was free trade of knowledge and blood between full and halfblood gypsies. But that ended with the Great Divide." Domick said. "Purebloods do not now teach their skills to halfbreeds. Therefore halfbreed wares are pale echoes of their work, based on little-known or half-recollected formulae and recipes. Invariably inferior, they bring scant coin whereas the purebloods make more than enough to live well from what remains of their work after the tithe."

"Why dinna Twentyfamilies gypsies teach th' halfbreeds th' craft-skills?" Matthew demanded indignantly. "A halfbreed mun have at least one pureblood in their line of descent. Dinna this tie mean anything to them?"

"Once, there was no difference between half and purebloods," Domick said. "But halfbreeds weren't as scrupulous about obeying Council lore as the Twentyfamilies. That caused a lot of strife. Finally, the Twentyfamilies leader had no choice but to announce the Great Divide cutting half-breeds off absolutely from purebloods. The Council accepted the division because it allowed them to control the troublemaking halfbreeds, without breaking contract with the Twentyfamilies. The Great Divide was a matter of survival for the purebloods. They had to maintain the exclusivity of their work because it was their only leverage. And they do not abuse the safe passage agreement, for they keep to themselves and are scrupulously honest. It is hard on the halfbreeds, though. It would not be so bad if they were permitted to settle and become ordinary Landfolk, but in spite of the division, people regard gypsies as gypsies. They resent the wealth and inviolability of the Twentyfamilies gypsies, so they take it out on the halfbreeds."

"There have been a number of incidents where halfbreeds have been beaten or attacked," Kella said, her eyes worried. "Your disguises are now dangerous because you are obviously not Twentyfamilies and, as halfbreeds, you are fair game."

Why had Domick not warned us of this in his reports? But before I could ask, Matthew spoke, "Why can't we *say* we're Twentyfamilies? Fer that matter, why dinna th' halfbreeds say it? There's enough color variation for that not to matter."

"Twentyfamilies gypsies would know you were an impostor regardless of skin color and kill you or report you to the Council," Domick said.

"How could they know?" Matthew persisted.

The coercer shrugged. "They just do. You might farseek them and find out how, if it mattered enough. Yet, what point would there be in it? Your gypsy can only be a halfbreed. To reach her people, you must be one of them."

That was true enough.

"The Faction wants gypsy traveling stopped, because they want all gypsies under their power," the coercer added. "Of course, the Council has a vested interest in keeping things as they are, because if they make the purebloods settle, the bribe tithe will cease."

"Naturally, greed would decide th' day," said Matthew, with a flash of cynicism.

"So, as Kella said, disguised as halfbreeds you will be the target of Herder ill-will, as well as persecution from ordinary Landfolk," Domick said. "And even among the halfbreeds you will have trouble getting information because, gypsy or not, you will be unknown to them. Given the climate, they are understandably wary of strangers. If, by chance, they discover you are not a gypsy they will probably kill you, thinking you are a Herder spy. Worse, if you approach the wrong halfbreed, you'll find yourself reported to the Council or the Faction, and hauled in for questioning."

I frowned into the fire.

"There is another thing you must consider," Domick went on inexorably. "I have heard no report of the affair in Guanette at the Councilcourt, but just because it has not reached the Council does not mean the Faction is ignorant of it. If they do know, they are certain to have spies watching the gypsy greens with descriptions of you in their pockets."

"I will keep the gypsy woman out of sight and go about as a boy," I said firmly, stamping ruthlessly on a little flutter of fear in my stomach.

"Best to abandon the gypsy disguise altogether, but of course the tan would give you away," the coercer said.

"I can brew something that will fade it faster," Kella offered.

I nodded. "It would not be a bad idea to have such a mixture on hand. However, given what you have said, I doubt any gypsy would speak to me unless I was obviously one of them, so I will have to remain as I am for the present. Maybe I can coerce them into thinking they know me."

Changing the subject, I told Domick how Dragon had come to Sutrium, and asked if he could send word back to Obernewtyn that she was safe.

"It will take a sevenday at least," he warned. "My reports go through Enoch and he daren't let himself be seen going up to the mountains anymore, since it's supposed to be plague-ridden and deserted. He'd be stoned if he was seen coming down for fear that he carried the disease. He'll have to wait until Ceirwan or someone calls by."

I shrugged. "Well, it can't be helped. The plague seems to have an effect on so many things."

"How was it at Obernewtyn during the plague?" Kella asked, and I realized how little she must hear of home and everyday events in Rushton's business-like missives. It would not occur to him that his spies might need to hear the small details of life in the mountains.

"It was not so bad in the highlands, but when it reached Darthnor and Guanette," I said, "we knew it would only be a matter of time before it got to us. Fortunately, before it did, Katlyn and Roland unearthed a Beforetime method of immunizing us. They used the blood of a Coercer novice, who had survived the plague, to make a potion to strengthen those who had not caught it."

Kella looked fascinated. "How was this blood potion administered? Surely you did not drink it."

"It was forced under the skin using a hollowed needle," I explained. "It caused us to contract a lesser variation of the plague and, in overcoming this, our bodies became resistant to the more virulent strain." I shuddered at the memory. Even a mild dose of the plague had been horribly unpleasant.

"Better a needle than the plague," Kella said, misunderstanding. Her expression was suddenly haunted. "It's so dirty here that people went down with the disease in the hundreds. So many died that there were not enough left to bury the dead. The corpses bloated and stank and the disease spread and spread. I blame the Herder Faction for it," she added, in sudden anger.

I was surprised. "How could the Herders cause a plague? Or do you really think Lud sent it on their behalf?"

"I didn't mean they caused it," she said. "How could they? I am sure it was nothing more than a disease born of filth and ignorance. But the Herders predicted it, so they must have had some sort of forewarning."

"Didn't they do anything to stop the disease?" I asked.

Kella gave a hard, humorless bark of laughter. "Stop it? Oh no. It was a Ludsend to them. They claimed only those hated by Lud would die." There was a terrible bitterness in her voice. "Are babies and old dodderers evil? Does Lud hate children and sick people, for they were the first to fall?"

"The strange thing is that so few of the Herders died," Domick said pensively. "It seemed to prove their claim that Lud was protecting them. They did not care at all when plague killed off the sickly and the weak, but when it began to eat up the strong, they were less delighted. After all, if everyone was killed, who would be left to be preached at?"

Kella laughed wildly. "They really started to worry when the crops were ready and there was no one to harvest them. What would they eat? Would they have to till and labor for food with their own white hands? The Councilmen were panic-stricken, of course, and right from the beginning the majority of them had barricaded themselves in their homes with supplies. But still many of them died as well."

She fell silent.

"What happened in th' end?" Matthew asked, as if looking for a happy ending to a bedtime tale.

Domick answered him. "It went on and on, until half the city was dead or dying, and finally the Herders told the Council to lock up the houses of the dead and burn them with the corpses inside."

Kella gave a gagging sob. "Yes. That was their solution. They told the Council to employ the purifying flames of Lud. So the soldierguards went out, burning any house where there had been plague, and quite a few where there was nothing, whether there were people inside, or not. Dozens were burned alive."

I swallowed back an urge to vomit as Domick moved to take Kella in his arms, his expression more mask-like than ever.

"I did what I could," Kella whispered into his shoulder. "But there were so many..."

The coercer met my eyes over her bowed head and for a moment there was a flare of some emotion in his eyes, but it was gone too quickly for me to interpret it.

"It was difficult," he said in a cool voice. "Brydda was bringing those of his people who had contracted the plague here and most arrived too late to be helped. Other times, there were so many needing healing that Kella had to choose between which life to save, and whom to let die. She almost killed herself trying to heal them all. She would not rest or eat."

"How could I rest with people dying every minute I slept? How could I eat in the midst of all that death?" she whispered.

Domick rose and led the weeping girl out, leaving me and Matthew to stare at one another.

"I dinna know it had been so bad," the farseeker said in a subdued tone.

I said nothing, for though horrified by Kella's story, I was concerned that people had been brought willy nilly to the safe house. Yet the thought gave me hope, for surely the rebels would not use it and Kella's healing skills so freely if they did not mean to ally themselves with us.

Maruman appeared from behind a cupboard and climbed into my lap again, curling himself to face the fire. I was fascinated to feel his mind curling around mine in much the same fashion as his body shaped itself to my lap.

"Maruman/yelloweyes guards ElspethInnle," he sent, as if I had posed a question.

Domick returned.

"I have coerced Kella to sleep," he said in a somber voice. His eyes met mine. "She is exhausted in body and spirit. You cannot know what it was like for her. She nearly went mad when she learned of the burnings. You must take her with you when you go. She cannot bear it."

"It doesn't seem to bother you," I said.

"I am not Kella," he responded flatly. "I am a realist. There was plague and the burnings ended it. Therefore the method worked."

"It was a brutal solution," I snapped. I did not like the coldness in his voice when he spoke of Kella, nor his apparent acceptance of the Herder Faction's murderous solutions.

"Brutal?" he said. "Perhaps. But this is a brutal world. Yet it did not endear the Faction to the Council, for all its success. Too many Councilmen died, and too few Herders."

Diverted, I frowned. "Then there is still conflict between the Faction and the Council?" I had sensed that, while inside the Herder's mind in Guanette.

Domick nodded. "There is a feeling among Councilmen that the Herders have too much hysterical power over the masses; that they are fanatical and dangerously extreme. Of course since the plague, they command the power of life and death—or so the ignorant are led to believe— so there is no question of the Council doing anything immediately to limit their power. But, I daresay, they will find a way to curb them in the end."

"Do you think the Council would ever disband them altogether?"

He shook his head decisively. "I doubt they will do more than pull a few teeth. Why bark yourself, when you can have a dog to do it? The Faction serves a purpose and the Councilmen know it. Look at them sending a pack of Herders to soften up the Sadorian tribespeople. Better to risk a few tame priests than their own precious hides."

And if the dog turns on his master?

For all that the Council imagined the Herders under their control, the Faction was an unstable body, with its own plans.

Domick stood up abruptly and reached for his cloak. "Come."

My bones ached and I was still cold, not to mention hungry, but I stood, lifting Maruman from my knee. The old cat gave me a haughty look and stalked away. I sent an apology, but he would not respond. I pulled on my sodden boots and took the cloak the coercer handed me.

"We will be back before midnight," he told Matthew.

The farseeker nodded and leaned forward, lifting both hands to the fire. I felt a stab of envy.

"Where are we going?" I asked, as we clumped down the dark stairs.

Domick's eyes glimmered in the darkness as we stepped out into the windy night, and his words were an echo out of the distant past: "You wanted to see Brydda Llewellyn, didn't you?"

IX

The streets were all but deserted as we passed through them like two shadows. Houses were sunk in darkness, but here and there were more of the blackened gaps I had noticed that afternoon. I shuddered, now understanding them in the light of Kella's story.

A woman peered out of a window at us, and I wondered whether I should have insisted we take the horses. Gahltha would be angry that I had gone without him, but Domick had argued that we would draw more eyes on horseback than on foot. Because of a rising trade in stolen horses, few rode at night.

Even so, Gahltha had ways of defending himself that would discourage any thief.

I realized, with a shock, I had grown so accustomed to the black horse's presence that I felt curiously vulnerable without him.

A curtain twitched as we passed another window and a memory surfaced. "Is there still a curfew in Sutrium?"

Domick lifted his head as if to dispel a dream and I wondered what he had been thinking about. "There is a curfew but it does not come into effect until midnight," he said. "It is not strictly enforced because there are worse things than soldierguards to contend with. Only fools asking to be robbed or murdered wander the streets after dark."

"Marvellous," I said sourly, wondering which category we fell into.

"Too many disappearances. Too many robbers," the coercer went on, as if I had not spoken. "Since the plagues and the loss of crops there is no work and little food. There are a legion of poor in the city. Some beg for their needs and others take what they want. Hard times make for hard folk."

Involuntarily I smiled, recognizing Brydda's love of neat sayings in the phrase. "One of the Black Dog's homilies?"

Domick gave me a startled look, then said defensively, "He has a way of putting things that makes them memorable. It is a fine and useful quality in a leader."

There was not the slightest flicker of humor in his voice. He had always been serious, seldom speaking more than was necessary or laughing aloud, but now it seemed to me he had built a deep wall of reserve about himself. I wanted to ask why, but something about his silence repelled intimacy.

"Do you see much of Brydda?" I asked instead.

The coercer gave me a wary glittering look as we passed under one of the few lighted street lanterns, and it struck me forcibly that there was something very wrong.

"I see him," he said noncommittally.

"How is he then?"

Domick was silent so long, I thought he meant to ignore the question, but at last he spoke.

"Superficially, he is the same as ever: brave as a lion, swift to laughter, loyal, proud and silver-tongued. But to my mind his policy of elusiveness is affecting his mind."

"You mean he is going mad?" I asked, startled.

Domick gave me a pale echo of a genuine smile, that fleetingly stripped ten years away from his face. "I mean it is affecting his way of thinking. He is the kind who needs to trust. He is happiest with loyal comrades constantly about him. Yet, for the sake of security, the Black Dog has chosen a lonely path."

He fell silent and I considered what he had said. No one knew better than I how loneliness tainted a person's thinking. Solitude could become an addiction; a canker of the soul, ever hungered for as much as it was loathed. All the years I had spent in the orphan home system after my parents were killed, I had kept myself apart—even from my brother Jes— fearing that someone would discover I was a Misfit. This had made it hard for me to trust or to relate to people, even when it was safe to do so. And, in spite of all the years of longing for friends, now that I had them, part of me yearned to be by myself again.

Yet, even as a child, I had been something of a loner, and in the orphan homes I had learned that friendship was dangerous. There had been too many informants among us; besides, orphans had been rotated during the Changing Times to prevent alliances. But Brydda had not learned the orphan's lesson. I could well imagine the effect enforced solitude would have on him. It saddened me to think of the laughter dimmed in the merry giant.

"What of Reuvan and Idris? Does he separate himself from them as well?" The handsome seaman and the blond boy had been his closest companions and he had brought them with him when he moved from Aborium to Sutrium.

"They? No. They are the only ones who know everything about his movements. That is a risk, and Brydda knows it, but they are what keep him sane. Yet, still, this life gnaws at him unhealthily."

"And you?" I asked impulsively. "Does it gnaw at *you*?"

Domick gave me a strange look, but made no response.

We fell silent as we passed an open verandah where an old woman swept her porch. She watched us go by, as if poised to run inside and bar the door. I felt her eyes following us through the rain until we passed out of sight.

We came into a street running right along beside the shore. A board-walk was built level with the cobbled street, but the ground dropped away beneath to a narrow rocky beach which ended at the sea. Rain fell into the water with a hissing susurrus. Again, I was conscious of a strong mental static. Clearly, the water was tainted in some manner. I did not recall this from my previous visits to Sutrium. Perhaps there had been a recent fire-storm?

The sea was so dark that it seemed as if we traveled along the rim of an abyss. This would be a good place for an attack but I resisted the urge to look over my shoulder.

Thoughts of one fear begot another for, without thinking, I asked, "Have you heard anything of Ariel lately?"

The name evoked in the coercer the same heavy silence it caused anyone who had been at Obernewtyn before Rushton became its master.

"He went to Herder Isle just before the plague struck," he said at length. "He was seen going there. It seems that he remains in the Herders' good graces, though I do not know why. They were as angry with him as the Council when the soldierguards sent to Obernewtyn found nothing. I would have expected them to cast him off as the Council did."

Ice touched my blood.

Though Rushton dismissed the Faction, concentrating his efforts on the Council, I had always felt the priests to be the more sinister body. For a time it had seemed that their day had come and gone, but the plague had turned the tide. And at this very time of changing fortunes, the demon-spawn Ariel had chosen to join them. I could not say why the thought of Ariel on Herder Isle disturbed me, but it did.

I mulled on that for a while, and old questions arose in my mind.

"You know it has always bothered me that Ariel was so certain Obernewtyn had not been destroyed by firestorm, that he sent the sol-dierguards," I mused, more thinking aloud than expecting an answer to this old paradox.

"His Talent must have given him the knowledge," Domick said.

I gaped at the coercer, astonished. Why had it never occurred to me that Ariel was a Talented Misfit?

Domick went on unaware of my reaction to his words. "Kella thinks he has empathy because of the way he generated fear, but I think he is a latent coercer. He couldn't be a futureteller, because if he had futuretold that Obernewtyn was not destroyed, he would also have foreseen us using Dragon to fool the soldierguards. I think he simply had a true dream."

True dreams were common among Misfits, and often contained fleet-ing flashes of the future.

My mind circled back to my own question: why had I never thought of Ariel being Talented? I had known he was a Misfit, but above finding him morally corrupt and sadistic, I had never considered what it was that had made him a Misfit.

Why?

The answer came swiftly.

Because I did not want it to be so.

I wanted to believe that all Talented Misfits strove for right and justice. Yet there were many who hid their abilities from themselves, de-spising them. It was why we tended to rescue children and young people, for they were more capable of changing their thinking, accepting their Talents as gifts to be nurtured and developed; of becoming part of our community.

I forced myself to think of Ariel as having a Talent. It left a bitterness in my mouth.

"To my mind, the real question is what made Ariel set so much store by a single true dream," Domick was saying. "Everyone knows how easy it is to misinterpret them, and how often they're just plain wrong."

I blinked, as his words penetrated. "Maybe he dreamed it more than once. After all, it *was* true."

The rain began to fall more heavily. The coercer looked up with a muffled curse and lengthened his stride. I drew up the hood of the cloak to stop water dripping down my neck and hastened to keep up, my thoughts running ahead of me.

Ariel as a coercer—even as a weak and unaware coercer—was a fearsome notion.

In the early days at Obernewtyn, there had been much concern over the morality of coercion, and even talk about trying to convert it to healing or some other use. But in its aggressive form, it had proven too necessary to our survival.

Instead, there had been a move away from separatism. These days, guilds aimed at training novices to use all of their powers, though Misfits still generally chose to specialize in one specific Talent as part of the process of becoming guilded. There had been some resistance to cross-guilding, until it was realized secondguilding often enhanced the primary ability. For instance, as a farseeker with coercion, I could coerce from a distance, instead of needing to be close to a subject, as a plain coercer must. And the combination of beastspeaking, farseeking and coercivity meant I could coerce animals without being close to them physically.

My thoughts returned reluctantly to Ariel.

I preferred to think of him as an unconscious coercer than as an empath. Obscene and impossible that he should possess the same ability as the blind, infinitely gentle Empath guildmaster, Dameon. If Ariel were an empath, it must be some twisted variant.

I felt my mouth open, for indeed he might be a Talented Misfit *with a defective mentality*. There were many born since the holocaust with warped minds, and not all were drooling imbeciles.

I shivered at the notion of a Misfit with empathy or coercion, driven by a defective will. Thank Lud, Ariel had never realized his abilities or used them consciously. How much more harm might he have done?

Domick plucked at my arm and pointed across the street to a dingy inn whose signboard proclaimed it incongruously: The Good Egg. "That is where we will make contact with Brydda."

"The last time I went into an inn looking for Brydda Llewellyn I was arrested," I said, following him reluctantly across the street.

"We will not ask for him openly," Domick said. "It is just a matter of ordering a certain obscure brew that will not be in stock."

"What if someone else gives the same order?"

"There is a combination of quantity and certain other stipulations that trigger the process which will signal the Black Dog. He will come as soon as he is able."

"Here?"

"Here, or to the safe house. We will wait a little, in case he gets the message at once and sends someone for us."

There was no time for more talk as the door swung open and a group of drunken revellers stumbled out into the night. Domick grasped my elbow, steering me past them and into the inn.

Though cavernous, it was ill lit as all such places were, for the people who came to drown in their cups seldom wanted to be seen doing it. The inn was surprisingly crowded for a city supposedly full of poor, but perhaps there was always enough coin for oblivion. The room reeked of cheap, sour fement and old sweat, but I was grateful for the warmth created by the throng, and glad to stop walking. My feet ached from the tramp across the city.

I took my cloak off with some trepidation, having no alternative but to let myself be seen as a girl because of the clothes I had put on in the safe-house bathing room. I could have completely coerced one or two people into seeing me any way I chose, but not a whole roomful. Coercing a large number of people was more of a general influencing, or accentuating what existed already in their minds. There was always the risk that someone with a natural mindshield would see through this less specific coercive cloaking, but only if their attention was on us at the moment I set it in place. Oddly, I had always found the cloak very effective even when there were unTalents with natural mindshields, because a group of people tended, more often than not, to operate as a single not very intelligent mind. I was not clad in very extravagant gypsy garments, but the tan of my skin marked me, so I made them see me as a full-grown gypsy woman rather than as a girl.

To my astonishment, Domick suddenly reached out and drew me into the circle of his arms.

X

"Ho, Mika!" someone cried.

Domick turned, digging his fingers into my shoulder.

"Join us," said a lean man with thin lips and close-set, crafty eyes that moved over me like prying fingers. "Who is your companion, my friend?"

"Her name is Elaria," Domick said in an arrogant voice, that startled me almost as much as his putting an arm around me. He slid into a seat, pushing me before him, and I found myself crushed up next to an old man with a grizzled face and faded blue eyes.

"Elaria, I am Kerry," the lean man opposite introduced himself with a leering smile. He stabbed a blunt finger at the old man beside me. "That is Col, and by me here is Oria."

Col merely grunted, but the blond Oria gave me a friendly nod which filled me with suspicion. Since when were people even civil to a gypsy? Far less a halfbreed.

As if voicing my thoughts, a thick-necked youth further down the trestle scowled at me. "Halfbreeds are thieves an' plaguebirds," he said loudly in a highland accent.

"You are a fool, boy, blighted with stupidity which is a greater affliction than plague, since one cannot even hope for recovery from it." Domick's eyes were contemptuous. "Would I walk about with a carrier of the curst plague?"

Oria and Kerry roared with more laughter than the witticism deserved. As the blond woman moved her head, I saw that her face was disfigured on one side by the savage spore of the plague.

"Ruga, you've been put in your place fair enough." Kerry leaned across the table to me and I fought the urge to slap him away. "She's comely enough," he approved. "But my taste don't run to gypsy flesh. Specially not one with a face as sober and sour as a judge."

"No doubt she finds you a sour eyeful, too," laughed the woman.

"Well, like I was sayin'," said the young highlander further down the trestle somewhat huffily, "I'm thinkin' of joining th' soldierguards. I'd just as soon step on a few necks as have mine stood on."

The oldster beside me gave a sneering laugh. "Join up and you'll just as likely find yourself warring with the tribesfolk in distant Sador. And I've heard they roast over their temple fires and eat them as who they take prisoner."

"There will be no war against Sador," Kerry said swiftly, his eyes flickering to Domick's face and away.

"The Council has sent Herders on a mission to make peace with the Sadorians," Domick said.

"Peace?" echoed the bleary-eyed Col. "The Council don't want peace, 'cepting maybe a big piece of Sador. And who knows what them Herders are after?"

An awkward silence ensued, then Kerry said with forced joviality, "Best keep your words for other company, old man. There's some here who might not take kind to your speculation."

"You have no need to worry about me," Domick said. "Fools blow air out of their mouths as often as their bums, and either way it causes a stink and comes to nothing."

I looked around at the people at the table and, seeing their expressions, understood suddenly why Kerry and the woman had behaved so oddly, fawning on Domick and being civil to his gypsy companion.

They were *afraid* of him.

Abruptly Domick rose and left the table, saying he wanted to order a drink. I tried not to look disconcerted at being left alone there, but I sensed the others at the table studying me covertly. Unnerved, I shaped a general coercive probe suggesting that I was defective. Given the general prejudice against gypsies, it was not difficult to plant a negative thought and, as the idea took root, they relaxed.

Only the plague-scarred Oria did not cease her scrutiny. I entered her mind at the subvocal level, and discovered she believed me to be a spy left by Domick to garner information. It was clear this disturbed her, but I did not trouble to delve deeper to learn why. I merely grafted into her thoughts a memory of having seen me before with different men at different inns, and of having observed enough of my behavior to judge me defective.

Her disquiet faded, and she dismissed me from her mind. Turning to the old man, her brow creased with exasperation. "You are a fool with a mouth big enough to lose yourself in, Col. Don't you know who that was?"

He shrugged. "Some official or other. What do I care who he is? I've seen him here before."

"And that makes him safe?" she hissed. "He works for the Councilcourt."

"He sweeps the floor an' runs messages," said the highlander, Ruga, from down the table. "I heard him say so once."

Oria sneered at him openly. "Of course he would *say* that."

The old man frowned. "Well, what does he do then? Is he a spy?"

I felt myself start, but no one noticed.

The blond woman leaned across the table and lowered her voice. "You heard what happened to Jomas?"

Col nodded, so I was forced to read the memory evoked by the woman's question direct from his thoughts.

A man called Jomas had spoken out against a Councilman, claiming he had charged his father with Sedition in order to obtain his farm. Jomas had been arrested and charged with Sedition the very next night, and tortured so savagely that he had never walked again.

"So what? Everyone knows they torture Seditioners," Col said.

Oria looked around before speaking. "Neither Jomas nor his father were Seditioners and well you know it. But the point of the story is that Mika was here when Jomas was mouthing off about that Councilman."

Col snorted. "And for that you'd have me fear him? This place is full of folk who'd sell their mother for the price of a mug. Anyone could have reported Jomas' mouthings."

"I went to see Jomas when he recovered," Oria said fiercely. "He told me *he* was there when they tortured him."

"He?" the oldster echoed, confused.

"He," Oria repeated. *"Mika."* She lowered her voice. "He is a torturer."

I was so shocked that my probe faltered in its hold on the group.

"We should not talk of such matters," Kerry said, his tone suddenly anxious. "People who talk too much have a way of disappearing into the interrogation rooms beneath the Councilcourt."

"Sometimes elsewhere," Oria added darkly, as I regained control.

Obviously there were rumors about Domick because he worked for the Council. But why would he let them believe he was a torturer when a little coercion could quash a rumor that must surely make spying more difficult? Someone else asked if it was true that the recruiters were looking to war in Sador.

"Course they are," Oria snapped. "But they're hoping the mission will bring the tribes to heel without it. War is expensive, but they want control of the spice groves . . ."

"That's not why they're recruitin'," retorted Ruga. "They want more soldierguards because of them rebels with Henry Druid gettin' too big for their boots."

"Henry Druid is dead," Oria interrupted. "He died in a firestorm in the highlands."

"I heard tell he was took to Herder Isle," Col said.

"You think everyone who walks out the door is spirited away to Herder Isle," she snapped. "The Druid is dead and Brydda Llewellyn leads the rebels in Sutrium. That is all that matters."

"Not Brydda. Bodera," Kerry began.

"What does it matter who leads them?" sneered Col, glaring into his mug. "I hope there is a war, whether it is with them demonish-looking Sadorians, or the rebels, and they all kill one another."

"They'll have their work to catch the Black Dog," Oria said, with a defiance that made it clear that she had rebel sympathies. "They fall over their own feet every time they try."

"Don't matter who hunts him," the old man said. "They'll get him in the end. He's just a man, an' sooner or later he'll make a mistake."

The table fell silent again as Domick reappeared bearing a small jug.

"I don't know how you drink that mucky syrup," Oria said brightly. "But if you ordered it more often, old Filo would keep some for you instead of your having to wait while he sends out."

The coercer made no comment. He drank with every evidence of enjoyment, then set the mug down and looked around the table.

"You should be careful of loose talk," he said casually.

There was something in his tone that brought everyone in the immediate vicinity to silence.

"There are those who are not what they seem," he went on, in a sinister tone. My heart began to thump. Now what was he doing?

"Take that man." He pointed to a drunkard, staring about owlishly at the nearest table. "He seems no more than a sot. But is he really? Perhaps he is something more than he seems. Perhaps he has drunk less than he makes out and flaps his ears for Seditious talk."

Oria laughed uneasily. "You jest."

Domick smiled and sipped at his golden mead.

Suddenly the oldster beside me slammed his fist down. "I'll not pretend! I am no Seditioner to sit here cowering. You think we don't know what you are?"

The room fell silent and all attention was on Domick, waiting to see what he would do.

"And what am I?" he asked in a soft, dangerous voice.

"I've a right to speak," Col blustered, the silence penetrating at last.

Domick supped the last of his drink, then he dabbed fastidiously at the edges of his mouth with a handkerchief. "You should use your tongue for less dangerous talk, old man," he said at last. "Fortunately for you I sweep, I write letters, and sometimes I deliver them. That is all I do. Anyone who would say otherwise . . . should think twice."

He rose, pulling me up with him. I kept my head down, trying to look moronish and insignificant. Domick nodded languidly to Kerry and Oria. "Perhaps, when next I come, the company will be better."

Kerry smiled stiffly and bade us walk safe.

∽

Outside I pulled on my cloak with suppressed fury. "Are you crazy? There is not a person in there who will forget your face or mine after that little display. And how is it so many people know you work for the Council? Is this some brilliant new strategy based on telling your business to every stranger you meet?"

Domick was looking out into the night, his face empty of expression. "A Council employee is often investigated in the interests of security. If I had no life to investigate I would be instantly suspect. I must have a background to fit my role and those people are part of it."

"You might have warned me," I snapped. "What if I hadn't been able to improvise?"

"Guildmistress of the farseekers, veteran of hundreds of daring and brilliant rescues, unable to improvise?" he demanded dryly. "Yet I would have warned you, had I expected them to be there."

"Perhaps they deliberately came tonight to avoid you," I snapped.

He shrugged. "That is likely true. They have no love for me. Why are you so angry? I would have warned you if I could, but once inside it was too late."

I opened my mouth to deny anger, then realized he was right. My temper had risen from fear.

"That was unnecessarily dangerous," I said, forcing myself to be calm. "You deliberately frightened them. Why?"

Domick's eyes were like the holes of the Blacklands as he stepped out into the night. "The people back there are not bad folk. They are just poor and ignorant. They speak too freely of matters better left unsaid. I am trying to teach them to keep their mouths shut."

"And what if there had been trouble in there? What would Mika have done? Would his job protect him if someone decided to take offense to his bullying?"

"You don't seem to grasp what it means to be employed by the Council," Domick said softly. "There is little it would not protect me against."

I snorted in disbelief. "Only those high up in Council employ warrant that sort of protection. Not a sweeper of floors."

"You think that after so many seasons' faithful service, the Council would not reward a loyal worker?" Domick asked quietly.

A chill crept along my veins. "You mean . . ."

He laughed hollowly. "Let us say that it is some time since I have swept a floor in the Councilcourt, Elspeth."

I licked my lips. "The people back there believe that you are a torturer. Why didn't you coerce them against believing such a rumor? What possible advantage could it give you to let them think it?"

"The protection and power wrought by fear," Domick said. "But even if the rumor had served no purpose, I cannot stop it. I could not coerce everyone to disbelieve a rumor that is so universal."

"This . . . this rumor that you are a torturer . . . how did such a thing begin?"

He did not answer and my heart began to beat unevenly. "Domick, what is it you do at the Council now?"

"I am not a torturer," he said at last, in a grim voice. Then his eyes went over my shoulder. "Look, there is Idris. Brydda has sent him to collect us."

XI

Idris bowed, his round face lit by the sunny smile that I *remembered from my last journey to the coast.* "It is good to see you again, Elspeth."

The young rebel had appeared outside The Good Egg wrapped up in a cloak, and gestured for us to follow. It was not until we reached a small dark hovel, a few streets away from the inn, that he had drawn back the hood of his coat to greet us. Brydda had sent him to fetch us.

"What is this place?" I asked, as the rebel turned to the door of the hovel. It seemed to be nothing more than an abandoned husk, and was surely far too small to be useful as a safe house.

"It is just a house," Idris said, forcing the sagging door open and ushering us before him. Inside the front hall it was dark and we stood in silence as he found and lit a lantern. The hall was empty, its walls scored black from fire. Idris removed his cloak and hung it on a wall peg, closing the door carefully after us. Following suit, I remembered that he had always been meticulous and slightly plodding.

He brought us through empty, musty rooms to the back of the place, saying, "There are any number of houses standing vacant since the plagues." He pointed to the door of an outbuilding from under which a slice of light showed. "They have proven very useful to us as temporary residences."

"Don't people wonder at seeing lamps in abandoned houses?"

Idris shrugged. "No doubt, but it does not matter. We rarely spend more than a few days in any one. This is the last night we will spend here." He pushed open the door.

The room behind it was a complete contrast to the great, warm home-like place Brydda had used as a headquarters in Aborium. It was bare but for a number of rough stools drawn around a little fire, a table

piled with scrolls and maps, and a small supply of firewood stacked up on
the floor. It was clearly hastily assembled and no attempt had been made
to render it comfortable. The room was dimly lit by a single guttering
candle stuck in a mug on the table, and by the warmer glow of the fire.
Black cloth had been tacked over the only window, but as soon as we
entered Idris extinguished the brighter lantern he carried, the gesture belying
his unconcern about being seen.

"Where is Brydda?" I asked.

In answer, the large backed chair directly before the fire swiveled to
reveal the big rebel holding a knife.

"Little sad eyes," he said in his rumbling voice.

Watching him sheath the knife and rise, I thought the old nickname
suited him better than it had ever suited me. The rebel leader seemed more
hugely bearlike than ever, hair falling almost to his shoulders in a great
shaggy pelt of midnight curls. Yet there was a tinge of silver amidst the
darker hair at his temples and in his beard, and fine lines about his eyes
that I did not remember. The unsheathed knife told its own story. This
life was taking its toll of him, as Domick said. Brydda was like a lamp,
with the flame burning dangerously low.

He gathered me into the affectionate ursine hug I remembered so
well. That at least was unchanged, and my heart swelled with a gladness
that startled me and made me feel absurdly like bursting into tears.

I watched as he greeted Domick with warmth, and was interested to
see that for a moment even the coercer lost some of his icy reserve.

"Let me give you both something to eat." Brydda gestured to the
fire where a battered pot hung. "It is only a broth, I am afraid. These days
we do not have the time or leisure to feast." The note of regret in his
voice was palpable.

"I will do it," Idris said, pushing Brydda's hand aside and lifting the
pot from the hook. He opened the lid and a delicious odor wafted out.
My stomach, ever ready to herald its state, growled loudly.

Brydda burst out laughing.

"I have not eaten for ages," I defended myself. "I do not feel so
hungry when I am traveling, and we have just arrived."

"I am the opposite," Brydda said ruefully. He accepted a mug of
soup from Idris and handed it to me. "I eat as though for ten men! Ah
well, we are what we eat, that is evident. And how was the road?"

His eyes sharpened at this. He had switched effortlessly from friend to Seditioner chief seeking information. I drank and thought a moment before answering. "It was emptier than usual. More soldierguards and less ordinary travelers. Toll gates were heavily guarded. I would say the Council is tightening up on travel; trying to keep a record of who is going where and why." I glanced at him from under my lashes. "Perhaps trying to prevent rebel groups from liaising with one another. And from what I heard at the inn tonight, your people are, at least in part, the reason for the increase in soldierguard recruitment."

Brydda nodded approvingly. "Little sad eyes I called you, but perhaps sharp eyes it should have been. A good summation. And what do you think all these clues suggest?"

"That you have stepped up your activities and have been careless enough to let the Council know it," I said promptly. "Or maybe you meant the Council to know it, for some reason. Or..." I hesitated to voice the third and obvious possibility.

"Or we have a traitor in our midst telling the Council they had best get ready for a fight," Brydda finished bluntly.

"And had they?" I asked quickly. "*Are* your people planning to move openly against the Council?"

Brydda made a vague gesture. "I fear it is true we may have a traitor in our midst, not that they would have much to tell the way things are organized now. Mind you, any news of our doings would affright them. But the increase in recruitment is less for fear of us, than the Council's way of dealing with the number of people without work since the plague. So many who would have found work on farms have come to the city. The Council would have been wiser to restore the farms. But they are also making sure there are plenty of soldierguards if it comes to war over Sador." Here his eyes sought Domick's and the coercer nodded confirmation.

I frowned at this further evidence of close interaction between the rebels and the safe house.

"The crime rate in the cities has tripled since the plagues, and the Council reasons that employing more soldierguards will reduce the number of people out of work and control those who have chosen robbery as a way of filling their bellies," Domick said.

The rebel chief drank some soup. "Not a bad stratagem, but of course one wonders where the coin is coming from to pay them..." He paused, seeming lost in thought for a moment.

"Then the increase in soldierguards has nothing to do with Seditioners?" I persisted.

Brydda gave me a swift look. "I did not say that. It is true the Council have begun to regard us more seriously as a threat to their autonomy and that may be another reason for their increase in recruitment. In part, this is unavoidable. We have heightened our profile among the people, for we will need them behind us when..." He stopped.

I turned to stare at the rebel chief squarely.

"Are you planning to attack the Council, Brydda?" I asked flatly.

"Of course. You knew that all along."

I felt my temper rise. "Do not play word games with me."

I heard Idris and Domick gasp aloud, but did not take my eyes from Brydda's.

"You mistrust me?" he asked sorrowfully.

"Never," I said. "But I think you mistrust *us*. Or you think of us as fools to be lulled with meaningless phrases and promises. Don't underestimate us, Brydda. We can read the signs as well as anyone and rumor says the rebels prepare for rebellion."

There was a charged silence, then Brydda sighed heavily. "You have long known that we meant to oppose the Council openly."

I said nothing, waiting.

"Will you believe me if I tell you that no date is named as yet for rebellion?" he asked.

I hesitated, then nodded. "If you say it, I will believe it."

"Good, for I do say it." The rebel leaned forward to throw some wood on the fire, then he looked at me again. "Rushton sent you to ask about the alliance, didn't he? That is why you are here?"

"One of the reasons," I admitted, ignoring Domick's involuntary movement at my side. "When we heard the rumor that the rebels were to rise, he wondered why you had sent no word of it to us. And then he wondered if the reason you had not spoken was connected to your delay in responding to our offer of alliance."

Brydda gave me a penetrating look, then he sighed. "Perhaps I have underestimated you. There *is* a problem with the alliance and that is why I have evaded Domick's queries. I hoped to be able to solve them and present Rushton with a united acceptance of your offer."

My heart did an unpleasant dance. "You won't accept us then?" My tone was colder than I had intended, but it was too late to retract it. And in the light of his words, perhaps it did not matter.

The big rebel leaned closer. "Elspeth, you talk as if it is *my* decision. It is not."

"You are their leader."

To my surprise, he shook his head.

"When first you knew me, I was the leader of a small but devoted rebel group in Aborium," he said. "I'm still not sure how I ended up running things there, but I did. Just after we met, as you know, I left the Aborium group to be run by my second, a stolid, reliable fellow named Yavok. I took no one with me but Reuvan and Idris."

Brydda was silent a moment, his eyes distant, as he looked into the past.

"While in Aborium, I had come to know the leader of the Sutrium group; an old fox named Bodera, whom I learned to admire tremendously. I had told him my dream of uniting all the rebel groups to overthrow the Council and when he heard I was to leave Aborium, he invited me to work toward that end with him. The most difficult thing is that each rebel group operates almost in isolation. Fortunately Bodera was one of the first rebel leaders, and he knew all the others. They respect him tremendously, so he was exactly the right person to serve as a focus. It was only because Bodera asked it that the other rebels listened to my ideas."

"Then he is the leader of the rebels?" I asked, remembering that Kerry had spoken that name in The Good Egg.

Brydda sighed. "No single person is the leader. That is what I am trying to tell you. But Bodera has great influence on the group leaders and, because of this, he was able to get the rebels to accept me as a sort of roving overseer, whose task is to bring the groups together long enough to fight the Council. But it has been an uphill battle. And when Bodera dies it is almost certain the whole thing will fall apart."

"Is he so old, then?" I asked, fascinated by this glimpse into rebel affairs.

"Old, yes, but it is not age that kills him. He has a peculiar slow form of the rotting sickness contracted when he was a boy on Council-farms. In those days, they sent children with their parents if they were charged with Sedition, rather than sending them off to orphan homes."

From my own days in the orphan home system, I knew inmates mined whitestick, a poisonous residue of the Great White. In its raw state the substance had to touch the skin in order to transmit its poisons and we had been given gloves to collect it. Sometimes I still woke at night sweating because I had dreamed of touching it by accident, as so many orphans did.

Once collected, whitestick was sent to the Councilfarms where it was treated to strip away the poisons so that it could be used in medicines and as a power source. The transformation of whitestick was dangerous, because during the process it emitted the poisonous radiations which, over time, caused the dreaded rotting sickness. This was why a long Councilfarm sentence was, in effect, a delayed death sentence.

Brydda blinked, searching for the tail of his narrative. "I have convinced Bodera of the need for an alliance with your people. But the two largest rebel-group leaders reject you."

"Do they give reasons?"

Brydda ran a huge hand through tousled curls. "You come to the heart of my reluctance to present you with the matter. Of the two who oppose you utterly, the first is Tardis who runs the rebel organization in Murmroth. He has taken over recently from his father, who was a stiff-necked bigot. Tardis responded to the proposal of an alliance between rebel and Talented Misfit forces with predictable repugnance. He wrote that Talent or no, Misfits are not true humans and he will not make an alliance with mutants. The one bright note is that, unlike his father, Tardis does not favor wholesale extermination of your people. His note said that we do not make contracts with cows or horses, neither do we kill them for being less than human." He smiled wryly. "I am afraid Tardis regards your ability to communicate with animals as further proof of your inhumanity."

"And the other rebel leader?" I asked quietly.

"Malik. He runs most of the rebel groups in the upper lowlands and around the Gelfort Ranges." Brydda's voice held a flatness that told me he disliked this man. "He is more violent in his rejection of Misfits than Tardis. He thinks you are freaks and should be eradicated like poisonweed in a kitchen garden. There are others who oppose you too, but they might be argued around. If not, they are less important. Tardis and Malik are the keys. There can be no alliance without the compliance of at least one of them, for they command the greatest numbers among the rebel forces. Without them, there will be no rebellion."

Brydda tugged at his beard, a familiar signal of his inner disturbance.

"Then there is to be no alliance?" I strove to sound undeterred.

Brydda sat forward in his seat in sudden agitation. "Do not think that! It is the very reason I have hesitated to tell Domick what has been happening. There is always hope."

"What hope?" I demanded. "That boy you had guarding the safe house reacted like I was poison because he thought I was a *gypsy*. How is he going to react when he knows I am a Misfit? We can't make your people accept us."

With a wave of bitterness, I thought of Rushton's assertion that we would do exactly that. But what real hope was there for Misfits to live normal lives, if even our own allies thought of us as freaks? If we did trick them into standing beside us in battle, what would it ultimately achieve? Not the acceptance we dreamed of. And how long would it take before loathing tolerance became hatred and, once again, persecution?

"There is hope in Bodera's support of you," Brydda disagreed. "And there is always the possibility that we can change the minds of the other rebels. One of the main problems is that the rebels think all Misfits are shambling mental defectives. Second," he said swiftly, forestalling my outrage, "your youth has convinced them that there would be no military gain in an alliance with you."

"And in the face of this, you can say that there is hope?" I asked incredulously.

"I believe so," Brydda reiterated firmly. "The first thing is to make my comrades think of you as normal human beings."

"A simple matter."

Brydda ignored that. "I think you should meet with them."

"Rushton already did that and it was obviously no use."

He patted my arm. "I meant you specifically, Elspeth. Rushton was introduced to them as your leader, but he is no Misfit. The rebels think of him as your keeper, as if you were a troupe of trained bears."

Rushton had not bothered to tell the rebels he was a Misfit. He scarcely thought of himself that way, because his powers were latent. No one had thought of telling Brydda the truth. I decided now was not the time.

"I think they need to meet a real Talented Misfit," Brydda said.

"To what end?" I snapped. "Would you parade a freak before them to confirm their prejudices?"

The rebel shook his head. "I would have them meet and speak with a lovely young woman gifted with remarkable abilities. Not a mutated monster. I have not dared explain Misfit abilities in much detail because they would only increase your monstrosity in the rebels' eyes. But if they could meet you and accept you, then we could show them what you can do. After that, your age will not matter, I warrant."

"You think a meeting with me will make them accept us?"

"I do not know," Brydda admitted. "Their prejudices are very strong, but it is worth a try."

I sighed. He was right. It was worth a try, only because the alternative was too bleak to contemplate. "When would such a meeting take place?"

Brydda's eyes sparkled. "There is to be a meeting of the rebel leaders soon. The day is not yet set, but it would be within a sevenday."

I felt a sick thrill of nervousness. "Where?"

"It must be held outside Sutrium," the rebel said promptly. He looked over his shoulder at Idris who, though silent, had stood close to Brydda throughout our conversation.

The boy nodded and Brydda reached out to ruffle his hair. In the wordlessness of this exchange, I saw the depth of the friendship between the pair.

"It is my strict policy to keep the locations of rebel meetings secret until the last minute so they cannot be revealed to anyone." The big man shifted forward in his eagerness. "Think of it, Elspeth, all you need do is convince one or two rebel leaders to regard you as human. At the worst, it will be a positive beginning."

I thought it more likely such a meeting would simply confirm the rebels' prejudices. People had a way of seeing what they wanted to. And in spite of all Brydda's precautions and countermeasures, the big man had said there was a possibility of a traitor being in the rebels' midst. Which meant a definite risk.

On the other hand, if by some slim chance he was right and I did manage to change the rebels' attitude to us, the risk would be a small price to pay.

"I will send word to Obernewtyn to see if the guildmerge will condone this meeting."

Brydda frowned. "I am not sure there will be enough time to send for approval. It is a great pity you have no birds here."

Idris smiled at my expression of bewilderment. "We have learned that if some birds are raised in a certain place, they will return to that place unerringly, no matter how far away it is that they are released. Each of the rebel groups now raises birds and we exchange them so that we always have the means to send messages swiftly. These are carried in tiny cylinders fastened to a bird's leg. It was done this way in the Beforetime."

Brydda slapped his own leg. "But wait! *You* would not need a homing bird, Elspeth. You could simply beast-speak your message to a bird and ask it to fly to Obernewtyn."

Before I could respond, the door burst open behind us.

Brydda whirled, drawing his knife again in one smooth-flowing movement and landing in a crouch. Idris had just as swiftly taken a sword from his belt.

It was only the seaman, Reuvan, whom I had met before in Aborium. His handsome face was red from exertion and he was so intent upon delivering his message that he did not notice me or Domick. "There is a drunk in an inn who claims Salamander is in Sutrium," he panted.

Idris was at the edge of my vision and I was startled to see his pleasant features twist in a spasm of hatred.

Brydda slid his knife home and turned to us. "I am sorry to cut short our supper but I must go at once. I will come to you soon at the safe house and we will talk again. But think on what I have said, Elspeth. The only hope of an alliance rests with your being able to alter the way rebels see Misfits. A meeting may be the only means of achieving that."

A moment later, we were outside in the dark, and alone.

"Who is Salamander?" I asked Domick.

"It is the name of the man who runs the slave trade," Domick said. His tone was stiff. "Why didn't you tell me you were here to find out about the alliance? Doesn't Rushton trust me now? Has he sent you to check up on me?"

I shook my head helplessly.

XII

I woke near dawn to the muted sound of rain falling. The air felt clammy, and I wondered what had disturbed me.

I let my thoughts drift and had the fleeting impression of an unfamiliar mind touching mine as lightly as the shadow of an intruder might fall on a sleeping form. I was startled to find Maruman's mind curled up around mine, and gently extricated myself.

I let my mind rove about the safe house but encountered no unknown mental pattern. I was surprised, though, to discover Kella hurrying along the corridor outside my sleeping chamber.

The door opened and she peered in, a lantern held high.

"What's wrong?" I asked, sitting up.

Maruman stirred in his sleep on the pillow by my head, and opened his golden eye. I had the odd impression that he had been awake all along.

"It's the gypsy," the healer said softly, so as not to disturb Dragon. "She woke me screaming."

"Wait." I jumped out of bed and pulled a thick shawl around my shoulders.

We ran along the corridor and into the healing chamber. As I approached the gypsy's bed I saw that her eyes were open, unfocused as Maruman's when he was in the midst of his mad dreams. Kneeling by the mattress I forced myself to be calm as her queer two-colored eyes swiveled to me. One eye was blue and the other a mottled brown.

"Can she see me?" I asked.

The healer shook her head. "She's not really awake. She's having some sort of nightmare, but her system won't be able to take the strain for long. She's broken the sleepseal."

"Is she going to die?"

"If this goes on, yes. I need to get into her mind to relieve some of the pressure, but as a healer I can't work against her will, and her mind is refusing me access." Kella's eyes narrowed. "*You* could get into her mind through her subconscious."

I looked down at the gypsy and felt a ripple of unease at her steady regard. "And do what?"

"Wake her," Kella said promptly. "I'll do the rest."

I licked my lips. They felt dry and rough.

The subconscious could not be shielded, so the deepest thoughts and desires that formed the basis of the gypsy's character would be laid bare to me in all their seething disorder, if I did as Kella wanted. We had agreed unanimously in guildmerge that we could establish no system of dealing with the unTalented until they regarded us as equals. As long as they saw us as freaks, we could not afford to have any scruples about using our coercive abilities to plunder their minds and make use of what we found there against them. It was war, Rushton had said, and we must win before making terms.

What Kella wanted me to do had nothing to do with enemies or war. The gypsy was not my enemy and the thought of entering her undermind filled me with revulsion.

My reaction was emotional and instinctive. When I had first been sent to Obernewtyn, Ariel and his masters had invaded my mind using a coercive machine. My only defense had been to enter into a partial mindbond with Rushton and use his latent abilities to strengthen me and shield my mind from their torture. Such a bond had meant a kind of mental nakedness, the thought of which even now made me tremble. Rushton had not abused the mindbond by blending entirely as bondmate lovers might, but the affair had left us uncomfortable, intimate strangers, and me with an abiding hatred of all such mindbonds.

"Elspeth," the healer murmured, drawing me out of my thoughts. "I know this is hard for you, but healers enter unconscious minds all the time and do not regard it as violation. It's simply a matter of not absorbing while you are in there—of separating yourself mentally."

I ground my teeth together. She was making a good point. To enter for healing purposes was hardly a brutal invasion. And in doing so I would be saving Obernewtyn and myself, if Maryon's predictions were true.

Steeling myself, I leaned closer to the gypsy.

"Do you hear me?" I asked aloud, still reluctant to begin. She made no response, either by word or gesture, to indicate she heard what I was saying. I sighed. "All right. I'll deepsense her and bring her out if I can."

I closed my eyes and called up a deepsensing probe, extending it delicately toward the gypsy. My mind butted gently against her shield then slid down the outside of it, seeking the point at which it would dissolve in the maelstrom of the subconscious. I would be able to enter freely there.

I was astonished to find the shielding continued right down into the subconscious. I quested against it, but it was no aberration. It was definitely the sort of shield unTalented minds produced naturally. After a little time I realized that it was an ordinary shield, which had been somehow displaced from the upper levels of the gypsy's mind. It was scarred and buckled and I began pushing coercively, testing until I found a weak place where I could enter.

Amost immediately I came upon a wall of forgetting. Again, this was not usually found at a subconscious level.

Puzzled, I examined it.

The wall had fused in places with the mindshield, but both showed signs of recent erosion. This suggested the original forgetting established by the mind had begun to give way, allowing whatever had been repressed by it to rise to the conscious mind. From what I could see, the gypsy's mind had reacted instinctively to protect itself, collapsing its shield on top of the memory in an effort to bury it. Obviously this had worked for a time, though it had left her unconscious. That must have happened when she was at the stake about to be burned in Guanette. Now the memory had begun to erode the fused barrier again, causing the fit that had so alarmed Kella.

Curious, I pressed myself lightly against the fused barrier, wondering at its strength. It was paper thin and before I could stop myself, I had slipped through into . . .

. . . a small room. I/we are alone. My/our hands and legs bound tightly. I/we cringe at the sound of Caldeko's screams. What are they doing to you, my love?

????

The Herder and the boy are bringing me/us to him now. Showing him to me/us. The thing that was once Caldeko is barely recognizable as human. The mindless keening that rises from it fills me/us with horror/fear.

Caldeko opens his eyes. His soul reaches out of them to us/me, begging for release.

The Herder smiles coldly. "Tell me about the Twentyfamilies, gypsy."

(How does he know?) I/we shake my/our head but I/we are afraid. (Block)

He waves his hand at the boy who does something with a brand.

Caldeko's shrieks fill my mind. Split me open.

I/we scream and struggle to reach him.

"Tell me his given name," the Herder says.

I/we dare not speak. Must not. But Caldeko is my/our soul's joy! I must answer.

Caldeko is suddenly silent.

"Fool," the Herder snarls at the boy, "you have killed him. If she will not speak to save her bondmate pain, she will never speak to save herself. Well, we will make her an example . . ."

Caldeko/beloved is gone in terrible agony because I/we would not speak.

The pain of the tearing/the guilt/the grief is unbearable. I push it down into the darkness because I cannot exist with it burning at me.

I make a wall of forgetting to bind it.

Peace.

Now I am at the stake. My arms are cut and bound. I am to die. I do not fear. I go to join my beloved. But, oh the thought of Caldeko gives the memory/the monster life, and it rises to savage me. (I betrayed/I failed)

I panic and reach. Again I have it trapped, but the new barrier is flimsy. It will not last long. No matter. Soon the flames will come and it will be ended.

But they do not come. I live. There is only one escape. Now I must go down and down into the deepest darkness. But something opposes . . . me . . . Everything . . . slows . . . down . . . I . . . am . . . weak . . . But . . . I . . . fight them and now, now it is easier. Soon it will be over.

The spiral begins. I go down. I want to go to escape the memories (I failed to speak/I betrayed/he died/I killed him).

I fall. I dive.

I hear the song. Death sings my name.

I felt myself pulled down; dragged with the gypsy woman in her search for death. I fought against her, struggling frantically to disentangle our minds. We were too deep. I sensed the humming magnetism of the mindstream.

Desperate, I drew on the dark strength of the violent power at the depth of my mind to tear us free from the pull of the mindstream.

I wrenched us away into...

...a pale shining room. I/we are looking at a man with skin as black and polished as an old tree root. He wears odd clothing. His eyes are frightened. He takes me/us by the shoulders and shakes me/us hard.

"We have no choice, Emma," he whispers. "We have to escape. If we tell them what they set in motion by their actions, Cassandra said they won't believe us. And there will be more experiments because, by telling them, we will have shown them what we are."

"But if what Cassandra foresaw is to happen, we will give them what they seek," I/we say.

"She said one of us will give in. One will reveal what we have kept hidden. But it need not be you or me. We can escape."

We/Emma open our mouth. "But where can we go? How will we survive? There will be radiation sickness when it comes—better to die at once."

"There are places that won't be hit so badly, where humanity will go on. We will join them. But Cassandra said we must make sure no one ever knows about us or what we can do."

"Oh God, why? Tell me why this has to happen?" We/Emma begin to cry hysterically.

The man squeezes our/her arm awkwardly, as if he is not used to such gestures. "I don't know. Come with the rest of us. We're going to go to the Reichler Clinic first. Hannah and Jacob believe the mountains will be safe. Cassandra has been in communication with Ines to say we are coming...."

... The mindstream tugged, dragging me/us free. I/we are close to the mindstream. It is pulling me/us down....

A familiar voice called to me, harsh and intrusive.

"ElspethInnle! Remember your promise. You must live to come when the oldOne calls!"

It was Maruman.

"How are you here?" I asked dreamily, drifting downward, mesmerized by the shimmering siren call of the mindstream.

"You mustnot go down anymore. Stop!" he sent urgently. I felt a searing pain on my hand, and at the same time I realized that I was on the verge of sharing the gypsy's suicide.

I fought to free myself, but again Maruman spoke. "Bring the funaga. Bring her, for she is needed."

I reached back and dragged the gypsy up with me. She screamed in fury and fought me. I drew on the murderous power hidden in my mind for the strength to reject the mindstream and to cling to her. I gripped tighter still. I could not hold her so close and remain separate. Our minds merged again...

... Something is holding/pulling. I am caught/something makes me live/stay/suffer.

Let me go. Let me die. I cannot bear it.

WHO ARE YOU?

I screamed and opened my eyes. My hand was hurting. I looked down at it. Blood welled from three savage slashes across my palm.

"Elspeth!" Kella was shaking me, white to the lips.

"What?" I felt dazed, confused, shattered. My mind churned with grief and guilt. Disjointed, impossible memories seethed in me. And my hand!

"What happened?" the healer demanded. "One minute you were sitting there calmly and the next you started to convulse. I thought..." She sank down on the edge of the gypsy's bed. "Lud, but you scared me!"

"I scared myself," I said shakily, pushing the heaviness of my unbraided hair from my face. I felt hot and cold at the same time and my hands were trembling uncontrollably. I dabbed at the blood.

"Maruman scratched you," Kella said. "He climbed onto your lap when you were in the gypsy's mind, and when you started to shudder and groan, he scratched you. He must have been frightened. I . . . I slapped him and he ran out."

"He saved my life," I murmured, remembering the combination of fierce pain and Maruman's voice that had wrenched me from the oddly seductive dive into death. That was twice now he had appeared in my dreams as a savior. How queer. I had gone too deep but he brought me out of it.

"Oh no," Kella said, aghast. "I slapped him!"

There was a small moan from the bed and I looked at the gypsy. Her eyes were open still, but now tears coursed down her cheeks, and her expression was aware, anguished. "I wanted to die," she whispered hoarsely. "Someone stopped me. . . ." She stopped, seeming to realize what she had said. "Someone?"

"It doesn't matter," I said wearily. "You're awake."

The gypsy buried her face in her hands. "Doesn't matter? You don't know. You can't imagine what I have done. . . ."

Her eyes glazed and her eyelids shut. I looked up to see Kella frowning in concentration. After a moment she nodded in satisfaction. "I've put her back to sleep. It's just a light sleepseal—not like the one Roland put on her whole body. She is out of immediate danger, but still terribly weak. I have closed her wounds and hastened the healing, and her body is responding. What on earth happened?"

I took a deep shuddering breath and looked down at the gypsy. There seemed no connection between the tempestuous, desperate will I had encountered inside her mind, and this passive form.

"She had locked a memory behind a wall of forgetting, but it was leaking all over the place. She was trying to die so as to escape it. Roland's seal slowed her down, but tonight she broke through. I was testing the wall, but I had neglected to erect a separating shield around myself. When I broke through, we just merged."

Kella's eyes widened. "And?"

"I relived the memory she was trying to escape. The Herder we rescued her from tortured and killed her bondmate in front of her to make her tell him the name of some Twentyfamilies gypsy. She refused to speak. When her bondmate died, she was convinced she had betrayed him."

I felt a surge of sorrow for the loss of a man I had never known; a residue of the accidental joining. "She thinks if she had talked, he would have lived."

Kella's eyes were curious beneath the compassion.

I shook my head sadly. "It was obvious the man had been tortured before they brought her in. He was on the verge of death and I don't think he even knew what was happening."

The healer was ashen. "Monsters," she whispered. "They are monsters to be capable of such barbarism."

Kella bent to draw the covers up around the gypsy and, abruptly, I remembered the odd sideways shunt that had hurled me into the depths of the gypsy's mind, and into one of the racial memories that Maryon said arose occasionally from the mindstream like bubbles. The memory was already blurred at the edges like a dream, and even as I groped for detail it dissolved.

But I did remember one thing. *There had been something in the dream about the Reichler Clinic.*

I shook my head. The foray into the gypsy's mind had drained me, and my own wits drifted with weariness. The previous day and night seemed to have been going on for years.

Kella washed the scratches Maruman had inflicted, worrying all the while about her treatment of him.

"He will understand," I said. We went into the kitchen and I took a poker and stirred the embers of the night's fire to life.

"Domick told me you met with Brydda last night," Kella said, hanging up a jug of mead to warm.

I nodded. Domick had spoken little on the journey back to the safe house. When we arrived he had stalked off to his bed, saying he had to go early the following morning to the Councilcourt. He was convinced Rushton had lost faith in him. I did not know what to say for, in one sense, it was true. Rushton had been puzzled about Domick's communications. But that had been explained by Brydda. Yet he had changed so much and until I had understood why, I did feel somewhat uneasy about him.

"Greetings, ElspethInnle." Maruman was sitting under the table, his yellow eye glinting. "I am glad you didnot take the longsleep."

"You saved me."

"Of course," he sent complacently. "Maruman guards the dream-trails."

"Elspeth?" Kella prompted, unaware of my exchange with the cat.

"I'm sorry. What did you say?"

"I said surely there is no hurry to return the gypsy to her people, now that she has wakened. You will be able to wait until she recovers completely."

Impulsively, I told the healer the part of Maryon's prediction dealing with Obernewtyn, and of the need to return the gypsy within a sevenday. I did not mention myself or the mysterious word whose meaning I must discover.

She was aghast. "But that is impossible!"

"I meant to ask Brydda about the best way to do it, but I didn't get the chance. I'll find a way."

"That's not what I meant," said Kella. "You cannot move her. Her system has undergone a terrible shock and she was already weak. She needs to be allowed to rest. . . ."

"There is no time," I snapped.

"Then she has even less time, for you will kill her if you move her in the next couple of days." There was a deep crease between the healer's eyebrows. "Does she have no rights of her own, Elspeth? Is Obernewtyn more important than her life?"

I bit my lip in sudden shame. I had not thought of the gypsy at all, only of myself and Obernewtyn. I felt sick. "You are right," I said. "I will not move her until you say it is safe. But, Lud, pray it is soon."

Kella's face softened. "I did not mean to criticize you. After all it is not for yourself, but for Obernewtyn that you fear." I flushed, but held my tongue. "In any case, you cannot return her until you find her people. That is your task, and mine is to heal her. I'll do my very best to have her well enough to be shifted before the days are up," she vowed, squeezing my hand.

Just then Dragon came in, and I was glad of the distraction. Her face and hands were unusually clean and her hair roughly braided. Her beauty struck me anew and, from Kella's expression, she felt the same.

"Hungry," Dragon said.

My stomach chimed in agreement. Kella laughed and rose to carve some slices of bread and cheese. My mouth watered as she toasted them, then for a time there was silence as we ate. Kella did not join us, but fed crumbs of cheese to Maruman as an apology. He sent to me that he felt no ill will for the slap she had administered but he accepted her offerings with feline fastidiousness, seeing she needed the reassurance.

"Good," Dragon announced at last, patting her distended stomach. Then she gave me an anxious look. "Dragon stay?"

"I suppose you must, but you're an awful nuisance," I sighed.

"Nuisance," she echoed with an identical sigh.

I stifled a grin and put my arm around her. "Dragon, I'm going to let you stay, but only if you promise to do exactly as you are told."

"Promise," she agreed after some thought. "Promise and stay."

"Is Domick still asleep?" I asked Kella.

At once the strained look returned to her eyes. "He has returned to the Councilcourt."

I nodded and looked into the fire, reflecting on his behavior at The Good Egg. Kella would be a great deal more worried if she understood more about what Domick did when he was not with her.

I wondered how the healer, with her horror of torture, would respond to the knowledge that people thought her bondmate a Council torturer. My own wild fear, that he really had become a torturer, now seemed absurd. No Misfit could stoop to that, not even a coercer.

Ariel's lovely vicious face floated into my mind, giving lie to that certainty, but I thrust it away. Domick was no Ariel.

Only then did it occur to me that Domick had not told me what he did now at the Councilcourt.

XIII

"Do you understand me/ElspethInnle, who stands before you?" I sent, framing the thought carefully.

The bird tilted its head and eyed me, but I could sense no thought from it, other than an instinct to eat and a subliminal memory of flight that filled me with restlessness.

"Well? Are you buying the creature or communing with it?" the stallholder demanded.

Resignedly, I handed him a coin and he passed over the cage. "You must be starting up a breeding pen with all them birds you keep buying. Store them in your wagon, do you, boy?"

I took the cage and turned away, ignoring him.

"You found one?" Kella whispered eagerly, coming over from another stall.

I shook my head. "I can't get any sense out of it."

The healer stared at me. "Oh, Elspeth! Are we going to free this one like all the others?"

"What else?" I asked in a disgruntled voice.

Brydda's suggestion of using a bird as a messenger had seemed a marvelous one. But I had quickly discovered that I could not reach the birds' minds. It was always easier to communicate with tamed or partly tame animals, so I had decided to search the numerous markets for a part tamed bird with which I could communicate and which would agree to carry a message to Obernewtyn. This search would also give me the opportunity to randomly coerce a large number of people for information about gypsies.

I found an astonishing amount of Herder-induced superstition and wild surmise, but very little real information. Landfolk despised all gypsies, but hated and envied the Twentyfamilies with a passion that surprised me.

Kella had accompanied me to the market to replenish her supply of herbs, leaving a disgruntled Matthew to watch Dragon and the gypsy, but she had lingered, drawn into my search for a messenger bird. In many ways, she was of more use here than I, for I had quickly discovered that the birds available in the market were not sentient in the way that Maruman or Gahltha were, and used a mode of communication closer to empathy than farsensing. I was able to receive only the vaguest images from their minds. Kella was able to use her slight secondary empathic ability to muster some response from them, but it was an emotional response.

After trying so many, I was beginning to believe that the Agyllians had the only avian minds capable of full communication with humans.

Those few who were able to comprehend farthought speech seemed to have no grasp of time, and very short attention spans.

However having felt, even dimly, a bird's longing for freedom, I had not been able to leave it caged. So far I had purchased fifteen of the wretched creatures and set them free, running our store of coin dangerously low.

Kella made a strangled noise and I thought she wept out of frustration.

Then I realized she was trying not to laugh.

I sighed, wondering why I was still trying, when it had been perfectly obvious for some time that the idea was doomed.

"I'm sorry for laughing. It was stupid," she said contritely.

She thought I had sighed out of irritation. "It's good to hear laughter," I said, and meant it. "It helps me to forget Maryon's deadline or that I must make some reply to Brydda, when he comes, as to whether I will meet with the other rebel leaders. Since these birds will not lend themselves as messengers to carry word to Obernewtyn, I will have to make the decision myself."

"Domick will have sent a message off this morning," Kella said.

"Nevertheless, it will take too long to arrive to give me any direction. I will be back at Obernewtyn by the time it gets there."

And perhaps I will return to die before the next Days of Rain; the thought crept insidiously into my mind.

I wished I had had the chance to tell Brydda about the gypsy and ask his advice. Lud only knew how long it would take him to call by the safe house. I racked my brain for some sensible way to find the gyspy's people, but nothing came to me other than finding out where they set their wagons up in the city, and going among them. I did not want to do that unless there was some other course, given my lack of knowledge. The other obvious alternative was to have Kella waken the gypsy again so I could ask her. But I was reluctant to do that. I still felt a twinge of shame at the selfishness of my attitude to the gypsy. Let her waken when she would.

Maneuvering the cage through the market throng, I noticed a ragged gypsy lad trying to sell something to a stallholder; a halfbreed by his poverty, the lad was clearly receiving short shrift from the trader, and departed finally with a doleful expression.

If I could coerce some general information out of this gypsy about his people, I would be able to face any number of them without quaking in my boots for fear that I was about to give myself away as an impostor. It was odd how blithely I had gone about pretending to be a gypsy, when I thought I knew all that needed knowing about them. Now, my ignorance terrified me. Swiftly, I shaped a light probe and sent it after the lad.

The probe slid away from his mind, blocked by a natural shield.

"Damn," I muttered, withdrawing.

"The poor thing," Kella murmured, her eyes following the gypsy too. "They are not allowed to farm or settle and no one wants to buy from them. No wonder they take to thievery. What else are they supposed to do?"

I thought again of our gypsy, and the whole question of half and pureblood. She was a halfbreed, but she had let her bondmate suffer torture rather than speak the name of a Twentyfamilies gypsy. Yet Domick had told me with absolute conviction that Twentyfamilies were estranged from halfbreeds.

I scowled. For a moment, I forgot my guilt and almost felt I hated the gypsy. I had saved her from the Herder flame only to see her try to suicide and draw me with her! Even if I had broken free and let her go, her death would have meant my own if the foretellings were true. It angered me that my life should hinge on a woman who valued her life not at all.

She had not wakened from her suicide attempt when I rose late in the morning. Over firstmeal I had thought this ominous, until Kella told me of the sleepseal she had imposed to give the gypsy time to recover.

"Does it have to be a bird?" Kella asked.

I blinked at her, having lost the thread of the conversation.

"Does it have to be a bird you use as a messenger?" she reiterated.

"Any other animal would move too slowly, and be as vulnerable as a human messenger," I said. "I might just as well send Matthew." The virtue of a bird was in its swiftness and its inviolability once it had taken to the wing.

"Gypsy pig!" a man hissed, as I brushed past him.

I ignored him, but Kella paled. Belatedly it occurred to me that I was endangering the healer by being with her. There was a definite antagonism in the eyes of anyone who looked at me. The Herders' slur campaign against gypsies had been more than effective.

The sooner we got back to the safe house the better.

Gahltha whinnied softly as we approached the public holding yard, and in spite of my tensions I smiled at the sight of him. I had asked Dragon to dirty him and the empath had surpassed herself. His coat was so matted and filthy that it was impossible to tell his color, and he smelled truly disgusting. I could not imagine what she had rubbed onto him to achieve such a repellent stench. For once, there had been no need to worry about leaving him alone since he looked and smelled far too disreputable to be worth stealing.

"Is the bird/sahric useful/capable?" Gahltha inquired politely. Sahric meant those who sing. I noted the coolness in his mental voice and realized he had not forgiven me for going to The Good Egg without him the previous night. I had promised not do it again, knowing he felt his guardianship to be a sacred trust from Atthis, but clearly he still felt slighted.

"I'm afraid this bird/sahric is no more capable of hearing me than any of the others," I sent, looking glumly at the cage.

I mounted him, and then offered my spare hand to Kella. She wrinkled her nose in distaste and volunteered to walk.

Suddenly, her eyes shifted to something beyond me, her smile vanishing. My heartbeat quickened.

"What is it?" I resisted the urge to swing around and look for myself.

"That gypsy who was watching us before. He's on the other side of the holding yard on a horse. I'm sure he is following us."

I forced myself to be calm and think. Mistakes were made when people panicked.

"Are you sure it is the same gypsy?" I asked at last. Kella was nervy and much given to morose reflections. When she had first claimed a gypsy was watching us, I had dismissed it as overactive imagination. Gypsies were too much on both our minds.

"I was sure before and I am surer now. He is looking directly at us," the healer said forcefully. She looked near to fainting. If the gypsy *had* only been staring casually, he would surely wonder at her white face.

"Perhaps I should beastspeak his horse and ask it to tip him on his head," I said. As I had hoped, her fear evaporated into concern at my flippancy.

"Be serious, Elspeth. He has obviously followed us through the market and he might now follow us to the safe house."

"He probably follows us because he finds you attractive," I said robustly.

She colored. "But I ... I ..."

"Oh, never mind. I won't tell Domick you have been flirting with gypsies. Or perhaps I will, since he neglects you disgracefully."

Her color deepened and then fled. "Oh Elspeth, he's coming around this way! I'm sure he's trying to see your face."

My heart bumped against my breast, but I kept my voice calm for the healer's sake. She sounded on the verge of hysteria. "This is what we are going to do," I said calmly. "You are going to go back into the market and pretend to shop. If the gypsy follows you, I *will* ask his horse to drop him on his head. If he follows me, Gahltha and I will lead him out of the city and give him a run for his troubles. Either way, stay at the market a little while and then make your way carefully back to the safe house."

Kella nodded, eyes wide and frightened.

I handed the birdcage down to her. "Take this."

She took it and moved off as I had bid. I waved, turning my head slightly and scanning the area with peripheral vision.

Sure enough, he was there; the same tall, rangy gypsy in costly blue silk that Kella had pointed out earlier. I was puzzled. What reason could he have for his interest in us, other than the slight curiosity value of a halfbreed gypsy boy walking with a Landgirl? He did not fit the description of the gypsy that Matthew had seen leaving Guanette. This was the only other reason I could imagine for a gypsy following us, and that would have been odd in any case since, in Guanette, he would have seen a girl when now I was dressed up as a boy.

From the corner of my eye, I studied the gypsy. His dark hair was bound back in a plait and the thong about his brow was stained to match his shirt. Kella had said the elaborate and expensive garments marked him as Twentyfamilies, but this did not seem conclusive evidence to me. After all, a halfbreed gypsy might be vain enough to spend his coin on such things.

I pretended to adjust my trews, watching to see if he followed the healer. Sitting astride his gray horse, he stared intently after her. But almost at once his eyes moved toward me. I dropped my glance and pretended to spur Gahltha.

"Head out of the city."

The black horse wheeled and, after a moment, I pretended to look back as if I had remembered something to say. Kella had gone and I shrugged and turned forward, but my heart was beating wildly. "He's right behind us," I sent.

"The grayequine ridden by this funaga who follows is named Sendari," Gahltha sent suddenly. "He/Sendari tells that he has not been owned/ridden long by thisfunaga. Thisone owns many equines, but none can make the mindtalking with the funaga as I do. He says thisone's hands and feet are skilled and gentle."

I frowned. His ownership of many horses seemed to confirm Kella's surmise that our pursuer was Twentyfamilies, but it still did not tell me why he was following me.

"Does Sendari know why thisfunaga follows?" I asked, just in case he did.

Gahltha paused, then reported the answer to my question. "He/Sendari tells that thisfunaga has ridden about much in these days soonest past, but he has arrived nowhere. He has spent much time standing/idle."

Watching, I thought uneasily. Looking for us?

"When he saw us, the funaga tensed/knees tight," Gahltha went on. "But he/Sendari does not know why the funaga follows."

I made up my mind to coerce the gypsy and sent my mind questing, but to my frustration I encountered yet another natural shield. Cursing, I withdrew, thinking it an odd coincidence that all three gypsy minds I had tried to enter possessed natural mindshields. Garth's theory that more unTalents were developing mindshields was beginning to look as if it might be true. But still, I doubted the increase in natural shielding was because of a few Misfits born capable of mindspeech among the hundreds of normal Landfolk. There must be some other reason for it.

I was indecisive. Short of turning and demanding to know what he was up to, there was no subtle way to find out the gypsy's motives. His natural shield would prevent my coercing him except at a subconscious level and there would be no gain in that. And I could ask him outright what he was doing, but I could have no way of coercing the memory of our meeting from him. On impulse, I decided to lose him.

"Let's lose him," I sent to Gahltha. Obedient, he broke into a fast canter along a road leading toward the farmlands east of the city.

I could hear the clatter of hoofs behind me, but Gahltha did not increase his pace, saying it would confuse Sendari's rider if we behaved as if we were being followed. He was right, for the gypsy made no attempt to overtake us, but rode at a distance.

Only when we reached the edge of the outlying farmlands surrounding Sutrium did Gahltha break into a full gallop, and I flattened myself to reduce wind resistance, thrilling to the race.

"He/Sendari follows," he sent.

"Can you outrun him?"

"There is no need," the black horse sent, with a faint echo of his old haughtiness. "Only the funaga race one another for no reason. Equines race for mate or lifesaving. Sendari knows that you are Innle. He willdo what is needed."

I was discomforted by the thought that the gray horse would let us get away because of his belief that I was a figure from beastlegend. I had been horrified the first time I had heard this notion in a Beastguild meeting, and had insisted I was not the person their myths referred to. I had tried endless times since to convince Gahltha I was not their heroic savior. It was enough that the Agyllians had co-opted me into their dreams and futuretellings without finding the animals were trying to do the same thing. But neither Gahltha nor any of the other beasts at Obernewtyn would listen. Any more than Sendari would, I realized.

We rode swiftly along the dirt road, then without warning Gahltha turned sharply, cutting across a long, sloping, grass plain. I clung tightly in case he stumbled on the rough tussocky ground and unseated me, leaving it to him to decide how to proceed.

Looking ahead, I saw that he was making for a thick copse further up the slope. He slowed only fractionally as we entered the trees and in moments we thundered out the other side of the stand onto open ground.

A rush of exaltation filled me as the ground blurred beneath us, and I gave a wild cry as we crested the hill.

Glancing back over my shoulder, I saw that the gray had fallen into a limping walk, just short of the copse. Even as I watched, his rider dismounted.

"He/Sendari has pretended lameness," Gahltha reported, coming to a halt too.

I saw the rider kneel to examine the leg and was impressed. Most men would have lashed their mount to death rather than lose a quarry.

As if he sensed my thoughts, the gypsy stood and looked up to where I sat on Gahltha. I could not see his expression but, as we turned to ride away, I had a mad urge and held up my hand to wave in a cheeky salute.

∾

The city center lay visible on the other side of the hill and we went straight overland, riding over farm fences and hedges at a full gallop and making for a main road snaking through the hills and trees. We came out wider than I realized, for when we reached the road, we were in full view of a gate *from the outside*. There was no possibility of withdrawing without looking suspicious, for the soldierguards manning the gate were gazing at us.

My heartbeat quickened, as we approached them for the second time in a few days. Fortunately, it was not the same gate I had entered before.

"Papers, boy," a burly soldierguard demanded. It was an expedition rule that each of us carry papers on us at all times when we traveled away from Obernewtyn, so that was no trouble. I dug in my pocket and proffered them without a word, concentrating on reinforcing the coercive suggestion that I was a boy.

The other soldierguard stared at me narrowly, but it was not until his eyes dropped to Gahltha, that I became concerned. He sauntered over and rubbed at the dried filth on the horse's coat.

"Got some white, does he, under all that muck?" he asked.

It was such a strange query that I probed his thoughts.

He was comparing Gahltha to a description that he had been given of Zade. Fortunately Zade was smaller and had white markings on his brow and back legs.

"All black," I said. Digging further in the soldierguard's mind, I found a description of a gypsy girl that was clearly me but, to my horror, there was also one of Matthew and the wagon.

Word of our rescue of the gypsy in Guanette had finally reached the Council.

"Been in the highlands recentlike?" the soldierguard asked, moving around and casually taking a hold of Gahltha's rein. I told myself firmly that there was no reason to fear—Gahltha did not fit the description he had been given, and I was nothing like Matthew. Even so, my heart pounded.

"I came from Murmroth way just yesterday, and just now from Kinraide by Rangorn," I said in a bored voice, coercing the soldierguard eyeing my papers to see yesterday's date on the entry stamp and a watermark from the Suggredoon ferry. I wrinkled my nose and gestured at Gahltha. "Mud keeps away the flying biters, but it smells none too good."

The two men exchanged a glance, and the one with the papers nodded. The soldierguard's subvocal thoughts told me he had decided that neither Gahltha nor I fitted the descriptions they had been given.

The larger of the pair shrugged, releasing the reins. "All right then, boy. Get on."

I rode off, trembling with reaction, and not just because news of the incident in Guanette had reached Sutrium at last.

While in the soldierguard's mind, I had learned that the Council intended to institute a gate search for the missing gypsy and her two rescuers the very next day. Each gate would have a copy of the original Normalcy Register, which recorded each child at birth after Herder inspection, against which to check the authenticity of travelers' papers.

This told me that either they thought we were heading for Sutrium with the gypsy woman and hoped to trap us as we entered or, worse, they knew we were here already, and meant to stop us getting out of the city.

XIV

It was just on dusk before we rode into the market square alongside the safe house. I had taken a circuitous route from the city gate in case we were followed.

I asked Gahltha to stop, and took a long careful look around the market. He moved restlessly under me, sending that his flesh itched and stank abominably and must we go so slowly?

"I have to make sure no one was watching us," I said firmly.

He trotted into the lane leading to the wagon-repair yard without comment. I slid off his back and removed the false bit and bridle, lighting a lantern. "I'll wash/brush you down," I sent.

We walked together to the high gate leading to the grassy courtyard. The walls made it look like an additional shed from without. At the far end of the yard was a real shed where hay and oats were kept. Jaygar was a shadow grazing in the deeper darkness alongside it, and lifted his head to greet us.

I hung the lantern from a nail, and stepped into the shed to find a brush.

"Clean Gal-ta?"

I started at the voice rising from the shadowy interior of the feed shed.

"Dragon?" I called softly, when my wits had regrouped.

The empath-coercer emerged carrying the curry brush. She looked even dirtier than usual, her face woebegone and tearstained.

"What are you doing here?" I asked her.

She held up the brush. "Dragon dirty Gal-ta. Dragon clean Gal-ta. Dragon waiting and waiting."

"Does Kella know where you are?"

"Kella sad," Dragon said earnestly. "Cryingcryingcrying here," she pointed to her slight breasts. "Water here," she touched one of her eyes. "Not see. Not hear Dragon."

I frowned. The empath's ability to receive emotions was improving dramatically if she could sense inner tears. "And Matthew? Where is he?"

Dragon scowled. "Matthew say: Dragon go away. Dragon go. Not need Matthew. Dragon wait here with Jaygar. Dragon loves Jaygar!"

I sent an enquiry to the roan.

"Mornir has been here since sundeath," he confirmed. "Water came from her eyes."

Dragon's tears did not surprise me. Matthew had been unremittingly cold to her since our arrival at the safe house, for he fiercely resented her presence. He was being childish, but it was a personal matter between them and I did not wish to intervene. Better if he and Dragon resolved their own difficulties.

Poor Kella's tears were somewhat more worrying, for her emotions were already stretched taut.

"See if you can do as good a job at cleaning Gahltha as you did in dirtying him," I told Dragon absently. "Come inside when you have finished."

She nodded and set to with the brush, seeming glad of something to do. I was sorry for her boredom and loneliness, but perhaps she would learn from it that disobedience did not always produce what was desired.

Domick, Kella and Matthew were in the kitchen. The Farseeker ward spotted me first.

"Thank Lud," he cried fervently, jumping to his feet. "We've been worried sick. I tried to farseek ye but there is so much static about. Maybe it's just from all these minds crammed together, but it feels like trying to see over Blacklands or tainted ground."

"Kella said a gypsy followed you at the market," Domick interrupted. There was no sign of the previous night's anger over what he perceived as Rushton's mistrust.

I told them what had happened.

"He definitely weren't th' gypsy I saw ride out from Guanette," Matthew declared. "*He* were old an' gray-haired. An' he weren't Twenty-families judgin' by his clothes."

My thoughts ran off at a tangent. The gypsy woman had refused to answer the Herder's questions about a Twentyfamilies man, though her bondmate was being tortured. Who had she been protecting and why? And how had the Herder known about it anyway? Could the Twentyfamilies man she had refused to name be the same man who had ridden after me from the market? But if he was Twentyfamilies, why pretend to be a despised halfbreed?

"Perhaps this gypsy simply mistook Elspeth for someone he knew," Domick said dismissively. "In any case you lost him and I have more important news. The Council is about to institute stringent new measures for checking papers in an attempt to catch two renegade halfbreed gypsies who set another gypsy free in Guanette, killing a Herder and two soldierguards in the process."

There was a tinge of righteousness in his tone.

"I know," I said mildly, and explained what had happened at the gate. "I am only surprised it has taken as long as it did for news of the rescue to get here."

"You realize this may make it more difficult for you to leave Sutrium."

"I doubt it," I said, leaving my own worries unvoiced. "I am sure these restrictions will be temporary. They will waste time, occupy a greater number of soldierguards and catch nothing. How long do you suppose they will support the expense of all this vigilance?"

"As soon as you begin to ask questions, the gypsies will know you came to Sutrium," Domick countered. "It won't take long for it to filter through to the Council or the Herder Faction after that, because information is as good as coin. Someone will talk and then the gates will be nets, waiting to catch you. And the soldierguards within the city will look for you as well. There will be random street searches and if you are wandering about...."

"I have no intention of wandering about," I said crisply. "Nor will I be asking indiscreet questions. And if I had to, I could have Kella waken the gypsy woman and she could tell me whom to contact."

To my surprise, Kella nodded easily. "If you want, I can break it now. It's only a light seal and it will not harm her to talk."

"I do not like the idea," Domick protested. "Why not simply put her in the street before waking her? She can make her own way to her people."

Kella gave Domick a fierce look. "What if she were recognized before she had time to find them? And how will she make her way anywhere? She is very weak."

"Her welfare is not our concern," he answered coldly. His eyes shifted to me again. "I don't understand why you are so determined to deliver her personally. Or why you have risked so much for her. She could report us."

"And what will she have to report?" Kella asked. "A wild story about being saved by gypsies who live inside a building in the city? In any case she is hardly likely to march off to the Council to tell her story, is she? And since we will not be dumping her in a street, she is unlikely to be caught by them and forced to speak." She stopped abruptly, staring at her bondmate. The tension between them was fraught with unspoken angers.

"As for letting her creep away herself," I said gently, "it would be a waste. I want to find out more about the gypsies and this will give me the perfect opportunity. Or so Maryon advised," I added, suddenly wearying of parrying words.

"Maryon did?" Domick echoed with less belligerence. "You did not say that the Futuretell guildmistress had spoken of this."

"Didn't I?" I asked offhandedly. I knew this was the perfect moment to tell Domick about Maryon's prediction, but his continued callousness about the gypsy's fate made me stubborn. I stood up and looked pointedly at Kella. "Shall we go and wake her then and see what she has to say?"

∾

The healer lay a gentle hand on the gypsy's brow.

The woman stirred almost at once, and opened her eyes. I was startled anew at their queer coloring. She gave me a deeply suspicious look, heavy brows drawing together forbiddingly over the bridge of her nose.

"Who are you?" she rasped hoarsely. "Where am I?"

"You are in a safe house," Kella said soothingly, giving her water to moisten her throat. "You have been very ill."

The woman's head turned sideways and she frowned up at Kella for a long moment before her odd two-colored eyes shifted back to me.

"I do not know you."

"I am a friend." I said, relieved that she had no memory of her previous brief wakening.

Her chin lifted. "I do not forget the name of a friend. Yet your voice sounds ... familiar." She sounded as if this were more cause for suspicion than comfort. "What is this place?"

"As I said, it is a safe house."

"*Whose* safe house? This Landgirl's? Or yours? A gypsy girl dressed up as a boy."

"I am no more gypsy than I am a boy," I said bluntly. "I dye my skin and dress like this so as to travel unnoticed about the Land. I was traveling through Guanette disguised as a gypsy when I came upon the burning. I stole you from a Herder who was about to roast you, and he was killed. Now the soldierguards are hunting me and you both. Your friend in the trees shot that Herder, not I, but the Council believes I did it."

Her eyes were suddenly wary. "My friend?"

"The gray-haired man who helped me get you out of Guanette," I said, bending the truth slightly.

Her eyes widened with alarm. "He *helped* you?"

I nodded, still narrowly skirting a direct lie. "If you tell us how to contact him, we will send him word that you are here."

Her eyes narrowed. "Where is *here*?"

"We are in Sutrium."

Her eyes darkened with mistrust. "You brought me all the way to Sutrium alone? Past the city gate and the soldierguards?"

"I hid you in our wagon."

She nodded as if such trickery were commonplace, and perhaps it was among her kind. "Why did you bring me here?"

"Why not?" I could not tell her Maryon had commanded me to bring her to Sutrium.

"Why did you help me in Guanette?"

"Perhaps because we may be of some use to one another, and might even become friends."

She closed her eyes. "I have no friends."

"Then a stranger did you an unbelievable service if that gray-haired man was not a friend," I snapped.

Her eyes opened, glinting. "As *you* have done? If he was a friend, why would he ride off and leave me with strangers?"

I felt my cheeks redden and realized I had underestimated her intelligence. "We became separated. He rode toward Sutrium," I said less aggressively. "Look, all I want to know is how to bring you to him."

Her eyes were abruptly cool. "I do not recall asking for aid. Then or now."

"You were in no condition to ask for help then. Nevertheless, I gave it and thought you would be pleased," I added, unable to prevent irritation from seeping into my tone.

"You interfered of your own free will," she snarled. "I was not afraid to die."

"No," I agreed shortly. "You were afraid to live."

There was a flare of pain in her eyes then. "I am not afraid of anything," she said, but there was a frayed edge to her tone. I guessed she was remembering snatches of her attempt to die, and wondering at her dreams, for so would she judge my communications with her subconscious mind.

Her eyes went from me to Kella and back again. "What do you want of me?"

"No more than to return you to your people." That was almost true. I tried to get into her mind again, now that she was conscious, but the block remained firm. Any further pressure and she would feel me.

"Why?" she demanded flatly. "I am no Twentyfamilies with a fat purse to reward you."

I decided to take refuge in indignation.

"You are a fugitive wanted by the soldierguards and the Herder Faction, and they are no friends of mine. I helped you and I expected no more than a little gratitude. Well, that is too high a price for your life, it seems. Instead you insult me and accuse me of sinister motives. Well, if you want to die, that is your business, but I have vowed to return you to your people and that is what I will do. With or without your help."

There was a prickly silence.

"Help me to dress and show me a door and you will not need to trouble yourself," she said stonily.

Again she had outmaneuvered me. "No."

She nodded, as if she had anticipated the answer. "If you will not let me go, then I am your prisoner."

I thought fast. "In your weakened state you are bound to be picked up by the soldierguards and questioned. You would speak of us and this place. Perhaps even lead someone here to us with your gypsy tracking-skills. I cannot risk it."

"Who are you?" she said again, her expression openly baffled. Then she seemed to think of something, and glared at me anew. "You needn't think I will tell you anything. . . ." She stopped.

"Anything about your Twentyfamilies friend?" I asked without thought. Instantly her face changed and my heart sank.

Angry at my own mishandling of the matter, I said bitterly, "I don't suppose you know what *swallow* means either?"

Her eyes widened in shock, the pupils swelling to devour the color. "Where . . . where did you hear that?"

My mind raced. "You said it in your sleep," I lied.

"It must have been gibberish," the gypsy said, closing her eyes again, her voice indifferent. "I do not know what it means, and I am afraid I can tell you nothing about my blood kin since I remember nothing more about myself than that I am a gypsy. If that gray-haired man you saw was a friend, I do not remember him either. Or even my name."

She was lying, but there was nothing I could do to make her speak.

"Well, perhaps in time you will remember. . . ." I said icily. "Just as I might recall why it was I bothered to save your life!"

I made a sign to Kella to put her back to sleep.

"Wretched, ungrateful woman," I snapped, as we left the chamber.

Kella shrugged. "You can't really blame her, the way things are for halfbreeds. For all she knows this whole thing could be an elaborate trap. You must admit it would look odd."

Which is the closest she would come to telling me I had been clumsy. I sighed and my temper faded. I had been stupid to expect the woman to fall on my neck.

"What is *swallow*, Elspeth? The gypsy did not speak of it in her sleep," Kella said, as we went back down the hall to the kitchen.

"Didn't she?" I murmured vaguely. I was thinking of how dramatically the woman's face had changed at the mere mention of the word.

Obviously it meant a great deal to her, and that intrigued me. What could it mean? Was it a password of some kind?

"Will you try talking to her again?" Kella asked, stopping outside the kitchen door.

"I think not. If she will not be forced to speak by the torture of her bondmate, there is no way she will tell her story to a pair of strangers with no good reason for helping her," I said. "Damn the woman for being so difficult. I will have to find her people the hard way."

"The hard way?"

I nodded. "I will have to go among the gypsies and probe at random in the hope of finding some clue as to where she might safely be taken. It must be time for luck to work for me rather than against. Domick was right that asking questions would be dangerous, but if I can't get to her people by farseeking, I will have no alternative."

I fell silent. The troublesome quest Maryon had sent me on was becoming more impossible. Fleetingly I was tempted just to give up. After all, the Futureteller guildmistress had, herself, said that futuretellings were often wrongly interpreted.

Yet, I could not just sit back and hope Maryon had made a mistake, when Obernewtyn's future and my own life were in the balance.

"Where do gypsies camp when they stay in the city?"

Kella gave me a quick, comprehending look. "They are permitted to camp on any green, but most go to the largest green over near the Suggredoon."

"Both half and pureblood gypsies?"

She nodded, clearly troubled. "Gypsies don't think in terms of physical boundaries, so in spite of the Great Divide Twentyfamilies camp alongside halfbreed wagons. But that does not happen often. Twentyfamilies gypsies come to Sutrium only in the Days of Rain, when they are to tender the yearly tithe. Otherwise they avoid cities." She hesitated. "If you go there you might encounter the Twentyfamilies man who followed us. Perhaps you could wait a few days until they have gone."

"I dare not wait," I interrupted. "I will have to risk it."

I sighed and wished Maryon's prediction had been more explicit about where in Sutrium the gypsy woman must be taken!

Domick and Dragon were seated at the kitchen trestle when we entered, but Matthew had gone. No doubt he had departed when Dragon came in. I shook my head in disgust.

"What happened?" Domick asked.

"She will tell me nothing. I will have to go among the gypsies after all, and see what I can winkle out."

"You must be careful," Domick said worriedly, and for a moment he seemed like his old self. "I spoke to you of Faction and Council spies but, remember, the gypsies themselves are dangerous to cross. They may value the woman, but your knowing about her makes you a risk. The best way to protect her and themselves would be to kill you. The fact that you are a gypsy might stay their hand, but if they guess for a moment you are not what you pretend to be..."

"I will be careful," I promised.

"Have you decided whether to meet with the rebels?" Domick asked, as I dippered a mug of fement from a pot just boiled and fragrant.

"I have," I said. "I am going to do it. Rushton wants to know where we stand with the rebels, and this meeting will give us an answer one way or the other. As soon as it is over, we will go at once to Obernewtyn."

Domick nodded soberly. "That is best. But be careful tomorrow, for all our sakes." He rose and reached for his cloak.

"You are going out again?" I asked, surprised.

"I have to go back to the Councilcourt. There is some sort of delegation from Sador arriving tonight."

"Sador," I murmured. There had been a lot of talk about the distant province of late; Herders taking a mission there, Councilmen coveting Sador's spice-bearing groves, rumor of war. And now a delegation of Sadorians. A year ago, no one but the few seamen who plied that part of the coast had known of Sador.

"I sent a report to Rushton when the Council sent Herders and a contingent of soldierguards to Sador, not long after the road was opened," Domick said, thinking my silence indicated confusion. "The plagues spurred them on. To begin with, they saw that it might be useful to have a distant province to retreat to if such a thing should come again. Now, there is also the lure of the spice groves."

"You said the Sadorians are sending a group to the Council?" I asked.

He nodded. "They are coming by ship. I expect they will request the removal of the Faction mission from their domain. They have been sending delegations to that effect from the first sevenday the Herders dwelt among them." He pulled on his cloak. "The Herders are interfering in the Sadorian religion and they don't like it. The Earthtemple in Sador controls how much spice is harvested, and it will allow only a small yield. It is my guess the Herders have been sent by the Council to erode the power of the Earthtemple and take it for themselves. Then they will increase the spice yield."

The coercer departed with a perfunctory farewell that obviously distressed Kella. I felt for her, but my mind was filled with all that Domick had said of Sador. Garth would be fascinated.

"I should alter my appearance again. I dare not go out as a girl since the soldierguards have my description, or I would have to have a coercive cloak the whole time and that's a risk with all of these natural shields growing in people." I was talking, to give Kella time to compose herself. "Since that Twentyfamilies gypsy saw me as a boy, I will have to think of something else. Perhaps I could remain a boy, but cut off my hair...."

"No!" Kella looked horrified. "It is so long and beautiful. Like black silk."

Glad to have distracted her, I was nonetheless embarrassed by her words. "I don't care about hair."

"But gypsies do," she said insistently. "They do not cut their hair—men or women."

That was true enough. I had forgotten for the moment. Well then. Perhaps I must go as a grown woman again. Or as an old woman. I had not tried that yet.

"Cut?" Dragon said. She was holding a knife in her hand and looking so hopeful that both Kella and I burst into laughter.

Dragon hooted along happily.

"What's so funny?" Matthew asked lightly, coming in with his hair wet from a bath.

Dragon's laughter died and her eyes followed the ward as he moved across the kitchen and peered into the pot.

"I hope that is not for us," he quipped, sniffing at the herbal preparation.

He could not have helped being aware of the empath's obsessive regard, but he made out that he had not noticed her.

"What about something to drink?" Kella asked Matthew.

He sat down and nodded.

"And will you sit and be waited on?" I snapped, disliking the lazy way he expected the healer to bring him his mug. He flushed and rose to help her and I found myself thinking of him as he had been when first I came to Obernewtyn, with his thinness and his limp and his quick dark gaze. A child then and not yet a man now, for all he looked like one.

"Dragon will drink," Dragon said, looking up at him with pathetic eagerness.

The farseeker scowled, but he filled a mug with the steaming liquid and handed it to her ungraciously. Dragon took it and drank with the solemn air of a Herder acolyte performing a sacred rite.

Matthew turned pointedly away and I felt my temper stir. He might not relish Dragon's adoration, but there was no need for him to be so unkind. He had used all of his charm to make her obedient when he was developing her powers so that she could defend Obernewtyn, but now he was refusing to deal with what he had set in motion.

If it was anyone's fault Dragon had fallen in love with Matthew, it was his own. He had used her affections to manipulate her and now he wanted to stamp them out because he had no use for them.

I forced my anger back, knowing Dragon would detect it if I was not more careful.

Matthew went to refill the empty pot from a stone jug on a bench and Dragon trailed across the kitchen in his wake, drawn as if by some force she could not control. The farseeker did not notice her standing at his elbow and, when he turned back, cannoned hard into her, sending both the full pot of fement and Dragon's mug smashing to the floorboards.

"Fer Lud's sake, ye idiot!" he exploded. "If ye'd drunk th' stuff instead of gollerin' at me like a fool, this wouldn't have happened!"

Dragon's face was white as paper. She turned and ran from the room without a word.

Matthew was left standing amidst the debris of broken mugs and steaming fement, looking from one to the other of us. "Ye dinna understand!"

"I understand that was unnecessary," I said coldly, furious that he expected me to pity him.

He paled and ran his fingers distractedly through his hair. "Ah Lud, damn it. Yer right. I'll go an' apologize."

"Why?" Kella demanded fiercely. "She should not be surprised. More fool her for expecting anything more of you."

"Kella I'm sorry. . . ." Matthew began, but the healer tossed her head, blue eyes flashing.

"Don't tell me!" she said stonily. "I'm not the one you should be talking to. You don't deserve her love, Matthew. She's worth ten of you but you're too stupid to see it."

"She's a savage," Matthew flared, stung by the disgust in her voice.

Kella laughed contemptuously. "You don't have the slightest idea about who or what Dragon is, even after all these months you've spent with her. She's a lot of things, but she's no savage. Eating with fingers and having dirty clothes doesn't make a person a savage. Cruelty and thoughtlessness do. That makes you the only savage here."

I was amazed to hear the gentle healer speak with such passion. Matthew glared at her, then turned on his heel and stalked out. A moment later the stair door slammed. I felt as though a firestorm had roared its destructive way through the room.

Kella let out a great sobbing breath and sank into a chair. I crossed to sit by her and lay a tentative hand on her arm. "Dragon will be all right. It wasn't as bad as all that. . . ."

The healer shook her head. "It's not Dragon, Elspeth. Matthew was wrong, but I should not have spoken to him like that. It . . . It is Domick. You saw how he was tonight. I've tried and tried not to see, but I can't lie to myself anymore. He no longer cares for me. Sometimes I think he hates me. He has changed." She looked at me with tormented eyes. "That is why you did not tell him what Maryon said, isn't it? I know it. Of course, I know. Oh Elspeth, I just want to go home to Obernewtyn."

She began to weep in earnest.

I stared at her helplessly. After a long minute, I crossed to the sky window and stared up. Rain fell lightly but steadily on the glass.

"Perhaps it is time for all of us to go home," I said softly to the night.

XV

I sank into the hot, soapy water with a sigh.

My backside and legs ached from hours of riding about Sutrium and I was chilled to the bone by the constant icy drizzle that had fallen.

It had been altogether a miserable and fruitless morning. I had gone to the biggest green, and then to as many other greens as I could find. At each, I had tried to farseek gypsies at random, *but every single one I had tried had been naturally shielded!* The two Twentyfamilies gypsies I had tried to penetrate were even more tightly blocked than the halfbreeds. I had been forced to assume that all gypsies possessed natural mental shields, though of varying strengths.

As I had done with the gypsy woman, I could have entered any of the gypsies at a subconscious level, but there was simply no point. I would not find what I needed in their underminds.

In desperation, for now there was no other course, I had tried to talk to some gypsies clustered around a well, thinking to draw them gradually to talk of the gypsy woman who had escaped the Herder fires, but Domick had been right. They were impossibly suspicious of strangers, even of gypsies who were unknown to them. I had not needed empathic Talent to be immediately aware of their hostility.

I might have kept on, but for the patches of static arising from the buildings. This had puzzled me until it came to me that the Council might be using stone from Oldtime ruins to build within the city. The amount of residual poison was not high enough to cause the rotting sickness, but it stole my energy having to circumvent it. The other problem was the mysterious, strong static given off by the sea and the Suggredoon. There were several smaller greens close enough to these to make farseeking difficult, if not impossible.

I had returned to the safe house an hour past, exhausted and dis-heartened, and convinced the only hope of success now lay in letting the gypsy go and following her. I was not sure that would qualify as returning her to her people, nor even if it would enable me to learn the meaning of the word *swallow*, but what else could I do?

The trouble was that it would be some time before she could walk unaided, let alone hike across the city on foot. Unless she could be ma-neuvered into taking Jaygar.

Kella had interrupted my depressive account to suggest a bath. "You can't think properly when you are all tied up in knots, cold and tense and miserable."

I had been too tired to argue, though peeling off my garments I had wondered how I could possibly relax.

I sank deeper in the hot water and felt some of the stiffness melt from my bones.

Strange, how little I could believe that I would die if I failed to return the gypsy. But perhaps imagining death was not a thing anyone could do easily.

I closed my eyes with a sigh. As sinew and muscle unknotted, even as the healer had promised, things began to look slightly less bleak. After all I had only been trying for a few hours. Surely there were gypsies with less than half Twentyfamilies blood, whose minds might be penetrated. I would try again.

It would be unwise to be seen moving about the greens and asking questions two days running. Since I could not cut my hair, perhaps I could tip flour into it to make myself seem older. Coercion would do no good, since so many gypsies had natural shields. That left physical disguise.

My mind drifted a little and I found myself wondering if snow would have fallen in the highest valleys yet. Gahltha and I had loved to ride through the early snowfalls, scattering the powdery whiteness high.

My thoughts moved down to the valley where Obernewtyn lay, as if I rode there on Gahltha's back. I visualized the farms and orchards visible from the foothills of the higher mountains. The last crops would be read-ying themselves for harvest and Alad's beastspeakers would soon be work-ing hard.

I smiled at a fleeting memory of picking berries with the farseeker novice, Zarak, and the irrepressible beastspeaker, Lina. Bonded in spirit as children, it was likely this would become formal as they grew up. Our laughter had disturbed Maruman, who had departed in a grumpy huff with rude things to say about noisy funaga. That had made us laugh all the more.

I thought of the brief summerday evenings, redolent with the scent of silvaein blossoms and talking quietly of the future with Dameon.

Unbidden, the image of Rushton came to me with a queer ache.

I saw him as he had been in my earliest days at Obernewtyn. Having hidden me from Ariel and his killer wolves at great risk to himself and his friends, he had told me how to escape from Obernewtyn. I had slipped away from his soft-voiced farewell, running as much from the intensity in his green eyes as from Ariel's wolves.

I had been little more than a babe then, all prickles and fears, and Rushton had been a man. No wonder I had been afraid of what I saw in his eyes.

The inner vision changed and, again, I saw myself departing Obernewtyn for the dangerous journey to the coast that had brought us Dragon and the treasures of the hidden Beforetime library. I had been angry with Rushton that day but, standing on the steps to Obernewtyn, he had waved to me.

And only a few days past I had, again, left him on the steps. But this time, he had not waved.

I blinked and the image faded, leaving me to ponder what it was about Rushton that made me feel suffocated and tense whenever I was with him, and yet think of him so often when we were apart. A queer contrariness, yet it had always been that way between us. When we had met, he had been pretending to be a farm overseer at Obernewtyn, hiding his true identity from Ariel and his masters. My first sight was of him carrying a squealing, struggling piglet.

The memory made me smile though, at the time, I had sensed his latent powers and feared that he had sensed mine and would report me to the masters of Obernewtyn. I had been no more content at his attentions than the pig! But he had not reported me, and in time we had become allies. Yet, in truth, we had never been friends.

I tried to decide what I felt for him. Not revulsion, or hatred or even dislike. It was ... I struggled for an emotion.

It was fear.

I stared unseeing into the water, shocked at the word that seemed to have risen up from my deepest mind. Once said, it would not be dismissed.

Was I afraid of Rushton?

Surely not. I had saved his life and he mine more than once. We shared a vision for Obernewtyn and the Talented Misfits of the Land, and once a partial mindbond. I would trust him with my life, so how could I be afraid of him?

My mind delved deep beneath layers of denial and deception to the truth. Yes, I was afraid, but not of him. *Of myself*. Of giving into that force that drew him toward me; of what it would do to me.

I thought of Dragon trailing helplessly after Matthew, and shuddered. Starkly, I heard the words Rushton had rasped to me once in delirium: *Elspeth love*. I had tried to rob those words of their meaning, and to tell myself his emotions were latent or distorted—that he did not truly feel love, but some lesser thing because of our mindbond.

But it was not true. None of it.

He loved me and I knew it. Had always known it.

And I?

I became aware that my hands were trembling violently where they rested on the rim of the bathing barrel. I thrust them under the water and wrenched my mind forcibly away from Rushton.

I thought of guildmerge, and my emotions calmed.

There was something infinitely reassuring about the thought of the huge circular room where guildmerge was held, with its enormous fires and towering bookshelves stuffed with volumes. It was the heart of Obernewtyn. No matter that it had once been a hellish laboratory where Misfits had been experimented on. We had made it into something new, driving out the demons of the past.

The memory I had conjured up was again so real that I could almost smell the smoke from the fire, and hear the crack of mountain pine above the hum of conversation. I seemed to feel Avra's breath tickling the hair at my neck, for the mountain pony always stood at my side during guildmerge. Sometimes she would reach down and touch her nose to Maruman, who invariably slept on my lap. Other times she would nudge Alad, signaling her desire to communicate, or to reproach him for failing to interpret her clearly enough.

Ceirwan always sat on my other side, saying little but measuring everything with his dark-blue eyes, storing up impressions for our own guild meetings.

Life at Obernewtyn revolved around the guildmerge and what it stood for: community and purpose. In contrast, Sutrium was dark and chaotic, devoid of hope or purpose. All at once, I felt a longing to be home at Obernewtyn as savage and powerful as a hot knife in my belly. The strength of it took my breath away.

Then the irony of it struck me just as forcibly, for I had been only too ready to leave for Sutrium. Ever had it been my way to long for Obernewtyn when I was severed from it, and yet to hate it when I was there.

I blinked in surprise, seeing this was exactly how I felt about Rushton.

How strange.

But perhaps not. I loved Obernewtyn, and the feeling it gave me of being part of something larger than myself, but often I felt absorbed and devoured by it as well. In many ways, I had used my secret quest to raise a barrier between Obernewtyn and my lone self. My fear of Rushton, if that was the right word for it, was the fear that the giving of myself to him would cause me to lose myself; that, in some queer way, I would be absorbed and no longer myself.

Shivering only partly from the chilled water, I climbed from the barrel and towelled myself vigorously. Better to worry about what to do with the gypsy than to think of Rushton. That was a far more immediate problem.

Dressing hurriedly, I went to the kitchen. A fire had been lit and Matthew was repairing a tear in his breeches.

Before I could speak, Kella rushed in behind me. "Dragon," she cried breathlessly. "She's gone."

Matthew jumped to his feet. "Gone? What do ye mean gone?"

"Just what I said," Kella said. "She refused to answer the door to her chamber this morning. I thought she needed time, so left her. But just now I noticed that the door was open and she wasn't in there!"

"Well, for Lud's sake," Matthew said impatiently. "She'll be downstairs with..."

Kella gave him a look of such searing fury, that he flinched. "Stop telling me and let me tell you! I've checked everywhere. The horse yard, the healing hall, the bath house, the repair shed. Even the empty chambers in the safe house. She's gone, I tell you."

Her eyes accused Matthew, and he paled. "It's my fault. I meant to apologize for shoutin' at her when she came out," he whispered.

"You should have gone in to her," Kella blazed. "That's the usual way to go about an apology. Or did you expect her to beg for that as well?"

"Kella..."

The healer swung to face me. "We have to find her!"

"Do you have any idea where she might have gone?" I asked them.

"To Obernewtyn!" Kella said at once, voicing her own longings.

"She...she might have gone to th' market," Matthew said hesitantly. "I...she's been pesterin' me since we got here to take her."

He flushed crimson under the healer's scathing look. "What are ye lookin' at me like I murdered her for?" he shouted, highland accent thickened with anger. "I'm nowt responsible fer her. She shouldn'a be here in th' first place."

"Well, maybe you'll be lucky and she'll be killed. That would teach her obedience, wouldn't it?" hissed Kella.

Matthew whitened to the lips.

"That's enough," I said, shocked at the cruelty of her words. "The thing is to find her, not to decide whose fault it is that she's gone. Matthew, you go out and look for her on foot. I'll farseek her and if I can't find her, I'll go out on Gahltha. Leave a channel open for me. I'll reach out to you," I said, knowing he might not be able to farseek me in the fog of static that was Sutrium.

He ducked his head and hurried out as I turned to the healer. "Have another good look around the safe house. See if she has taken anything from the chamber with her."

She nodded and ran out.

I sat down on a chair and composed my thoughts, blocking out all apprehension and shaping a probe to Dragon's mindset. If she was near, and not on badly tainted ground, the probe would locate her.

It took less than a minute.

She was wandering through the stalls in the central trade market of the adjoining district. I fixed her position in my mind and then farsought Matthew.

"I will go there straight away," he sent, his mind leaking emotional surges of relief and anger.

Kella came in. "I couldn't find her, but she has taken nothing with her."

"She is in a market in the next district. Matthew has gone there on foot. I'll go over with Gahltha and bring her back."

"Thank Lud," Kella murmured.

I hurried along the hall and down the stairs, farsending to Gahltha as I went. Fortunately I was clad in boyish clothes, so there was no need for me to waste time in changing. Only the gypsy who had followed me would know me in that guise and, if I had outwitted him once, I could do it again.

Gahltha was waiting, snorting with impatience at my slowness.

"You have forgotten the coldmetal painmaker," he chided, as I vaulted onto his back.

With a curse I dismounted, found a bridle in the wagon, and buckled it on him with an apology.

"Do not sorrow for forgetting the fetter, ElspethInnle. Would that all the funaga would forget. Where is the little mornir?"

I sent Gahltha an explanation as I remounted and, as soon as we were clear of the little square, he broke into a brisk trot. It had stopped raining, but the drains ran swiftly, filled to overflowing after a day and night of rain. In seconds, the chilly breeze had leached all the bath's warmth from my bones.

I resisted the urge to ask Gahltha to go faster, knowing it would attract too much attention. I could have used a coercive cloak to stop anyone noticing it, but the more obtrusive the behavior, the more energy required to hide it. The effort of cloaking a wild gallop over any distance would virtually drain my immediate energy, and I had the sudden, uneasy premonition that I was going to need my powers very soon.

I chafed at the delay, my mind filled with visions of Dragon wandering through the market with her unforgettable face and hair. If anything alarmed her, she would resort instinctively to her phenomenal power, calling up the dragonish illusions for which she had been named.

I breathed a sigh of relief as the market came into view at the end of the street but, drawing nearer, I felt a stab of dismay. This was a far larger market than the one beside the safe house. If anything were to happen here, hundreds would witness it. The feeling of danger increased as Gahltha brought me to the perimeter of the crowds.

The empath could not have chosen a more perilous time to come to the market; late afternoons were traditionally the busiest part of the day. Hoping for a bargain, men and women shopped as late as possible, for it was well known that traders believed that a day without a sale offended Lud, and that they would be punished by another poor day to follow.

I never ceased to be amazed by their paltry image of a Lud who would care for the sale of this bit of fish or that stretch of cloth.

The horse-holding yard was filled to capacity, which meant I would have to tie Gahltha to the less secure bars along the outer edge of the corral. Gritting my teeth at the delay, I led him into a side lane and scooped some mud from the bottom of a drain. I had almost finished smearing it over him, when I heard footsteps.

I knelt and pretended to examine his fetlock. Peering covertly behind, I nearly fainted at the sight of a troop of soldierguards marching along the lane.

There was nothing to be done but to concentrate fiercely and produce a general coercive cloak that would stop them noticing me.

"Seems as if we ought to have more to do than play nursemaid to some Herders," grumbled one of the soldierguards at the front of the column. "Council wants to keep them happy because of them financin' th' Sador business," another muttered.

The Herders were financing the invasion of Sador? Could it be so? Where would they come by such coin?

"More like they don't dare move against them, for fear they'll get Lud to send another plague."

"It was nothing more than coincidence that they predicted pestilence and the plague came," snapped another soldierguard. "Council'll put them in their place before long and that'll be an end to our nursemaiding them."

"Will it? Herders have coin aplenty, so I've heard, and they ain't averse to greasin' soldierguard palms. I ain't fussy as to where coin comes from. Long as I get some."

"Shut up and get a move on," called a lean, surly-looking captain at the back of the column.

Their voices faded as they passed out of the lane and I leaned against Gahltha's noisome flank, weak-kneed with relief.

Gathering my wits, I farsought Matthew to warn him that there were soldierguards in the market, and possibly Herders as well. As my probe touched him, a panicky burst of images and words surged painfully into my unprepared mind.

I blocked the chaos and requested the use of his eyes. Instantly, Matthew made himself passive so that I could literally see through his eyes. It was a difficult maneuver, but one we had perfected through long use.

He was standing at the far side of the market in the midst of a crowd of people facing one of the market speaking stones, onto which people climbed to advertise wares or make announcements. Standing atop it was a Herder, red and gold armbands marking him as one of the more important priests in the Faction hierarchy. Two brownband Herders stood on either side of the speaking stone like guards.

But none of this explained Matthew's panic.

"Look!" His voice rose in my mind. His head turned and I saw Dragon. Standing out in the open between the crowd and the speaking stone, blue eyes ablaze with fury, the flame-haired empath was standing protectively in front of two small children. She resembled some avenging goddess out of a Beforetime story, the sun burnishing her red-gold mop of curls and her face glowing with unearthly loveliness.

Her mouth moved, and only then did I realize that she was shouting *at the Herder priests!*

XVI

Sick at the magnitude of the disaster unfolding, I flung myself onto Gahltha's back, bidding him to carry me to the other side of the square. Passing through the center of a trade market on horseback was forbidden, but I used my coercive power recklessly, forcing people not to "notice" us, and clearing a path.

I saw that the group of soldierguards had taken the easier and longer route around the perimeter of the market, and prayed for something to delay them.

"What in Lud's name has happened?" I demanded of Matthew.

Rather than explaining, he sent a vision of a woman and the two children being manhandled by the Herders. There was no sound but it was clear enough. The woman had shouted something at the redband priest and had been struck to the ground. One of the brownband Herders had grabbed at the little boy, who had screamed in terror and clung to his sister.

Dragon had flown from the crowd of watchers like a spitting fangcat defending its young, and the beleaguered Herder had retreated with alarm.

"I arrived just as it began," Matthew sent. "The priests were collecting boys to be taken and trained as acolytes on Herder Isle, and the mother refused to let them take her son." There was a pause. "The main Herder has just told the brownbands to take both children. I'm afraid Dragon will . . . Uh oh!" Matthew sent frantically.

By now I was close enough to hear the empath-coercer's clear childish voice, and I craned my neck in order to see her over the heads of the crowd. She had her arms about the two cringing children and was glaring at the approaching Herders purposefully.

"Don't," she cried in a warning voice, that froze my blood. "Don't dare!"

Then she dropped into a fighting crouch she must have learned from watching the coercers train, and bared her teeth at the priests.

They fell back again in astonishment, and there was a murmur of amazement from the crowd.

I could not repress a groan. Dragon would vision. I was amazed she had not done so already. I had to stop her unleashing her incredible powers in front of so many witnesses.

"Lud preserve us," Matthew sent despairingly along the probelink between us. "Th' soldierguards are here!"

I turned on Gahltha and, sure enough, the troop which filed past me in the lane had reached the speaking stone. Their captain was looking around, taking in the fracas at a glance.

"What is going on?" he demanded, marching up to the senior Herder.

The priest pointed to the woman sprawled at his feet, now awake and dabbing at her bloody mouth. "That woman has interfered with Faction rights," he accused, in a shrill furious voice. "And that creature attacked us." He pointed to where Dragon stood with the two children. He turned back to the soldierguard captain, then stopped, frowning. I looked, and saw that the soldierguard captain was gaping thunderstruck at Dragon!

Something in that look filled me with fear, and I directed a savage coercive bolt at Dragon, augmenting it with the destructive power at the depth of my mind. A simple coercive probe would have no chance of breaking through her mental shield. I had no time to fashion a subtle arrow of it, and my probe clubbed through her shield, obliterating it and knocking her instantly unconscious.

She slumped to the ground and the two children screamed in fright.

Their mother leapt to her feet and pulled them away from Dragon, just as the soldierguard captain stepped toward her.

Without hesitation, I stamped coercively on his will. The rough nerve control I imposed would fade swiftly, so I had little time. I sent a swift instruction to Matthew and another to Gahltha.

Immediately, the black horse reared up with an ear-shattering equine scream. People on all sides scattered wildly to escape the flailing hoofs.

The senior Herder shrieked as Gahltha rolled his eyes and snorted dramatically, dancing dangerously near to his skinny shanks.

"Someone has fed my horse prickleberries!" I cried, pretending to have no control.

Gahltha bucked, lashing out with razor-sharp hoofs and the three priests dived away from the speaking stone with cries of terror, apparently convinced he was on the verge of the hysterical and lethal deathrage caused by ingesting the poisonous weed.

"Captain?" One of the rank-and-file soldierguards tapped his superior and the captain stirred, for this was enough to break the trance I had imposed. He looked around, then his eyes widened in fury and he cracked his fist into the other man's face. "Fool!" he raged. "The red-haired girl. Where is she?"

Time had run out.

"Go!" I sent, and Gahltha bolted out of the square and down a feeder lane.

"A gypsy youth took her!" I heard someone cry out and cursed, for I had thought no one noticed Matthew scoop up the unconscious empath in all the fuss.

Using the little that remained of my store of mental energy, I sent to Matthew, telling him to try to find somewhere to hide until the fuss had died down.

He sent that they had taken refuge in a burned-out house. I took the location from him. They were still close to the market.

"Are you sure it's safe?"

"Safer than on the street," Matthew sent fervently. "Besides, they'll never think I'd hide so close."

I hoped he was right. "Is Dragon all right?"

"She's unconscious," Matthew said. "How in Lud's name did you . . . ?"

"You stay put and I'll bring Gahltha," I interrupted.

I used the last of my reserve to drop a complete coercive cloak over Gahltha and myself, wishing I had time to rest. But even thick-headed soldierguards would work out that Matthew and I were the same gypsies wanted for the murder of a Herder and two soldierguards in Guanette: unfortunately my diversionary tactics had obliterated my coercive suggestion that I was a boy.

By morning the streets would be crawling with squads combing the city for us as the gate search surged inward.

The clouds cleared from the sky, and the sun shone properly for the first time in days. Everything in the sodden city steamed as we made our way in a wide arc around the market where Dragon had confronted the Herders, and into the next district.

Coming around a blind corner, I found my way blocked by yet another of the small markets dotted throughout the city.

My first instinct was to circle it. I had had enough of markets. But it was not long until dusk and I did not want to waste any more time. Dismounting, I took Gahltha's rein, leading him behind me. It was not forbidden to have horses in the lesser squares, only to ride them there.

Brushing along the aisles, my eye was caught by a table laden with swatches of colorful cloth. I stared, for I had never seen cloth dyed so brightly before.

"Sador dyes..." I heard a stallholder tell a customer.

One of the pieces on the stall table was deep green, with a sheen as soft and yielding as the coat of a newborn pup. I ran a thumb over it, fascinated by the alien texture. Was this Sadorian as well?

"Get yer dirty paws off it, yer halfbreed slattern."

I dropped the material in shock, feeling as if I had wakened from a drugged sleep. What, in Lud's name, had I been thinking of to stand about admiring a piece of cloth with half the city out looking for me? I knew what was wrong of course. I was almost dazed with tiredness. It always happened when I used the strange power at the depth of my mind.

Now that the wretched trader had identified me as a girl, I could not make myself into a boy in his eyes, but I could stop anyone else from seeing me.

I began to back away, weaving a general coercive net, but the burly stallholder lumbered from behind his stand with unexpected speed and pushed me hard, sending me stumbling back against Gahltha's warm flank. Anger filled me, hot and unreasoning as fire.

I choked it back, realizing too late that I had let my coercive cloak fall again. Since it worked by heightening and enhancing disinterest and inattention, there was no way I could reinstitute it with so many people goggling at me. Especially not with my energy so depleted. I must slip away and regain my precious anonymity.

"If you won't let a customer feel the cloth she might buy, I'll move on," I said pacifically, and backed away.

"Since when did halfbreeds buy when they could steal?" sneered another man, blocking the way from behind.

His skinny companion leered and stepped in my path when I tried to sidle by them. "And since when was a gypsy civil and honest at the same time?" he asked in a sinuous, high-pitched voice. "If you ask me, this one speaks too soft to be trusted. And why does a girl wear trews, except for ease to run when she has stolen something?" He looked around at the gathering little crowd, seeking their support.

Several nodded and I began to feel uneasy.

I let Gahltha's rein slip from my fingers.

"Shall I/Gahltha bolt/rear, ElspethInnle?"

"No!" Using the black horse as a diversion yet again would be as good as posting a sign to say the gypsies wanted for the market fracas were still close by. I dared not risk it with Matthew and Dragon in hiding so near.

"Find Matthew and Dragon and take them back to the safe house," I sent, giving Gahltha a mental map of their location.

"Gahltha must protect Innle," he protested.

"No! There are people here with knives and arrows and they would think nothing of killing you. Obey me," I commanded. "I can take care of myself in this."

Reluctantly, Gahltha withdrew. Fortunately, no one noticed he was riderless and apparently ownerless because all attention was riveted on me. "I think we ought to give her a good whipping just to teach her what we think of gypsy thieves," said the thin man, who had stopped me leaving. He unlaced a long whip from his belt with a practiced flick of his fingers.

Two louts cheered and offered to lay on the first stripes to show how it was done and other people crowded nearer. As ever I was astonished how ordinary pleasant-faced Landfolk would delight in seeing a whipping.

I looked around and my skin broke into gooseflesh, for I had no alternative but to let myself be manhandled and whipped.

I clenched my teeth and steeled myself, invoking a coercive suggestion that the thin man should use the whip lightly. At the same time I cursed and struggled as anyone would when the two louts grabbed me and ripped the gypsy shirt to bare my back.

"Now we'll see ye dance." The thin man laughed and flicked the whip. It whistled viciously through the air and I screamed when it struck, though I felt nothing, for I had erected a mental barrier to net the pain.

I would experience the sting when there was no need to keep my wits about me.

The whip struck again.

"A weak blow," cried the cloth trader, and he strode out to commandeer the whip. I reached out a coercive probe to soften his blows too, but, to my horror, he was naturally shielded.

I could not reach his mind without his knowing it!

"I'll show you how she dances to my music," he promised, and swung his arm as hard as he could.

The whip hissed, tearing into my skin. I felt no pain, but I screamed, writhing inwardly at the thought of the agony I would have to endure when the barrier was dissolved.

He struck again and again, with no sign of stopping and I thought he might kill me. Perhaps this was the death I had been promised if I did not learn what *swallow* meant. Maybe Maryon had misjudged the number of days or misread her vision. Maybe my time was already up.

"Dance gypsy! Give us a show!" cried the trader, as he lifted his arm again. His lips and eyes shone with lascivious pleasure. "I thought gypsies loved to dance."

"That is so," said a caressing masculine voice, and suddenly I was free, falling forward and grazing my knees on the cobbles.

Clutching my shredded clothing, I turned to see the dark-haired gypsy, who had ridden after me the day before. This time he was on foot and the two louts who had held me were sitting at his feet with dazed looks.

The trader gave a roar of anger and rushed forward. With lightning swiftness, the gypsy stepped aside and plucked him up by the scruff of the neck. The oaf must have weighed as much as Gahltha, yet the gypsy held him dangling in midair as if it were no effort at all.

"You have made a mistake, Littleman," he was saying to the dangling trader, in a lecturing voice. "A gypsy dances as an expression of pleasure in movement or song, or for a lover. Not for moronish illbreds who would not know beauty or grace if it bit them on the bum."

I was astounded that a lone gypsy would speak that way to Landfolk.

He could only be a Twentyfamilies pureblood to behave with such arrogance. No one made a move to intervene. In fact, people began to edge away.

The stallholder was by now purple in the face and in imminent danger of suffocating, his jerkin screwed tight around his neck.

"What is that you say, Littleman?" the gypsy asked with exaggerated politeness.

"Erk!" the man squeaked, clawing at his collar.

I stifled an incredulous giggle as the gypsy put his ear to the trader's mouth. "Your pardon? You say you want to apologize to this girl? Do I hear you aright?"

The trader shook his head, then changed his mind and tried to nod. "What was that?" The gypsy hauled him closer, with the result that the cloth around his neck was drawn even tighter.

"Ahhk," the trader gasped, batting his arms as if he were a bird about to fly away.

"You'd best put him down before you kill him," I said, beginning to be worried. The trader's eyes were rolling about in an alarming way and his lips were quite blue.

The gypsy ignored me. "Ahh! Now I understand. You wish to apologize by gifting a piece of cloth to her."

"Ug," the trader said dully.

"A fine gesture," the gypsy said, opening his hand and letting the man fall in a gasping heap at his elegantly black-booted feet. "Now what cloth was it that you wanted?"

I stared up into his bold, laughing eyes. "Uh. I don't think..."

"The green?" he said, as if echoing my words. "A good choice. It will suit you." He took up the cloth I had touched and held it up to my face. His knuckles brushed my cheek and I flinched.

"You startle like an unbroken pony," he murmured.

The blood rushed to my cheeks and he laughed, turning back to the trader who had risen unsteadily to his feet. "The green it is. Now wrap it up little fellow and I will consider amends made and say nothing to the Councilmen."

The trader took the cloth in trembling fingers, rolled it up and slid it into a paper sleeve. The gypsy took it and threw a few coins on the ground.

I was stunned at his audacity and thought the Twentyfamilies' tithe to the Council must be magnificent indeed to let him get away with such high-handedness.

Suddenly he reached forward, grasped my arm in a powerful grip and propelled me behind the stall and down a side street. A few paces down the street, he thrust me into a shadowy doorway and pressed himself against me; I panicked and struggled.

"For Lud's sake and mine, girl, be still," he said in a hard urgent voice.

"Let me go!" I cried.

"Shut up," he hissed.

"Shut up yourself!" I flared, temper overcoming fear. He pulled me against his chest and closed a hard hand over my mouth. "Shhh," he said quietly and distinctly into my ear.

Then I heard the sound of running feet on the cobbles.

I froze.

"I tell you it was the girl from the other market. The one on the black horse that caused all that fuss," panted a man's voice nearby. "The captain said there is a big reward for her or one of them other two who was with her."

"It couldn't have been one of them," said another in a gravel voice. "That trader said the gypsy who stopped the whipping was Twentyfamilies. They don't get mixed up with anything that ain't Lore. 'Sides if it were the girl from the market who rode that black horse, where is it?"

Their footsteps and disgruntled voices receded. When the gypsy released me I spun away from him angrily and rubbed my lips where his fingers had mashed them against my teeth.

"It would be polite for you to give your name to your rescuer," he said.

I glared at him. "I didn't need rescuing!"

"No? Then you wanted to be whipped? I apologize for intervening, but there are gentler pleasures." The wicked expression in his eyes made me step back involuntarily.

"I suppose you caused all of that trouble over at the other market a little while ago as part of your quest to be whipped. It must have disappointed you to have escaped so easily. What have you done with your horse, though?"

My heart jumped. "I don't know about any other market or a horse."

"No?" He smiled. "Then I must have been mistaken in thinking you rode a black horse from the city just yesterday dressed as you are now, to appear as a boy."

I flushed.

"All right. I ride a black horse and I wear boyish trews. So what? Why did you follow me yesterday? And why did you help me just now?"

"So I did help you then?" he asked mockingly.

I scowled and gathered my will to give him a coercive mental jolt, hard enough to penetrate his mindshield, but, without warning, he stepped forward and kissed me full on the mouth.

Wit and breath fled at his audacity.

"If I had known it was so easy to silence you, I would have done that sooner," he said, releasing me.

I scowled, mortified and furious that I had not pushed him away. Did he think because he was Twentyfamilies he could kiss anyone and they would like it? Childishly, I rubbed my hand across my mouth.

"Revulsion rendered me silent," I snapped. "Why did you do that?"

Heavy eyelids drooped secretively over his eyes. "Because I wanted to," he said.

I did not know what to say to the simplicity of such an answer.

His mouth shifted into a lazy, curving smile. "But what I want to know even more, is why you are pretending to be a gypsy."

Part II

The Twentyfamilies

XVII

"What are you talking about?" I demanded scornfully, gathering myself to run if he tried to catch hold of me again. "Of course I am a gypsy."

"Your back is bleeding," he said mildly. "You need treatment and there is a gypsy rig close by here where you can clean up. I will take you there, if you wish. . . ."

I bit my lip, mistrusting his apparent indifference.

I did not like the gypsy, even though he had rescued me from a very unpleasant situation. Yet I dared not cross the city on foot in bloody disarray. Aside from that, here was the opportunity to learn why he had followed me the previous day. Moreover, this might be my last and only chance to locate the gypsy woman's blood kin before Maryon's deadline.

"Very well," I said.

His lips twitched into a faintly ironic smile.

As we walked I took good care to stay out of the reach of his long arms and a little behind him, but, true to his word, he led me to a rig set on a tiny green not far away from the market. Alongside it, four horses grazed.

I was shivering, but not from cold. The pain from the whipping was locked behind the mental barrier I had set up, but there was no way to block the shock of it from myself.

One of the horses was Sendari, whom the gypsy had ridden the previous day. To my discomfort, he scented me as we approached the rig and trotted over to push his soft muzzle against my hand. I could not reach his mind to ask him to withdraw, so I stroked him and pretended not to see the startled look the gypsy gave us. In some situations it was safer to say nothing than to try explaining the inexplicable.

The rig itself was magnificent. Every panel of wood was intricately carved in an elaborate scene. It made our own poor wagon seem fit only for firewood. The carvings were unusual, and reminded me vaguely of the stonework of the mural in the Reichler Clinic under Tor. Then again, they were also like the carvings that had once graced the huge entrance doors to Obernewtyn.

"It is very beautiful," I said, meaning it.

He nodded. "This is the skill of my family. It is a very ancient art." He caressed a ridge in the dark, smooth wood.

"This is *your* rig?" I asked, wishing that I could simply read his mind for the information I needed, but of course with a natural mindshield he would sense my intrusion.

"Maire!" he called suddenly.

An extraordinarily ugly crone poked her head through the brocaded curtain. Her skin was much darker than the man's and her hair hung snow white to her waist in stark contrast, but she had the same black, penetrating eyes. Squinting against the dusk light, she eyed him with disfavor. "What do you want?"

"This girl was whipped by some louts in the market. Her back needs treatment. Can you heal her?"

The old woman sniffed and raked me from crown to toe with her sharp eyes. "Can I? Yes. But should I? Will I?"

She took up a battered box of woven reed, climbed from the wagon and hobbled over to the smouldering remains of a fire. She was tiny and wore a bed dress of deeply embroidered silken material the color of the summerday sky. Setting the box on a log, she flicked a derisive glance at the man. "I suppose you rescued her. Your father would be delighted to hear what a hero has sprung from his loins."

When he made no response, she glared back at me. "Well? Are you going to show me your wounds or do you want a body servant to strip you? I daresay your rescuer would oblige."

I felt myself redden, but turned and shrugged to part the ripped shirt. She gave an exclamation that told me the wounds were as savage as I had feared. It also made me realize the weakness I was feeling might not be due to overuse of my Misfit powers alone.

"Am I a bird to fly up?" the old woman shrilled. "Kneel down, for Lud's sake!"

I did as she asked, thinking how much she reminded me of Louis

Larkin, kindness hidden behind a shield of irascible carping. Tutting and muttering to herself, Maire bathed the flesh, then gently peeled away the cloth stuck to the wounds. Rummaging in her box again, she withdrew a bottle and a moment later the unmistakable odor of herbal preparations filled the air. The old crone was a herb lorist. I jumped at the feel of cold ointment on my bare skin. She slathered it on with a liberal hand, then stuck a dressing over my whole back.

"'Tis done," she said, slamming the box shut.

I thanked her and pulled my shirt about me as best I could.

She watched me with an odd expression on her aged face. "You are a tough one, girl. Not a flinch for all the nerves exposed and hurt. No Twentyfamilies would have done as well, for all their infernal pride."

I saw, too late, that I should have pretended discomfort when she was working on the open wounds, but the forbidding had prevented me feeling anything and I had been too preoccupied to remember. Well, it was done.

I made myself shrug. "Halfbreeds are tougher than milky pure-bloods."

She snorted. "Except that you are neither."

I felt the blood drain from my cheeks.

"I am a gypsy halfbreed," I said faintly.

She cackled ironically. "So you say and so those rags you wear would have it, but it is not true. There is nothing in your face from Twentyfamilies stock. Not darkness of eye; not thickness of lips, nor any other physical characteristic that belongs to my people."

"I am a halfblood. I throw to my mother," I declared, watching the man from the corner of my eye. His expression had not changed, though the old woman's question exactly echoed his own accusation.

"Why were you whipped?" Maire asked.

"I touched some material and the trader selling it objected."

I wondered why she did not reiterate her accusation. The gypsy man had changed the subject in exactly the same way when I denied his accusation, rather than demanding proof or arguing the point. It struck me that these gypsies were shifty folk, who sidled about things rather than coming on them bluntly. I began to wonder if it had been such a good idea to come after all.

"Gypsies are not popular in these times," the man said in a neutral voice. "What is your name?"

"Elaria," I said. I felt as if there were undercurrents here concerning me, which I could not read.

The man shook his head. "That is not your true name."

Fear skittered along my backbone. How did he know that?

"Do Twentyfamilies know everything then?" I sneered, drawing indignation from a little surge of anger. I did not like to be called a liar, even when it was true.

"Has no one told you that Twentyfamilies gypsies have the gift of truth?" he asked.

I licked my lips. "Truth?"

"Twentyfamilies know when a lie is being told. As you are lying."

My heart began to pound, for suddenly I remembered Domick's warning about making sure the gypsies did not guess I was an impostor. What if the gypsy had saved me on a whim and would now kill me? Perhaps he would even present my body to the soldierguards and claim the reward. I had no energy in reserve with which to defend myself.

Then I scowled, for how should he know if I spoke true or not? He was no Misfit coercer to read my mind. I would have known by now if he were. He was guessing, or somehow I had given myself away. I would stall until I had power enough to force them to let me go.

The gypsy laughed suddenly. "You've spunk enough, for all your face reads like a book. Well, if you don't believe in gypsy powers, then let us say I know you lie because you lack the signs by which our kind know one another."

"What signs?"

His smile broadened. "That question marks you a liar even more than the absence of the signs."

"What signs?" I demanded, putting my hands on my hips.

In answer, he rolled up one sleeve.

I stared at the elaborate painting on the inside of his wrist and up his arm. Three birds were depicted flying in a spiral of black and green, shot through with red.

My mouth fell open with astonishment for it was *the exact design* Garth had shown me on the plast documents from the Reichler Clinic in the city under Tor!

The arm painting was executed in greater detail, but there was no doubt that it was the same. But what on earth could it mean? The sign on the plast documents had been the identifying mark of a research cell in the sinister Beforetime organization, Govamen, which had experimented on Beforetime Talents.

How in Lud's name had a *gypsy* come to wear it?

And could it possibly be coincidence that I, who had seen the design under Tor, should see it again so soon? Both gypsies were looking at me so oddly that my heart skipped a beat. I searched my memory for the thread of the conversation. "I...What if I were to say I have no arm picture because it was washed off?"

The gypsy lifted his arm and spat on the painting, then he scrubbed hard at it. This had no effect and told me that the paint was indelible.

"All right," I shrugged, thrusting the monumental puzzle of the arm paintings to the back of my mind. "So, I don't have one. What of it? Not all gypsies have them."

At least, the gypsy in the safe house did not bear any such markings.

"You did not let me finish before you rushed in to tell me how your *arm paintings* washed off. This is a mark worn only by those of the Twentyfamilies and entitles us to pass through the gates of any city unsearched and untouched. No mongrel halfbreed would wear it." There was a note of bitter self-mockery in his tone as if these words were not his, but someone else's, and this robbed them of offense.

He lifted the same sleeve higher to show me a metal band around his upper arm. "This is what I meant to show you. All gypsies, full and halfbreed, wear these; yet, when I held you in the lane, I felt nothing. It tells anyone who might wish to know, if you are bonded or promised or no."

I flushed, at the same time remembering the gypsy woman's metal band.

"And what of this?" He showed me a woven band on his thumb. "All gypsies wear these too; weaved into the ring are signs telling the line of their descent. We bear these and other such things about us so that we may exchange knowledge about one another without the Landfolk hearing it. Do you still claim to be a gypsy?"

"Believe what you will," I told him stubbornly. "That is what my father told my mother, and he left in such a hurry he did not have time to teach my mother the finer points of gypsy culture. Her family threw her out when it was learned she carried a halfbreed child, and so she brought me up alone in Rangorn. Then she died," I snarled, so carried away by the part I had imagined for myself that I felt bitter for the sake of my poor mother.

"The Twentyfamilies left without leaving his name, I take it," Maire asked, her eyes inscrutable.

I felt I had misspoken, but it was too late to change my story. "So my mother said."

She nodded and gathered up her box. "I will give you a shirt to wear in place of that." She hobbled back to the wagon.

"Well," said the gypsy man, "that is quite a story."

I did not know what to make of this, so I said nothing.

"Do you know that a girl fitting your description rescued a gypsy halfbreed from the Herder flames in the highlands?" he asked casually.

"That is nothing to do with me," I said.

"No?" He squatted down to poke at the fire, and the flames lit his face.

Only then did I register that the sun had fallen below the city skyline. The gypsy's sleek dark hair and hollowed cheeks gave him a devilish look as he fed the fire until it blazed high, sending showers of sparks into the sky. I stood awkwardly watching him and wishing the old woman would hurry up with the shirt. The sooner I got away the better, but still I felt weak—my mind was taking longer than usual to recover.

"They say there is a rich reward for the wanted girl."

My heart began to bump.

"It is my guess that the girl who caused the ruckus in the market today and this Guanette gypsy are one and the same. What do you think?"

I shrugged, not trusting my voice to remain steady.

It was no great surprise he should have heard the rumor about the affair in Guanette before it was common knowledge. Gypsies probably kept their ears to the ground in the same way Misfits did, listening for the approach of trouble. No surprise, either, that he should put two and two together and guess that the girl wanted from the market fracas was the same one who had rescued the gypsy. But he could not *know* that I was the same girl, whatever he suspected.

"Tell me, was it you, or the boy you were traveling with, who stuck a knife in the Herder in Guanette?" he asked casually.

"It wasn't us...."

I stopped, aghast that I had fallen into such a simple trap. I took a step backward, but at the same moment the old woman stepped out of the dark and thrust a shirt into my hands.

"This is the girl from Guanette?" she asked the man.

He nodded and said lightly, "She rode a black horse then, though not the magnificent creature she outrode me on yesterday. The lad with her traveled in a false gypsy wagon."

The old woman turned to me, and I did not know whether to run or stay before the anguished intensity of her expression.

"Is she alive?" she whispered. "The woman you cut from the stake?"

I opened my mouth to say I didn't know what she was talking about, but the glint of tears in her old eyes stopped the lie.

"She lives," I said impulsively, softly.

"Praise be." She grasped my hand.

"You ... you know her?" I asked, to give myself time.

The crone nodded, mopping her eyes with the end of her bed dress. "Her name is Iriny and she is ... is very dear to me. I had feared her dead. Where is she? Is she in the city with your companion?"

Instantly, I regretted the impulse of pity that had made me tell the truth without thinking it through first. Yet, this surely was the solution to my problem of what to do with the gypsy woman, for clearly these people knew who she was and cared for her.

"She is in Sutrium," I conceded, trying to decide how best to proceed. "She is very weak."

"Dying?" the man asked abruptly.

"Not now. But she almost did. She seemed to want to die."

"Ahh," the old woman moaned, and rocked herself back and forward. "My poor girl." She fixed me with a sudden fierce stare. "Where is she? I must see her."

"She is in good and healing hands."

"You will take me to her now," the man said, advancing with a threatening air.

"No!" Maire said. She looked back to me with frank entreaty.

"I will bring her to you," I promised, ignoring the man and his threats.

"When?" he demanded.

"As soon as it is safe to bring her across the city," I told him coldly. "The soldierguards are looking for me and her. Tomorrow it will be worse because of the business in the market today."

"That is so," he said darkly, his eyes troubled. "Yet we Twentyfamilies are to leave Sutrium in three days."

I blinked in wonder at him, for the Twentyfamilies departure from Sutrium coincided exactly with the end of the sevenday deadline. Was this, then, the reason for the deadline Maryon had set?

The gypsy took my silence for a question. "On the reckoning of our history, we began our journey to the Land on that very day eons past. It is our custom to leave Sutrium always in the final hours of that day in remembrance, and as a sign of good faith to the Council. You see, it was also on that day that we made the agreement of safe passage. We regard it as an auspicious day for journeys."

"Yet I will remain until Iriny comes," Maire said, in a voice that brooked no argument.

He nodded. "And so shall I, *if* there is need. But the sooner we can get her out of the city the better, and it will be a simpler matter to get her out in a group than as a lone Twentyfamilies wagon leaving later than it should." He gave me a sharp look. "I will organize a rumor to say that you and your companion have left the city with Iriny. It will not take too long for the soldierguards to run after the scent and leave the city free. When this happens, bring her swiftly and safe to us and I will reward you in good coin."

"I'm not interested in your coin," I snapped indignantly. "I did not save her life for coin and I wouldn't bring her to you if I thought you meant her harm, no matter what you offered."

He looked genuinely taken aback and, indeed, I was surprised at the extent of my anger.

"He is a fool as all men are," Maire said dismissively. "Put on the shirt."

I did as she bid, turning my back to strip off the ripped shirt and don the other. When I was finished, she looked at me, then went to the wagon and brought back a bundle of clothing.

"What are these?" I asked, as she put them into my arms.

"They are Twentyfamilies skirts and gee gaws. Wear them when you return and no one will trouble you. But make sure it is night when you come. A dark night, if you can. And speak to no one, unless you cannot avoid it; especially avoid Twentyfamilies gypsies." The old woman gave me an imperious little push. "Go now," she said. "Walk safe and bring her with you when you come again to us."

A thought occurred to me like a burst of lightning on a dark night. "I don't want coin as a reward, but there is something I would ask. . . ."

"Of course," the gypsy said, his eyes flashing with triumphant cynicism.

"I want you to tell me all about Twentyfamilies gypsies and half-breeds," I said. "I want you to tell me how you came to the Land and everything you can remember about where you came from before that. And I want you to paint that mark you wear on *my* arm and tell me what it means and how you came to use it."

The man looked at me in blank astonishment, "Only Twentyfamilies bear that mark. . . ."

Maire prodded his arm. "She knows that, fool. Can't you see she means to pass herself off as a Twentyfamilies gypsy?"

The man's eyes widened in disbelief. Then he gave me a narrow stare. "You would play a dangerous game, girl. Do you know that Twentyfamilies are by lore permitted to kill impostors?"

"How should anyone know me for an impostor with such marks and these clothes?"

He smiled. "I would know."

I ignored that. "There is another thing. I also want to know about *swallow*."

His brows shot up. "Who told you of Swallow? Did Iriny speak *his* name in her delirium?"

His name! So Swallow was a person. I had not expected that. I ignored the question, because answering it would reveal the extent of my ignorance. Instead, I gave them both a challenging look. "Do you agree with my conditions?"

After a long tense moment, the man gave an unsmiling nod.

The old woman touched my hand. "Bring her safe to us and you shall have what you want. Better still, you shall meet Swallow if you wish it."

The man made a negating gesture, then shrugged. "So be it. But do not bring Iriny here when you come."

"Where then?"

He frowned in thought. "Sometimes the best way to hide a leaf is in a forest. Do you know the main gypsy green?"

I nodded.

"Bring her there, then. That is where we will wait for you."

I nodded and walked away down a lane without a backward glance. As soon as I was out of their sight I threw a full coercive cloak about me, and set a probe to detect anyone who followed, but no one came.

Only then did I dare to relax and allow myself to feel relieved at having all but completed my appointed task.

With some effort, for I was not yet much recovered, I farsent Matthew using an attuned probe. It located him at the safe house and I felt a surge of relief that they had returned there safely. Perhaps the streak of bad luck that had dogged us since leaving Obernewtyn was over.

"I guessed you'd sent Gahltha, of course, but I had no idea why. What happened to you?" Matthew sent, his thoughts tingling with curiosity.

"I will explain when I get back."

The farseeker offered to ride out with Jaygar and Gahltha to get me, but I refused, reminding him that it was on dusk, and horses ridden after dark would only call unwanted attention. Despite the long, frightening day, and the dangers of being abroad as a halfbreed, I did not mind the walk. In truth, tired as I felt, I was glad of the time to think and to be alone. So much had happened in a single day and, to crown it all, after searching fruitlessly for the gypsy woman's people, I had been rescued by them. I could not imagine how the gypsy man had guessed that I was the gypsy from Guanette. Nor how he knew so much of what had happened there— unless he knew the older gypsy who had shot the arrows.

But why would a Twentyfamilies gypsy, who was supposed never to break lore, be prepared to receive and harbor a halfbreed condemned to death? And how could she, Iriny, be precious to Maire when the two breeds were supposed to be estranged?

And then there was the triple-bird painting on the gypsy's arm—an exact replica of the one exposed under Tor only a sevenday or so past.

Well, all questions would be answered when I brought Iriny to them. I was puzzled about the man, Swallow, trying to see how knowing him would stop my death.

My mind drifted wearily and I felt depressed. In spite of all my efforts, Maryon's vision had come to pass without much help from me. I wondered suddenly how much foreknowledge of the future really altered anything. Seeing where a path led did not enable you to alter its destination. On the other hand, without the futuretelling, I would not have come to Sutrium.

Garth and Fian would be amazed when I showed them the triple-bird mark they had unearthed in a dead Beforetime city. My demand that the gypsies set their mark on my arm had been an impulse, because it was a guarantee of safe passage anywhere in the Land. With luck, Katlyn and Garth might come up with a suitable duplicate so that any of us could disguise ourselves as Twentyfamilies and take advantage of the safe-passage agreement they had negotiated with the Council. With such a mark, one would need only the smallest trickle of coercive energy to reinforce a taboo that was already established. Who knew what we might achieve under its protections?

Given the lethal penalty for pretending to be a Twentyfamilies gypsy, I would also have to find out more about the signs gypsies used, so that the disguise would be perfect. We would have to use it sparingly, though, and with great care, lest our own activities reduce the protection it offered.

My mind shifted away from gypsies to the incident at the market with Dragon and the Herders. Despite the potential for disaster, it had come to nothing, and yet for some reason, the mere thought of it filled me with a premonition of danger.

I concentrated on what had happened, trying to pinpoint exactly what had made me so uneasy. It had something to do with the way the soldierguard captain had stared at Dragon. His eyes had been covetous, yet it seemed to me that there had been more than lust in his face.

I pictured the man's long nose, the jutting cheekbones and narrow gray eyes. Gradually, the face assumed the expression I had seen at the market and the blood ran like a glacier in my veins.

Dragon had never been to Sutrium or indeed to any city. She had spent her whole childhood in a deserted Beforetime ruin, and had not left Obernewtyn since I brought her there.

Yet the soldierguard Captain had looked at her *as though he recognized her*!

XVIII

I *arrived back at the safe house in time to see the rebel, Reuvan, mounting a* tan mare. I recognized the horse as one which had come to Obernewtyn for refuge the previous wintertime, and this drove all thoughts of the soldierguard captain and the gypsies from my mind.

"Greetings, ElspethInnle," the mare sent, its dark-flecked eyes solemn.

"Greetings, Halda," I responded, concealing my surprise.

Ever since Brydda's beloved mount, Sallah, had chosen to remain with him after he freed her, the Beasting guildmaster, Alad, believed the Beast guild had been supplying mounts to the rebel network so that beasts could organize their own rescues or sabotage. Animals would often come to Obernewtyn claiming that Sallah had sent them, and asking for Avra. Most would remain only a little time, supposedly to be trained to live in the wild, before going out into the vast mountain wilderness.

Alad was convinced that some were trained in a different sort of survival and sent back to Sallah. He believed she was the leader of a lowland arm of the Beast guild and a sort of animal network of spies.

I had thought this unlikely, but seeing Halda made me wonder, for she had been one of the equines who was supposed to have gone into the wild. Reuvan had not noticed my approach, so I coughed to get his attention. When he turned, the flesh was bloodless beneath his tan.

"What is it?" I demanded, wondering if there was ever to be a moment in Sutrium unmarred by disaster.

"Idris is missing," he answered in a hoarse voice. "Brydda sent me to see if he had come here."

"Was he sent to the safe house?"

The seaman shook his head and took up the rein. "I must go. There are other places he might have gone if he were injured. Brydda asked me to try them all."

"Can I help?" I asked.

Reuvan appeared not to hear me. He lifted his hand in a distracted farewell gesture and urged Halda on.

I hurried upstairs and into the kitchen.

"Where have you been?" Kella cried, jumping to her feet.

Matthew rose too, his face pale and set. "Idris . . ."

I nodded wearily. "I know. I've just spoken to Reuvan. Did he ask you to farseek Idris while he was here?"

"It would ha' done no good fer him to ask me to farseek anyone here. Too many minds an' too much holocaust tainting."

"But *he* would not realize that," I said impatiently. "I suppose he was too distracted. I'll try."

I shaped a probe to Idris' mindset, but since I had never farsought him before, I did not know his exact mind signature, which meant it was not a strongly defined probe. Forced to compete with the miasmic static rising from the sea and river, and from various areas of the city, I had no great hopes of locating him.

I opened my eyes and shook my head. "I didn't find him, but I'm still weak from the business this afternoon."

In fact, though I did not say it, I felt as if all of my energy were being siphoned away through some secret channel. I forced myself to concentrate.

"Did Reuvan say how Idris disappeared?"

"Apparently he dinna come back last night from some errand he had been sent upon," Matthew said.

This puzzled me. Reuvan had seemed dreadfully upset considering Idris had been missing only a single night. Any one of a dozen harmless things might have delayed his return.

"Greetings, ElspethInnle," Maruman sent.

The old cat was curled on a blanket beside the hearth. I went to kneel beside him and to warm my hands at the fire.

"I am tired," I sent.

He turned one flaring yellow eye to me and, for a fleeting moment, there was a mindless emptiness in it. Then his gaze sharpened. "You are tired because yourbody heals its hurts. This is a place/barud where there is much hurting. Nomatter. Soon we will leave."

I stared at him. "What?"

"Soon we/you will go far away. Very far..." His eye was cloudy again. I felt a surge of alarm at the thought that the old cat was on the verge of another of his fits of madness. Yet he had not long ago returned from a period of wandering madness, and the attacks did not usually happen so close together. Perhaps he was simply tired. Lud knew that could make you a little mad.

"I/Maruman amweary," the cat sent, as if to confirm my thoughts. "The h'rayka searches in the dreamtrails of ElspethInnle, and I have fought many battles to guard the way."

Abruptly I was wide awake.

Maruman had lately spoken often of these dreamtrails, and though he would not be drawn to explain exactly what he meant by the term, I had got the impression they were as real to him as a road. He often spoke of meeting the Agyllians on the dreamtrails. But it was not his talk of dreampaths that disturbed me. H'rayka, translated loosely from beast thoughtsymbols, meant one who breaks and rends. Atthis had told me that if I did not find the weaponmachines and disable them, another human whose fate path twinned my own, whom she called the Destroyer, would find and activate them, raining a new doom on the world.

And now Maruman said a Destroyer was searching my dreams. Could Maruman mean that he had dreamed the Destroyer was searching *for me*?

I shivered, for I had never considered that the Destroyer might be someone I would have to confront. I had seen our search for the weapon-machines as a sort of parallel race. Surely Atthis would have warned me if I was to be hunted by this person.

Another possibility occurred to me. What if Maruman was trying to tell me that the Destroyer had begun to search not for me, but for the weaponmachines? This seemed far more likely.

But, perhaps, I had misunderstood Maruman altogether. I looked into his eye.

"Maruman, who/what is h'rayka?"

"H'rayka is the one who brings destruction," the cat sent.

I felt a rush of pure terror, followed by fury, for if my interpretation was correct, and Maruman had just warned me that the Destroyer was searching for the weaponmachines, why was I wasting time in Sutrium?

Why hadn't Atthis called me?

"The oldOne called," Maruman answered my despairing deep-thought disconcertingly. "You do her bidding here in barud-li."

I stared at him. "I do the bidding of Maryon/tallone."

"Maryon/tallone hears the ashling of the oldOne/speaks the oldOne's words toInnle."

I struggled to stay calm. "Are you ... are you saying *Atthis* sent a dream to Maryon to make me come to Sutrium?"

"A path forms itself like snow in the high valley of the barud," Maruman sent dreamily. "First there is this piece of whitecold and that piece, and they are alone and nothing. But soon they join and they cover the earth."

The obliqueness of his answer exasperated me, for past experience told me that this was his way of indicating that he was sick of a subject. Any further questions would be met with increasingly obscure answers.

The old cat gave me a sly look, then curled to sleep.

I tried reading his subvocal thoughts, but could not penetrate the drifting mists of distortion.

I sat back on my heels and stared into the fire.

Could it be true that Maryon's vision had been *sent by Atthis*? If so, then the need to return the gypsy to her people must be somehow connected to my secret quest to find and destroy the weaponmachines. Or perhaps the return of the gypsy had been nothing more than an excuse to get me to Sutrium. Yet the deadline Maryon had given fitted with the Twentyfamilies departure, and I had learned, at least in part, what *Swallow* meant.

Frustrated, I tried thinking it through from another direction.

Maryon's first trance had produced a warning for Obernewtyn, while her second and deeper futuretelling had concerned me. Perhaps Atthis had caused only the second trance. But why bother to send messages through the futureteller instead of speaking to my mind directly? I had sworn to heed her direction, so it could not be through fear that I would refuse to obey.

Yet there was a precedent. The first time Atthis summoned me had been through Maruman's mind. In any case, if Maruman spoke the truth, I had no more cause to fret at leaving Obernewtyn, or fear I would not be there when I was summoned.

It struck me suddenly that rather than spending my time worrying about my destined quest, I should simply live and trust in the fates to bring me where I was needed.

I stared into the flames, with a feeling of having perceived a tremendous truth.

For a moment, in spite of weariness and concern over Idris and the rebel alliance, I felt a sense of clarity and purpose such as I had not experienced since standing on the high peaks of the Agyllian ken. It seemed to me that simply by existing, I fulfilled the purpose of my life.

"There is blood on your shirt," Kella said, sounding startled.

"Some louts in the market whipped me," I said.

"Let me see," she commanded.

I flapped my hand for her to leave me be. "It has already been cleaned and treated—by a gypsy herb lorist."

In a tired way, I enjoyed the amazement in their faces. I let them speculate a moment before telling them what had happened, leaving out only the gypsy's kiss. It shamed me to think of it, as if somehow I had wanted it, or made it happen. Nor did I complicate matters by telling them about the triple Guanette bird design, nor the mysterious Swallow.

But what I had told was enough to have them all agog.

"When will ye take her to them?" Matthew asked.

"When Kella says it is safe for her to travel. After that business with Dragon in the market, all the eyes in every rat-hole and cranny of the city will be peeled for gypsies, so even if she was able to move now, I'd wait a day or so. Unfortunately, they saw you take her so neither of us will be able to move about too easily, and certainly not together."

"Iriny," Kella said, for I had told her the name of the gypsy. "Strange to give her a name after so long. She is sleeping naturally now and her wounds have begun to knit nicely."

I nodded and looked around. "Where is Dragon?"

"Sleeping still," Kella said. "It's not surprising. You must have had to hit her hard to knock her out right through her shield. I didn't even know that was possible."

The stair door slammed and Domick came in. Kella recounted the day's events to him, but the coercer seemed more concerned about Idris than anything else.

"When did Reuvan say he was seen last?" he demanded.

"Last night. Or mayhap yestermorn," Matthew said.

"He has only been missing a night," I pointed out, as the coercer began to pace back and forward. "Surely, this is a little soon for everyone to be panicking."

"Did ye try farseekin' him?" Domick demanded.

"I did, but it was an unfocused probe and I could not find him. There are lots of blank spots in the city where the ground must be tainted. And the sea seems to be throwing up static as well, and that makes it hard to focus along the wharfs. Or he might just be sleeping. You know it is much harder to find a sleeping mind even with an attuned probe."

"He might also be dead," Domick murmured.

I glared at him. "Do you take pleasure in being so miserable and hopeless?"

His hard eyes met mine. "In suggesting Idris is dead, I offer hope. If he is not, he may very well wish he were."

"Wh ... what?" Kella gasped faintly.

"None of you seems to have grasped what Idris' disappearance may mean," Domick said. "If someone has him and questions him, he will be made to tell all he knows ..."

"The safe house," Kella whispered, lifting a hand to her lips. "He knows where it is and all about us."

"He knows everything about Brydda and the rebels too," Domick reminded us brusquely.

I groaned, seeing more than that. "Lud save us. *He knows about Obernewtyn!*"

"He'd nivver give us away," Matthew said stoutly.

Domick turned a bleak look on the Farseeker ward and suddenly they seemed decades apart in age.

"You don't have any idea, do you? Faced with a skilled torturer, you or I, even Rushton himself, would tell all. And Idris is a boy. Make no mistakes, if those who have him want information, he will tell them everything he knows."

XIX

After a heated discussion, we decided not to abandon the safe house immediately, but to wait until first light in the hope that Idris would be found. At the coercer's urging, we spent the night packing into woven boxes Kella's precious store of herbs and herb lore preparations, and her healing implements.

When we were almost finished, Kella went to waken Dragon so that she could apply the skin dye. After the way the soldierguard had looked at her, we dared not let her remain undisguised. Domick took out a city map which showed the location of the nearest green.

"I wish you would reconsider," he said.

"I wish you would stop suggesting it," I snapped.

The coercer wanted us to go directly to Obernewtyn to alert Rushton and help evacuate. I had argued against doing anything so drastic before we had clarified exactly what the rebels knew of Idris' disappearance. After all, Reuvan had not suggested there was any danger to us or to the safe house.

Kella pointed out that he might have been too distraught to think of warning us. "He seemed almost dazed when he left the safe house."

I was sure that Brydda would have sent someone to warn us if there was any need and had said so, arguing that we could lose ourselves quickly and easily in the morning bustle of traders moving into their places at the markets. If we stole away in the night, someone was certain to report it. We had also agreed not to go to Obernewtyn at once, but to the nearest green, to wait and watch. If there were no raid on the safe house, we would return to it after a while; if there was a raid or any suspicious activity at all, Matthew would ride at once to warn Obernewtyn while the rest of us would follow in the rig.

"You must go back to Obernewtyn too, if the safe house is lost to us," Domick told Kella, who had come in and was now rinsing dye from her fingers.

"What about you?"

"I will stay at an inn as Mika."

"I will stay with you," she said stubbornly.

"Mika has no bondmate and I don't want you connected with him, in case something goes wrong and he has to disappear."

Kella blinked hard at his peremptory tone, and turned away to pull the last of her dried herbs down from the wall racks. His words reminded me of something else.

"Domick, didn't your last report mention people just vanishing without trace in Sutrium?"

The coercer nodded.

"Maybe, whatever happened to those other people is what happened to Idris. And since these disappearances have nothing to do with the Council, then surely we need not fear..."

"We don't know that the Council has anything to do with them," Domick interrupted.

"But your report..."

"Contained conjecture as well as facts. I simply said that I had heard nothing to make me think the Council was behind the disappearances. But I don't hear everything that goes on and, sometimes, the very fact that I have not, means only that people have been warned to hold their tongues." He shrugged. "There are so many factions within the Council and the soldierguard ranks, all with their own plots, and if I have learned one thing in the time I have spent here, it is that sooner or later everything is linked to everything else."

There was something profound in his words, which struck a note of response in me, but it was swamped by a wrenching weariness.

"You remember when we went to see Brydda the first night you got here?" Domick went on. "Reuvan came in and spoke of Salamander."

I nodded. "You said he was something to do with the slave trade."

"He is its leader. Salamander buys the people who disappear, and the increase in disappearances corresponds with an increase in the demand for slaves."

"Buying them from whom?"

"The rumor is that the disappearances are the work of an organization which specializes in kidnapping or removing people for a price. I think it is likely that Salamander set it up himself, to ensure his supply. No one in the slave trade knows what he looks like, because he is fanatical about keeping his face and identity secret. He delegates like a king to a whole herd of people and rarely appears in person. When he does, there is almost no prior warning. It has long been rumored that he is a Councilman or some other high official. No doubt he is well aware that the mystery surrounding his identity creates an atmosphere of terror and suspicion, and keeps his people silent and obedient."

"I didn't know the slave trade had a leader," I said, amazed.

"It did not—until Salamander came on the scene. Once, it was only the odd ship that stole people from the Land and sold them to lands over the seas which were supposed not to exist.

"Then a ship with a flag showing a flaming salamander began to attack any vessel known to trade in slaves, sinking it. One crew member would be kept alive, tortured, then cast ashore to tell the story of a ship with Beforetime weapons that spat fire. In no time the trade virtually ceased, for no one wanted to make themselves a target for such a nemesis."

I had a sudden vision of the hatred that had flared so unexpectedly in Idris' mild eyes when Reuvan had said Salamander was in Sutrium.

"Idris' family were taken by slavers, weren't they?"

"His sisters," Kella said. Her shoulders were hunched forward and there were dark shadows under her eyes. Whenever she looked at her bondmate, there was pain in her eyes.

Domick was oblivious. "If Idris has been taken by the slavers, he will be tortured for information that could be used, before he is sold. Blackmail is another of Salamander's specialties, and you can be sure he will know the value of a Seditioner with inside knowledge of the rebel organization. He would sell it dearly to the Council, and perhaps even Idris himself. So we are back where we started."

It was a grim prospect, for Idris and for Obernewtyn, and we fell into a weary staring sort of silence contemplating it. This was broken when Domick slammed a hand on the arm of his chair.

"Look at us sitting here and yawping into the fire like a herd of defectives! Don't you see that it doesn't matter who has Idris? If I am right, someone may be on their way here now! How will we make a run for it with Dragon and the gypsy unable to walk?"

He was right. I stood up and flung the dregs of the fement onto the fire. It gave a vicious hiss and belched a sullen cloud of smoke.

"All right," I said shortly. "Let's get everything down to the wagon."

Kella continued the last bit of packing while Domick and I transferred the boxes downstairs. Matthew took them from us and packed them into the cramped interior of the gypsy rig, sweating freely in spite of the chill air.

"If Idris is made to talk, won't he mention this room you keep?" I asked.

Domick shook his head and motioned for Matthew to take the other end of the box he carried. "He knows nothing about it."

"But he knows about you."

"He knows about Domick," the coercer corrected. "Not about the Council worker, Mika. Even a physical description of me will fit a number of others. And if he does tell them of a spy in the Councilcourt, I will know they are seeking me long before they realize which one I am, and vanish."

He had it all worked out and no doubt he was correct, but one part of me wondered if this new Domick was not pleased for an excuse to hurry us all out of Sutrium.

"But why risk it at all?" Matthew demanded, shoving a box in place against the others.

The coercer's voice was curt with dismissal. "Because my position is too valuable to abandon lightly. Apart from that, if Idris is brought to the Councilcourt, I might be able to wipe his mind so he may not be able to speak of the rebels or of us."

The ease with which he proposed to erase the boy's mind shocked me. I stared at him for a moment, half-tempted to loose a farseeking probe in case any surface thoughts drifted free of the coercer's mindshield. It would not be ethical to probe him, but if he were careless I might learn what had so altered him. What stopped me asking him outright was the fear that whatever was wrong arose from his relationship with Kella. And no matter how it hurt her, and chilled me to see him this way, the changes did not seem to be affecting his work for Obernewtyn, and therefore were none of my business.

The sleepless night and the long day that had preceded it were taking their toll and I thought longingly of my bed upstairs. It was hard and lumpy and bits of straw poked into me in the night, but I could think of nothing more wonderful at that moment than to have the freedom to sink into it and pull the covers over my head while there were still a few hours of night left. Sometimes I longed fiercely to have only myself to worry about.

"After what happened with Dragon yesterday, all the gypsy greens will be under observation. It would be safer for you to go straight back to Obernewtyn," Domick went on relentlessly, as we made our way back up to the kitchen.

I lost my temper. "Do you suggest we take the gypsy back with us to Obernewtyn? And if the greens are watched, then the gates will be watched too, which means the risk of being identified as we leave will be doubled."

"Returning her to her people is surely less important than keeping Obernewtyn safe," Domick persisted. "As for the gates, you can coerce yourself past them because you know who to coerce. In the city you will have no idea who watches with hostile eyes and, if you are recognized, you will still have to pass the gates to escape."

I shook my head in exasperation and brushed past him to enter the kitchen again. Domick went on and on like water dripping on stone. Everything he said made sense—if Idris had been taken by someone who would ask about us.

"The gypsy cannot be taken on the trip back to the mountains just yet," Kella said, having heard my words. "After a couple of days of rest and quiet..."

"I am sure she would prefer a little discomfort to being captured along with us and burned at the stake!" Domick interrupted coldly. He looked around the empty kitchen. "Surely everything must now be packed, Kella, or must you also bring such necessities as the bathing barrels?"

The healer's shoulders slumped as he turned on his heel and stalked out, and I wondered how long her love for the coercer would survive his insensitivity.

"He is rough in saying it, but right," I said gently to her after a moment. "It will do the gypsy no good to be healthy if the soldierguards get hold of her. There are times when we must endure what comes and take our luck. Go and prepare her to be carried down to the wagon."

"A trip into the mountains might kill her...."

"We are not taking her back to Obernewtyn. I will return her to her people. She *must* be back to them before we leave."

Kella's eyes widened, then she nodded soberly, remembering Maryon's deadline. Or Atthis'. It was possible I had already done enough to save myself and Obernewtyn in finding the gypsy's people and learning that Swallow was a person, but there was no way of telling.

Therefore, the gypsy must be taken to Maire. The trouble was that Kella and Matthew would have to come as well.

I was still trying to make up my mind if it would not be best to have them wait somewhere for me, when Domick departed, saying he was expected at the Councilcourt.

Dragon trailed into the kitchen. In spite of the muddy dyes Kella had used to disguise her hair and skin, and a wan, woebegone expression, she was lovelier than ever. She put her hand to her forehead and rubbed at it fretfully.

"Are you all right?" I asked.

She blinked at me, her blue eyes pink-rimmed. "Head hurts."

Small wonder after the ruthless jolt I had given her, I thought ruefully, drawing her to warm herself by the fire. It was not much of a reward for her courage in defending the woman and her children, yet what else could I have done?

Kella entered, frowning. "The sleepseal on the gypsy will hold only a little while longer. Seals are progressively less effective when they are applied close together and because she woke as I was setting it in place, her mind is fighting it. It will hold for a few hours. No more."

"It will do. I'll get Matthew to help me bring her down in a minute." I nodded at Dragon. "Is she all right? She says her head hurts."

Kella examined the girl, looking intently into her eyes and touching her temple lightly. Rummaging in a basket, she made a soothing herbal mixture and we both watched as Dragon drank it.

"She'll be fine once the herbs begin to work," the healer said softly. She glanced around the kitchen at the bare walls and sighed. "I suppose we might just as well go at once. I have sometimes longed for something that would send me back to Obernewtyn, yet now I am sad. I cannot imagine this place without me."

"Nor can I," said a gruff, familiar voice.

We both whirled to see Brydda Llewellyn standing in the kitchen doorway.

"Brydda!" Kella cried gladly, and flung herself into the rebel chief's arms. The big man hugged her, then gently put her away from him.

"The soldierguards are searching the city for a gypsy girl and boy who freed a woman from a burning in Guanette. They are picking gypsies up all over the city and questioning them. The descriptions they are giving out fit you and Matthew too well to be anyone else. They also tally with reports dozens of people gave after an incident in a city market where two gypsies and a red-haired Landgirl attacked Herder priests about their business."

I felt sick. Not only had they connected the market incident to the one in Guanette, Dragon's description was now being bandied about. Thank heaven, we had thought to disguise her.

"Brydda..." I began, but he cut me off as if he had not heard me.

"I thought it must be you, so I came to... to warn you." There was an odd twitchiness in his manner.

"Has Idris come back yet?" I asked, with sudden foreboding.

He shook his head.

"Then we must leave here at once in case the soldierguards come," I said firmly, and tried to propel him back toward the stairs. It was like trying to push a mountain sideways.

"The soldierguards won't be coming," he said.

Matthew came into the hallway behind us, but his welcoming smile faltered as he took in the strangeness of the older man.

"Something is wrong, but let him tell it how he will," I farsent, forestalling his questions.

Dragon was staring up at the giant rebel in wonderment. Clearly Kella's medicine had done its job. He stirred under her gaze and frowned down at the empath. "So it *was* you in the market, Dragon. What a little beauty you are...."

"Bir-da," she said shyly, coming toward him as if beguiled.

The rebel's eyes lost their feverish look, as he dropped to one knee to make himself her height, but she would not be coaxed nearer.

"Brydda, if the Council have Idris, they will force him to tell them about this place...." I spoke more in an attempt to draw the rebel back to normality, than in expectation of an answer.

"Idris will not talk," Brydda interrupted.

I bit my lip. After Domick's chilling assertion that a skilled torturer could make anyone talk, I did not understand his conviction that Idris would not be made to speak. Especially since a friend had once before been tortured to betray him.

Unless his suppressed Talent had told him something.

I was trying to decide how best to frame a query, when the big rebel rose with catlike grace and moved past us to the dying fire. Kella and Matthew exchanged worried glances as he lowered himself onto a chair.

Dragon sidled gradually nearer until she came to lean against his knees and stare into his face. He did not appear to be aware of her at all.

"I am so tired...." he said, rubbing his fingers in his eyes.

"Brydda, how can you know the soldierguards won't come here?" I asked, coming to stand by the fire too.

The rebel did not answer, but, fascinatingly, Dragon's face twisted with the emotions she was receiving from the big man. Her ability to receive emotions had been slower to develop than her power to transmit them, but physical contact enhanced all Talent. Brydda had no idea of what was happening because the empath's face was turned slightly away from him. It was disturbing and oddly grotesque to read the movement of a grown man's thought in Dragon's mobile young face.

First there was grief and guilt, then anger and frustration, and at last a sort of wretched despair.

"It does not matter how I know, only that I do," he answered at last, face impassive.

"Do you know who has Idris?" I asked, keeping one eye on Dragon.

Her face again mirrored the rebel's inner turmoil, and I felt a deepening disquiet. Who could have taken Idris for Brydda to react so strongly?

The big man was staring into the red embers of the half-extinguished fire, still redolent with fement. "Idris was investigating something for me when he disappeared," he murmured at last. "He asked me to use him. But I should never have done it."

"Who do you think took him?"

A terrible weary despair dragged at Dragon's youthful features, making of them a grotesque mask.

"You have heard of the disappearances in Sutrium?" Brydda asked.

"Yes. Do you think that is what happened to him, then?"

He gave a croaking laugh. "My curiosity is what happened to Idris. My infernal hunger for knowledge. I overheard a sot at an inn boasting about knowing Salamander. I bought the fellow a drink and it took me no longer than that to know he had lied. The slavemaster would never trust his face to such a ninnyhammer. I needled him a bit just for the sake of it, and he wound up telling me that his master knew Salamander. I had a feeling there was some truth in this, so I decided to have him watched. He shut up after a bit, as if he realized he had said too much. I did not want to frighten him off, so I played the gull for him. I got roaring drunk and let him rob me before I was thrown outside."

This sot must be the drunkard Reuvan had spoken of when he burst in on us that night at the burned-out-way-house. The rebel's eyes had grown cold as sharpened icicles. "Idris volunteered to keep an eye on Salamander while I organized a roster of watchers. The sot was lodging at the inn and Idris had only to watch him and note the name of anyone who spoke with him while I was gone. I did not expect anything significant to happen."

He gave me a bitter look. "*Stay put and watch*, I said. But the sot went out about an hour after we left and Idris followed. I was so busy gloating over having finally caught hold of Salamander's elusive tail, that I took no account of the fact that Idris wanted the slave trade destroyed with a passion far greater than mine..."

"Do you think this man realized Idris was following and took him prisoner?"

"He was a drunk and, for all his smallness, Idris was strong and tough."

"Then... what?" I asked, when he fell silent.

Brydda did not answer. His face was as still as if it had been a carved image. Kella pinched me and pointed to Dragon. The flame-haired empath was staring out blindly, tears coursing down her cheeks.

A heavy dread settled in my stomach, as it came to me that Brydda had been speaking of Idris in the past tense.

Kella had reached the same awful conclusion. "Idris is dead, isn't he?" she whispered.

The big rebel jerked convulsively at her words. "Dead? Yes," he said flatly.

Dragon's face twisted, revealing the emotions the big man would not express, and she began to tremble. I signaled Kella to get her away from him.

"Are you sure?" I whispered.

The rebel turned dry eyes, hectic with self-hate and grief, on me. "I am sure. His body was found this morning washed up on the banks of the Suggredoon."

Dragon let out an anguished howl, voicing the jagged spike of Kella's shock.

"We'll find whoever did it," Matthew vowed, through gritted teeth.

I gave him a pointed look. The last thing we needed was high drama at such a moment. He rose and went out, muttering that he had to unpack the wagon. Kella went too, taking Dragon out of the range of Brydda's searing anguish.

"Salamander killed him," he said, when we were alone. "I have sworn I will crush the man and his foul trade once and for all, in the boy's name."

I bit my lip, but I knew I must say the unsayable. "Brydda. Idris might ... still ... have been made to speak, before ..."

The rebel shook his head emphatically. "His body was unmarked and he would not have spoken unless they had forced it from him. He would never ... never betray me willingly or easily." The last words were voiced in a savage rasp, and I blinked my own sudden tears away.

"If Idris was not questioned, why was he killed?" I asked. "Surely Salamander would have sold him as a slave?"

"Idris followed the sot to a meeting with the slave supplier, who, in turn, must have been watched by Salamander," Brydda said, after he had regained control of himself. "No doubt the slavemaster killed Idris because the boy saw his face; killed him as a routine precaution, thinking him no more than a curious lad who had seen more than was good for him. If he had suspected Idris was a spy, Salamander would have had him tortured. That tells me Idris was killed as thoughtlessly as if he were a fly or an ant in the wrong place at the wrong time."

"Why are you so certain it was Salamander that did it?"

Brydda's face was grim with certainty. "A tiny lizard shape was carved into his forehead—Salamander's murderous trademark."

I felt a sick wave of horror. "I'm so sorry," I whispered, knowing there was no way to console the rebel for the loss of a boy he had loved like a son.

Brydda took a deep shuddering breath, and seemed incredibly to compose himself to a bleak serenity. "I will not grieve while Idris' killer breathes. Salamander will pay for the boy's life with his own blood!"

I shuddered inwardly at the mad, cold fire in his eyes, revolted by the notion that one death could compensate for another. But I understood the guilt-driven anger that motivated him.

The rebel chief turned burning eyes on me. "That is why I came tonight. You can help me to trap him."

I blinked, startled. "Salamander?"

He nodded grimly. "You can use your powers to lead me to him."

"When?" I asked warily.

"Now," the rebel said.

XX

"Now?" I echoed, incredulously.

Brydda inclined his head and rose slowly, as if his bones were stiff and pained him. Yet the emberglow from the dying fire rendered him mysteriously younger. "Come, I will explain as we go."

"I won't go without knowing what I'm getting myself into! You are my friend, but I have a responsibility to Obernewtyn."

He stared at me for a long moment, then sat back down, grief and fury extinguished with visible effort. "Listen well then, for there is not much time. There was information on Idris' body about a meeting...."

"Surely, Salamander would have found any message when he searched the body. It must be some kind of trap...."

The rebel shook his head emphatically. "It was not a message to any eyes but mine. Idris and I have a special code in case ..." The momentary eagerness in his face faded to a grim recollection of the boy's loss. "The message said that a Councilfarm overseer, called Evan Bollange, had approached the sot just before he left the inn, offering five able-bodied Councilfarm workers whose deaths had been staged. The poor wretches had been smuggled into the city, drugged and hidden under the boards of a manure cart. A time and place were named for a meeting between Bollange and the sot's master to discuss terms. The drunk claimed there was a high demand for slaves in the lands beyond the seas, and seemed to feel his masters might pay a higher price to ensure a steady supply of them."

The Council had in the early days maintained the Land was all that remained unpoisoned of the world, while the Herders preached that it was all Lud had seen fit to spare of the corrupt Beforetime. Seafarers had long known this to be a lie, but they had a rigid code of silence imposed by the Council—even so, word had leaked out. The red-haired Druid arms-

man, Gilbert, had told me once that there were many places in the wide
world other than the Land.

Brydda went on, "I am certain the sot went out of the inn that night
to let his master know of the meeting date with Bollange. He was a minion,
chosen precisely because he *would* boast, for an organization that is too
secret will have no clients."

Brydda's eyes were hard and suddenly purposeful. "Like all such, he
was disposable. He was found the day after Idris vanished with his throat
cut—no doubt payment for his carelessness in letting himself be followed.
Such culling is not uncommon among Salamander's people. There was now
no trail to the slavemaster but, in his arrogance, he made a mistake. He
let us find Idris' body, never knowing there was a message on it, telling
the time and place of the rendezvous that had been set up between Bollange
and the slaver supplier. That rendezvous is before dawn this day, in an inn
on the other side of the city. If you will help me, we must leave at once."

"Are you going to spy on the meeting..."

"I have no intention of spying," Brydda interrupted, his eyes aglitter.
"I intend to intercept the Council worker *before* he arrives at his meeting
with the slave supplier, and take his place."

"You would pass yourself off as the overseer?"

He shook his head. "There is every likelihood that the sot described
Bollange to his master. Therefore, I will be his brother, Arkold Bollange."

"You must be mad! The slave supplier will never believe such a far-
fetched story!"

"I do not expect him to," Brydda said calmly.

"Then what is the point of it? If he does not believe you, he will
tell you nothing about the slave trade or Salamander."

"I doubt he would tell me anything if he did believe me. But fortunately it does not matter, because you will come with me as my assistant
and *read his mind*. He must know enough about Salamander to reach him
at need."

I gaped at his audacity. "What if the slave supplier decides to just
kill the overseer's unlikely brother and his gypsy assistant?"

"That is a risk," Brydda agreed, sounding as if he were admitting
that it might rain. "But I doubt he will do that, even if he is extremely
suspicious, because Salamander will want the slaves." He stood up suddenly. "Will you help me?"

I sighed, then stood too.

"Rushton will be furious. He will like this no more than that I have decided to take your advice and meet with your rebel leaders."

Brydda's eyes widened. "Good on both accounts! Opportunities must be seized upon when they arise. We need leaders, truly, but sometimes decisions need to be made on the battlefield in the heat of the moment by rankless fighters. Without those capable of making such decisions, any force might founder. Rushton would appreciate the need and your ability to rise to it and make a decision without consultation."

"I wonder," I murmured dryly, pulling on my boots.

I went to my chamber, donned a hooded cloak and plaited my hair.

When we came down into the wagon-repair shed, Gahltha stirred in the wagon harnessing and farsent a stern reminder of my promise not to go out without him.

"He insists I ride him," I told Brydda, unbuckling the straps that bound the black horse to the wagon. "If there is trouble he is a savage fighter. Jaygar has been trained to fight as well and he offers to bear you too."

Brydda shrugged. "I had thought to walk, but if we take the horses, we can get away fast if something goes awry." He signaled his thanks to Jaygar.

I was silent, impressed that the rebel did not simply accept Jaygar's offer as his rightful due. He genuinely regarded the horses as equals. Though he rode Sallah often, and in fact had stolen her from a Herder cloister, he never took her for granted. Sometimes I was convinced he had accepted my Misfit powers solely because, through me, he had been able to devise a finger signal language that enabled him to communicate with horses. He had been delighted when the Beasting guildmaster, Alad, had asked to learn the language so it could be taught gradually to all at Obernewtyn who were not beastspeakers, and to the beasts themselves.

As we rode out into the early morning, I wondered if Alad was right about Sallah being the lowland beast-leader and, if so, whether Brydda had any idea of it. It would not surprise me at all to find he had allied himself with the equines over his own kind.

The streets were all but deserted at that hour, and we did not see any soldierguards, but nonetheless I was unable to rid myself of the feeling that we were being watched.

Certainly we made a strange enough couple, a gypsy boy on a magnificent, if dirty, black stallion, and an enormous dark-haired man wrapped in his oil cloak and mounted on a stocky roan.

"I scent no funaga," Gahltha assured me.

I relaxed fractionally, reporting this to Brydda.

"Nor should there be," he said quietly. "I am taking us through parts of the city that are virtually deserted except during trading hours."

Brydda ceased his scrutiny of the streets to look at me for a moment. "I will send birds off as soon as we return to let the group leaders know about the meeting with you. It will take a few days for them to reply, though they have birds as well, because they will confer and scheme before responding."

"Is it wise to let the rebels know in advance that I am to come?" I asked. "Especially if there is a traitor among you."

"That there is a traitor is not yet certain. But even if there is, we must ensure that as many rebel leaders as possible come to hear you speak. Otherwise the report they hear will depend upon the bias of the teller. And even if they were favorably inclined toward you, it is easier to dismiss secondhand reports as exaggeration. I will write so that every rebel leader feels they will miss out on something vital, unless they attend. The rest will be up to you."

There was no sign of Brydda's earlier shattered disorientation; the big man was shielding himself from the pain of Idris's loss by concentrating on plans and schemes.

We froze at the sound of scuffling, then relaxed as a cat darted out and disappeared in a shadowy alley. This reminded me that I had not seen Maruman since the previous morning.

"I/Gahltha will keep youInnle safe," Gahltha sent gravely.

He thought I was afraid without Maruman. In fact, I was afraid *for* the old cat, but there was no point in explaining. I would find him when I returned to the safe house.

The rebel was silent now and I was certain his thoughts revolved around Idris. I said nothing, knowing that no words would ease his pain. I remembered how deep the hurt of Jik's death had cut into me. Words had not helped then—and sometimes I had longed for silence as much as forgetfulness. Time had abated the immediate wrenching sorrow I had felt at the boy's death, yet even now the thought of it sometimes made a dull ache in my chest, like a long-healed scar echoing its birth.

Suddenly Brydda signaled Jaygar to stop.

"Idris' message said the overseer had been told to seek out the street of five inns," the rebel said, looking about. "We are almost there so we should assume we'll be watched beyond this point. We will wait here to intercept the overseer."

"Do you know what he looks like?"

He shook his head. "There are three paths leading into the street of five inns. Two come from the other direction and one from the direction of the inn where the sot stayed. I am sure he will come this way for he will almost certainly have been staying near the inn. There will be few enough people about at this time but you must tell me when he comes," he added, touching his head to indicate that he meant me to use my farseeking powers.

It seemed a vague sort of plan. But then Brydda had a "knack" of guessing right, so I held my tongue and let him lead the way into a narrow lane between two high buildings. We dismounted and the horses moved deeper into the lane to wait.

"What am I to do when I have him?"

"You must turn him back," Brydda said softly. "Can you do that, so that he will not know what has happened?"

I sighed. "I will try, but his mind might be . . ."

"Someone/funaga comes," Gahltha sent urgently.

I froze and at once we heard a quick light step. It was a woman carrying a basket, and a few minutes later two boys ran by. Then, on the third sound of footsteps, I sent my mind flying out and breathed a sigh of incredulous relief to find the wiry little man coming down the street was indeed the very person we were waiting for. Best of all, his mind was wide open to me.

Gently I rifled through his memories before coercing him into forgetting why he had come out. In the gap left by what was erased, I took an older memory of a rousing night's drinking from his memories, and re-established it as the memory of the previous night. I pinched a nerve and gave him a headache to match, then sent him around the next corner and back to his lodgings bewildered and disorientated.

"It's done," I said aloud. "He has forgotten everything about this meeting, and believes he has been out carousing. I have made him forget about the slaves too. He now thinks they really did die in an accident. You will have to free them, though."

"You know their location?"

"Of course."

"Good," Brydda said grimly. He cast a look at the sky. "We had better go on. The instructions said the overseer must stop at the public trough and drink, to identify himself."

We moved out into the street on foot, leaving the horses to wait, and made our way into the street of five inns. There was a dirty-looking trough about halfway along, and Brydda stopped at it and cupped his hands to scoop some of the brackish water to his mouth. I let my mind loose, but I could detect no watcher. It made my skin creep to think that Salamander might be somewhere about us, watching from a window or a pool of shadow.

A ragged boy stepped out of a doorway and I gasped in startled fright. His eyes skated along the empty street, passing us, then returning to settle. His lips were blue and he was shivering violently with the cold or fear. His eyes slid to me uneasily, then back to Brydda. "There was to be one man walking alone."

"It is none of your affair," Brydda growled. "What are the words you have been told to say to me?"

The boy seemed reassured by Brydda's roughness. "You are to go to the last inn in this street, and ask for the man in the best room."

He turned and darted away down a lane.

"He was frightened," I murmured, but Brydda had begun to walk again.

The last inn proved to be a cheap roomhouse with a room attached for casual drinking. I grimaced, for compared to it the frowsy Good Egg had been positively luxurious. A rank smell assailed us at the door, rising from piles of stinking refuse to one side.

I gagged at the stench as Brydda knocked, wondering what had possessed me to agree to such a mad scheme. My powers would do us no good because I could feel that the wretched place was constructed of rock lightly tainted with Beforetime poisons. Fortunately, this would not matter once we were inside the walls, as long as they did not lie between the slave supplier and ourselves!

"I/Gahltha am here. I will kick the wall down if you do not return," the black horse sent stoutly. I felt slightly less afraid, knowing the fierce black horse meant exactly what he said.

After a long wait a man with yellow-stained teeth opened the inn door a crack and squinted out at us. Brydda drew a little scrolled note from his pocket and handed it through the opening. "Give this to the man in your best room."

The innkeeper grunted in derision, but he took the note in his grimy fingers before slamming the door shut.

"What was in it?" I asked.

"A note from my brother, Evan, introducing me as his proxy. And now we can do no more than wait and keep our sword hands free."

We waited in silence and I spent the time adopting various creative ways of breathing, in an effort to filter out the foul stench of the place.

The door opened again and the man indicated that we were to enter. Brydda gave me an encouraging pinch as I preceded him. If possible, the smell inside was worse and it was all I could do not to vomit. The rebel seemed completely impervious to it. I gulped and was glad I had an empty stomach.

The innkeeper brought us to a room with a brown door and held out a dirty paw. Brydda dropped a coin into it, then knocked, and the innkeeper scuttled away as if he did not want to be there when the occupant appeared.

This made me very nervous.

The door opened a slit.

"Enter," a papery voice rasped, and a shiver ran up my spine at the sound of it.

At first, I thought the chamber windowless and unlit, but it was simply that Brydda's bulk had blocked the light of a cheap lantern shaded to throw its light toward us, leaving the rest of the room in darkness. The windows, if there were any, had been blacked out.

The only thing I could see clearly was the pitted surface of a wooden table, and two enormous scarred hands with thick, powerful wrists resting on it. Between the hands were a wickedly curved dagger, carved with odd symbols, and the little scrolled note Brydda had sent in.

The atmosphere of threat in the room was almost palpable and my heart began to gallop as Brydda stepped forward. "I am Arkold Bollange, Sirrah. . . ."

"You do not resemble your brother?" the man behind said, his skepticism patently obvious.

"Different fathers, Sirrah," Brydda said, and it was all I could do not to goggle at him in astonishment. In the blink of an eye, without the benefit of even changing his shirt, the rebel had transformed himself into a self-important fool whose pompous facade barely concealed the sniveling coward lurking beneath.

I did my best to shape myself into the sort of cringing nitwit that I imagined such a man would choose as a servant. At the same time, I loosed a probe. It moved sluggishly because of the taint in the walls and floor. The first thing it told me was that the man seated behind the table was not alone. There were three others standing against the wall behind him.

I bent my mind upon one of them and learned that he and the man next to him were hired killers. The third was known to them only as the slaver's assistant. The two hirelings carried knives, unsheathed, and had instructions to kill instantly after a certain combination of words.

I tried the slaver's assistant, but his mind was shielded.

"Why did not your brother come himself as was arranged?" the slaver was asking Brydda.

"As he wrote in that note, Sirrah, Evan feared he was being followed and sent me in his place. I am here only as an emissary to discuss, ah, price."

"Who is this gypsy?" The slaver's voice cracked out like a whip and I jumped.

The two men with knives tensed and so did I.

"My servant," Brydda blustered. "You could not expect a man of my stature to go about in an area like this without even a body servant? I can't very well use my own people. You need not worry about him though. He is defective except for a peculiar strength with his hands and feet that make him a useful guard in spite of his small stature."

Again the silence, and I prepared myself to coerce the two with knives if the slave supplier gave the signal to kill.

"Very well," he said at last in his sibilant voice. "But I do not want him brought again. I do not like gypsies, full or halfbloods. They are trouble and they are carriers of disease. Get rid of him."

"Of . . . of course, Sirrah," Brydda babbled.

The slave supplier became businesslike as he spoke of the price he would pay for each slave, and how this would increase with the number of slaves offered. The men in the shadows relaxed.

"How will I reach you if there is a problem before then?" Brydda asked.

"There will be no problem," the slaver said with chilling finality.

"Of course not," Brydda babbled idiotically. "I understand perfectly."

The slave supplier stood and even his hands were swallowed up by the shadows. A moment later, a bag of coins fell onto the table.

"This is an advance on the payment for the five. You will get the remainder when I get the slaves if they are sound-limbed and not defectives."

"I assure you..." Brydda blustered.

I summoned a coercive probe swiftly, realizing I had been so busy listening to the interchange that I had forgotten what I was there for. Sending the probe to the slave supplier, I was flabbergasted to find my way barred by *another farseeking probe*. Wrapped delicately around the slaver's mind, the alien probe had taken on the shape and feel of the host mind and in some places was indistinguishable from it.

Unwilling to disturb the probe until I knew its purpose, I cast about until I found its source. It was the man in the shadows whose mind I had been unable to read. The slaver's assistant *was a Talented Misfit!*

I hovered uncertainly, my mind reeling with shock. I had promised Brydda to get what information I could about Salamander, which meant getting past the othermind.

I clenched my teeth and readied myself to attack.

"Collection of the slaves will take place in two days," the slave supplier was saying. "Here is a map. The shed where you are to bring the slaves is marked on it. When you hear a knock thus..." He rapped in a sequence. The movement brought him into the light for a fleeting second and I had a glimpse of bad skin, dark-brown eyes and a vicious slash of a mouth before he moved back into the shadows. "Then you will open the door. Do you understand?"

I braced myself for a battle and let an aggressive coercerprobe fly toward the slaver's assistant. To my complete astonishment the othermind opened to me!

XXI

When we came outside, the sky arching above was a deep, icy blue and there were few stars, for the sun was near to rising. We could only have been inside the inn a short while. I felt as if we had been in there for years.

Gahltha whinnied a welcome and I stroked his neck in mute affection, realizing unexpectedly that whatever the enigmatic stallion felt for me, I loved him.

"What did you find?" Brydda asked, as we mounted up.

"Another mindprobe," I said. "Wrapped around the slave supplier's mind."

Brydda turned to stare at me. "Are you saying there was a *Misfit* among those who skulked in the shadows of that room? Protecting him?"

"Not just a Misfit. A Talent, and not protecting, though that is what I thought at first. Trying to get into his mind. I traced the mindprobe back to its owner. Do you remember Daffyd, who brought Dragon to Obernewtyn when I was ill?"

"The Druid's armsman? The probe was his?"

I nodded, then we both fell quiet, perforce, for we had come to a lane where people were bustling about preparing for the day's trading. In one tiny market square a fire had been lit in a metal barrel and cloaked men and women stooped over it, warming their fingers. They were busy and preoccupied with their own affairs, which made it a simple matter to weave a coercive net that would make it difficult for anyone to keep their eyes on us. I wondered at the absence of soldierguards, given the events of the previous day.

I thought of my first meeting with Daffyd; a chance encounter, if such meetings were ever really chance. I had been waiting in the Council-court to undergo the Misfit trial that would see me sentenced to Obernewtyn. Daffyd and another man had been waiting to see about a trade permit for the high country. I could not recall what words had passed between us that day as we sat there but, somehow, Daffyd had given me the courage to hope.

I had never forgotten his brightness in that dark moment.

We had met a second time after I had been taken captive by the fanatical ex-Herder, Henry Druid. Daffyd had been one of his armsmen. It had been there, at the Druid's secret encampment in the White Valley, that Daffyd and a number of others had been simultaneously awakened to their Misfit Talents, and emotionally enslaved by a powerful Misfit baby, Lidgebaby; there that he had fallen in love with Gilaine—daughter of the Druid, and despised by her father for her muteness.

I had shown them and their friends how to free themselves from Lidgebaby's powerful overmind, in return for their help in escaping the camp. When the firestorm razed the Druid camp to the ground, Daffyd alone had escaped.

Discovering the loss of his friends, he had been heartbroken, but he remained with us in the mountains for some time. He had left us during the last summerdays after Maryon had dreamed of his friends. He had been convinced they had survived, and was determined to find them. Maryon had told me the dream had been vague and the faces unclear, but Daffyd had not cared.

We had not seen nor heard from him since. Until now.

"Elspeth?" Brydda murmured with faint exasperation, and I realized we had entered a street that was empty.

"I'm sorry, I was thinking about Daffyd. Yes, it was his probe. I am sure that his working for the slave supplier has something to do with his friends from the Druid camp."

"Didn't he tell you why he is working for the slavers?"

"There was no time. I farsent him the location of the safe house, and he said he would come when he could."

"It is a pity we did not know that he worked for the slavers all along. It would have saved reading that slave supplier's mind. I doubt that was a pleasant experience."

I licked my lips. "Brydda, I didn't farseek him. I couldn't. His mind was sensitive and he would have felt me at once. Daffyd stopped me just in time. He has spent months trying and still he has not managed it."

"If he has been working for the slave supplier for so long, he must have some notion of where Salamander is," Brydda said.

"I think not, since he is trying to get into his mind for that very reason: to find Salamander. That much he did tell me."

The rebel said nothing.

"I'm sorry, Brydda."

"I know you are not to blame, Elspeth," he said heavily, "but if Daffyd does not come by tomorrow night with the knowledge of Salamander's whereabouts, we will have lost the chance to stop him."

"But surely we can follow the slave supplier until he meets with . . ."

"You don't understand. Two nights hence, when I do not take the five slaves to the abandoned warehouse as agreed, Salamander will guess something is wrong. Knowing his reputation, there will be a short and savage bloodletting during which anyone with any connection to him will be slain. That slave supplier we met tonight will be one of the first to go if he knows what Salamander looks like, or how how to reach him. And perhaps Daffyd, too, though his ignorance might protect him. So you see, there will be no one to follow back to the source."

"Daffyd will come," I said, crossing my fingers.

∾

The air was damp with the promise of more rain and dark clouds obscured the waxing moon as we came in sight of the safe house. In the gaps between clouds, the sparse morning stars were winking out one by one.

"What did you do with the gypsy woman you rescued in Guanette?" Brydda asked suddenly, changing the subject.

"We brought her to Sutrium to take her back to her people. She is ill," I added. The furrow between the rebel's brows deepened appreciably when I told him that I had made contact with the gypsies and meant to return her to them in person.

"You take a terrible risk and I do not understand why," he said. "Gypsy folk have no loyalty or allegiance except to their own. What possessed you to interfere in the first place? After all, the woman was a gypsy, not a Misfit."

I frowned, disliking his inference. Brydda caught my expression and misinterpreted it. "I am sorry. I have no right to question you. But I am only concerned. Perhaps you don't realize . . ."

"It is you who doesn't realize," I interrupted him gently. "We undertake rescues to bring Talented Misfits to Obernewtyn where they will be safe, but that does not mean we callously ignore the plight of all others. There are many we have helped escape the soldierguards, who were not Talented, and others who were not Misfits at all, but simply ordinary Landfolk in need. We don't see ourselves as a race apart, as the gypsies seem to. We are people, even as you are; even as the Councilmen and soldierguards are, for all they behave as if they are cousins to Lud. We think of ourselves as normal human beings and we want others to think of us in that way too."

Brydda looked ill at ease. "I was only concerned that you risked yourself for one who will not show gratitude."

"I hope you are wrong," I said, "but I did not do it for gratitude."

We rode into the yard, dismounting to the squeak of leather and the jingle of metal buckles on the harness. There was a coolness between us. I felt Brydda blamed me for failing to farseek the slave supplier, and I was disturbed more than I liked by the big rebel's words about gypsies.

When the horses were released into the grassy holding yard, Brydda bade them thanks in his finger signs, saying aloud to me that he would not come up. "Reuvan expects me back by sunrise and it is moments away. Where are the drugged Councilfarm workers being kept?"

I told him the cellar's location that I had taken from the thoughts of Evan Bollange.

"I will return tomorrow night," the big man said. "Let us hope Daffyd has come by then with some news for us."

As I watched him stride away, a cat yowled forlornly some streets away, startling me. I thought of Maruman again, and farsought him with an attuned probe.

It did not locate him.

There could be any number of reasons for that. I knew the cat's mind as well as my own, but if he had fallen into one of his mad states, his mind would change its shape, rendering him as good as invisible to a probe which was specifically shaped to his sane mind. Or he might be sleeping or prowling over tainted ground or water.

Or he might be in trouble.

The early morning chill seemed to have seeped into my bones as I farsent Gahltha and Jaygar, asking if they had seen the battered old cat leave the safe house. They had not.

I cursed myself for not watching him more closely.

"What could/would you have done?" Gahltha farsent gently. "The yelloweyes wanders where he wills."

There was truth in that.

Instinctively I glanced up, seeking the pitted face of the moon. Maruman had always attributed his darkest foresight to it, and I had come to see it as a bad omen too. As if summoned by my thoughts, the moon suddenly sailed clear of the clouds.

I felt a mindless rush of fright at the sight of it glaring down on me like the eye of some unearthly hunter. But even as I laughed at my melodramatic imagination, I felt oddly unsettled, and it took me a long time to sleep.

∾

I woke just before midday.

Gray daylight streamed in through the sky windows of the safe house sleeping chamber, but there was no warmth in it. I stretched under the covers, then sat up reluctantly, reaching for my robe. Ariel's face came into my mind, and I froze in the act of climbing out of the bed, remembering that I had dreamed of him.

We had been in the stone tunnel again.

The stone tunnel was a recurrent image from my dreams and once I had asked Maryon what it could mean. She had replied that it was either a place where I would one day go, or it represented me or some aspect of me.

I belted the robe, letting the dream flow back into my mind. This time, instead of pursuing me with a knife or some other horror, Ariel had been walking beside me, his hand nestled in mine, small but very cold. He had smiled up at me as we came to the part of the tunnel where the doors of Obernewtyn flamed.

With the strange logic of dreams, it had seemed perfectly reasonable to me that the doors I had commanded be burned, should exist here.

"Why did you burn them?" the dream Ariel had asked in his piping, eager voice. His eyes had seemed to bore into mine with hypnotic intensity.

"Because there was a map carved into the design," I had answered. "I did not want anyone to find it."

This was the truth. Everyone at Obernewtyn believed the doors had been burned to free the inlaid gold in the design so that we could make guildleaders' armbands from it. But my true object had been to destroy the hidden map carved into the doors, which showed the location of a cache of Beforetime weaponmachines.

Louis Larkin had once told me that he remembered, as a boy, hearing Marisa Seraphim purchase the great doors. She was long dead now, but there was a painting of her at Obernewtyn. She had been very beautiful but everything in the picture spoke of her brilliance and will, and nothing of her heart. Her diaries had revealed a woman as clever and ruthless as a teknoguilder without soul.

In the dream Ariel's face had possessed that same brilliant, soulless quality, as he moved forward to peer at the doors.

Drawing on my slippers, I wondered what it meant that Ariel asked such questions in my dreams. I had the powerful feeling that he had asked something more, but I could not recall what or if I had answered. The questions had ended when I had heard Gahltha's cool mental voice calling my name. He had emerged from the shadows behind me in the tunnel, dark and even more magnificent than in life.

"Ride on me," his mind spoke to mine.

I had responded instinctively, vaulting onto his back. We had ridden a road which led eerily up into the clouds and the sky, leaving Ariel and the dreamcave far below. We had ridden impossibly high, until Gahltha sent to me that he was unable to go further. Before I could say it did not matter, he bucked violently, sending me flying up like a stone from a catapult.

I had screamed in fear, but all at once an Agyllian bird flew beneath me. I clutched convulsively at the warm feathers and thin bones.

I had thought the bird was Atthis, except the Eldar was blind and too small to bear me. This bird was pure white, rather than red and enormous like the Agyllians.

"Things bear their spirit shapes on the dreamtrails," a voice had whispered, but so faintly I could not tell whose it was. The bird bore me silently ever up and out, through a swirling rainbow of color and light that ended only when I awoke.

It had been a peculiar dream. Not an ashling, for all its vividness; perhaps no more than the distorted summation of a long day of turmoil. Even so, it was hard to throw off.

I took refuge in practicalities. A swift farseeking scan told me Matthew and Kella were busy shifting the boxes from the rig back into the safe house. There was no sign, yet, of Daffyd. Or, indeed, of Maruman.

I gathered up my clothing, careful not to waken Dragon who was still sound asleep. I crept from the room and padded along the hallway to the bathing chamber to splash my face and neck before dressing.

My eyes looked out of the mirror at me, bloodshot but alert. That was when I realized with horror that I had done nothing about the mental barrier I had set up to catch the pain of the whipping in the market. I knew better than any, the danger of allowing too much pain to build up for, when freed, it had an accumulative impact—the pain from simple leg cramp left for too long could become a crippling agony.

My heart thumped with apprehension as I began carefully to dismantle the barrier. I went very slowly, so as not to flood my senses with too much of the stockpiled pain at once. It was always difficult to regulate the flow.

To my surprise, nothing at all leaked out of the minute gap I had made. Puzzled, I removed the barrier completely, but there was not even a slight ache waiting to be endured.

My face looked out at me from the mirror, blank with astonishment. Stored pain could not be released without my experiencing it, so what had happened? Had the herbal ointment Maire had applied to the wounds somehow absorbed or counteracted the pain? Or had I dismantled the barrier and endured the pain in my sleep? A pain barrier *could* split open of its own accord, though it happened rarely. But it was hard to imagine anyone sleeping through it.

On the other hand, it might explain the queerness of my dreams and the sluggishness that had filled me on waking.

Well, I had no complaint if that had been the case. I wished it would always be so easy. Trapped pain was more severe than in its raw form because it was concentrated. Letting it loose deliberately required a large dollop of mental discipline. Relieved to have been let off so lightly,

I decided not to push my luck and disturb Maire's bandages. Instead, I simply put a clean shirt on and went to the kitchen.

Over a late firstmeal, I told Matthew and Kella what had happened in the meeting with the slave supplier.

Not unexpectedly, Kella disapproved. As a healer she did not accept the notion of revenge. To my surprise, Matthew also chided me.

"Ye know Rushton would nowt approve. An' ye should at least have let me know where ye was goin'."

This caution was so unlike the farseeker that I stared at him.

His eyes fell away from mine, but I caught a swiftly shielded memory of Dragon with her arms about the two children in the market. This Dragon was not the dirty urchin Matthew usually saw when he looked at the empath-coercer. She was older and her eyes shone with courage. In its own way, it was no more a true picture of her than the old one had been, but at least it was no longer derogatory.

Matthew had always peopled the world with villains and heroes, and his head was stuffed full of wild scenes of courage and drama. It had been so, for as long as I had known him. The fleeting and idealized memory of Dragon defending the children suggested her mad-headed bravery in trying to protect them had forced a change in his attitude to her. Clearly, he was finding that confusing enough to distort his other cherished attitudes. Well, it was about time he began to realize that life was not all perfect heroes and heroines and undiluted quests for good.

Domick arrived during midmeal. He was unsurprised to hear about my encounter with Daffyd, saying only that he had expected the armsman to turn up sooner or later. He had come to tell me that the search for the renegade gypsies had been shifted to Rangorn. "There is a rumor that you were sighted up that way and three troops of soldierguards have been despatched to search the area."

That explained the absence of soldierguards on the street that morning. I was impressed. The gypsy who had rescued me from the whipping might be arrogant and conceited, but he had said he would get the soldierguards out of the city, and he had done it.

Even so, I could not help being puzzled by the scale of the search, and I said so.

"It can be no great grief to the Council that soldierguards died in Guanette or even that we escaped with a half-dead gypsy woman. From what I heard at the inn the other night, there are plenty of men ready to take up the yellow cloak for a few coins. What does it matter that one gypsy escapes the fire? Or that one Herder dies?"

"Th' Council mun have some reason fer orderin' a sizable search," Matthew said.

The coercer shrugged. "*If* they ordered it. The soldierguards may have done it on their own. They have the power, and given that some of their men were killed in Guanette, they might want revenge."

"Rank-and-file soldierguards are a mercenary lot," I disagreed. "They fight for coin, not for justice or loyalty to their fellows. I cannot see it troubling them that a soldierguard or two died. They would simply give thanks to Lud that it had not been them."

"I think you are making too much of the number of soldierguards sent out," Domick said impatiently. "You said yourself they are recruiting more soldierguards—they may simply be using this search as a training exercise."

I refused to be soothed. "I want you to find out who set the search in motion, and why it is so large." I thought of something else. "You might also look into the Council's relationship with the Faction since the plagues. Yesterday I overheard a soldierguard talk of secret rewards offered by the Faction for information that could be used to discredit the Twentyfamilies gypsies...."

"There are always rumors of rewards," the coercer said dismissively. "The soldierguard captains start them half the time. They are nothing more than that—rumors aimed at getting information from dolts who imagine they will get something for their troubles. But the size of the search may be the Herders' doing. The fact that gypsies killed one of their people would enrage them and they might be putting pressure on the Council to strengthen the search."

Especially if they believe a Twentyfamilies gypsy was involved, I thought. If they could prove that, it would destroy the accord.

"I want you to find out for sure whose doing it is," I said firmly. "And where the coin is coming from to recruit all of these soldierguards. I heard a soldierguard say the Faction is going to fund a war against Sador. If the Herders are splashing bribe coin about, we must know from whence it comes."

Domick snorted scornfully. "How would the Faction have coin for bribes or to finance wars? They might well be using their renewed power with the people since the plagues to force the Council to organize a search. But what coin they have is extorted from their congregations. It would not be enough to bribe one soldierguard let alone a captain. You make too much of this and worry where there is no need. The search is concentrated on Rangorn, as I told you, so what does it matter? They will not find you there."

There was an arrogance to Domick's surmising that dismayed me. Yet, he might be right that I was overreacting. After all, how much did they know that would hurt us?

In Guanette, two gypsy halfbreeds had helped another escape a burning, killing two soldierguards and a Herder. Violent, perhaps, but not unheard of. And in a Sutrium market, a young girl had leapt to the defense of two frightened children. Unlikely, but not impossible.

My intervention on Gahltha at the market was less explicable. If only Matthew had not been seen taking Dragon, Gahltha's fit might have been judged coincidental, but we had obviously helped Dragon escape. Two gypsies helping a Landgirl was definitely odd and putting this together with the Guanette fracas and my whipping, I could see why someone might begin to wonder about gypsies; why a larger than usual number of soldierguards might be sent out. But since there had been no obvious use of Misfit powers on any of the three occasions, it must be seen as a mystery relating to gypsies, not Talented Misfits.

∽

After the meal, the coercer returned to the Councilcourt, and Matthew accepted Kella's offer to learn how to bake bread.

I had made up my mind to take the gypsy woman to Maire at dusk, when the world was shadowy and people were too busy going home and getting their supper to pay much attention to anyone else. That would allow me to arrive at the gypsy green right on dark, as Maire had suggested. I decided to spend the afternoon trimming the horses' hoofs and reshoeing them. This was done whenever we came to the city, for it was the only time horses were forced to walk on stones and cobbles. In the mountains they had no need of metal shoes.

The afternoon shadows were long, striping the yard, when I hammered the last nail into the last shoe and stretched the taut muscles in my back. I took a comb and began to smooth Jaygar's tangled mane, thinking again of the way the soldierguard captain had looked at Dragon. Domick's underthoughts had suggested I imagined that knowing expression. Instead of feeling indignant, I began to wonder about his carelessness in shielding his thoughts. I hoped this new sloppiness did not manifest itself during the time he spent at the Councilcourt.

I would let Rushton make the final decision whether to bring Domick in. Regardless of his usefulness as a spy, my own instinct said we ought to bring him back to Obernewtyn. Surely, with Domick's inside knowledge, someone else might be insinuated in his place. It would be wise to have someone else trained, just in case something ever went wrong.

For a second I had a remarkably vivid vision of the coercer lying slumped in a Councilcourt cell, hair long and matted, his body covered in sores and filth. I thrust the revolting image from me and made the warding-off sign, for I believed as Maryon did, that things could be made to happen by thinking of them too much.

I finished the roan's mane, acknowledged his thanks and turned to Gahltha, my thoughts circling back to Maruman, and the hazy look in his eye.

Was he wandering, mindless, in Sutrium? Again, I wondered if I should have restrained him for his own good? Since I loved him, hadn't I the right to stop him from harming himself?

With something of a shock it occurred to me that this was the sort of thinking that had caused Gahltha to try to stop me helping the little mare, Faraf. And which had once caused Rushton to forbid me to go on dangerous expeditions.

I would never exchange safety for freedom, I thought, regardless of the danger. I had the right to risk my life as I chose.

"Truly danger is part of freedom/freerunning," Gahltha sent unexpectedly, sounding as if the thought startled him. "It is easy to forget this when it is not us/me."

The equine's aslant way of using his mental abilities had allowed him to bypass my shield and hear my deepthoughts because we were in physical contact. I had forgotten for the moment, but was not annoyed. We had grown much closer than the wall of formality Gahltha erected between us implied.

"It's easy to have one rule for others and another for myself but there's no honor in such double standards," I sent mildly.

"Honor?" Gahltha snorted. "That is a littleword for a great thing. Funaga have freerunning thoughts. But instead of admiring/joying in them, you would cagethem with words. Some things will not be tamed to words."

I smiled a little, thinking to myself how Maryon and her futuretellers, or Dameon in his most reflective mood, delighted in such complex ethical and moral discussions as this. They never tried to come up with a final answer. For them the reason for such a mental journey was in the wordy road traveled.

But it was not enough for me to admire words and ideas as beautiful abstractions. I had to see how they could be applied. And I knew only too well that what worked in words was often very different when you tried to apply it to a real situation. In essence, freedom of choice sounded a fine and noble thing. But in reality?

Putting away hammer and brushes, and making my way back upstairs into the safe house, I admitted wryly that it was difficult to be philosophical about Maruman and his right to freedom when I only knew I loved him and wanted to protect him.

The kitchen was filled with the exquisite fragrance of freshly baked bread, and Kella and Matthew were so engrossed in examining the results of their afternoon's work, that they did not notice my entry or, a moment later, Dragon's.

"The first one was like a lump of stone," Matthew laughed. "I will take it back to Obernewtyn and offer it to Gevan as a new kind of weapon."

I had crossed quietly to the fire when I caught a movement at the door. I turned to watch Dragon glide into the room, hollow-eyed and pale underneath her murky skin-stain. Her eyes swept the room, coming to rest inevitably on Matthew, but there was no vestige of the adoration that had hitherto marked her regard for him. She stared at the Farseeker ward as if he were a window opened on a barren landscape, whose existence she had not before noticed.

Something in her bleak regard chilled me to the bone.

Matthew sensed her eyes, but the moment he looked up, she looked away. Kella gave an exclamation and hurried over to her.

"How do you feel, love? Does your head still hurt?" She rubbed her floury hands on her apron to clean them, then curled an arm around the empath's shoulders, drawing her close.

"Hurts," Dragon echoed dully, standing passive in the healer's embrace.

Kella's brow creased in thought, and she shifted to her bench and riffled through a disordered pile of herb parcels to mix another herbal infusion. Once this had been swallowed to the last drop, the healer tried to get Dragon to eat something, but the girl showed no interest. She said listlessly that she would rather go back to sleep, and the healer led her out.

Frowning, Matthew lay a damp cloth over two more loaves he had just kneaded. Only then, when he was done, did he notice me standing by the fire.

He flushed and I wondered at his thoughts.

Kella came back and, noticing me, offered to slice some bread for supper. I nodded and moved to help her.

"What will Brydda do if Daffyd doesn't come tonight?" she asked.

"He will come," I said firmly, refusing to give voice to my fears. "In the meantime, when we have eaten, I am going to take our gypsy home."

XXII

Daffyd had not come by the time I was ready to leave, and resolutely I dismissed him from my mind.

"I am taking you to your people, Iriny," I told the gypsy.

She started at hearing her name, but her strange twin-colored eyes were defiant and shuttered. "Do as you will," was all she would say.

I explained that we had given her a sleepdrug so that she would not be able to tell where she had been kept, nor how long the journey had taken to the gypsy camp.

"I don't care if you give me poison," she said, and there was a flash of pain that told me her mind was on her bondmate. Her eyes closed as Kella imposed another sleepseal.

It was strange, watching her fall into a deeper sleep. The gypsy had been with us for almost three sevendays, yet we knew as little of her now as when she had come among us. There had been no true exchange. Now we would never know, for there was scant likelihood of our ever meeting again.

Matthew and Kella carried her between them down to the cart and installed her safely in it while I changed into the elaborate Twentyfamilies attire Maire had given me. The loose, wide-necked shirt was designed to slide off one shoulder or the other, but it exposed the bandages on my back. The other shirt she had given me was stained with blood so, after a moment's debate, I unwound the bandages gingerly, reasoning that since there had been no pain, the wounds must be a good way to healing. To my surprise, they had healed completely. I was unable to feel any scabbing; I would ask Maire about the ingredients she used in her miraculous ointment. It must be that, in absorbing and dissipating the pain of the whipping, the salve had also healed with uncanny swiftness. Roland would give much to have the recipe for an ointment that would enable the draining of built-up pain without danger.

Buckling a thick belt with its dagger pouch about my waist, and sliding a knife into it, I came down to the rig to find Kella packing blankets around the unconscious gypsy.

She stood back to survey her handiwork critically. "You should be fine," she murmured.

Matthew was in front of the wagon, holding out the leather harnessing so that Gahltha could back into it. His skin twitched with loathing as the farseeker buckled the straps that bound him to the false gypsy rig.

"Well!" Kella said, her eyes widening in admiration as she noticed the elaborate gypsy clothing.

I laughed self-consciously and flipped the full Twentyfamilies skirt to reveal a multitude of red and green petticoats. "Elaria has never been so well dressed."

"If only Rushton could see you like that," she giggled, then she flushed at my astonished look and began to fuss with the blankets.

"Let us go," Gahltha sent tersely. "I/Gahltha do not like the feel of this funaga bond."

We departed and though the moon had risen early, it was low on the horizon and, as on the previous night, ragged drifts of dark cloud made the evening a matter of shifting ambiguities and anonymous shadow. I set about erecting a formidable coercive enhancement of the rig to make it seem more fitting as transport for a Twentyfamilies gypsy. The last thing I wanted was to be stopped because the rig did not match the rest of me!

As it happened this was hardly necessary, for there appeared to be no soldierguards about and the few people hurrying along, huddled deep in their coats and cloaks, paid no attention to me. It was a freezing evening and I found myself shivering in the light gypsy attire. I had not worn a cloak because I wanted the Twentyfamilies clothing to be completely visible. I dragged a blanket around my shoulders from the back.

With little to do but sit and shiver, my thoughts wheeled back to Kella's words and their meaning.

The healer had long been aware that something lay between Rushton and myself; perhaps because we had traveled on expeditions before, and because she possessed empath as a secondary ability. No doubt her relationship with Domick had given her some insight into such matters. Sadly, they seemed to have come the full circle—beginning at utter odds, but gradually caring for and respecting one another and now distant strangers.

What *would* Rushton make of the gaudy Twentyfamilies clothes? He had told me once the gypsy clothes made me look like another person: wilder and more reckless. In truth, I did feel bolder in gypsy clothes, but the Twentyfamilies attire made me feel different again; more than Elspeth Gordie and more than Elaria the halfbreed.

In my mind's eye, I saw Rushton standing in the misty mountain dawn, watching me ride away, his expression brooding. A waiting look, yes, but also a questioning look. And what sort of answer would Elaria of the Twentyfamilies make to that unspoken query, dressed as I was?

"Funaga play too many games/hide much," Gahltha sent. "Beasts have not somany/faces for truth-hiding. Whynot say what is true, be what is true, be what is true? Why hiding/pretending/untruthtelling?"

"I don't know," I sent soberly. "Perhaps because the truth is sometimes frightening."

"Truth is fair/light/bright. Lies are darkness/fear/ignorance."

I could not argue with that. "Sometimes it is hard to know what the truth is. And sometimes truth is pain. Easier to hide the truth and make a secret of it, than to face it."

"Truespoken," Gahltha sent.

We came out from a narrow street and I was glad to see before us the dark wilderness that was the largest of the city greens at night. Fires bloomed like orange flowers in the darkness, illuminating here the side of a great shaggy tree, or there the edge of a wagon. The faces of the gypsies were as pale blobs clustered about each separate campfire, hemmed about by ragged shadow, the spaces in between fires pitch dark. The green had seemed smaller when I had come there in the daylight, and more ordered.

As Gahltha picked his way down the uneven rows of gypsy wagons parked in clusters with a little cooking fire at the center, the darkness was filled with spicy food smells and strains of music—singing and the languid strum of gitas, sprinkled with frequent bursts of laughter. At one campfire, I saw a girl and a boy dancing closely, spinning away and back to one another in graceful accord.

"Gypsies dance for a lover. . . ." The gypsy's words came to me like a caress and I thought of his kiss and flushed, thrusting the memory from me.

A warmth and a camaraderie filled the night around me. I squinted my eyes as we wove about, trying to distinguish the elaborately carved wooden rig that belonged to Maire. We passed several Twentyfamilies rigs, but none resembled hers.

After a time I began to despair, for aside from the difficulties of seeing in the dark, the wagon rows were crooked and folded hither and thither about on themselves. This meant several times we had found ourselves going the same way we had passed already.

"Gahltha/I can farseek Sendari?" Gahltha offered.

At the same moment, an older Twentyfamilies gypsy stepped from the darkness and called out to ask my name. I chose my words very carefully. "I . . . I call myself Elaria." This was true enough.

He came nearer and I had the same sensation as I had with Maire, that he was looking not at me, but somehow *around* me. Suddenly, I was very glad of the darkness.

"I am seeking Maire, the healer," I said, feeling myself tense in case the name provoked a reaction.

The man nodded mildly. "Well, she is here, but that is all I can tell you. Usually she sets her wagon over yonder."

I nodded my thanks. Even so, we needed directions from Sendari to find the wagon, which was parked under a tree that seemed to wrap its branches around the rig protectively. A fire had been lit, and thick cuts of wood set on end about it as rough stools.

The gypsy man who had rescued me from the whipping was seated at the fire. Beside him sat a plump, dark-haired gypsy girl and opposite were two gypsy men, one like enough to be the girl's brother. The three were clearly Twentyfamilies—richly clad and with a certain haughtiness in their bearing. I wondered if one of them were Swallow. There was no sign of the old woman, Maire, but I supposed she was inside the wagon.

Hearing Gahltha whinny to the other horses as we drew closer, the gypsy man looked up casually, then his eyes widened. He jumped to his feet, dismissing his companions with an imperious flick of his fingers. The two men went at once, giving me impassive looks, but the girl glared, first at the gypsy, then at me, before flouncing off into the darkness.

"You look better in these than in the boyish trews you wore last," he said, when we were alone.

If I had been Maruman, hackles would have risen on my neck. "I have brought Iriny," I said tartly, climbing down. "She is in the back of the wagon."

I moved to open the curtain and show him, but he caught my arm to stay me and looked about before letting me go. "Have a care. We do not want anyone seeing her."

"You could have said so without mauling me." I rubbed my arm, though in fact he had not held me tightly. I merely wanted to make the point that I did not want him grabbing at me.

He smiled, flashing white teeth, but before I could think of something cutting to say to wipe the leer from his mouth, he had crossed to Maire's wagon and hammered on the carved panel.

"Maire!"

The old gypsy emerged in a pale night dress and woolly shawl, her white hair hanging long and loose like skeins of cloud about her neck and shoulders. Her expression sharpened when she caught sight of me. "You have brought her?" she asked eagerly, climbing down with sudden agility.

I nodded and, to my astonishment, she flung her arms around me and pressed me to her withered bosom. "Lud keep you, girl!"

After another long look around, she and the man lifted the unconscious woman from the cart carefully, laying her gently on the ground by the fire. Maire knelt by her and opened her eyelids with a gnarled finger.

Finally she looked up at me. "Is she drugged?"

"No," I said. "She is sleeping. Our healer said she would wake tomorrow."

Maire looked impressed. "She is so accurate at diagnosing?"

I shrugged, and let her make what she would of that as an answer. To my relief, she bent and continued to examine Iriny, paying especial attention to the scarred inner forearms.

"These are healing well," she said approvingly.

I was gratified for Kella's sake. "I daresay they'll heal faster with your miraculous potions."

"Is she all right then?" the man demanded, interrupting our courtesies in an impatient voice.

"Haven't I just said so, you idiot," Maire snapped, with a sudden return to her old manner. "Are you going to stand there huffing like a fool, or get her into the wagon before she dies of cold?"

Obediently, he bent to lift Iriny gently into his arms, staring down at her with a tender expression far removed from his earlier supercilious haughtiness. He climbed into Maire's rig and the old healer followed, leaving me alone.

The dark grass and the flickering flames of the campfire bent beneath a cold wind that plucked hair from my plait and flapped the elaborate gypsy skirts about my knees. Suddenly I felt very alone.

"Not/never alone," Gahltha sent from the darkness with all the intensity of a vow.

The gypsy man climbed from the wagon, a glint in his eyes that I did not trust. "I suppose you want your reward now?"

"Since you will leave tomorrow, yes," I said. "First, I want to know who Swallow is. Maire said I could meet him."

"And so you have," the gypsy said. "Swallow is one of *my* names."

I tried to hide my surprise. "One of your names? What does that mean?"

"Nothing more than I said. Swallow is one name, just as Elaria is one name. But there might be others a person would wear in different circumstances."

I scowled. "What does Swallow signify, then?"

"Swallow is the man you see before you."

"Then you will not keep your bargain?"

He crossed his arms over his chest. "You asked to meet Swallow. Here is Swallow."

I wanted to shout at him for playing words against me, but I was too busy wondering why knowing who he was could save my life. Perhaps he was less important than whatever this name signified. I used the name Elaria to hide my true identity. Maybe Swallow did the same. Well, it was clear enough he had no intention of telling me more about the name and I had surely fulfilled Maryon's quest. I had returned the gypsy woman to her people and I had learned what Swallow meant.

I put my hands on my hips. "There was another part to this bargain, *Swallow*. You promised to paint onto my arm one of those pictures you have on yours. Unless you have found reason to renege on that promise now."

Instead of becoming angry at my implication that he was a cheat, his smile merely broadened. "Gypsies always keep their promises. But perhaps we should discuss it first...."

"There's nothing to discuss," I snapped.

He gave me an amused look and shrugged. "Very well."

His tone was so meek that I was instantly suspicious.

"Sit down and I will prepare what is needed," he murmured.

I sat, watching warily as he went over and reached into a trunk set on the side of Maire's rig. He came back with a woven box somewhat smaller than the healer's box of potions, and sat opposite me. Opening it, he withdrew a series of sharp needles and some little glass bulbs of color.

"Where are the brushes?" I demanded.

"Brushes?" The gypsy gave me an innocent look, but the flames reflected in his eyes danced.

"The . . . the brushes you use to paint the design on. And what are those?" I pointed to the sharp little skewers laid out neatly alongside the box. They reminded me unpleasantly of the little spikes Roland had used to inoculate us against the plague.

"They are what I use to apply the design," the gypsy said, attaching a spike deftly to the top of one of the bulbs of color. "The picture is created by a series of tiny stabs, which allows the color to seep beneath the skin and set. First I prick out an outline of the design, and then I fill in the color. Usually the process is carried out over many days, but since you want the whole thing at once, it will take the entire night."

I felt foolish and angry. "You did not tell me. . . ."

His eyebrows tilted up. "No? It must be because you did not want to be told anything. Traditionally the designs are marked onto Twenty-families gypsies when we are swaddled babes and too small to be afraid."

I bridled. "I'm not afraid. What are you doing?"

"Putting them away," he said calmly.

I took a deep shaky breath and did not speak until I was certain my voice would be steady. "Not before you keep your promise." I pulled up the sleeve on my shirt and held out my arm.

He stared at me, for once apparently bereft of witticisms.

"Well?" I snapped, angry because I was beginning to feel sick with apprehension. "If it is going to take all night, you had better get started."

"You want me to use these on you?" he held up one of the sharp spikes.

I nodded, not trusting to the firmness of my voice.

His eyes glimmered and slowly he took out the bottles and needles that he had put away.

I swallowed a great lump of terror and looked away from the needles into flames that seemed to shudder with fear.

∾

"In the Beforetime, it was called a tattoo," Swallow said. There was no mockery in his voice or his eyes now, but I would not have cared if he had sneered openly at me.

My arm felt as if it were on fire. Some obscure pride had made me endure the pain rather than sealing it away behind a mental net. Each single prick had not been so terrible, but now my arm felt as if it had been savaged by a hive of virulent bees. Only the strange, long story he had told me as he worked had helped me bear it. Garth would be fascinated to hear that, contrary to common gossip, the gypsies had come from the sea, led by one who had vanished when they reached the land. And though it had taken hours to tell, I sensed there was much left unsaid.

Swallow passed his arm across his forehead, wiping away beads of sweat gathered there. For a moment our eyes met, then he bent over his design again. I tensed involuntarily, trying to prepare myself for another endless series of needles, but he released me almost at once.

"It is done. Of course, you won't see the full effect until the scabs form and fall away."

Then he gave me such a queer, searching look that I felt uncomfortable. I glanced down for the first time and a wave of nausea struck me at the sight of the raw and swollen welts.

What have I done? I thought in dismay.

"Maire!" Swallow called, dropping the needles into a pot of water suspended above the fire. I took a deep, steadying breath. The stars had faded. It was the second night in a row I had been awake to see the dawn.

He moved to the wagon again and rapped on its side. "Maire! Wake up. It is done."

The previous night the gypsy healer had called us a pair of fools before stumping off to her bed.

"It offends her sense of fitness," Swallow had said, eyes gleaming with mischief.

Maire emerged from the wagon dressed this time, and wearing a full apron. She ignored my arm and looked critically into my face. After a moment she shook her head.

"It is madness. Well, let me see."

I held my arm out obediently, hoping she would apply some more of the miraculous salve she had used on my back after the whipping, but instead she only mixed me a foul potion to drink.

Swallow laughed at my expression. "The cure is worse than the ill when Maire is displeased."

She gave him a scathing look and bent to examine the tattoo. "It is a good job, though I would as soon not add to his conceit by saying so."

Swallow grinned, then his eyes turned back to me and narrowed into the same discomfortingly searching gaze. He rose. "And now to complete the process, an honorary toast offered by the D'rekta. I am not he, but I will do, as the heir apparent."

Maire gave him an astonished look as he crossed to the wagon and climbed inside. After a moment, she took a bottle from her basket and sprinked a sweet scented powder onto the tattoo, then she bandaged it carefully, and instructed me to leave it untouched for some few days.

"What is a D'rekta?" asked, when she was done.

Maire gave me a haughty stare and for a minute her resemblance to Swallow was startling. "The leader of the Twentyfamilies. Each D'rekta is the eldest blood descendant of the first, who led our people from the lost lands. The present D'rekta is Swallow's father, but there is little love and much duty between them. . . ."

This meant Swallow was the son of the leader of the gypsies and therefore descended from this original leader.

I gestured to the bandaged tattoo. "Why did he do this?"

"No doubt he thought you would be frightened off when you knew what was involved. It seems he underestimated your courage, or over-estimated your common sense."

Swallow returned carrying a small box; not a woven square this time, but a box made from wood and carved in the same wondrously intricate style as the wagon itself.

"The making of the Twentyfamilies mark is generally toasted by the D'rekta," he said. He opened the box and removed a jeweled goblet from its velvety recess. It was the most exquisite thing I had ever seen, all streaked with iridescent green and purple and globs of shimmering gold. If this was a sample of Twentyfamilies tithe ware, I did not wonder that the Council would keep their pact. He took out a small corked vial made of the same dazzling material, unstoppered it, poured a measure of the liquid it contained into the goblet, and raised it to me. "I am for you, as you are for me."

He drank and I heard Maire's indrawn breath when he refilled the glass and offered it to me.

"No!" Maire said in an outraged voice. "You make mockery of the ancient promises."

He looked at her, his face deadly serious. "There is no mockery in what I do, Maire."

The old woman glared. "Have you gone mad? She is not Twentyfamilies. Nor is she even a gypsy for all her talk. Indeed, we know nothing of her other than that she saved Iriny. For that I thank her, but she is no part of our destiny."

Swallow took the healer's withered hand with a tenderness that made a nonsense of their bickering. "Trust me, Maire. She may not be a gypsy, but she is part of the ancient promises."

Her face sagged with shock. "But how can this be . . . ?"

"What is all this?" I demanded, but they ignored me, seeming to commune or to pit their wills in some silent way.

The old woman broke away first. "So," she said in a subdued tone.

Again Swallow offered the goblet to me. "Drink."

I shook my head. "Not until I know what I am drinking and what it means. I won't be bound by something I don't understand."

The gypsy's dark eyes bored into mine, but I gave him look for look, and at last he set the goblet down. "The toast I offered is an oath of fealty to the ancient Twentyfamilies promises, by those whose fate is bound up in them. As is yours."

"I know nothing of these promises. And, as you have said, I am no gypsy. What could they possibly have to do with me?"

"I will tell you," he said with a queer fierceness. "This night I have done a thing," he gestured at my arm tattoo, "that, were it known to my father, would see me hunted to death by my own kind. Anyone seeing it on you and discovering you were an impostor, will know a Twentyfamilies made it, for no other has the secret. That will end the truce between the

Council and my people. If you are captured and tortured, you will speak of it, and me and Maire, and again our lives would be worth nothing. Nor the lives of my people, for we will be forced to settle and become part of this Land."

I shook my head impatiently. "If giving me this was such a terrible thing, why didn't you just refuse?"

"It was the reward you named for returning Iriny."

"Even so, you might have refused."

"It was a promise," he said sternly.

I shook my head. "I don't understand. Your people are supposed not to break Council lore or have anything to do with those who do. What is Iriny to you that you would risk so much for her?"

"She is my half-sister," he answered flatly. "Before my father bonded with my mother, and before he was D'rekta, he loved a halfbreed gypsy. She who bore Iriny. It mattered not with whom he bonded, since he had an older sister who was to inherit the D'rektaship. But when she broke her neck in a fall, my father was forced by duty to set Iriny's mother aside, and choose a Twentyfamilies woman, so that he could get a pureblood child. He chose a Twentyfamilies cousin to Iriny's mother and I am their son."

Again there was a flash of that deep bitterness in his eyes. "Swallow is not my formal name, but a pet name I was given as a child by Iriny."

I blinked, suddenly convinced that Swallow was the Twentyfamilies gypsy the Herder in Guanette had wanted Iriny to name. I resisted the urge to warn him, for how would I explain knowing it? Let Iriny tell him when she woke.

"My daughter bonded with the D'rekta, but there was no love between them," Maire said.

I stared from one of them to the other. "He is your grandson, then?"

Maire wrinkled her nose, seeming to recover her equilibrium.

Swallow gave a hard-edged laugh. "There is too much division among our people. When I am D'rekta I will dissolve the Great Divide. The answer to the halfbreed problem is not to sunder ourselves from them, but to make them understand why we must remain separate from Landfolk. When I am D'rekta, any gypsy who swears fealty to the ancient promises will be one of us whether they be purebloods or no. But, until that time, I must appear dutiful and seem to believe in tradition. It is only as Swallow that I am free to help Iriny and, through her, the halfbreeds."

"Swallow is the name you take on when you are among the half-breeds!"

He nodded. "I help them as best I can. Unfortunately my sister does not confine her good works to halfbreeds, hence her plight in Guanette. Landfolk are not overgrateful to those who aid them. I warned her but Iriny does not care about her safety."

"You do?" retorted Maire. "And do not speak ill of Iriny. She is an angel."

"She was almost a dead angel," Swallow said.

"How did you know we had her? Iriny, I mean," I asked curiously.

Swallow's dark eyes glimmered with amusement. "The day you rescued her in Guanette, I was the archer in the trees."

My mouth fell open. "You! But Matthew said your hair was white. At least..."

He grinned. "A little flour ages a man dreadfully. I heard Iriny and Caldeko had been taken and I came to help them as Swallow. I was too late for Caldeko, but I was determined to save Iriny, even if it cost my identity. If caught, I meant to kill myself before I could be questioned for, regardless of the Great Divide, she is blood kin and I love her. I was in the trees waiting for the chance to arrow that Herder when you walked out of nowhere claiming to be her sister."

I felt myself flush. "It was all I could think of...."

"Do not mistake me. When you spirited Iriny from Guanette, you saved me having to reveal myself. That was the first debt I owed. Then you healed her and brought her here. Even the Twentyfamilies sacred mark did not seem too great a price for all of that."

Fear fluttered through my mind, for it occurred to me that he could keep to the letter of his promise and ensure his own safety if he now killed me. My unease increased as I thought of all that he had told me. If he meant to kill me, it would not matter what he revealed. Why else would he have said so much? That had been no part of our bargain.

I flinched as his hand snaked out, but he only pulled me to sit. "You are swaying on your feet," he said gruffly. "Sit down girl, for I mean you no harm. The toast I offered you promised fealty, not treachery."

"Why have you told me all of this if you mean to let me go?" I demanded.

He smiled. "You have a grim view of gypsy justice, if you think that is how we keep bargains. In part, I have told you what I have so that you would know how important it is to keep the tattoo hidden except where it may be safely shown. It will aid you. But it is a protective charm only so long as the Council and Herders believe that only purebloods bear it."

"I worked that out already, but why the toast? And what did you mean by telling Maire I was part of your ancient promises?"

Swallow's eyes shifted to where Gahltha stood in the wagon traces.

"That day in Guanette, I saw a horse come to you, though you made no sign nor did you call to it that I could hear. It knelt at your side as if to pay you homage and received Iriny's body gently. And when you mounted and were struck by the knife, it rode from the village without letting you or Iriny fall. That seemed surpassing strange and an omen of some force to me. I rode direct to Sutrium for I had to be present at the Council tithe and my absence would be the cause of dangerous questions. I thought you would follow and let it be known about the greens that you had Iriny.

"When no one came, I began to wonder if you were a gypsy after all. In retrospect, there were discrepancies—the things you had said to the Herder and your behavior . . . But I could not begin to imagine who would choose to mask themselves as the most despised creatures in all the Land, for so the unlucky halfbreeds style themselves."

I kept my expression still and polite.

"The only answer I could come up with was one who had a greater secret to hide," Swallow said.

XXIII

"I guessed that you and your friends were Seditioners or escapees from a Councilfarm," Swallow went on. "I do not ask you to tell me if I am right. Yet when next we meet, there will be no lies between us."

"Next time...?"

He held up a hand. "Let that rest for a moment." He lowered his hand and hesitated, as if trying to frame what he would say in words. "You asked why I include you in the ancient promises. Know that there are those among my people with the sight—an ancient power passed down from the first D'rekta, which sometimes allows those who possess it to see what will happen before it comes to pass."

Futuretelling? His eyes caught my involuntary movement and he stopped, but I said nothing.

"This seering is a strange power and perhaps a fearsome thing. My people do not invoke it lightly for if it were known, those possessing it would be burned. One of my people with such power told of Iriny's capture. When I returned from Guanette, the same seer told me that she would be brought safe to Sutrium by those who held her, but he could not tell if she would return safely to us.... So I waited and set those I trusted to watch for you and your wagon. They saw nothing but one night a voice spoke in my dreams, such as the first D'rekta heard, telling me that if I would find Iriny, I must go at a certain moment to a certain market."

From the edge of my sight, I saw Maire gape at him, and understood this was as much news to her as to me.

He looked at her. "You know I am no seer and so it seemed madness to obey a dream voice. Yet, Maire, there was such power in it that it was not in me to disobey. When I came where the voice had bidden me, I saw you, Elaria, dressed as a boy, with a Landgirl buying birds. I meant to speak with you when I rode after you, but you outrode me."

The gypsy's face was pale and tense, his eyes looking inward, dark with wonder.

"The voice spoke again into my dreams that night, sending me to another market, lest all promises be broken. That is exactly the words I dreamed: lest all promises be broken. What could it mean but the ancient Twentyfamilies promises? I obeyed and so came to find you being whipped. 'Save her,' the dream voice had told me. 'She is everything to you.'"

We stared at one another. I thought my expression must mirror his, pale and shocked. Two people, I thought, sent out by seers to find one another. There was a terrifying symmetry in it. Worse, I thought I knew whose voice had commanded Swallow to my aid; that voice of power which spoke in dreams.

"When I obeyed the dream voice, you must believe that it was not because I feared to die." He said this as if he needed to say his thoughts aloud. And perhaps he had, for I had no doubt voices in dreams could drive the unwary to madness. Perhaps he had feared he was losing his reason. "I obeyed the voice because . . . such voices of power speak for higher reasons than to save the life of one man or a girl—even if horses do bend knee to her, or become lame."

I felt myself flush.

He nodded gravely, as if my silence was an answer to something. "I obeyed, too, because it ill behoved me to disobey; I, who must someday carry the weight of the ancient promises of the Twentyfamilies, for they are also matters of high destiny."

I wanted to laugh, to bring us down from such heights, but his expression was deadly serious and forbade such cowardly evasion. And a voice inside asked me who I was, of all people, to sneer at his talk of destiny and high things. Was not my own life ruled by the very incomprehensible mystic forces he was striving to name?

"Last night as I held your arm and made the tattoo, I knew that the time of the ancient promises foretold by the first D'rekta draws near." He looked to Maire.

The healer paled. "Can it be so?"

"I saw a vision," he said. "I saw this girl speak the words of the ancient promises in the place where first they were made."

"No," I whispered, backing away. Not again, I thought incredulously, fearfully. Not another mysterious fatebinding. First the Agyllians had bound me to their quests and then the beastkindred claimed me for their legends, and now the gypsies would chain me with their ancient promises.

"Yes," Swallow said. "And more. I will stand by your side when that day comes. I feel the weight of that meeting across my soul and across the fatepath of the Twentyfamilies like a great heavy shadow."

Something burned in the gypsy's face that frightened me for it told that he truly believed his words, and believing a thing so passionately must bring it to pass.

"This is madness," I said, but even to my own ears the words lacked conviction.

"Do not fear this," Swallow said. "I will consult the seer again and perhaps when next we meet, I will know better what is to come. And we will meet again; sooner than you think, and I will stand at your side in battle."

He glanced around. Here and there people had begun to emerge from their wagons and stir their cooking fires, for the sun had risen, not bright and red as on the day before, but wanly, veiled in gray cloud. I saw this as from a great distance.

"The green begins to stir though it is early, for this day we of the Twentyfamilies go from Sutrium. You should leave now, before full light. People are more inquisitive under the sun's honest glare." He took up the little jeweled cup and offered it. "Will you drink before we part?"

My skin rose into gooseflesh. Learn what Swallow means, Maryon had charged me. Or Atthis. Well, I had done that, and perhaps this toast was part of it. I felt powerless to resist the fey forces that seemed to drive this man as much as they drove me.

I shivered and reached out to take the cup, drinking a little sip of the bittersweet elixir in it. He took it from my cold fingers, leaning near. "Have courage, girl. Never did I dream that I would live in such a time and, even less, that I would be part of the ancient promises, yet so it must be. There is great honor in such a fate."

There was a wild joy in his eyes that frightened me as much as anything he had said. An exalted recklessness.

"Come," Maire said briskly. "Before you go, let me look at the whip marks to see how they are healing."

She had stood apart from us during the matter of the drinks, as if she did not want to hear what passed between us. I was relieved at her words, for they brought me back to earth, and freed me from the searing radiance of Swallow's face.

I rose to face the old woman, composing myself. "The scars are healed already, thanks to your salve."

Maire snorted, so I turned and lifted my shirt to show her. There was a long curious silence, and I craned my neck to see the tiny woman. My heart bumped against my ribcage at the look on her face.

"What ... what is it?"

She let my shirt fall, her expression bland. "Nothing. You are right. The whip marks have healed."

I searched her face, but there was nothing of the amazement I had seen a moment before. I had imagined it perhaps. After all, why would the mere sight of my back healed by her own potions give rise to such a look?

"I ... I'd better go," I said to her. "I hope Iriny recovers completely." I turned to Swallow, forcing myself to meet his eyes; their black longing. "I do not think we will meet again, but I thank you for this." I touched my arm gingerly. "I swear that I will be careful and sparing in my use of it, and that no harm will come to you because of it. Goodbye."

He bowed. "I will say only: ride safe, for whether you believe it or no, we will meet again."

Gahltha made no comment as I climbed into the wagon, though he had been privy to much of what had taken place. I had felt the light touch of his mind several times through the night.

Well, why would he object, I thought somewhat bitterly. He, too, believed I was part of higher matters, and relished his own role in them. Too bad that I had no choice.

As we passed from the green, I glanced back through the forest of wagons to Maire's elaborate rig. Neither she nor Swallow was to be seen, and even as I watched, the last ragged flame from the fire into which I had stared for so many hours, flickered and died in the rising wind.

∽

Threading through the streets back to the safe house, I felt bewildered by all that had taken place. The tattoo had, in the end, been the smallest part of it. Why was it that whenever I looked for answers, I only came away with more questions?

I thought of Swallow's dream voice summoning the gypsy to my aid. Surely it could only be Atthis? She had sent him to save me from the whipping. But why not simply warn me in advance of the danger? Why had she seen fit to let Swallow believe I was connected to these ancient promises? So that she could use him, just as she used Gahltha and Maruman's belief in beastlegends to make them watch over me?

I shook my head, wondering for the thousandth time why the bird always worked in such secretive ways.

The tattoo on my arm throbbed and I hoped it would heal as well as my back had. I imagined Garth's amazement when I showed it to them at Obernewtyn and told them that *swallow* was not a password as we had imagined, but the outlaw name of the future king of the gypsies, a man who, incidentally, bore the very mark they had found on documents in the Reichler Clinic Reception!

I would say nothing of the other things that he had told me; I would say I had been given the mark in gratitude for Iriny's return. Swallow's impassioned words and the oath of fealty seemed to belong to the hidden part of me—the secret self that obeyed dreams and commands from blind birds.

I was exhausted. No doubt the legacy of the long night and the painful process of receiving the gypsy tattoo. I closed my eyes and pulled the blanket tight about me.

∾

Gahltha sent to me that we were back at the safe house, and his voice in my mind was like a jab in the ribs. Incredibly, I realized I had drifted off to sleep sitting up.

I still felt tired; this irritated and puzzled me. I always seemed to be tired lately, as if there was some hidden but constant drain on my energies.

Gahltha almost ran the wagon headlong into Matthew, who was coming out the gate at a breakneck pace mounted on Jaygar. I braked the wagon and the rig slewed to a halt.

"Where have ye been?" Matthew cried, his accent thicker than usual. "I were about to go out lookin' fer ye."

I stared at him wearily, too tired to be bothered with his histrionics. "I have been with the gypsies. You knew that. And what do you mean charging out of the gate like that. You might have killed someone."

I brought the wagon properly into the yard and climbed down to release Gahltha from the harness. He did not trot away but turned to nuzzle at me.

"Elspeth, it's Dragon . . ." Matthew slid clumsily down from Jaygar's back.

"What is it?" I asked. "Has she run off again?"

"She . . . she were complainin' that her head hurt earlier. . . ." Matthew passed a shaking hand over his eyes as if to erase a nightmare.

Suddenly I was wide awake. "Tell me?"

He opened his mouth but, before he could speak, tears spilled down his cheeks.

I swung around and ran into the shed and upstairs to the safe house.

"Dragon!" I yelled, slamming open the door. "Dragon, where are you?"

Kella emerged from the healing hall, her face grave and sorrowful.

"Dragon . . . is she . . . ?" I stammered, suddenly as inarticulate as Matthew.

"Inside," Kella said.

I followed her into the healing chamber on shaking legs. She cannot be dead if she is here, I thought numbly.

She lay on the mattress bed nearest the door. The gypsy had occupied the same bed, and it was as if one pale corpse had been exchanged for another. The empath-coercer's red-gold hair lay like frozen flames over the pillow.

"What happened to her?" I whispered.

Kella shook her head. "I don't know exactly. I was not in the kitchen. Matthew was there with her. They were arguing. I was coming up the stairs, and I heard a thump, then Matthew burst out of the kitchen yelling that Dragon had fainted."

"She *fainted*?" I cried. "Is that all? You scared the living daylights out of me! Matthew met me at the gate as if someone had been killed."

"Elspeth, you don't understand," Kella said. "This is no ordinary sleep. Dragon has fallen into a coma. *I can't reach her!*"

XXIV

"How long has she been like this?" I demanded.

"Not more than half an hour," Kella said. "It happened not long after we had eaten firstmeal."

I felt sick. "A coma. I don't understand. How could it just happen like that for no reason?"

From the corner of my eye I noticed Kella open her mouth and then close it again.

"What is it?"

The healer bit her lip. "It's possible that you damaged the blocked part of her mind when you forced your way past her mindshield to . . ."

"Are you saying I caused the coma?"

"You go too far and too fast," Kella said, the softness of her tone a protest at my stridency. I resisted an urge to shout at her that it did not matter how loudly I talked—Dragon would not hear it. Kella pulled the covers around the empath-coercer's neck and gestured for me to follow as she left the room.

In the kitchen, the scent of food cooking only served to heighten my feeling of unreality. A fire blazed on the hearth, but it was some minutes before my mind registered that Brydda was sitting in a chair before it.

He rose to greet me.

"I had gone out to the market to get some milk and was returning when I bumped into Brydda," Kella explained. "We were coming up the stairs together when we heard them arguing. When we came into the kitchen, Dragon was lying on the ground."

"I struck too hard," I said.

The healer sighed. "There is no certainty of that. Damage to a blocked memory is not uncommon. Sometimes an eruption occurs spontaneously, but once disturbed, the memory inside will develop and shift until the block is shattered. Often that is the best thing, but Dragon's memory block is very deep-seated. The chances of her mind being able to deal with a flood of unresolved memories is slim. The whole healthy mind would be sucked into a sort of mental whirlpool revolving around whatever has been repressed. Eventually all normal thought would be absorbed and there would be nothing left in her mind but that single matter replaying itself again and again."

My skin prickled with horror as the meaning of her words sank in. "You mean she will be defective when she wakens?"

Kella held up her hands. "I said that *would* have happened, but Dragon's mind retreated, which is the best thing that could have happened under the circumstances."

"You call a coma the best outcome?"

"Everything is relative," the healer said firmly. "At some level Dragon obviously sensed the block was damaged and likely to break open, and willed herself inside it. This means that, right now, she is caught up in a loop of blocked memories: reliving what she has repressed over and over as she tries to resolve whatever caused her to block it out in the first place."

"Then she'll come out of it when she has sorted herself out?" Brydda asked, struggling with unfamiliar concepts.

Kella shook her head helplessly. "That is what we must hope. But there is no predicting how long it will take. It could take a year or a day or a minute."

I stared into the healer's face, seeing only my own culpability. With a flash of despair I thought of Jik and Cameo and wondered if it would always be my fate to lead those around me to destruction.

"Elspeth, you blame yourself too much," Kella chided.

I glared at her. "Too much? How much should I blame myself then? And who will take the rest of the blame? Dragon?"

"Perhaps," the healer said quietly. "It may be that this is indeed her doing."

"It is my fault she's in a coma," Matthew said, hearing the last as he entered the kitchen.

Kella gave him a weary look. "I wish the pair of you would stop fighting over who is to blame and listen when I say the coma might be a natural development."

"Natural?" he murmured.

She nodded vigorously. "Exactly. Sooner or later this would have happened because Dragon *never intended* to forget her past. She didn't push her unwanted memory into her subconscious, the way the gypsy woman tried to do.

"She encysted it in her *conscious mind*—forgotten, yet not forgotten. She stored it as if whatever she has suppressed contained both something unbearable and something precious."

I tried to decide if her words contained hope or absolution, but my weariness had returned with redoubled force. I felt numbed.

"I have to get some sleep," I mumbled, but did not move.

"I am sorry for what has happened to Dragon. Truly I am," Brydda said sincerely, shifting forward to look into my face. "But life rarely permits us time to regroup or to mourn. I have come here because I need your help and, sad as this is, it does not change my need."

"Again?" I asked with bleak irony. "I could not help you last time. And I have been out all night. Even if I wanted to I couldn't summon any power just now...."

The rebel shook his head. "I do not need you until tonight. You can sleep until then."

"What then?"

Brydda's expression hardened. "Daffyd has not come and I am supposed to take the slaves to the warehouse for the slave supplier's people tonight. I mean to deliver them as agreed, so that I can track them back to Salamander. Eventually they will have to come to him. I cannot have them followed because Salamander will certainly have someone watching. He would be a fool if he did not. But you could use your mind to track the slaves safely."

"I could," I said. "If they are not shielded and if they are not taken over tainted ground or water. And if a thousand other things that could go wrong don't."

Brydda looked taken aback at my fierceness.

I tried to explain. "It is difficult enough to farseek a Talented and a known mind this close in a city streaked with impenetrable tainted areas and among all these other mind patterns, let alone someone who is both unTalented and unknown."

Matthew sat forward, a flare of eagerness driving away the despairing guilt of moments before. "Th' slave you use as a marker need not be unknown or unTalented."

I stared at him, uncomprehending.

"I could take th' place of one of th' slaves," Matthew said.

I stared at him, slightly sickened by his eagerness. He took my silence for approbation. "Ye'd have no trouble keepin' a probe on me. Ye could do it from here."

"No," I said. "If you are taken over water or to some place that is tainted, I would lose contact with you. . . ."

"Nowt fer long if ye follow physically as well," Matthew interrupted. "Further back than anyone would bother with, but close enough to feel where I am, even if ye can't farseek me, I'd have my mind open to ye all th' time."

"It's out of the question," I said.

"Very well," Brydda said firmly, stopping Matthew's protest before it was uttered. "But you will trace the slaves?"

"If I lose them, they will be condemned to live as slaves."

The rebel's face hardened. "As they would have done had I not intercepted them. Perhaps they would think it fair chance, since I am trying to stop this foul trade altogether."

"The end justifies the means?" I asked cynically. "Have you given *them* a choice?"

The rebel frowned. "As far as they know, they are still captives held by slavers. They are resigned to their fates. This is the real world, Elspeth, and I am doing the best I can. I will not lose this chance," he added harshly.

I sighed. "I will track them. But I'll have to come to the warehouse so that I can get a fix on one of their minds."

Brydda rose and took a scrap of paper from his pocket. "Here is a map to show where it is. The slave supplier said he would send his people to pick up the slaves before dawn, so I suggest you arrive well before that. I will be waiting for you."

"He also told you to get rid of me, so it will be better if I do not come inside."

Brydda frowned. "I doubt he will come in person, but perhaps you are right. We should not take the chance. You will have to get into position somewhere outside. Will that be close enough?"

I nodded and committed the route and warehouse location to memory before handing the paper back.

"You should assume you are being watched as soon as you get into the area."

"Am I nowt to come then?" Matthew asked, caught between pleading and demanding.

Brydda looked at me.

"You had better come with me," I decided. "When we arrive, you will go inside the warehouse with Brydda and pretend to be his assistant. With different clothes and in the darkness, you can pass yourself as a seaman's lad. The skin stain has faded enough. With you inside, I can use your eyes to see what is going on there, and communicate with Brydda even as I track the slaves."

The rebel nodded. "When you let us know where they have been taken, we will ride after them." He frowned. "No. On second thought, Salamander may have the warehouse watched for some time after the slaves are taken to ensure we don't try to follow. I will have some rebels stationed nearby. Can you ride to them and tell them where the slaves are?"

I nodded, feeling incapable of more. Brydda stood and squeezed my shoulder. "Get some sleep," he murmured, and departed.

∽

"Ye should have let me do it," Matthew said sullenly after he had gone. "There would have been no risk."

"There is risk in everything," I said, thinking of Dragon. I stood up.

"Wait!" Kella protested. "You haven't told us what happened about taking the gypsy..."

Kella and Matthew were both staring at me expectantly. I yawned and rubbed at my eyes. "I'm too tired to go into it all now, but I took her back." I looked at Kella. "The gypsy healer said you were a good healer."

She flushed with pleasure.

I stumbled down the hall and into my bedchamber, falling into the bedding fully clothed. Dimly, I wondered if it was possible that there was something wrong with me. I felt incredibly fatigued, and this was not the first time. I had felt the same unnatural tiredness after being struck by the acolyte's knife in Guanette, and again after the whipping. Perhaps this time it was because of the tattoo. Every time I was injured, my mind and body seemed to withdraw....

My mind drifted and I dozed, shifting in and out of sleep....

So much had happened: Dragon in a coma; Daffyd's failure to appear; Idris' death; Domick's and Kella's estrangement. And behind everything it seemed to me that a shadow loomed; a hint of some greater disaster.

I flung my hand out, seeking the comfort of Maruman's rough, warm fur, but the place where he slept by my head was cold and empty. I wondered, with an ache, where he was, and if he was safe.

"Sleep the shortsleep...." I heard Gahltha's voice in my mind. "I/ Gahltha will guard the dreamtrails in place of Maruman/yelloweyes."

And sleep claimed me again.

∾

I woke to darkness and Matthew shaking me urgently.

"Whaa?" I grunted, feeling as groggy as if I had been drugged.

"Wake up, Elspeth. It's time to go."

Time? Then I remembered Brydda's request. Incredibly, at least thirteen hours must have passed if it was night.

"Get the horses ready," I said, sitting up and rubbing my eyes.

My limbs felt stiff and sore, but there was no need to dress since I had gone to bed fully clothed. I was much refreshed though it felt peculiar to wake in the middle of the night as if it were morning. The numbing exhaustion had vanished altogether.

In the kitchen, I splashed my face with water and accepted the bowl of hot, sweetened oats Kella pressed into my hands.

"Is Dragon...?" I asked, when I was done, half hoping I had dreamed the nightmarish business of her coma.

The healer shook her head gravely. "I will watch over her. There is nothing you can do here. Do what has to be done, but be careful. Getting yourself killed will not bring her back." In her agitation she brushed against my tattooed forearm. I flinched, only then registering that there was no pain.

"What is wrong with your arm?" Kella asked.

I shook her off. "Nothing. It is Cameo we should be worrying about. Not me."

"Cameo?"

I blinked, startled at myself. Cameo had died at Obernewtyn long ago. An odd slip of the tongue. "I meant Dragon," I corrected.

At that moment Matthew yelled from the bottom of the stairs for me to hurry up. I pulled myself together, bade the healer farewell and hurried down to him.

In the lantern light, I saw that he had dressed himself as a seaman's lad. His skin was some shades darker than it ought to have been, but in the night he would pass. Mine was far darker because I had continued to use Katlyn's stain but, with a little coercion, the seaman's disguise might be one I could make work for me.

Gahltha suggested we both travel across the city on his back and I concurred, since one horse would be easier to cloak than two.

"Let's go," I said.

XXV

Thunder growled in the distance and it began to rain.

I felt a prickle of unease, for lightning played havoc with farseeking powers and it would make retaining a link with one of the slaves that much more difficult.

As usual, Matthew's emotions caused his shielding ability to deteriorate sharply. This, combined with our close physical proximity, meant that I was shortly awash in his remorse over Dragon's coma.

Strengthening my shield to block his emanations, I felt a touch of anger that he would wallow in his guilt, after having treated Dragon so shabbily.

"Get down now," I said. We were still several streets from the warehouse, but I wanted to take no chances. "You had better get your mind fixed on what is ahead of us, rather than on what cannot be helped."

I ignored the farseeker's sudden rigidity and the belated mortified strengthening of his mental shield as he dismounted.

"I have farsought the warehouse. So far as I can make out, no one is paying any attention to it but, just in case, you had better walk from here. After a bit I will follow. I will farseek you when I am in place to find out where Brydda's people are waiting."

Matthew nodded, then he shuddered violently.

"What is it?"

"I dinna know. I felt as if someone walked over me grave. Maybe ye should come inside too. Anyone might spot ye in th' street."

Touched by his concern, my irritation at him faded.

"I will make sure no one sees me," I promised. "I have to stay out here so I can get away without being seen, to let Brydda's men know where the slaves have been taken."

Matthew still hesitated.

"Go on," I urged, giving him a push. He turned to go. On impulse I called, "Be careful."

"You be careful too," he called in a low voice, and loped off.

I let a small farseeking probe drift with him and, when he had got inside the warehouse, signaled Gahltha, who turned into a lane a short way along the street. I dismounted and he moved swiftly into the shadows at the end of the lane. It was a single-ended alley with no doors opening out into it which meant no one would come up behind me. On one side the sloping roof of an adjoining building had sagged into a dip at the center, and thereby cast a deeper pool of shadow. This was where Gahltha positioned himself.

I stayed at the street end of the lane and leaned against the corner in the shadows. From this point I would be all but invisible even without coercion, and I could see both ways along the street leading to the warehouse. There was no sign of life. I set loose a general farseeking net which would alert me to any movement in the streets, then shaped a probe to Matthew's mind signature and sent it flying in the direction of the warehouse.

As soon as he felt me, the farseeker opened his mind to permit me access to the synapses and nerves that would enable me to see through his eyes.

I occupied these only passively for the moment, taking in the cavernous warehouse lit by a single lamp as Matthew looked around slowly to show me the interior of the warehouse. The view was wavering and indistinct as if I was peering through a stream of water, but the image would sharpen if I took active use of his sight.

Dimly, I watched Brydda approach. The big man's face looked slightly less battered than usual and it took me a moment to realize Matthew's hero worship of the older man was coloring his view. If I took over his sight, I would see Brydda clearly. Or rather, I would see him as *I* saw him. Intrigued with this thought, I wondered how much my own view was shaped by my emotions.

They spoke for some minutes, but I could not hear what they were saying, then they came down to the end of the warehouse.

"He is taking me to see the slaves," Matthew sent.

The five men stood passively in a little group and I was puzzled by their stillness until Matthew sent to me worriedly that they had been drugged by Brydda to prevent their being questioned by whoever came for them, and giving the whole thing away.

I suppressed a surge of consternation at this news. After all, it was my fault I had not thought to warn Brydda that drugs would bar me from the slaves' minds.

Matthew and Brydda spoke again at some length. Through the far-seeker's eyes, I saw the rebel's look of surprise. Then he shrugged and nodded.

"What is he saying?" I asked Matthew curiously.

"He is saying the drug will take about three hours to wear off."

"I will have to . . ."

I broke off at the touch of Gahltha's soft muzzle against my shoulder. At the same time I became aware of the warning tug of my farseeking net. I had been so engrossed in what was going on inside the warehouse that I had not felt a thing. Thank Lud for Gahltha!

"Funagas come," he sent succinctly, before moving back into the inky shadows at the end of the alley.

Of course, whoever was coming might be nothing more than an innocent passer-by, but it was the middle of the night. My senses told me that there were two people walking swiftly along the street toward the warehouse, talking in low, intent voices. I poked my head out a fraction. They were some distance away but I could see in the light of the single street lantern that they were both men; one was small and slender, while the other was at least twice his companion's size.

I shaped a probe and tried to enter the larger man. He was a Misfit, but not Talented. His mind was buckled and distorted—hopelessly defective. I could pick up nothing more than a miasmic desire to cause pain, but I could not enter it.

Shuddering I withdrew, and entered the smaller man's mind. It was something of a relief that he was neither defective nor naturally shielded. It was a moment's work to learn that he had been hired by Salamander, but when I searched deeper for a memory of the incident that would show me what the slavemaster looked like, there was nothing to be found. He had simply been approached in an inn by a beautiful, dark-haired woman bearing a note with Salamander's mark. It offered a relatively large amount of coin for what seemed to him to be a minor job. He had hired the defective because of his strength and brutish appetites, and because it never hurt to have a bit of muscle on your side.

His thoughts showed that he admired the ruthless efficiency of Salamander, as much as he feared him. Apparently the slavemaster had a reputation of being generous with those who performed their given tasks well, and utterly vicious to those who failed.

He did not expect to fail, though.

His instructions were simple. Just before midnight, he was to go to the warehouse where he would find a man named Bollange waiting with five men. Though it had not been said, he understood that these were to be sold as slaves. The woman had given him a bag of coin, which he was to give to Bollange once an examination of the slaves had pronounced them sound of limb. He was to bind and gag the slaves, then bring them outside where a wagon would collect them.

His final instruction was to kill anyone who tried to follow or stop the wagon.

I mouthed a curse at the realization that here was another dead end. He did not know who would come to take the slaves, nor where they were to be taken. Withdrawing, I sent out a roving probe.

Several streets distant, I found what I was looking for—a man sitting in a closed wagon, waiting.

I was relieved, knowing there would not now be any need to track the slaves. I could simply read their destination from the wagon driver's mind.

Unfortunately, when I tried to enter him, a strange buzzing vibration distorted his thoughts so that I could not negotiate them. I tried again to enter at his subconcious level and, though this was also slightly distorted, I gained entry to him, and rose up through the levels to his conscious mind. His thoughts at this level were chaotic and only by chance did I encounter the driver's thought that the slightly hallucinogenic quality of the Sadorian spiceweed he was chewing was pleasant. It had been gifted him from the same dark-haired emissary from Salamander. That explained the queerness of his mind.

Unable to gain a hold, my probe slithered loose without being able to learn the slave's destination. When I tried to re-enter, his mind barred me even at the subconscious level. This suggested that the spiceweed produced a certain sensitivity to mental intrusion.

Glumly I withdrew into myself; if I could not gain a hold on the driver's mind when he was stationary, I had no hope of keeping track of him once he began to move! How unlucky that he should be eating the spiceweed.

The only solution now was to track the wagon physically, using my coercive powers to hide myself and Gahltha from any watchers. With this decided, I made up my mind to move further from the warehouse as soon as the two men had gone inside, to ensure I would not be seen when I moved to follow the wagon. There would be no time to inform Brydda's waiting rebels.

By now, the two had almost reached the part of the street where I was hidden. I drew back slightly into the shadows, willing them to hurry up.

To my consternation, they stopped right in front of the lane where I was concealed. At first I thought they had spotted me, but when they began to converse, I realized they had simply stopped to confer.

A slight coercive enhancement of my hearing enabled me to make out their words.

"If something goes wrong, Salamander'll have our guts," said the smaller of the pair.

His huge companion wagged his great shaggy head. "Salamander angry. Bad," he grunted.

"Yes. Bad enough. You'd better stay out here and keep watch. I'll go inside and see Bollange. If anyone comes along, kill them."

"Kill," the hulk echoed.

"Exactly. Now when I come out with the slaves, you stay where you are. Understand?"

"Stay?"

"Stay and watch, I'll pretend to leave and you stay and watch for a while. That way we'll see if this fellow has traitoring on his mind. If he has, we'll get a bonus for putting him out of the picture. You got that into your skull, Lill? You stay and watch until I come back."

"Lill watch?"

The second man nodded. "Yeah. And if anyone so much as pokes their nose out the door, you know what to do."

"Stay?"

"No, stupid! You kill. Get it? If anyone comes out, kill them."

"Wait. Watch. Kill," the brute repeated the words lugubriously.

"Right. And don't mess up or Salamander'll kill both of us. Now go and hide. That alley looks like a good spot."

He pointed straight toward the lane where I was hidden!

Frantically I tried to coerce the shambling giant against the idea, forgetting that he was defective and therefore impenetrable. By the time I thought of coercing the second man to change his instructions, he had already gone striding off toward the warehouse.

There was nothing but for me to remain utterly still as Lill bore down on me. I dared not even shift back to where Gahltha was.

My heart was yammering and I wondered that the brute could not hear it as he entered the lane, a mere step or two from where I was standing.

For a minute we were literally face to face and I thought my heart would batter its way right through my chest.

Fortunately, he barely glanced down the dark end of the lane. Turning as I had done at the corner, he set himself up to face the street and the warehouse.

"Stay. Watch. Kill," he muttered to himself.

Behind him in the shadows, a bare handspan away I could feel the crawl of sweat down my back. Trying to be calm, I shaped a probe and sent it to Matthew to warn him that I was trapped in an alley by a man whom I could not coerce, and dared not confront physically without alerting Salamander that his network had been contaminated, setting off the very bloodbath we were at pains to avoid. I told him swiftly about the second man approaching the warehouse, and about the carriage driver.

Dimly, I registered the sound of knocking at the warehouse door.

"Tell Brydda not to send the slaves because I have no way of tracking them. Have him quibble about the coin . . ." I sent urgently, knowing Matthew would have to speak to Brydda before the hired thug was inside the warehouse. After that he would have no opportunity.

I slid along my probe and into Matthew's waiting mind. The interior of the shed swam dimly into focus. I was startled to find that Matthew seemed to be standing behind the Councilfarm workers. Was he trying to keep himself out of sight?

"What is happening? Did you tell Brydda?"

"Everything is fine," Matthew sent with admirable calmness, and my panic subsided slightly. "Are *you* all right out there?"

"I am so long as I don't move a muscle or make a sound."

"Lucky ye've no need to move with a farseekin' probe."

My heart began to thump again. Could he have possibly misunderstood me? "Matthew, I told you I can't farseek the carriage driver and the slaves are drugged."

"You can now," the farseeker interrupted calmly. I've taken th' place of one of th' slaves. Ye need nowt blame Brydda," he said, feeling my anger. "I told him ye'd changed yer mind. As things transpire, it's lucky I did."

I could not deny that but, even as my fury faded, I was filled with a terrible foreboding.

"Matthew, if something goes wrong…"

"Nothin' will go wrong. Ye'll trace me, an' when ye can move, ye'll lead Brydda to me an' th' slaves."

I bit my lip. It sounded simple, but life seldom went according to plan. On the other hand, we had no choice now. The slave supplier's hired thug was inside the warehouse, and Matthew was committed to his course of action. It was not the time to tell him that sacrificing himself was no way of atoning for his treatment of Dragon.

The slave supplier's man was now examining the slaves, feeling their limbs and making them walk about to ensure they were not lame. Matthew's eyes did not look at him directly and this annoyed me until I realized he was deliberately letting his gaze wander as if he were drugged like the others.

I had a single clear glimpse of the squat fellow with his mouthful of blackened teeth as he peered right into Matthew's face. As his lips moved, I wished I could hear through Matthew's ears as well, but we had not yet found a way to achieve that.

"What is happening?" I asked Matthew.

"He is talkin' to me an' I'm pretendin' not to hear or understand," the farseeker reported.

The man turned away and spoke to Brydda at length.

"He's claimin' we're all defectives. Brydda is arguin' that we are drugged," Matthew sent after a brief pause. "Now th' slaver is sayin' he has no instruction to say we're meant to be drugged. He says there'd be no need since he's supposed to gag an' tie us."

There was another pause.

"Brydda's makin' th' fellow think he's a coward. He said he was nowt takin' any chances on us tryin' to run away or fight him. It looks as if he's bought it. Yes, he's givin' Brydda the bag of coin."

Abruptly I withdrew from the farseeker's mind conscious of a warning tug on my senses. At once, I became aware of the clatter of carriage wheels on the cobbled street.

The carriage driver had come for his passengers.

In front of me, Lill flattened himself to the wall as the wagon rattled past the lane opening. It was a square closed rig without windows; once Matthew was inside, there would be no using his eyes to orientate myself.

I crossed my fingers hard that nothing would go wrong.

I returned to Matthew's mind and found he had now been bound and gagged along with the other four. "The slave supplier has told Brydda to stay inside the warehouse until daylight. If he comes out before that, Salamander will have him killed."

My heart sank at the thought of being forced to stay perfectly still in the lane all night.

"Now he's bringing us outside. . . ."

Through the farseeker's eyes, I saw the wagon and the surly carriage driver. He said not a word as he climbed down and unbarred the back of the carriage. The slave supplier's hired man loaded in the five, including Matthew, and slammed the door shut, plunging the interior of the wagon into darkness.

I left a probe with Matthew and withdrew to my own mind to watch the carriage trundle past again.

The slave supplier's hired thug strode off down the street, and Lill shifted forward stealthily to watch the warehouse. I prayed Matthew had warned Brydda not to leave and waited with my ears peeled for any sound in the street.

"Wait," the brute muttered in a disgruntled tone after some time, and he relaxed slightly. Only then did I relax too, realizing Brydda must know not to come out. There was nothing more to do but to wait until the other man came back for him.

My probe was still securely locked into Matthew's mind, and I tested it for the thousandth time.

"Dinna hold on so tight," he protested, with a mental wriggle.

Apologizing, I loosened my grip.

"I think we're stoppin,'" the farseeker sent suddenly. "Perhaps..."

The carriage door was flung open so I was as blinded as he was by the brightness of a lamp; Matthew blinked rapidly, trying to restore our vision.

As his eyes adjusted, I saw the face of the man holding the lamp and a feeling of terror assailed me, for it was the very same soldierguard captain who had seemed to recognize Dragon in the market!

❧

"Who's there?"

The surly grunt dragged me instantly back to my own body as the hulking Lill turned to peer into the shadowy lane. I realized with dawning horror that I had gasped aloud!

He dropped a great paw to his belt and withdrew a long-bladed knife, squinting to see more clearly as he took a careful step forward.

One more step and he would literally fall over me, but his eyes were on the end of the lane. He had no idea how close I was. I was paralyzed with terror.

"Move/shift," Gahltha sent sharply. A split second later he gave a shrill whinny and charged the thug.

The man issued a bellow of fright and stumbled backward, dropping the knife as the black horse leapt at him and over into the street. He turned his head to watch Gahltha gallop away into the night and, as he did so, I sprinted lightly to the sagging roof and hauled myself up onto it. The sound of hoofs on the cobblestones drowned any noise I had made, and I lay completely still.

There was a long silence as the thug got to his feet and retrieved his knife. He turned and came down the lane, brandishing it purposefully. Fortunately it did not occur to him to look up and when he found no one in the lane, he shrugged in bafflement, muttering to himself about abandoned horses as he returned to his position at the head of the lane.

I lay for some moments shivering, before I realized that I had lost contact with Matthew.

I remembered the soldierguard captain with renewed shock, and sent out an attuned probe to find Matthew, wondering what on earth a soldierguard was doing with slavers.

The probe would not connect.

With burgeoning fear, I tried again and again, concentrating fiercely on Matthew's mental signature.

It would not locate.

On the verge of panicking, I swept the entire area surrounding the place where I had last had contact with the farseeker.

Nothing.

XXVI

The giant, Lill, abandoned his post several hours short of daylight, after a sudden downpour. Drenched to the skin, I hurried into the warehouse to tell Brydda what had happened. The cloudburst had ended by the time we came out, and Gahltha emerged from his own hiding place to carry us to where Brydda's people were still waiting for me in an abandoned house. The rebel leader had given them instructions to scour the area where I had lost contact with Matthew, convinced the slaves must have been taken from the wagon and shifted indoors somewhere over tainted ground.

I had ridden back and forward in the area, too, farseeking Matthew until the heavens opened up again as the season showed its claws. Torrential rain fell so heavily that it obscured the surrounding streets like a gauze curtain and the lightning flashing high above rendered me all but mind-bound.

There had been nothing but to return to the safe house and break the news about Matthew. Brydda had come with me, leaving his own people to continue searching.

We were now huddled over a fire lit hastily by Kella, trying to figure out what might have happened to the farseeker ward. The noise of rain on the tin roof was thunderous and water ran in a gurgling torrent along the roof guttering.

"Maybe you couldn't farseek Matthew because he is asleep," Kella offered timidly.

I coughed and pulled the blanket closer about me. "I was inside his mind when he saw that soldierguard captain, Kella. Matthew recognized him just as I did. There would be no way he could just drop off to sleep after that. Not in such a short time. I was out of touch for a couple of minutes at most."

"I meant he might have been put to sleep," the healer persisted. "If he were drugged you would not have been able to farseek him."

"I would not be able to *communicate* with him, but if I was close I would have felt his presence. Anyway, as far as the slavers knew, he was already drugged," I said. "They would not bother to do it again, surely."

"Maybe you made a mistake about where they were when you lost touch."

I shook my head.

"All right. Then maybe more time passed than you reckoned. The Suggredoon is not far from where you lost them," Brydda pointed out. "If they put the slaves on a boat while you were out of contact you could not have reached him because of the water being tainted."

I looked at him in surprise. Domick must have told him about the static from the Suggredoon and the sea. I wondered if he knew what was causing it.

"A boat could not have come up to the river wharf because it would have been low tide and there is a barrier of exposed mudflats," Reuvan disagreed.

I said nothing, numbed by so much catastrophe. Idris dead, Dragon comatose, and now Matthew had vanished. My throat ached with despair.

"Then he must be somewhere near to where you lost him," Kella said despondently.

I had ridden Gahltha up and down the streets in all directions for as far as a carriage could have traveled in the few minutes we had been out of contact, but there had not been the slightest twinge. He could not have got any further than that, even in a speeding carriage. I looked down at my hands clasped together in my lap feeling a strong urge to weep.

Matthew's face floated before my eyes, the thin limping boy I had first met, and the young man he had become, alternating eerily.

"It is as if he was just snuffed out of existence," I murmured, then was aghast at what I had said.

Yet the slavers had killed Idris. Why not Matthew as well? I blinked away a horrid vision of the farseeker's body washed up on the tide.

"What if the soldierguard captain recognized Matthew from the market? He would know straight away something was wrong. Maybe he suspected a trap and just . . . just . . ." I could not speak my worst fear.

I found I was weeping after all.

Brydda clasped me in his big arms. "If this soldierguard had known the lad, the last thing he would do was kill him outright. Salamander would want to question him, wouldn't he?"

My eyes widened as an incredible thought occurred to me. "Brydda . . . what if the soldierguard *was* Salamander!"

I broke off in a savage fit of coughing that scratched my throat and made Kella eye me sternly. She was distracted by Domick's arrival and as he divested himself of his sodden cloak, Brydda told him what had been happening.

"As to how and why Matthew vanished in such a short time, I think you are right in guessing he is not far from where you lost contact with him. Salamander would not risk the wagon being stopped and searched by soldierguards. He would have instructed his people to get them somewhere safe until he was ready to take them."

"Unless the soldierguards were part of it. After all, there was that soldierguard captain," Reuvan said. He explained my notion to Domick that the soldierguard might be Salamander.

Domick looked startled.

"Whether he is or not means nothing," Brydda said. "Domick is right. Salamander does nothing in haste and he never exposes himself or trusts anyone. He would have the slaves taken somewhere, so he can watch and make sure it is not a trap. That's the way he works. Slave ships depart from Morganna, so Matthew and the others will have to be got out over the Suggredoon. That means they must travel by the ferry, or by a hired riverboat. Since we cannot find where they have been hidden, we will set a watch on the Suggredoon."

"They might be taken inland first, and across the river at the Ford of Rangorn," Reuvan said thoughtfully. "It might be wise to watch all of the city gates."

"Salamander will have to figure out the least dangerous way to get five drugged and bound men out of the city gates. That rules out the ferry since the slaves would have to walk on if they were to journey that way. Drugged slaves would be obvious at once."

"Not necessarily," Domick said. "With some drugs the five slaves would simply obey instructions to walk onto a ferry or out of Sutrium, and be rounded up outside by their masters later."

Reuvan and Brydda looked thoughtful.

"I have never heard of such drugs," I said.

"They are brought in from Sador," Brydda said. "They are another byproduct of the spice groves."

"I have not had the chance to make a report about them to Rushton yet," Domick said. "They enable you to function normally in every way except that you are utterly docile and suggestible. It is much simpler to deal with obedient puppets than with unconscious bodies or men and women who have been drugged into a shambling idiocy. This soldierguard captain would certainly know of them well enough, since the Council have them using it on prisoners."

"If that soldierguard stopped the wagon to give them such a drug, that would have prevented me locating Matthew, even if he was still in the wagon," I said, sitting up straight.

"But it doesn't make sense that he would drug them," Kella objected. "You said the other four slaves were already drugged and Matthew was pretending. Why would the soldierguard bother doing it again?"

"How would this soldierguard *know* they had been drugged?" Reuvan demanded. "You said there was no conversation between the man Salamander had hired and the carriage driver when the slaves were transferred from the warehouse to the wagon. And there would be no way of telling, with the slaves gagged and bound, who was drugged."

"A drug would not stop me from sensing Matthew if I was near. I went all over that area. If he was being hidden somewhere there, drugged or not, I would have felt him."

"If it were an ordinary drug and he were close by, that is so, but if he were also on tainted ground, you might not have picked him up. And even if you had, your probe would not have recognized him because of the drug distorting his mind patterns. If Matthew were given such a drug, even if your probe touched his mind, it would read it as the mind of a stranger."

I nodded slowly. "You know, I have been thinking about whether that soldierguard could be Salamander. It would be just like him to appear at different stages in his own plan as a minor player. What better way to keep his eye on things?"

"It would expose him to risk though," Brydda said.

Domick nodded. "It would, but perhaps he would see it as a necessary risk. And perhaps the reason the wagon was stopped was not so much for him to administer a drug, but in order for him to check on his purchases."

"All right," Brydda said, sitting forward in his seat. "Now we are getting somewhere. If we assume the carriage driver was instructed to take them to a certain place, and then this soldierguard, who might or might not be Salamander, met him and administered a Sadorian drug, what then?"

"They were moved indoors?" Kella suggested.

Brydda shook his head slowly. "Salamander has done everything in a roundabout way. That is part of the secret of his success. The obvious thing would be to have the carriage brought to its destination, but maybe they were only part of the way there when it was stopped. Maybe the soldierguard took over from the carriage driver—paid him off or even killed him—then drove the slaves somewhere else himself."

They all nodded.

"But no matter where they are or how they got there, the slaves will have to be moved from the city to Morganna. I think we ought to concentrate on that and forget trying to find them in the city," Brydda said.

I felt hope stir in me. "If Matthew is drugged, as soon as it wears off, I'll be able to farseek him."

Domick sighed heavily. "I am sorry to be a doomcrow, but whoever has them might not let the drug wear off. And even if they give it a break, which they would be wise to do if they do not want to damage their slaves, then you would need to be farseeking at the right moment to reach Matthew. Even you cannot farseek indefinitely."

"It will not hurt to try. How soon before a single dose of this Sadorian drug wears off?" Brydda asked him.

"Several hours, more or less," the coercer said, after some thought. "It might have worn off already. The drugs react differently with each person. Weight and how much has been eaten and drunk would need to be taken into account for even an approximation. But the other thing we have to consider is that the soldierguard may have got a good look at Matthew—his dark skin would stand out in the daylight—and if he did not recognize him before, he might have done so now."

Brydda thumped the table in excitement. "But don't you see that will work for us! If this soldierguard recognized him from the market, he would definitely let the drug wear off so that he can be questioned."

For the first time Domick looked convinced. "You are right. They would be fools not to interrogate him." A darkness flickered in his eyes.

"How frequently can you farseek in a day?" Brydda demanded, looking at me.

"If I were fresh, every hour or so." I turned to Kella. "Can you drain the fatigue from me?"

The healer stood up and put her hands on her hips. "Are you mad?"

"I am not planning to scan the whole of Sutrium," I snapped. "I will be using an attuned probe and it will only take a few minutes to send it out. Either it will find Matthew or it won't. It may be our only chance to save him."

Kella's ire faded. "I can only drain your fatigue the once. You have not eaten all night and it would be better if you slept a little. Later . . ."

"Later may be too late," I interrupted her grimly.

The healer sighed and held out her hand. I gave her mine and relaxed completely as her Talent hummed through my body. Gradually, the night's tensions drained from me into the healer, and with them the chilly stiffness from all the hours of waiting motionless on the roof and the queer lightheadedness I had begun to feel.

When I opened my eyes I felt as if I had just woken from a sound night's slumber. Kella's eyes were closed as she dissipated the fatigue poisons she had drained from me.

I closed my own eyes again and concentrated on shaping a probe tuned to Matthew's mental signature. Sending it out I kept my fingers crossed, but before long it was obvious it had not located him.

On impulse I sent out a searcher probe. Starting at the place where I had lost touch with Matthew, I let my mind fly out in ever-widening circles, dipping fleetingly into every mind I encountered just in case I happened upon a mind or group of minds that were oddly distorted. If that happened, Brydda could check if it were Matthew and the four slaves.

I moved gracefully in a spiraling mental dance, because awkwardness wasted energy. I kept fanning out until I felt my little store of energy fading, then I withdrew into my own mind and opened my eyes.

The others were all staring at me hopefully. I shook my head, not trusting the steadiness of my voice. Brydda began to pluck agitatedly and absently at the beard hairs beneath his jutting chin as I described the many tainted areas in Sutrium. When I spoke of the wall of static rising from the Suggredoon, he looked puzzled.

"That is only your first try," Reuvan said. "It is quite likely this drug has not even had a chance to wear off yet. And we can search the areas you can't farseek in."

"That is true," Domick said, getting to his feet and pulling on his coat. "I must go back to the Councilcourt," he added, in answer to our questioning glances.

"But you've been there all night," Kella protested. "And you have eaten nothing."

He glanced about and took up one of the loaves Matthew and Kella had baked together. "This will do. I have no time for more."

The healer stared at the loaf as if she wanted to cry.

"Is something happening at the Councilcourt?" Brydda asked. "Surely you do not always work such long hours."

Domick shrugged on his sodden cloak. "The Council is shifting us about at random to see who moves easily and who resists. It is a thing they do occasionally. A security measure. In fact I have been thinking I might stay at an inn for the next few nights, just in case I am under investigation. That is what I came to tell you."

He did not look at Kella when he spoke and her expression told me this was the first she had heard of it.

Reuvan rose, saying he must leave too; Kella stood up swiftly, saying she would walk them both out. Her face was pale and set.

XXVII

"He is so cold," I said to Brydda, when we were alone.

The rebel gave me a stern look. "Do not blame Domick for being good at what you and your people have asked him to do, Elspeth."

I shook my head. "Does being good at spying mean he has to be so cold and remote? So hard?"

"Of course it does," Brydda said sharply. "Spying requires a person to turn themselves inside out in their efforts to pretend to be what they are not. In a sense Domick has had to become the enemy, and that means he must work against the very things he believes in most passionately. He must do and witness things that are abhorrent to him, and yet pretend to approve. And he is in constant peril. Of course it has changed him. How could it not? If he had not hardened, what he does would have destroyed him."

Shocked and chilled, I thought of Domick's knowledge of torture methods and his certainty that anyone exposed to them would talk; the rumor of his presence in the torture chamber. "Sometimes you have to endure a lesser wrong in the way of dealing with a greater evil," he had said.

"Oh, Domick," I thought, "was that why you reacted so strongly whenever anyone spoke of torture?" He had said he was not a torturer. But of course he must have seen terrible things—torture and death and executions, experimentation with new drugs. He was spying in the Council-court, for Lud's sake. What sort of naive idiot had I been to think he would simply sweep floors and gather up the odd secret?

I was suddenly stricken with a feeling of black despair, hopelessly muddled by what was right and wrong. Nothing seemed clear cut; we did evil in the name of good, and good was done in the name of evil. Perhaps we *were* some sort of aberration that deserved to be wiped out.

Brydda rose and threw a knot of wood on the fire. "I have received replies from almost all of the rebels as to whether or no they will attend your meeting."

I nodded without enthusiasm. A meeting with the rebel leaders was just one more possible disaster in the making.

Brydda gave me a level look. "You *are* going to meet with them still, I trust?"

I nodded apathetically. "I'll go, but I just don't see that it will change anything."

"Not if you go with that attitude," he said shortly. "It will be held in Rangorn. I will not tell the others the location until the day of the meeting. Less chance of a leaking mouth."

I was startled out of my dejection. "But Rangorn is thick with soldierguards scouring the place for me!"

"Exactly, which is why it will be the safest place to hold a meeting. By the time we get there they will have given up searching and left. No one would dream anyone would dare anything unloreful there after all of that." He smiled disarmingly. "There are plenty of good reasons for choosing Rangorn but, in truth, I have an urge to see the trees I climbed as a boy."

Like me the big rebel had grown up in Rangorn, though oddly we had not met in those days. It was hard to imagine the burly rebel as a tree-climbing boy, but I saw that he was only half joking.

"The meeting will take place in six days," he added.

I gaped. "So soon?" I felt sick at the thought of being solely responsible for the decision the rebels made on the all-important alliance. With the way my luck had been running, they would be bound to vote no decisively.

He nodded. "On the eve of the meeting, I will transport the rebel leaders to Rangorn. Until they arrive, none of them will know where they are going. I have only informed them that the meeting will be outside the city and probably in the upper highlands."

He hesitated. "I think it would be best for the time being to let the rebels believe you are truly gypsies. If they knew the truth, they would want to know the whereabouts of your stronghold. It would not occur to them to ask about a gypsy stronghold because of the non-settlement agreement." He frowned. "Speaking of gypsies, what happened to yours?"

"I took her back to her people."

He misunderstood my shortness. "I told you they would not be grateful."

I shrugged. "What am I supposed to do at this meeting?"

"Answer their questions as best you can and remember that the aim is to make them think of you as a Talented human rather than a Misfit," Brydda said promptly. "When the question of your abilities arises, I would speak of farseeking as the power to communicate over long distances with others who possess the same power. Say nothing of mindreading or coercing unTalents. You might explain beastspeaking since that is unlikely to frighten them and they have already heard mention of it. And empathy since it is fairly harmless, but I would not mention futuretelling at all. And don't let yourself be pressured into demonstrations."

"You want me to impress them without scaring them?"

"In a sense," Brydda agreed with all seriousness. "The main thing is that you establish yourself as normal and human in their eyes."

"But you'll be there, won't you?" I asked, puzzled that he was giving me instructions as if he would be absent from the meeting.

"Of course," Brydda said. "But if I appear too much on your side they will feel threatened. It would cause them to see me as a rival and ultimately that would endanger the rebellion. Certainly, it would not serve you. That is why I chose to have the meeting in Rangorn—it is neutral territory because no rebel leader controls it."

I frowned. "Why would your rebels need neutral territory when they are allies?"

"An ally is not a friend. At best, these are reluctant allies. You must remember that these rebel chiefs are working toward smashing the established order."

"Yes?" I said blankly.

"Well, think about it. What happens when the current power structure of Herder Faction, Council and soldierguards is obliterated? Who will run things?"

"You mean, they're worried about which of them will be in charge when it's all over?" I asked incredulously.

"It is something that must be considered," Brydda said. "This is not a fairytale where everyone lives happily ever after. Following the rebellion there will be chaos and, in the midst of it, a struggle to decide who will have power over whom in the Land. Many of those who rule the various rebel groups are prepared for that and are determined to come out on top. For that reason there is great rivalry between the most powerful rebels. Indeed, some of the rebel group leaders hate one another more than they hate the Council or the soldierguards!"

"But that is stupid," I said.

He smiled sadly. "Stupid, yes, but it seems it is the nature of humankind, to want control of one another. Why do you think I prefer the company of horses? Of course, in some ways, the rivalry is my fault. Before I brought them all together with the notion of revolution, there was no competition because no one imagined it would be possible to get rid of the Council. No one thought further than simple survival. Now, of course, they think of afterward. . . ."

"Is that what the man you have joined wants? The Sutrium leader?"

"Bodera? No. There would be no point. And his son, Dardelan, is too young to be regarded by the rest as any sort of competition. That is what gives Bodera his neutrality and his best advantage." Brydda fixed me with a hard look. "It is because of this that I have been able to set the rebellion in motion. As to this meeting with you, make no mistake, they come more to keep an eye on one another than to give you a hearing. But they *will* hear you."

With a faint chill of apprehension, I thought of Rushton's certainty that the future of the Talented Misfits would one day lie in the hands of the rebels. And what if those rebels were like Tardis or Malik?

As if he read my thoughts, Brydda said, "I have not heard yet from Malik. Bodera predicts he will send his refusal at the last moment to be difficult."

"Your Bodera sounds like a wise man," I said. "I would like to meet him."

The big rebel smiled with affection. "Truly he is worth meeting, but the rotting sickness has distorted his features dreadfully and he dislikes being looked at. You will meet his son, Dardelan, though and he is very like his father. He will attend the meeting in Bodera's stead."

"To remind the other rebels that he, and not you, is his father's chosen successor?"

Brydda nodded. "The rebel leaders are a suspicious lot and it will not hurt to reassure them."

"Who else will come?"

"Tardis will send an emissary. That is not good, but it is better than nothing at all. There are few responses from the upper lowlands Seditioner groups because Malik has a strong following in the region and he has yet to respond. They will vote as he does, and only after he does.

"Malik sees Tardis as his most serious rival because the Murmroth group is the largest next to his own. The west-coast bloc is made up of three separate rebel groups from Port Oran, Halfmoon Bay and Morganna, each with their own leader. About half the time they work together well. They have been struggling for some time to amalgamate into a single group. The trouble is that none of the three leaders wants to step down for the other. They spend too much time locking horns in their own little power struggle, each trying to convince the other two to allow them to lead the triptych. They have promised to send representation but, if one comes, I daresay all will come: Radek, Madalin and Cassell. None will want the others to gain an advantage over them. The bloc has the numbers to rival Malik or Tardis, but much of their force is spent in internal divisions.

"Naturally the other major groups encourage the discord for they have a vested interest in keeping the situation as it is, though for the sake of the rebellion it would be best if one leader takes over."

On one level I listened with fascination to the internal machinery of the rebel network, but on another I was conscious that Brydda was talking as much to take my mind away from thinking of Matthew as anything else.

"Elii of Kinraide is a strong leader but his numbers are small...." Brydda was saying.

I stared at him, wondering if this could possibly be the same Elii who had guided me and other orphans from the Kinraide orphan home to harvest whitestick. Then again, Elii was not an uncommon name.

"...as well as Bram and Jakoby of Sador."

"Sadorians!" I was startled out of my lethargic drift.

He nodded.

"I don't understand," I stuttered. "What do the Sadorians care about our struggles? The Council has no jurisdiction over them."

"Not yet it doesn't," Brydda said darkly.

Abruptly all the gossip I had heard of the distant region coalesced in my mind. "They support the rebellion because they don't want to be absorbed by the Land and ruled by the Council!"

"Exactly. It is inevitable that this will happen if the Council's might is not curtailed, and the Sadorians are too intelligent not to see it. I approached them, but..."

"You went to Sador?" I interrupted.

The rebel nodded, smiling reminiscently. "It is a strange place— nothing at all like the Land. There they worship the earth, and human life is seen as short and unimportant. Ever since the road opened to Sador, the Sadorians have had to endure Faction missionaries. Interestingly, like the gypsies, they are nomadic.

"Bram and Jakoby are simply two of the wisest of the tribal leaders. There is little strife among the tribes mainly, or so it seems to me, because they do not own the desert they call Sador. They shift about constantly so there are no boundary disputes or territorial struggles. And when there are disputes, I believe they have devised some sort of ritual to mediate."

"How did you get them into the rebel alliance?"

"I simply pointed out to them that if they do not want to be forced to fight for their land, they must help us fight the Council." He shrugged. "But I think they had already made up their minds. They are a very practical people."

"I wonder what they will make of me?"

Brydda's expression was unexpectedly wry. "I doubt they will come. I have asked them more out of courtesy than anything else. At present we are allies only in principle—not in practice. But we will see."

For a moment his eyes were distant and distracted. Then he sighed and suggested I try farseeking Matthew again.

The probe returned without locating him.

∽

Three times before midmeal, and then three more times in the afternoon that long gray day, I farsought Matthew, each time to no avail. Rain fell intermittently and Reuvan came with progressive reports as the rebels scoured the tainted areas I had named, but found no trace of Matthew or the others. Brydda remained with me, talking when I was not trying to farseek. By dark, I felt exhausted and strangely hot.

Drawing up a mental probe for the eighth time, I shaped it to fit Matthew's mind with difficulty. When I sent it out, the probe felt heavy and unwieldy. It did not surprise me that such an uninspired search did not find him.

Opening my eyes, I seemed to see the flames on the hearth through a gray haze and even shaking my head required a tremendous effort of will. I felt dizzy and it seemed to me that I must be too close to the fire, but that I had no energy to pull myself away.

"Elspeth?" Brydda said from a long way off.

The room began to sway and dim and there was the sound of voices, but it was too hard to understand what they were saying. I closed my eyes and it seemed the flames were inside my skin. For a terrifying moment, I thought I was burning at the stake.

"Damn you! Where is it?" cried a disembodied voice.

"Elspeth!"

I dragged my eyes open and looked up to see Brydda's bearded face hovering above mine. The world rocked and there was a thumping sound. It took a moment for me to understand that the rebel was carrying me down the hall in his massive arms.

"Must...keep trying..." I said, struggling feebly, though I could not for the life of me recall what was so urgent.

"...fever..." Kella's voice drifted past my ears.

"Sleep," Brydda said with gentle insistence. "Sleep..."

∽

I dreamed again of the dark tunnel. This time I was being pursued. Something huge and savage was pounding along the tunnel after me, closing the gap between us with impossible speed.

"Begone!" Gahltha sent, leaping out of the darkness behind me. I whirled, as he reared in the tunnel, blocking the way. But in the dream there was something different about him. Before I could make myself understand what it was, I found myself again on the threshold of the flaming doors. Incredibly, the Teknoguildmaster was beside me.

"It's amazing, isn't it," Garth demanded, "what can be concealed when it is right in the open?" He looked at me. "Of course, you realize what it means?"

I shook my head.

"It means that you are really a gypsy."

His words seemed to come from a long way off.

"The gypsies keep the signs," someone whispered.

I knew the voice and tried to sit up. "Atthis! Why don't you speak to me?"

Hands pushed at me and I fought against them.

"Atthis?"

"Sleep," said a familiar voice. "Sleep and heal."

"Who?" I croaked.

"Sleep..."

∾

I woke, groggy and lethargic. Staggering to the bathing room, I plunged myself entirely into a barrel of icy water. The cold took my breath away and I washed swiftly, aching and gasping, before getting out and rubbing myself hard enough to make my skin tingle.

Only as I dressed, did I let myself think of the nightmarish events of the previous days and acknowledge that my memories were not nightmares; that Dragon really was in a coma, that Matthew had really vanished. And Maruman.

I looked back at my bed and wondered what had become of him. It had been days since I had seen him last.

In the kitchen Kella was nursing a cup of spiced milk. There were dark shadows under her eyes when she looked up, but the amazement in her expression startled me.

"What is it?" I asked.

"You... you're all right?" she stammered.

I stared at her, bemused. "Of course I am. Why shouldn't I be?"

"Last night you had a terrible fever, you were delirious and pouring with perspiration. Brydda carried you to bed. After everything that has happened I was afraid..." She shook her head. "I can't believe you look so well!"

"It must have appeared worse than it was—or I'm tougher than I look," I said. "Where is Brydda now?"

"He left before first light." The healer frowned and answered my unvoiced question. "None of his people has found any trace of Matthew."

Depression fell over me like a blanket. "And Dragon?" I stared into the fire as I spoke, and tried to keep my voice even.

"No change," Kella said in a low voice.

She poured some milk and sat it near my hand, but I pushed it away. She shoved it firmly back. To my surprise the warm creamy liquid tasted delicious.

"Have you seen Maruman?" I said.

"No. I suppose he has gone exploring. You know how he is. Almost as bad as a teknoguilder."

"I just hope you're right. I'm going to try again for Matthew." I closed my eyes and shaped a probe, letting it fly with a prayer. I cast it far, right to the edge of the Suggredoon and the sea rim, but there was no response.

I could have wept.

I opened my eyes and saw my own despair writ large on the healer's face.

"What are we going to do?" she asked in a frightened voice. "Brydda says you must leave Sutrium in a few days to meet with the rebels. Will you go if Matthew has not been found?"

Or Maruman? I thought.

"I have agreed to this meeting and I have no choice but to go."

I was hoping Maruman had been drawn to his old stamping ground in Kinraide and had made up my mind to go through the village on my way to Rangorn. I would ask Sallah to check in the beastworld if anyone had seen the old cat.

As far as Matthew was concerned, I refused to believe that he would not be found in time. He must.

But there was something else to be broached. I looked at the healer levelly. "I want you to come with me when I go back to Obernewtyn."

"What about Domick?"

"We need him here for the time being," I said.

"Why shouldn't I stay with him?" Kella's voice was defensive, truculent.

"Your face is becoming too well known to people who dwell hereabouts. This is a good safe house and we don't want to endanger it by overusing it. Domick can keep an eye on it, but he will be staying at an inn for the time being."

I gave her a quick look and saw that she was unconvinced. "Aside from that, I need you to look after Dragon."

The protestations died on her lips. I did not labor the point. Sipping at my warm milk, I watched the healer over the rim of the cup.

"It need not be forever," I said softly, when the silence had gone on for too long.

"Can't we all stay here until Matthew is found? I can care for Dragon here," she asked. "We can't just abandon him."

It was her last defense, and a good one, touching on my own guilts and fears. I bit my lip hard enough to draw blood, but let no sign of my anguish show. "I have to go to this meeting," I said.

"Everything is going wrong," Kella announced in sudden despair.

Hearing her voice my own thoughts produced an unexpected reactive surge of stubborn optimism. "No."

The healer looked startled at my sudden belligerence.

"We have to have hope. It is the least we can do. Matthew is missing, but wherever he is, he will trust that we have not given up on him. He will believe that we are searching and he will be doing his best to find a way to reach us. We Misfits are hard to kill."

Kella smiled, a quick genuine twitch of her lips. "You are proof of that."

I smiled back, for once feeling no discomfort about the reference to my return from the high mountains. "We have all proven it."

Hope ignited in her eyes, and I was surprised to feel my own heart lift fractionally.

"You really think everything will be all right?"

She sounded very young when she asked this, and I smothered a resurgence of doubt. "Of course. You'll see. It's only hopeless when we've given up hope."

"And Domick?" she asked after a minute.

I looked at her quickly; the animation had died from her face. "You know something is wrong with him and so do I," she said. "I am not a fool. I tried to reach him. To get him to talk to me, but bit by bit he

withdrew. Now we are like strangers. If I leave now..." Her eyes shone
with tears but pride kept her from shedding them.

"Whatever is the matter with him has something to do with his
spying," I said, considering my words carefully before I uttered them. "It
is something he needs to work out on his own, or I am sure he would
have told you what was wrong. But he still loves you."

"Then I should not leave," Kella said quickly.

"That is exactly what you should do!"

I hesitated, then decided she needed some hard words to stiffen her
backbone. "Why do you suppose he has been spending so much time away
from the safe house if not to be alone—to get away from you? Perhaps
he feels smothered by your worrying about him so much."

I did not believe this. But Kella needed to come home, and Domick
wanted her to go. Perhaps her presence was a strain he could not bear on
top of everything else.

Kella looked stricken and I wondered if I had misread her, but after
a moment her face settled into determined lines. "Maybe you're right," she
said at last. She was silent for a time, her brow furrowed in thought. "All
right, I will come back to Obernewtyn. Domick will know where to find
me when he wants me."

"Good girl," I said, heartened by her courage, and wondering if I
would have had as much in similar circumstances. "Now all we need to
do to complete the day is find Matthew."

"*I know where he is,*" came a familiar farseeking voice.

XXVIII

I jumped to my feet, knocking the chair to the ground.

Kella gaped at me in amazement. "What is it?"

"Daffyd is in the yard below!" I cried aloud to her. "He's just farsent that he knows where Matthew is!"

Her eyes widened in joy. We hurried downstairs.

I stopped dead at the sight of the ex-Druid armsman waiting just outside the repair shed. He was wearing an oiled cloak, glistening with rain.

At the inn Daffyd had been concealed by the darkness, and, before that, I had not seen him for an age. Like Domick and Brydda, I saw now that time and whatever straits he had undergone had altered him. He had lost none of his tan, which suggested he still lived an outdoor life, but there was a new intensity and a depth of pain in his dark-brown eyes that made me wonder what he had been doing since he left us. He was taller than I remembered and thinner, the skin on his bones so scant that he looked frail—his flesh too weak to contain his spirit. But when he embraced me, I felt his indomitable will in the sinewy strength of his arms, and was reassured.

There had always been unquenchable fires in the quiet armsman.

"I am sorry I did not come sooner but they are very watchful," he said. "Even now I dare not be gone too long or Ayle will become suspicious."

He nodded a greeting to Kella.

"Ayle?"

Daffyd flashed me a picture of a man and I recognized in him the bitter-eyed slave supplier Brydda and I had met at the inn.

"You said you know where Matthew is," I said eagerly.

Daffyd gave me an assessing look. "I do, but before I tell you where he is, you must make me a promise."

I stared at him, bemused. "What?"

"I have spent much time working my way painstakingly into the slaver's organization, waiting for a time when Salamander would expose himself. That time is near and I can't let you do anything that would stop him appearing."

"Is Matthew with Salamander?"

"Ayle has Matthew and the other four slaves, but Salamander is to pick them up. If you would free him and the others you must do it at the last minute. You don't have any idea how suspicious and fanatical Salamander is. If he gets the slightest notion that something is wrong, there will be a lot of dead people and dead ends and, believe me, Matthew and I are likely to be among the cold ones."

"I'll be guided by you," I said quickly. "We will not act until the last minute."

"Do you speak for Brydda as well?"

"I can't speak for him," I said after a slight pause. "But he has also been searching for Salamander because he killed Idris. He won't want to frighten him away anymore than you do."

"Salamander kills like other people breathe. I suppose Brydda wants revenge."

"He wants to smash the slave trade," Kella said.

"That is a fine desire," Daffyd said. "But this is a trade that brings a river of coin into the hands of slavers. Killing Salamander will not put an end to it altogether but I wish him luck. My quest is somewhat more personal, and as important to me as Brydda's is no doubt to him." There was something unbending in his face now, as he weighed things in his mind.

"You are still looking for Gilaine and the others?" I temporized.

"Always," he said, the terse word a vow.

"Then Salamander has them?"

"Not now. But he had them and he is my sole link with them." He frowned, seeming to make up his mind. "Matthew is being held with a whole lot of other slaves in a warehouse on the banks of the Suggredoon, waiting to be picked up by Salamander."

"One of the river wharfs?" Kella asked eagerly.

Daffyd nodded, but his eyes did not leave mine.

"Then we were right. He means to use the Suggredoon to get them out of Sutrium," the healer said.

"Matthew is drugged then?" I asked.

"He was," Daffyd said. "I near died when I spotted him among the others. I was afraid he might give me away—he did not look drugged, you see. When I could touch him, I tried to farseek him to find out what he was up to. That was when I discovered that he had been drugged. I had to sweat it out until the drug wore off to find out what was going on! I was terrified there was some plot afoot that would destroy any hope I had of getting at Salamander.

"I managed to get the job of redosing the slaves and I let Matthew's dribble onto the ground and kept my fingers crossed he would not give me away before his mind was clear. Yesterday was the first time we were able to exchange stories. I promised to come and find you, but it has taken this long to think of an excuse that would not cause suspicion." He glanced outside where it had begun to rain again.

"I don't understand," I broke in. "I've farsought Matthew every hour all day yesterday and this morning. If he was free of the drugs, how is it that I couldn't locate him? Is he on tainted ground?"

Daffyd shook his head. "The place where he and the other slaves are being held is built to extend out over the Suggredoon. I think there is something tainted in the water because sometimes the fish glow at night, or they are grotesquely deformed."

I opened my mouth and huffed a sigh of relief. That explained everything. Probably whatever was tainting the river had also affected the sea along the shore. And from Daffyd's description of Matthew, it looked as if Domick had been right about the slave suppliers using Sadorian drugs. As we had theorized, the drug must have been administered by the soldierguard in the time that we had lost contact, distorting Matthew's mind signature so that I could not find the wagon. The only mystery was why the soldierguard had stopped the wagon part way to administer the drug dose.

"How does the soldierguard captain fit into the whole thing?"

Daffyd gave me a blank stare. "What soldierguard captain?"

I did not want to divert Daffyd when we had so little time so I

shrugged dismissively. "How did Gilaine and Lidgebaby end up in Salamander's hands?"

Daffyd's eyes gleamed with obsessive fire. "Well you might ask, for
it is a strange and dark story. And long. Too long for these few moments.
Suffice it to say that they were sold to him as slaves. I have infiltrated the
slave trade specifically to reach Salamander, so that I can learn where they
were sold, and to whom."

He looked around again, as if he feared someone might have followed him. Taking me by the arm he drew me deeper into the warehouse,
and out of sight of the yard gate.

"The very day after you and Brydda met with him, Ayle told me
that Salamander had sent word that he would come by boat to collect the
slaves you were to deliver and a lot more besides. There was to be a change
in the way things were done. A streamlining, Ayle called it. In future, all
slaves were to be brought to a single spot in Sutrium—this would be
regularly changed. The slaves would be picked up by boat and taken over
the seas to be sold."

"Straight to sea from Sutrium? No more routing them through Morganna?" I asked, my mouth dry.

"Ayle said nothing of that, but I would guess this slave boat will
stop at Morganna as well. He is to manage the sorting house in Sutrium,
and I suppose there will be another sorting house and another Ayle in
Morganna—maybe one in every coastal town. Ayle told me because he
wanted to boast at his promotion, and since I had made it my business to
have him trust me and think me utterly loyal and devoted to him, if slightly
thick-headed, he was telling me that his good fortune was mine too."

Daffyd's eyes narrowed. "But as soon as I heard Salamander would
come in person, I knew it was the chance I had waited for."

"Chance?" Kella murmured, voicing the question shaping in my own
mind.

The armsman flicked a look at her. "I mean to farseek Salamander
when he comes for the slaves, to learn where he has taken Gilaine and
Lidgebaby and my brother. If that does not work, I will force him to recall
by cruder means. If he has truly forgotten, he will pay for his amnesia with
his life."

"Hard to believe that Salamander would come to pick the slaves up himself," I said. "It seems so out of character for him to expose himself like that."

Daffyd shrugged. "He is setting a new aspect of the slave trade in place, and he does not trust any other to do it properly. In any case, while he is aboard the ship he will be in no danger. I daresay he will not come ashore longer than it takes to load the slaves and it is likely he will be masked. But a mask will not keep me from his mind."

He looked a little mad, and I decided it was not the moment to ask what he would do if Salamander had a natural mindshield.

"Why is he taking them from the river wharf, when it means he will have to pass the ferry checkpoint before getting to the sea? Why not take them from the sea wharfs?"

"The sea wharfs are guarded much more stringently by the Council. Mostly the river is used for smaller vessels that do not go out too deep, and the ships which go back and forward to Herder Isle and Norse Isle. It will have to be a considerable size of vessel to take so many slaves though, and that will surely excite enough attention to cause him trouble."

"So many slaves?" I was puzzled.

Daffyd laughed bitterly. "I told you, Ayle's warehouse is to be the new sorting house. Every day more slaves are brought in to await Salamander's ship. There are more than one hundred already waiting for collection."

"*One hundred!*" I echoed, astounded.

"It is nothing to what will be coming, according to Ayle. These are early days."

"How long before this ship comes to take the slaves?" I asked with sudden foreboding.

"Ayle said tomorrow."

"Tomorrow!"

Daffyd nodded grimly. "Remember, you must not act until the last moment."

I nodded, thinking this *was* the last minute! We would be lucky to get anything set up in such a short time. "Does Matthew have any ideas how we might get him free?"

A rare crooked half-smile. "I think Matthew thought you and Brydda would come up with those minor details."

I shook my head in exasperation. "Well, without seeing things, the best I can come up with is for Matthew to commit suicide by jumping into the river."

Kella and Daffyd gave me amazed stares.

"Is there something wrong with that plan? Your Ayle doesn't sound as if a slave's suicide would cause him too much concern, and I doubt the taint in the water will harm Matthew as long as we get him out quickly."

"It is a fine plan given the nearness of the water and the fact that the slaves will not be brought out of the shed until they are to be taken aboard," Daffyd said. He looked again from the repair-shed door into the driving rain. "I must go back now. Is there anything you want me to tell Matthew?"

"Tell him to be ready," I said decisively. "How many guards are there?"

"Only four. The slaves are easy to handle with these new drugs. The other guards and are I doing little more than feeding and watering them as if they were herd beasts waiting for slaughter. But Salamander will probably have a few people of his own." He pulled the hood on his cloak up, and turned to face me, his eyes shadowed. "Remember your promise."

He strode away without waiting for a response, and was lost behind the curtain of rain, even before he had reached the gates to the repair yard.

I turned back to look at Kella.

"He is so full of hatred," she said. "I have only slight empath Talent, and yet it burned me."

"He loves Gilaine and he is emotionally linked with Lidgebaby. I had forgotten his brother was in the camp, too. I wonder how they got into Salamander's hands in the first place. And how they escaped the firestorm that destroyed the Druid camp."

"What are you going to tell Brydda?"

"Yes, what?" Brydda asked, stepping out of the shadows behind us.

We both whirled to face the big rebel.

"It seems I do not have to decide that question," I said coolly, not liking the fact that he had deliberately hidden himself and listened to words that had not been intended for his ears.

"Perhaps it is lucky for us both that you do not," Brydda said with equal coolness. He shook his head and the harshness melted from his expression. "I did not mean to overhear. I did not recognize Daffyd and so I hid. Only when you spoke did I realize who he was, and by then it was clear he would not welcome my presence."

"What will you do then?" I asked.

"What would you have me do?"

"You heard what Daffyd said. He wants to find out where Salamander took Gilaine and the others. I would ask, as he did, that we do not get in his way."

The rebel's eyes were somber. "Perhaps I have given you some cause to doubt me, but I tell you now, and my life on this, you can trust me. Daffyd wants Salamander alive so he can milk him for information, and I want him dead. Both our wishes can be met."

"What did you have in mind?"

Brydda smiled a feral smile. "Rescuing Matthew and taking Salamander captive, so that we can question him to our heart's content. And when he has no more to tell us, then I will deal with him."

I shuddered and wondered if there was ever any other way of dealing with hatred and violence.

"Well?" Brydda prompted. "Do we see how a sly Salamander deals with the Black Dog's teeth?"

I looked at the rebel steadily. "If I don't agree?"

He frowned. "You gave your word. I was not meant to hear what I heard and we are friends. Therefore by virtue of that friendship, I will abide by your decision."

I felt ashamed of my doubts. "You are a better friend than I am," I said. "I will say yes, but I must warn Daffyd."

"Can you farseek him now?" he asked.

I thought for a minute. "I might catch him before he returns to the warehouse, but I think it would be better to wait until your plans are firm. He will want to know how and what you mean to do. The only trouble is that the warehouse where the slaves are being held is over tainted water, and Daffyd is inside most of the time, which means I won't be able to farseek him any more than I could Matthew. But maybe if I go there, I can somehow get him to come outside."

"I will come with you. I will need to have a look at this shed and the river wharfs, and it will give me the chance to answer any questions Daffyd might have about my plans."

"We will have to go there tonight since the slaves are to be picked up tomorrow. There will be fewer people about then as well."

"I will call for you before dusk then."

"All right. Did you come for anything in particular?" I added, as the big man turned to go.

He slapped his head. "Of course. All of this drove it from my mind. I came to tell you that Malik has agreed to meet you, but that he refuses to come unless the location of the meeting is changed."

"But you said they did not know where..."

"They don't. But he proposes his own location. He says the meeting should occur on truly neutral territory and has named Bodera's home in Sutrium."

"Oh Lud," I said uncertainly.

"Malik sent his letter direct to Bodera, which suggests that, in spite of all my efforts, he has begun to see me as a rival."

"What did Bodera say?"

Brydda scowled, "Unfortunately he thought it was a good idea. He is proud to think that his home is neutral territory. Also he feels we should accede to Malik's wish for the greater good. If Malik is refused, he will believe I am the reason for it and there is cause to feel I am a danger to him. The worst of it is that Bodera is right."

"Then what is the problem? If he is not troubled..."

The big rebel ran an agitated hand over his unruly thatch. "It is dangerous to have these sort of meetings in a permanent place that we use. And, apart from that, the location of the meeting will be known in advance of the day which increases the chance of treachery."

"How much danger will there be?"

He shrugged. "Not so much as all that, I suppose, since none of the leaders would risk giving away a secret meeting at which they themselves might be taken prisoner or slain. The other thing, of course, is that the rebels do want the rebellion to occur and a raid at Bodera's house would immediately put an end to it." Brydda shook his head. "I don't know. Maybe I am worrying over nothing but I think it sets a bad precedent. And I don't like putting Bodera in danger."

"I suppose I must accept the risk if you and the others do. When will the meeting take place now?"

"On the same day," Brydda said. "The sooner it is over, the better I'll feel."

XXIX

I spent most of the day sitting by Dragon's bed, holding her hand.

I had brought her out of a different kind of solitude to Obernewtyn and, now, she was lost to us again, locked behind the fortress of her own mind.

In the late afternoon, the rain clouds parted to reveal a watery sun. I donned fur-lined boots and a thick cloak just the same, determined not to freeze as I had done the last time I kept a midnight vigil outside a warehouse.

I went down to ask if Gahltha wanted a blanket.

"I/Gahltha am not cold," he sent.

"Maruman/yelloweyes has been gone longlong days," I sent, wondering as always, why the beasts called a one-eyed cat yelloweyes. Well, I did it just as unthinkingly. Perhaps because, like Dameon, the old cat often saw better than those of us with two eyes.

Gahltha gave me a level look. "He does what he/yelloweyes must."

I frowned into his dark eyes. "Do you/Gahltha know where he/Maruman is?"

"The voices of his chaos/madness call him when they will and he/Maruman must hear them. The strain of guardianship caused the voices to call."

I frowned, confused. "Guardianship?"

"Of the dreamtrails. I/Gahltha know that it is not easy. Yet I have-sworn to Maruman/yelloweyes that I would take his place. I didnot know how until he/yelloweyes showed me. The dreamtrails are strange/dangerous. There are beasts like none that walk the earth on them, and shapes that hide/conceal other shapes, yet one grows better at it."

I wondered if I was understanding him correctly. In my mind's eye, I saw the black horse leap into the dream tunnel, urging me to run while he fought off whatever it was that followed me. Maruman's H'rayka? A dark unease filled me at the thought that somehow those nightmares were real.

"Are you/Gahltha saying that Maruman/yelloweyes asked you to look after me . . . my mind or my dreams, and then went away in his madness/mindchaos?"

"Did I not sayso?"

Was it possible I was being somehow stalked in my dreams? But how, and by whom? Again I heard Maruman talking of the H'rayka, seeking me on the dreamtrails. I shivered, for if the one who stalked me was my mirror image, the Destroyer, wouldn't they possess the same powers as me?

"Sallah comes," Jaygar sent politely.

I turned to see Brydda ride into the yard on the white mare, Sallah. The golden afternoon sunlight gave her a dazzling regality. I was surprised Brydda did not try to hide her beauty as I did Gahltha's. But perhaps his size was enough to dissuade thieves.

"Greeting and hail, ElspethInnle," Sallah sent formally.

"Greetings," I returned, embarrassed at the thought that the white horse might have communicated to Brydda her belief that I was the incarnation of a savior figure in beastlegend.

"Beastsecrets are not for the funaga," Sallah sent with clear reproof.

"Am I not funaga?"

"You are Innle," Sallah sent.

"Are you ready?" Brydda asked.

I nodded and Gahltha came forward so that I could mount him. Wordlessly we rode out into the yard where Kella waited by the gate to say goodbye.

"Be careful," Jaygar sent after us.

"Always," Gahltha returned.

∽

It was chilly already and I was glad of my cloak. Gladder still that the rain had stopped. With luck it would remain clear until we were safely back at the repair shed. I offered to knit a coercive cloak, but Brydda did not think it necessary. On the way to the river piers, he told me that the soldierguards were now at Kinraide where I had been supposedly sighted.

"I had some of my contacts there report a sighting of you. I wanted the soldierguards out of Rangorn when I thought the rebel meeting would be held there, and they were showing no signs of going," he said.

Mention of the soldierguards reminded me of something else that was nagging at me. "I am still worried about that soldierguard captain. Don't you think it odd that Daffyd knew nothing of him, when it was he who opened the slave wagon and shone in the lantern? Maybe he is Salamander."

"It is possible, but soldierguards are mercenaries," Brydda said. "They work for whosoever can afford them and they have a history of being notoriously easy to bribe. The slave trade could not have been developed in the way it has, even by Salamander, without officials being paid to turn a blind eye. It is quite likely that this soldierguard captain was hired to supply and administer the Sadorian drugs and generally to smooth the way for Salamander's activities, and no more. It is odd that he stopped the wagon in the street to give the drug, but maybe he does not want to be seen either."

"That still doesn't explain the way he looked at Dragon."

"No," Brydda said in a carefully neutral voice. "But, Elspeth, a look is easy to misinterpret. Probably what seemed a knowing look was only fascination or even wonder. There are not many who are as beautiful as Dragon."

I said nothing, but I was not persuaded that I had been mistaken. Even now I could call up that hawkish face and its look of stunned recognition. Perhaps the slave-master would have an answer for me.

"We are almost there," Brydda said presently. "We had better dismount. I have a few rebels in a house close by. They have been watching the place all day. We can leave the horses there and go the rest of the way on foot."

I gave him a quick look, disturbed by the thought that he had already set his people in place.

"Just in case of trouble," he promised, sensing my disquiet. "I wanted to have some idea of the movement of traffic about these river piers. I had no particular knowledge of them."

His reasoning was sound since he would have little enough time for investigating the area before the morrow.

The house turned out to be yet another of the city's burnt-out hovels. I was glad to find that only three rebels awaited us in the yard behind it. Reuvan was one of them. Beside him was a tall lanky fellow I had not seen before with woolly brown hair and a beard to match. The third was the blond woman with the plague-scarred face whom I had met at The Good Egg with Domick. I searched my memory for her name— Oria. I was gratified to realize I had been right in thinking she had some affinity with the rebels. Fortunately, she was engrossed in the examination of a map and had not seen me enter. For Domick's sake, I swiftly erased my face from her memory. Better if no one knew his Councilcourt identity. When Brydda introduced us she gave me a searching look, but there was no recognition in it.

"What have you found out?" Brydda asked her briskly.

She flicked her fingers at the bearded man who had a steady, seasoned look about him, and drew us into a room whose windows had been blackened. He lit a small lantern and unrolled the piece of paper Oria had been studying.

"Here is the sea," he rasped, stabbing a brown-stained finger at the paper. "There are four pier warehouses which are leased privately from the Herder Faction by traders. They are spread apart a little so that carts can draw up between them. As you see, there are the same number of piers. Each warehouse has its own and here, opposite, there are sheds for storage—one for each warehouse. They are quite often leased out separately. A rough road runs between them."

"The Faction owns the pier sheds?"

Oria nodded. "They bought them recently from the Council, and the wharfs. They use the river to travel straight from their cloister, on the edge of the Suggredoon, to Morganna and Aborium and then to Herder Isle. The Council controls all of the main sea wharfs and warehouses, as well as the ferry that checks the river boats, but they leave the river to the Herders now. Of course, other boats use the wharfs to ship wares in or out and pay the Herders for it. Small vessels mostly. The Herder ships are the largest that use the wharfs."

I nodded, but felt chilled at the thought of being on property controlled by the fanatical Herders.

"The pier manifest says there are only two ships due in tomorrow. One of them must be the slave ship," the bearded rebel put in. "Unless it comes in unscheduled."

"Is the pier empty now? Can we get any closer?" Brydda asked.

Reuvan shook his head. "A Faction boat docked about an hour back and there are at least a dozen burlymen and seamen roving about. We'll have to wait until they're done but it should not be too long—they are loading straight away."

Oria touched Brydda's arm and there was a clear look of devotion in her eyes, though her voice was brisk and businesslike. "The other thing is that troops of soldierguards have spent the day running some sort of training exercise on the banks of the river right by the warehouse that juts out over the water. Their camp is not far from here. Once it is dark, they will certainly be leaving too."

"I wonder if the soldierguards are making Ayle nervous," I murmured.

"No doubt he is thanking his lucky stars that the exercise was run today rather than tomorrow," Brydda said with sharp humor. "Imagine them trying to shift a hundred slaves under the noses of dozens of soldierguards."

"A hundred," Oria murmured. "It is hard to believe how brazen this is."

"Since we have to wait anyway, I might try to reach Daffyd," I said, sitting on an upturned box to make myself comfortable.

"I doubt he will be out in the open with so much going on," Brydda said. He looked at Reuvan. "Do you have any food? I have not eaten all day and . . ."

His voice faded as I closed my eyes and shaped an attuned probe to Daffyd's mind signature. The mental static was very strong this close to the water, which meant I had to concentrate fiercely to keep my mindprobe intact. Given Brydda's warning, I did not expect it to locate the armsman so I was shocked when the probe not only reached its target, but Daffyd reacted as if I had thrust a brand into his mind.

The intensity of his response was blistering.

"I have prayed and prayed you would come," he sent frantically. "Elspeth, it was a ruse! *They're loading the slaves aboard a ship right now!* They're going to leave as soon as it's done!"

XXX

"We dare not go any closer," Reuvan whispered from just in front of me. "The soldierguards are still there marching back and forward like a lot of fools. I can't think what they are doing but they will have to go when it gets dark. We should wait until then to go nearer!"

"This is madness," Brydda said softly. "Burlymen and soldierguards all milling about while the slavers openly load an illicit cargo of drugged slaves."

"Daffyd didn't sound as if he was making a mistake," I said softly. "He sounded panic-stricken and deadly serious."

"Keep your voices down," Oria warned. "Sound carries far and easily by the water."

"We have to get closer," Brydda said in a frustrated voice. "Ask Daffyd if he can..."

I shook my head. "I can't reach him. I just tried. He must have gone back into the warehouse and the static from the tainted water is like a stone wall."

"Lud damn it!" the rebel chief hissed.

"I don't understand," said the brown-bearded rebel. "The only ship on the manifest for tonight is *The Calor Lady* and, like I said, that is a Herder ship."

"That is the least strange thing about this whole queer affair. Herder ships are for hire at the right price, like any other," Brydda said. He looked at me. "Can you hide us somehow? We need to get closer."

I glanced instinctively at Oria and the other rebel. Their faces showed slight curiosity but nothing more and I wondered how much Brydda had told them of me.

"I can cloak two of us," I said.

"Wait here," Brydda instructed the others.

"Just a minute," I said quickly. "I can feel Daffyd again."

I closed my eyes and the general probe I had left in case the farseeker emerged sharpened into an attuned probe. As soon as this reached Daffyd, he was able to communicate with me again. Like Matthew, his farseeking power was too weak to combat the static from the Suggredoon.

"You'd better do something now if you are going to, Elspeth," he sent urgently. "Matthew is in the last lot and they are going to load them shortly. Once he is on the ship, you will have no hope of helping him unless you brought an army."

"What about Salamander?" I sent. "Have you managed to farseek him?"

"No!" Daffyd's mental voice was savage with disappointment and rage. "He has not come ashore and I cannot reach him over the damn water!"

"Ask him about the soldierguards and the Herders," Brydda hissed into my ear.

I shook my head angrily for he had distracted me and it was difficult enough to focus in the static.

"Daffyd?" I sent. "Why are they boarding them on a Herder ship?"

There was no answer.

"He's gone, but he said they're going to load Matthew any minute."

"What about Salamander?"

"He hasn't left the ship."

Brydda scowled. "The man has the instincts of a fangcat. It is almost as if he knew we were waiting for him." He took a deep, steadying breath. "Well, let's get nearer."

He led the way and I concentrated on cloaking us coercively as we emerged from behind the pile of crates and made our way through a narrow lane toward the water. I could smell the faintly brackish scent of the Suggredoon and hear its rush before I saw it. The static from the tainting was incredibly strong and I wondered what had caused it. Certainly the upper reaches of the river were clean.

The row of sheds came into vision and, through the gaps between them, I could see they were separated from the river by a stone walkway. Right on the bank were the warehouses, facing away from the river. The warehouse jutting out over the water was furthest away from us and set back a little from the rest. People were moving about in front of it and, even from that distance, I could see the huge front door stood ajar.

Tied up alongside it was a ship, its three masts and a small part of its bow visible behind the bulk of the warehouse. From the movement of people about it, the gangplank lay on the warehouse side of the ship.

Brydda pressed my arm and pointed past the ship to an open field, where fifty or so soldierguards in full regalia were marching in formation. They were paying no mind whatsoever to the slave ship being loaded.

The whole scene was bathed in the ever-deepening pinkish gold light of the pre-dusk. In less than an hour, the sun would set.

"It can be no coincidence that the soldierguards are here," Brydda whispered.

"Do you think they were hired by the slavers?"

"Not this many," Brydda said. "Too much risk of someone talking." He gave me a searing look. "Of course, a soldierguard captain might have some hidden reason for ordering his troops to perform their exercises here."

I bit my lip and wondered again about the soldierguard captain.

"Can you get us any closer?" the rebel prompted.

I shook my head decisively. "There are burlymen loading a wagon from that shed just up there. You can't see them from here, but they are there. I felt them with my probe. Too many to coerce into blindness."

Brydda and I stared at one another, and with dawning horror I saw resignation shape itself in his eyes.

"We have to help Matthew," I cried.

"Shh," he said sternly. "I know how you feel but it is impossible to attack openly. If he is to be rescued, it can only be by stealth and wit. Even with your powers, there are only five of us, six counting Daffyd and Matthew makes seven—if he is in any state to fight. We are vastly out-numbered. There must be ten or more seamen manning that ship, in addition to the slavers' hirelings and the burlymen."

"There are nine—if you count the equines as two more," Gahltha sent sternly, and I turned to see that the black horse had followed us.

"I/Gahltha hid myself," he sent imperturbably. "Sallah watches over the other funaga."

"Hell!" Brydda started in fright when he noticed the horse. "What in the name of ...?"

I shook my head impatiently, knowing two horses would not tilt the balance in our favor in an open battle. I spotted Daffyd coming from the warehouse with a small group of shuffling slaves. He led them along the pier and then vanished between the building and the ship.

"Elspeth!" Daffyd sent as soon as he felt my probe. "I'm taking this group to the ship and Matthew is in the next lot. It doesn't matter if you cause a fuss because Salamander is out of my reach anyway. Help Matthew...."

His voice faded and the contact dissolved. I guessed he had stepped onto the gangplank and out over the water. So long as they were on the ship over tainted water Daffyd was mindbound, as I or any farseeker would have been in his place.

I sent a swift command to Gahltha and pulled myself up on his back. At once he started forward, evading Brydda's grasp.

"Elspeth!" the rebel hissed, not daring to come out in the open after us.

"Stay still and no one will see you," I said over my shoulder, and urged Gahltha forward.

"Elspeth, there is nothing you can do!" the rebel hissed. "For Lud's sake, come back."

Gahltha's hoofs clattered on the pier boards, drowning out his frantic whisperings.

"Go along the pier/ride slowly," I sent to the equine.

"Matthew!" I sent. *"Matthew!"*

But, of course, there was no answer.

Closer to the warehouse, I could see *The Calor Lady* properly. It was an elegant vessel with slender lines and its name stamped in red on the bow. Underneath was the distinctive Herder insignia. Given what Brydda had said, it had probably been hired for the occasion to encourage people to mind their business. Though why I could not see, since they were brazenly loading slaves in public with soldierguards paying no mind to them at all!

The vessel rested low in the water, underlining Daffyd's warning that most of the slaves had already been boarded. No doubt the armsman had contrived as best he could to put Matthew's boarding off to the last moment. If this were imminent, it meant the ship's departure also loomed, as well it must if they meant to catch the out tide, cross the sandbars at the river mouth, and reach open sea by nightfall.

I came level with the burlymen I had sensed. They had been engaged to load bales of wool onto a wagon from a shed opposite the first of the six warehouses backing onto the river. But they had ceased their labors to watch the loading of the slaves. I felt dizzy with confusion. They were watching as if it were nothing out of the ordinary. This was a lot more than corrupt officials turning a blind eye!

"Good riddance, I say," said one of the two burlys at the forefront.

His thickset companion nodded and I could not stop myself staring at them. Since when had slavery gained such general approval?

"Reckon the Herders should have rounded 'em up a long time ago. Waste of space they are," the first man reiterated.

His silent companion nodded again.

"Can't see them succeedin' in healin' this lot, though, no matter that they say Lud'll help 'em. Even if they do have skilled healers on Herder Isle. Once a defective always a defective, I say."

I struggled to keep my face expressionless, but suddenly I understood what was going on. No one knew the slaves *were* slaves! Those watching thought that *Herders* were taking a load of defectives to their Isle for treatment. That was why the soldierguards were doing nothing, and why the whole thing could be done in broad daylight without fear. And the new Sadorian drugs meant none of the slaves behaved as if they were drugged.

My heartbeat quickened as the two burlymen turned to stare at me.

"Gypsy slut. Ought to round them up too," said one.

This time the other was prevailed upon to grunt his assent. I felt sick. I had been so concerned about Matthew that I had forgotten to maintain my coercive enhancement of my boyish apparel. At any minute I would be sure to be recognized by the soldierguards. I inserted a sharp coercive command to the burlymen to work and they reacted as if galvanized. This was dangerous because later they would remember me. But in the face of everything else, this seemed a minor problem.

Then I coerced an image of myself as a sun-browned seaman's lad. It took a steady surge of power to hold the image, and this, along with trying to combat the sea static, was proving a frightening drain on my mental energies. Soon I would have no reserve of power.

Yet what else could I do?

I sent to Gahltha to slow down as we came level with the warehouse from which the slaves were being led. At the same moment a man brought a small knot of people outside and I slowed to let them go before me, glad of a reason to delay.

"Elspeth!" Matthew sent.

I stiffened, for if the farseeker could reach me, it meant he was among those that had just been brought out.

"Matthew!" I sent gladly, urging Gahltha up beside them.

"Ride on past fer Obernewtyn's sake!" he sent urgently.

Startled by the intensity of his command, I obeyed.

As I passed around the outside of the little clutch of people, casually I glanced down at them. The farseeker was *less than a handspan* from me, his expression carefully blank.

"Go slowly/be lame," I sent and Gahltha began to affect an exaggerated limp.

After a few steps I pulled him up and slid off his back, pretending to examine a hoof. With a careful eye I measured the distance between myself and the little group of slaves. Matthew was only three or four steps away.

"It's no good," the farseeker sent suddenly. "This time I've got myself in a fix ye can't get me out of."

"What are you saying?" Fear made my mental voice strident. I pretended to pick a rock from Gahltha's hoof.

The man who had brought Matthew and the others out went back to close the doors, leaving the slaves standing alone in a little group. Matthew turned his head to look at me.

"Ah Elspeth, ye know ye mun let 'em take me," he sent. "Ye can't fight them all yerself."

"Brydda is with me and Sallah and there are three rebels besides. And some horses."

"Against dozens of soldierguards and burlymen, not to mention the ship's seamen?"

"Then I'll create a diversion and you can run for it. I'll pick you up and we'll ride clear on Gahltha."

"How? I'm shackled to these other slaves ankle to ankle, an' wrist to wrist. There's no time. Right now these slavers think I'm nothin,' an' I'd as soon keep it that way."

"Then I'll make a fuss to stop them boarding. I'll pretend to recognize one of the others. I'll say you're not defectives—that's what every-one watching thinks. Better to be taken to the Councilcourt by the soldierguards than spirited away to Lud knows where on a slave ship. And maybe then Domick..."

"Listen to me," Matthew sent. "Th' soldierguards are mixed up in this somehow. The soldierguard captain that drugged me in th' wagon was th' very one who came to th' market an' tried to take Dragon that day. He's part of this slave racket an' I bet all of those soldierguards bein' here are his doing too. I dinna think they would take us to th' Councilcourt if you made a fuss. I think they'd just bundle us aboard, an' then you an' Brydda would be caught as well as me."

"Matthew, they're taking you away on a ship!"

"I know," he sent calmly. "An' ye'll let 'em because we both know that this time we're outnumbered. Look, I'm nowt afraid. Wherever this ship goes an' whatever happens there'll be other ships, an' I'll be comin' back on one of them. I swear it. Tell Daffyd I'll keep a lookout for his Gilaine."

"Get a shift on, lad," said a surly voice right behind me.

I froze recognizing it as the voice of the slave supplier, Ayle. I did not dare turn around. I could not coerce him, of course, because he was mindsensitive. I tangled clumsy fingers in Gahltha's mane and, without turning, hauled myself on his back.

"Go," I sent, and the black equine moved forward.

Daffyd appeared right in front of me. He paled at the sight of me but my whole mind was too tightly focused on maintaining the contact with Matthew to let me communicate with him.

"What's wrong with you?" I heard Ayle demand of him, and held my breath for his answer, slowing Gahltha.

"Seasick..." Daffyd muttered, passing me.

Ayle bellowed with laughter. "Well, here's the last lot. You can kiss the ground when yer done." There was a little pause, then the slave sup-plier's voice reached out to me. "You hear me, boy? Get a move on. You've no business here."

"Go!" Matthew sent.

I heard Ayle's purposeful tread behind me.

"Please!"

With a heart as heavy as a stone anvil, I spurred Gahltha and he moved forward. After a few steps I glanced back and saw Ayle retracing his steps, shaking his head and muttering about half-wit gypsies. At the same time I saw Daffyd take up the leading chain of the last little group of shackled slaves and move toward the gangplank of *The Calor Lady*.

"I love ye, Elspeth," Matthew sent fiercely, meeting my eyes. "I'm sorry about Dragon an' all...."

His mental voice faded as he reached the gangplank and walked out over the water.

Every instinct in my body rebelled against riding away, yet I knew Matthew was right. There was nothing I could do to help him.

∽

Almost at once the gangplank was withdrawn. The seaman standing ashore threw off the ship's mooring knots and leapt aboard as the vessel swung to catch the out tide. *The Calor Lady* drifted from the shore, borne by the swift-flowing tide that would take it to the sea, sails snapping and fluttering as they were slightly unfurled to turn the ship.

Matthew was no longer visible. He had been taken below like the other slaves but I could not take my eyes off the receding vessel. I was stricken by the feeling that I had failed the farseeker ward and would never see him again.

A tall youth with white-blond hair and a great flapping black cloak came out on deck and leaned against the rail, staring back at the shore.

As I watched, he ran his fingers through his hair.

He was extraordinarily beautiful; long boned and slender, probably younger than me by some few years, with skin so pale it seemed to gleam in the fading sunset. That sort of fairness is not common in men and I stared. The only other I had ever seen so was Ariel, but perhaps his boyish beauty had faded as he grew.

My mouth fell open with shock and I stared at the blond youth with incredulity, suddenly remembering where I had seen that languid hand drawn through fair hair before!

The mannerism was Ariel's.

I only ever thought of Ariel as a young boy, but I had not set eyes on him for years. Of course he would be grown near to manhood now. I told myself it was impossible; that this was another blond youth. Ariel had traveled to Herder Isle to become a priest.

"This is a Herder ship!" a voice screamed in my head.

My eyes hurt with the effort of trying to see more clearly, but the light was fading to a golden dimness and the distance had grown too great. I could see no more than the white blob of the youth's face turned toward the river's mouth. But even as I watched, I saw his head turn until it seemed to me that he was looking straight at me.

Part III

The Sadorian Battlegames

XXXI

I *concentrated on walking, putting one foot in front of the other and keeping* up with Brydda. It required all of my energy. Listening to his words was more than I could manage.

It was early morning, and the dismal start of what looked certain to be as chilly and miserable a day as the one before. Five days since Matthew had been lost to us. The streets were blurred with a light drizzle of the sort that penetrates as damply and effectively as heavy rain.

We were making our way across the city for the long-planned meeting with the rebels at Bodera's home. Since leaving the safe house, the rebel had offered a monologue of advice and warnings, but somehow I could not make myself care about the meeting enough to hear what he was saying. Matthew's loss meant much more to me than any political alliance.

And Ariel's face haunted me.

"Malik arrived with Brocade of Sawlney and letters of authority which allow him to represent and vote on behalf of Vos of Saithwald and Lydi of Darthnor, and Tardis has sent a man called Gwynedd," Brydda was saying.

I nodded but scarcely heard the big rebel's words. Matthew's face seemed to float before my eyes, borne on a tide of grief and regret. My mind circled back for the hundreth time to our abortive attempt to rescue him. Not once had I imagined we would fail. It was useless to wish now that I had thought it out more carefully; been less certain of outwitting the ruthless, clever Salamander.

I had thought of a dozen perfectly good ways to get the Farseeker ward from his captors, that had not even occurred to me at the time, and somehow that made it all the worse.

"Elii of Kinraide and Zamadi of Berrioc have come too, but the real surprise is that Cassell has come without Madellin or Radek. You will recall I told you that he is the leader of one of the three rebel groups that make up the western bloc?" Brydda's eyes sought mine. Did I remember?

Yes, I nodded.

Reassured, Brydda took his brown eyes back to the way ahead. "Well, then, his presence alone may mean that Cassell has gained control of the group and that it has at last been welded into a unit—in any event, it will give Malik cause for concern."

I pulled my cloak tighter to stop water dripping from the saturated tendrils of hair down my neck, and glanced up at the heavy gray sky. Matthew had always disliked the Days of Rain, saying they drowned a man's spirit and dragged at his soul.

Ariel's face came to me, again, the lips tilted into a mocking smile. At first, he looked exactly as he had done when I met him; sweet mouthed with soft white skin, and a golden nimbus of fair hair floating like a halo around his head. He had been as beautiful as an angel, but the radiant exterior had concealed a heart that was rotten and black to the core. And then his image changed, aging and altering until the face that stared at me was that of the dazzling blond youth on the deck of *The Calor Lady*.

I was tormented by endless imagined scenarios in which Ariel came face to face with Matthew, whom he had known when they were both orphans in the old days at Obernewtyn. What would happen when Matthew, who had wanted to kill Ariel for torturing little Cameo to death, learned he was on the same ship as his most hated foe?

I could only pray that with so many slaves, Matthew's face would be lost in a sea of faces for, in spite of the Farseeker ward's courage and strength, he was no match for the vicious subtleties of Ariel.

"The biggest surprise, of course, is that Jakoby has come. . . ."

The odd name slipped through the haze of despair. "Jakoby?" I said aloud. "Isn't that one of the Sadorian tribe leaders?"

The rebel nodded approvingly. "Jakoby came by ship. From what I can make out, the Sadorians had no intention of attending this meeting until one of their Templeguardians had some sort of significant dream and so they decided at the last minute to send someone. There was not time enough for a land journey, so it was a ship or nothing."

"Because of a dream?" I asked warily.

"Some matter of smoke shapes and feathers burning." Brydda dismissed this with a flick of his fingers. "The sort of ritual whose outcome can be read to mean anything—I expect the Templeguardians wanted to get our measure so they came up with a guiding dream."

I swallowed, my mouth dry at the thought of guiding dreams.

"Anyway, Jakoby has come. Other than that, Dardelan will stand in for his father as I told you...."

My mind began to drift again. Jakoby had come by sea, and Matthew had been stolen away by the waves.

Brydda stopped suddenly, swinging around to look into my face. I met his searching gaze possessedly but, without the slightest warning, my eyes filled with tears. Fortunately the street we were walking along was empty for, within seconds, I was sobbing my heart out into the rebel's chest.

"Elspeth, girl," Brydda said, patting my back with awkward gentleness and drawing me into a doorway. "I am truly sorry about Matthew and I know his loss is a mortal blow to you," he said.

"You don't understand. It's all my fault," I choked. "First Dragon and now this. And last time I came to the lowlands, it was Jik. I'm not fit to lead an expedition. Everyone I care about dies or is hurt terribly."

Brydda put me from him and looked into my face with stern sadness. "I know how it is to feel responsible for the death of a friend," he said. "But we are their leaders as well as their friends and leadership often means putting people we care deeply for into danger."

"But that's wrong," I said in a hoarse voice.

"Which is more wrong? That a leader risks those he cares for, or that he cares nothing for whom he risks? And those who follow us are their own people; they make a choice to follow us and we must honor it. As we love them, we must accept that their deaths come from their choices—not ours, else we are no more than moon fair puppeteers, and they, sawdust dolls."

Involuntarily I shivered, but Brydda seemed as oblivious of the cold as he was to the rain.

"Matthew chose to join Rushton's cause," he continued. "You do him no honor to grieve and put on funeral weeds. He has powers that will stand him in good stead wherever he goes."

"But *Ariel* was aboard the same ship!" I said, feeling sick all over again at the thought. Wherever Ariel went, disaster and sorrow followed. "And if Matthew is taken by the Herders..."

"You run before you walk!" Brydda cried. "Let us look seriously at this certainty of yours that the youth you saw on *The Calor Lady* was Ariel. You said yourself you did not know him at first. Beauty is not such certain proof that he is Ariel."

I blinked the rain from my eyes, wondering if it was possible I had let fear smother all hope and common sense. Could I have been mistaken?

"And if the youth was Ariel, why would he notice one slave among so many? Or even recognize Matthew if he did happen to see him? The lad has grown from boy to man since Ariel was at Obernewtyn."

"It was a Herder ship and Ariel went to Herder Isle."

His eyes searched mine. "*The Calor Lady* is a Herder supply ship, Elspeth—it does not actually belong to the Faction, any more than do other vessels that wear their insignia. The mark simply means the ship has a contract of supply with them, and so they have first call on it. The slavers obviously hired it to authenticate their cover story of transporting detectives. It is even possible the Herders have been paid to turn a blind eye—that might well explain their sudden readiness of coin to splash about. Perhaps the ship simply serves two purposes—to travel to Herder Isle on its normal business, and then to journey on to...wherever to deliver the slaves. I doubt Herders have any real part to play in this scheme other than that."

He gave me a slight shake.

"Now dry your eyes, Elspeth, and take hold of your will. Let Daffyd discover what he can. Until then, put what has happened from you. There is work to be done and this meeting is important to all of us. Prepare yourself for it."

"How?" I asked miserably.

"The same way we all do at such times," Brydda said harshly, the calmness suddenly drawn aside from his eyes as if it were a veil, revealing raw pain. "Do you think I have forgotten Idris already? Of course I have not. I fear some part of me will always be grieving for him. But I cannot let grief get in the way of a cause that both Idris and I believed in. So I act. I pretend. And some of the time I am able to forget that it is a pretense and, for that little period, I forget my pain."

"Act?" I echoed blankly.

He shook me again. "Pretend, Elspeth. Pretend that you are clever, wise, brave, calm, courageous—in the same way that you pretend to be Elar the gypsy, or Elaria the gypsy girl."

A man and a woman came out of a door nearby with a child between them. The parents ignored us but the little girl looked deeply into my eyes, seeming to search for something.

"We are almost there," Brydda said, when they had gone out of earshot. "They are expecting you to be a fumbling half-wit, and I have made no attempt to question their misconceptions. Their surprise will give you an advantage. For Obernewtyn's sake, you must show your best and most impressive face, as well as your most human one. This is not the time to be cold and withdrawn. You must give them something to warm to. Once we are in there, I cannot be seen to instruct or direct you— especially since Malik already suspects that you are my pawn."

I took a deep shuddering breath, then I drew on an expression of determined calmness and turned it to the big man.

"Hmmph." Brydda's lips twitched in a faint smile. "Well, that is not so good, but it will do to be going on with."

When the rebel turned a corner to go down a lane that was too narrow for me to walk alongside him, I fell behind. At once the false smile fell from my lips and eyes. If he wanted acting, then acting he would have—but I would not pretend to myself.

As we walked I tried to recall Brydda's warnings about subjects to be avoided, and what I must and must not say; his advice on how to behave if this or that happened. My mind seemed to whirl with a tempest of words that would not connect.

Matthew, where are you? I thought with a fresh stab of sorrow, and prayed that Daffyd would have some good news for us, when he finally appeared. I was troubled by the fact that he had not come to the safe house yet, but I suspected he would be blaming himself for Matthew's loss.

"We are here," Brydda said suddenly. His tone was light but his eyes betrayed tension. He flung his hand to indicate a tall cream wall in which was set a heavily carved wooden door. He paused with his hand poised over the gate lever to look at me.

"Are you all right?"

I nodded resolutely, though in truth I felt like sitting on the footpath and howling.

Brydda merely nodded and pushed the gate open. I was surprised when he did not knock but maybe he was so well known in this house he did not need to observe the courtesies. Beyond the gate though was not a hall, but a little lush wilderness in miniature, open to the sky. It reminded me with painful insistence of a leafy glade where, during breaks from the summertime harvest on the farms, Matthew, Cameo, Dameon and I had often gone to sit before Rushton took over Obernewtyn. Matthew and I used to lie flat on our backs, searching the clouds for images of the future, of our hopes and our dreams.

My eyes misted but I blinked half-savagely, as a thin boy a few years older than me came through the trees to meet us. Either he had been waiting or the door had given him some silent warning of our approach. He had a long serious face, flyaway gingerish hair and sad blue eyes that were unchanged by his smile.

"Welcome, my friend," he said in a warm, unexpectedly deep voice, clasping the rebel's hand. Then he bowed formally to me.

"You are Dardelan?" I guessed.

He nodded. "I suppose it is not hard to guess. Brydda probably told you that I am by far the youngest rebel you will meet today. A fact that Malik has seen fit to mention in at least a dozen ways since his arrival," he added ruefully to the big rebel.

"I am Elspeth Gordie," I said, holding my hand out to him.

He shook it solemnly, then led the way along a little winding path to the terrace of a graceful-looking residence.

"This is a wonderful idea," I said, waving my hand behind us as we passed into an overheated hallway. "Much better than building up against the street. Far more private."

"The Beforetimers used to have many such walled gardens—one to each residence or so my father says," Dardelan murmured, ushering us inside. "They were very keen on privacy. I must apologize for the heating. I know it is too hot but my father's illness makes him very susceptible to chills."

"It is nice to be warm," I said politely, though in fact I felt stifled by the hot, closed atmosphere of the house.

"Brydda told me of your father's illness," I said on impulse, thinking of the teknoguilder, Pavo. "I had a friend die of it, too. I am sorry."

Dardelan nodded acknowledgment, and his eyes held a measure of speculation that told me I was not what he had expected. He led us through the house via a dark hall into a huge sunken room. It was windowless, being at the center of the dwelling as near as I could make out. Two lanterns cast a murky light over the occupants of the room.

A subdued hum of conversation fell into silence as they became aware of us and I felt myself suddenly to be the cynosure of all eyes. I bore the visual dissection in dignified silence, blinking and waiting for my eyes to adjust to the dimness.

After a long pause a handsome older man, with smooth gray hair and eyes the same shade, rose and stepped forward into the lantern light.

"So, the Misfit," he said in a sneering voice. There was an arrogance in the way he eyed me from head to toe. I waited for him to introduce himself but when he did not, taking into account his deliberate discourtesy and arrogant bearing, I guessed he was Malik.

I lifted my eyebrows and stepped further into the room. "I will move closer to the light so that you may get a better view, should you wish to count my teeth and toes."

An astounded silence met my words, then an elderly man gave a startled bark of laughter.

But Malik was too experienced a player to let this pinprick upset him. "You are even younger than the stripling," he said disparagingly, as if my words had been callow rather than clever. And, in addition, he had managed to turn the words into a sideways sneer at Dardelan.

"To be young is not necessarily to be weak," Brydda said pleasantly. "Whereas to be old...but you know what it is to be old, don't you, Malik. It renders the mind resistant to anything new."

As he spoke he moved to stand near Dardelan, symbolically allying himself with the youth, rather than with me. I was, I realized suddenly, truly alone.

Malik gave Brydda a stiff smile. "I am older, it is true, but I am proud of my years, for age brings caution and experience and wisdom and these things are well in one who would command. But perhaps that is why you surround yourself with children and freaks, Brydda. With such an obedient and malleable following, you would have no need of age or its virtues."

Dardelan colored slightly but, wisely, he held his tongue.

"I am no leader," Brydda said mildly.

Malik snorted and it must have been as obvious to the others in the room that he regarded Brydda as a rival. The big man could not afford to lie down and let the other man walk over him, yet to fight him would seem to prove Malik's insinuations. No wonder he stayed silent.

Malik's eyes swifted back to me. "Does it speak, we wonder?" he inquired brightly. "Or has your parrot exhausted its meager repertoire, Brydda? Perhaps you should have toiled harder to gift your little pet more words to play with."

I had to bite my tongue to keep from showing anger before I spoke. "I speak when I have something to say, not to admire the sound of my voice," I said flatly.

The rebel's eyes glittered with malice, but his smile did not falter.

"Malik, this is Elspeth Gordie," Dardelan introduced us. "It is impolite for us to speak to a guest without using her name."

"She is no guest of mine, boy," Malik snapped. "I have higher standards. She is a gypsy halfbreed and a Misfit to boot."

The man who had laughed earlier leaned forward in his seat, and I realized that prematurely gray hair made him appear older than he was. His face was unlined and I guessed his age to lie between Brydda's and Malik's. He was far less robust in appearance than either of them, yet there was a craftiness in his eyes that suggested the muscle he used to reign was one of brain rather than brawn.

"There is not much to you but skin and bones, child," he murmured. "Are they all like you, these warriors Brydda says you would bring to strengthen us?"

I saw then the part I was meant to play at this gathering. I was to be a pawn for these men to score against one another. Anger drove away my dreary sadness. I would be no one's pawn. I made myself smile.

"Do you measure your followers by their mass, Sirrah?" I asked sweetly. "We Talented Misfits measure ourselves by our deeds, and surely you of all people would concede that size does not always indicate courage or cunning or even strength." I let my eyes fall momentarily to his own slender frame.

It was difficult to tell in that half-light, but I thought his pale cheeks flushed slightly. "I am Cassell," he said at last. "And talk is cheap."

"That may be so of rebel talk, Sirrah," I rejoined promptly. "But my words bear my honor. Therefore they are valuable indeed."

This time his brows raised. "Well, you can talk a good fight."

I sensed I had won a slight victory, but did not press the point. A movement on the other side of the room caught my eye. When the man who had made it rose, it was all I could do not to gape. It was the Elii I had known as a girl at the Kinraide orphan home. It had always been predicted by the guardians there that Elii would die of the rotting sickness as his father had, for he had led orphans questing for whitestick. But he showed no sign of ill health. Nor did he show by word or gesture that he remembered me.

For that I was grateful, since he had not known me as a gypsy, but as an orphan. And perhaps the simple answer to that was that I had changed too.

He shook my hand and looked into my face, and I remembered that he had always been prone to judge by instinct rather than by the words people offered. The man alongside him had a stern, ascetic face and disdainful eyes, and wore his hair in two flaxen plaits. Dardelan introduced him as Tardis' representative, Gwynedd.

"This is Brocade," Dardelan said, moving me past the silent Murmrothian to a hugely obese man, who did not trouble himself to rise. He might have been brother to the Teknoguildmaster, except that where much of Garth's bulk was muscle, Brocade was like a plump, overstuffed powder puff. He was got up with as much lace and silk as any maiden would wear on her bonding day. From Brydda's lecture, I remembered this man was a staunch ally of Malik's and resisted the temptation to ask Cassell if this was the sort of size he liked behind him.

Brocade had a haughty, self-important air as his eyes swept over me disparagingly. "The creature is very badly dressed considering the importance of this meeting," he said in an affected tone. "Are all your Misfits the same color as you? I am not fond of that darkish skin color for it is known that as a rule such belongs to people of inferior mentality."

I was too dumbfounded by this absurdity to response.

"This is a very interesting observation, Brocade. I must be sure to mention it to Bram and the tribes when next we speak."

The drawling and unusually accented female voice arose from the darkest end of the room. I turned with the rest to see a woman unfold herself from a couch as gracefully as a cat. Standing, she was at least a head taller than any man in the room and possessed of considerable exotic beauty. Her skin was the color of yellow-gold and her tawny eyes were slanted up at the outer edges like a cat's. Her hair was straight and black as combed silk, and cut perfectly level at her jaw and across her brow. The hair and eyes, and an amused feline smile, made her appear more catlike than ever.

Yet the look she bent on Brocade was anything but amused, and he swallowed convulsively, numerous chins wobbling in alarm as her fingers slipped casually to the hilt of an ornate knife in her belt.

"I did not mean to insult your people," he bleated. "Your color is not the same as this creature's."

"What has color to do with anything?" Jakoby asked, for I knew it must be her. She wore voluminous trews, a long tunic belted at the hip, and flat sandals.

Her fingers caressed the hilt of her knife absently and Brocade followed the movement with bulging eyes.

"I meant no offense," he stammered.

"None taken," Jakoby said pleasantly. "Provided you retract your statement. But if you wish to stand by it, then I must demand a bout to see whether your pale skin really reflects greater wit than other colors."

"A... bout? You can't mean I should wrestle you? A woman?"

Her brows arched. "Is my gender also cause to think me inferior?"

"No! I... I... I retract!" Brocade stammered, mopping his damp brow with a scrap of silk.

Jakoby gave a throaty laugh of derision, then she turned to me and held out her long hand. I put mine into it, expecting her to shake it, but instead she stared into my eyes, seeming to weigh it in hers thoughtfully. Then she turned it over and examined the palm minutely. After a long moment she closed my hand into a fist, but kept it in her own hard grip, looking again into my eyes.

"A good hand, girl. One that must grasp many threads of destiny. A hand whose owner is at once open and true, and yet who is the keeper of terrible secrets, and a seeker of them."

Before I could wrench my hand away, Jakoby released it and turned to face the rest of the room.

"I vote for an alliance with this girl's people," she announced.

XXXII

There was a moment of astonished silence before Malik leapt to his feet with a snarl of fury.

"I do not know how things are done in Sador, Madam, but here we talk before deciding such issues as whether to ally ourselves with the likes of this creature."

"You talk. I have decided," Jakoby pronounced imperiously.

If the moment had not been so fraught, the look of baffled and impotent fury on Malik's face would have been comical.

"Jakoby, we honor you and know that your ways are different," Brydda interposed smoothly. "Were we in your Land, we would abide by your customs. But this is our Land and here decisions among allies are made by a majority decision of a vote, taken from all participants after everyone has had their say."

The Sadorian grunted and flung herself into a seat with feline grace. "Very well. Talk," she said in openly bored tones.

Malik looked perfectly furious, and the other rebels were clearly discomforted by her contempt. I tried wildly to imagine this domineering gold-skinned woman at a guildmerge where everything was decided by consensus, and failed utterly.

"Lady," Dardelan said. "You are a chief in your land. This, my father told me, is the Sadorian way; to choose the best and brightest by means of ritual challenges, and then to allow them to lead without interference. But this is not Sador, nor is it Sadorians whom you will battle. The Council, the soldierguards and the Herder Faction are Landfolk and perhaps in this light you may concede that there will be times when we will know better how to deal with them. Maybe you will learn something useful from observing our ways, just as we will learn from you. Isn't that the advantage of an alliance?"

Jakoby made no response to this speech but she had lost her bored expression.

"On behalf of the western bloc, I would like to say..." Cassell began, but Malik cut him off by snorting rudely.

"On behalf, Cassell? Do you have signatures over letters from Radek and Madellin explaining their absence and entitling you to represent them?" Malik demanded.

"We have come to an understanding...." Cassell began, but Malik interrupted him again with a loud laugh.

"An understanding—a very vague and useful term, is it not?"

Cassell flushed with anger but he was not quick enough to compose a cutting rejoinder.

I glanced at the Sadorian, wondering how she felt about their petty bickering. It was no great advertisement for Land ways, but it was not like this in guildmerge. I tried to pinpoint what it was that made the two organizations different, since both ruled by consensus, but I was distracted when Elii rose to speak.

"I want to know what these Misfits can do," he said in his gruff accents. "I thought that was what we were here for."

"That is what I was trying to say earlier when I was interrupted," Cassell interposed, with a dark look at Malik.

"I am not concerned with her tricks," Malik said flatly.

"I would like to hear what Elspeth has to offer," Dardelan said diffidently.

Brocade laughed coarsely. "No doubt you would but we speak of war, boy, not bedsports."

Dardelan flushed bright red and I felt the blood in my own cheeks.

"If you would conduct a war the way you conduct this meeting, I think it best if you stick to bedsports," I snapped.

Brydda's eyes warned me to be careful; that a display of temper would undo any favorable impression I had managed to make.

"I suppose Misfits know better how to run a meeting than human beings," Malik sneered.

Anger surged through me. Malik's continued attempts to label me, and his implication that we were neither normal nor human would not stop until I had answered him decisively. Yet I would remain calm and dignified if it killed me, I vowed.

The effort of keeping my temper leached all emotion from my voice and when I spoke it sounded curiously toneless. "We do not consider ourselves abnormal but only possessed of certain additional abilities. We lack nothing that any other human being has in the Land, excepting perhaps a place in the order of things. It is the Council who names us Misfit, along with dreamers and defectives. I do not know whether we conduct meetings better, but do I know that our aim when we meet is not to use words as sly daggers, but to exchange information." Sensing I had their undivided attention for the moment, I shifted to address the room, rather than Malik.

"I came here today to offer you the opportunity to find out how my people can help you win your rebellion against the Council. Yet, I am treated with as little courtesy as if I were your enemy. You insult me and sneer and from this I might judge that you wish me to depart."

Malik's eyes sparkled with triumph, and anticipation of his disappointment enabled me to infuse a sweetness I did not feel into my words. "Yet, in case not all who are in this room share Malik's opinions and attitudes, I will speak my piece in spite of all his efforts to stop me."

I hurried on before the furious rebel could cut in.

"I have told you that we have additional abilities and that is so. There are among us those who can communicate mind to mind over some distance. These we call farseekers. In a rebellion, with one such at your side, you could constantly exchange information and intelligence between yourselves, and seek advice without leaving battle posts."

I sensed I was speaking well, for all but Brocade and Malik had lost their skeptical looks and were listening intently—even the silent Gwynedd.

"Others among us have the ability to empathize; that is to receive or transmit feelings. Such an ability at your command would enable you to strike fear or doubt into a soldierguard captain at the crucial moment in a battle, or even to send love and friendship into the hearts of attacking forces to confuse and distract them."

Malik laughed, but no one paid any attention to him. I felt a wild thrill. I had them!

"Some of us can communicate with beasts and that would enable us to project instructions and conflicting commands to enemy horses, thereby defusing a mounted charge."

"That fingertalk of Brydda's," Malik sneered.

I shook my head, refusing to let him shake my confidence or control. "Brydda's success at his fingerspeaking is admirable, but communicating with beasts for those who have the Talent, is generally done via the mind as with farseeking. Were I an empath I could reach out a voice from my mind to the horse on which a soldierguard is mounted and, provided my request was polite and reasonable...."

"Polite," Cassell sounded startled and amused.

I looked at him gravely. "I find courtesy serves in any situation. Don't you?"

He looked faintly abashed.

"Of course," Malik jeered, drowning out whatever answer he might have made. "We could all take a lesson from this and curtsy to our dogs and goats before breakfast."

Brocade guffawed loudly. "I think I can conduct my forces without advice from my horse."

I resisted the urge to suggest his horse could probably do a better job, and went on to point out that, apart from our additional abilities, there were others among our number who had trained themselves as warriors, and who were prepared to stand beside the rebels and fight.

"Are there other abilities?" Jakoby asked.

I glanced at her, but did not let her catch my eyes. "Some of us have herb lore and are healers," I said, keeping my fingers crossed that she would not persist. "All of our abilities we would place at your disposal if we were allied, in the hope that by defeating our common enemies, the Land will become a place where we can all live in peace, without persecution or slavery."

"A pretty speech," Malik sneered. "But the heart of the matter is that you wish to trade your dubious and unproven additional abilities for acceptance among normal humans." He turned his burning eyes to the others.

"We oppose the Council because of its misuse of power, not for its attempt to clean the human race of holocaust poisons and mutations. If we accept aid from these Misfits, we must give up trying to cleanse our race of deformed mutants. It says that, hereafter, we will permit any freak or defective obscenity not only to live, but to exist alongside us, to share our Land, our food, our crops; to bond with our sons and daughters."

There was a charged silence and I felt frozen by the hostility in the faces that turned to me.

"She is a Misfit and I see no monster," Dardelan said softly. "Is she the kind you mean when you speak of freaks and mutants, Malik?"

The boy had formidable subtlety and I wondered what the father must be like, to have such a son.

"She is not visibly deformed," Malik conceded with ill grace. "But what of those she represents? No doubt they have sent her precisely because she was the most comely among them. After all, they would not send a monster, would they?"

"There are none among us whom you would see in a crowd and know as Misfits," I said. "None of us is physically deformed."

I stopped for this speech soured my mouth. I could not compromise what I believed, not even to win these people.

I looked directly into Malik's eyes. "But were such a one to come among us, grossly deformed or not, we would not turn them away excepting that they were deformed of spirit or soul."

From the corner of my eye, I saw the Sadorian shift involuntarily as if the words held some goad, but her face when I looked was impassive.

"See!" Malik declared. "She has said that she and her kind would accept grossly deformed mutants, as long as they possess these Talents. And how many generations before we would be reduced to a herd of howling beasts with such a philosophy? Rather the Council should continue to prevail than that. The thought of allowing mutants to exist alongside normal decent Landfolk is an obscenity to me, and one I could never condone.

"But," he went on quickly, striding to the center of the room, "if your own values and decency are not enough to let you see what the ultimate outcome of this alliance must be, then think on this: these Misfits are little more than children for all the abilities they claim. Is that not so?"

He shot me a look of icy interrogation.

"The majority of us are young, that's true, but . . ."

"There you are. Condemned out of her own mouth," Malik cried. "Are we to act as wet-nurses to monstrous children in the very midst of battle? Is it not a burden rather than an asset that we would gain in shackling ourselves to her people?"

"Youth means nothing," Elii said sharply. "I was a youth when I set up my rebel group. It's guts and brains that count, not age—and this girl sounds to me as if she has enough of both. I've no love for mutants, but she is no freak and if her people can do what she says they can, then they would give us an advantage the Council and the soldierguards could never counteract."

There was a moment in which I thought Elii had actually won them over for me.

"Your brain is surely addled from whitestick," Malik snarled. "Oh, yes, by all means invite these freaks to fight alongside you, Elii. And while you are at it, employ the cripples and the scum that clog the lanes of every city street and would as soon cut our throats as guard our backs. But in the remote chance that you would win with such a force, remember that you will not easily set them aside when war is done.

"I will seek out instead the best and worthiest to fight behind me and, though my force be less in number, it will prevail for it will be made up of true humans, not distorted copies and ghastly shadow creatures. Every one of my force shall know what they are and be proud of it."

"Your instinct for drama never ceases to enliven our meetings," Brydda said, as if the whole of Malik's impassioned diatribe had been nothing more than a puppet show for the rebels' amusement. "However, it might be as well to point out that this meeting is not to decide the future of the human race, but merely to ascertain if this girl's people can aid us when we rise against the Council."

His dry business-like tones diminished the effect of Malik's wild rhetoric, but the gray-eyed rebel was not done yet.

He stepped up to Brydda, his eyes narrowed. "I am not a fool," he hissed. "You want these Misfits to join us and you connive with soft words and wiles to this end for some secret purpose of your own that eludes my reasoning." He swung to face the others. "Ask yourselves that too, my comrades. Why does Brydda Llewellyn support an alliance with them? Is it that he seeks control of the rebel forces with their help?"

"My father also favors an alliance," Dardelan said coldly. "Do you also claim Bodera had secret purposes?"

Malik gave him a startled look, as if a duck had suddenly defended itself against a vicious dog.

"Do we need them?" Cassell asked, and the others turned to stare at the older man.

"I ask if we need these Misfits, regardless of how useful they will be. Can we win without them? It seems to me that is a question we ought to be addressing."

"There are more soldierguards than there are of our people," Brydda said. "The simple answer is that we need everyone that we can get."

"No!" Brocade shrieked. "I say we dare not take them among us, no matter how great is our need. Misfits are despised by Lud. If we accept them, it is the same as rejecting Lud and we will be punished with another plague or some worse thing than that. Lud will visit disaster on us and perhaps because of their eldritch aid, we will lose when we would have won."

I cast a look around the room and saw that all of the rebels, even Elii, were looking thoughtful. I had underestimated fat Brocade badly.

I swallowed, and found my mouth dry with fear and tension and too many empty words. In that moment I glanced at Malik. His eyes looked straight into mine, filled with naked loathing. His eyelids fell like shutters over the expression, but the hatred was burned irrevocably into my mind. In that instant, I understood that there would be no winning Malik's vote and no compromise. Not ever.

"Cassell was right in asking if we need them. I say we do not! This is a war we will wage and, to win it, we need only strong, committed adults, good armor and weapons and the warriors to use them. But most of all we need strong centralized leadership."

The others were all nodding approval, the question of alliance shunted neatly aside.

"I say we strike soon, before the new intake of soldierguards is fully trained," Malik went on forcefully, and I realized he was on the verge of taking over the meeting and perhaps the rebellion. With his smooth handsome face and eyes that glowed with confidence, he looked the picture of a leader of men. I knew then, as if by futuretell vision, that if Malik assumed the mantle of leadership now, after the rebellion, Misfits would be doomed. He and his people would hunt us down and destroy us.

The rebels had begun to argue and discuss the merits and disadvantages of different seasons to mount a successful rebellion. I glanced at Brydda but his face was blank and unhelpful. Well, he had warned me that I could not expect his aid—especially not when Malik had practically accused him of using us to seize leadership.

I noticed that alone of all those in the room, the Sadorian woman was watching me from her shadowy corner, yellow eyes glinting. This reminded me vividly of Maruman and, oddly, gave me the courage to do what I did next.

"The question of alliance has not yet been voted upon," I said loudly and firmly.

Malik gave me an irritated look. "Children should be at play, not meddling in the affairs of their elders and betters."

I was fleetingly puzzled, then I realized he would not want anything to remind the rebels of the powers I had earlier outlined. Well, I would play his game and beat him at it.

"Then let us speak plainly as children are wont to do," I said, still loudly. "You, Malik, wish to set yourself up as the leader of the rebellion and of all these others sitting here, because you think you are better than them, and because you desire the power that would accrue to such a position after the battles are over."

Malik flushed, then whitened, to hear me name his ambitions so nakedly and shorn of all softening or justification. Even Brydda looked aghast. It seemed that in the world of men and battles, only the truth was too shocking to be mentioned aloud.

But Malik was caught because, without looking like a fool or a liar, he could not deny what I had said, when every person in the room knew it must be true.

"Each person has their expertise," he said at last, through clenched teeth. "Mine is to lead."

For a moment the capricious balance of power was tilted in my favor. I looked into Gwynedd's blue eyes. "What of Tardis? Does he also not possess the ability to lead? What of . . ." I stretched my memory. "What of Yavok and indeed of any one of you in this room? Are you not all leaders of your groups because you possess exactly that same expertise to lead as Malik? And, in that case, why should he be set above you?"

"One must rule in wartime," Malik snapped. "In the end, a single person must be put above the rest. A rebellion must have a commander to whom all intelligence is sent. Once the battle begins, only one person can direct its course; can have the power to say go or stay, fight or retreat. A horse cannot have two heads or ten and, if it must have one, then give it the one who knows the trail best. I am a warrior. I know tactics and I know the feel of battle."

"Malik is right. Sooner or later we must choose one to lead us in battle and that is his strength," Elii said.

It was well said, but I had a final card to play in this game of words and Elii had brought me neatly to it.

"Why choose at all when, with my people by your side, each of you may lead your own forces and confer whenever you need? With farseekers to link you, there is no need for one warlord! Why not go on as you have begun—each ruling your own people, and conferring through mine when there is need? And then, when the war is won, choose one among you whose gift is peacetime rule, if you decide it is necessary."

"It makes sense," said Elii. "If each of us conducts our own share of the war, then what need have we of a leader in the aftermath of the rebellion? Could we not continue to rule our own provinces?"

"Bodera sent Brydda here to convince us with his silver tongue to join together because divided we were nothing more than thorns in the Council's side. With great eloquence he spoke of the need for us to be welded into a single unit with a single aim. Remember those words? And now he would have us splinter into tiny groups. Do you not wonder why? Could it be that divided we will be easier for him and his mutants to conquer?" Malik demanded.

Brydda stood up, his own face showing anger for the first time. "I did not know Misfits like Elspeth existed when this was begun. But since they do, it seems to be wise to look at what they can offer us. But the decision is not mine to make, whatever Malik implies. It is yours and I am nothing more than Bodera's and Dardelan's man."

"All I am offering is the means for you to retain independence," I said.

"I, for one, know my master would prefer to retain control of our people," said Gwynedd in a thin, ironic voice. "It would surprise me if any rebel leader would say they wished someone to rule over them."

"Without having to decide who is going to run things, we might better concentrate on winning our battle," Dardelan put in.

"So speaks the wisdom of the ages," Malik sneered.

"I speak for my father," the young man said quietly.

"Again, I offer an alliance with my people," I said. "We will allow ourselves to be dispersed among you...."

"No!" Malik snapped, banging his hand on the table. "Who is this girl to offer alliance to us? Is she the ruler of her people? I think not. Why does not her master come among us, or is he so grossly distorted that he cannot be seen?"

"Some of us have met him," Cassell said mildly. "He is not a Misfit at all."

"Well, what sort of man is he that chooses to rule freaks? And I ask you again, how do we know that these mutated brats can do what she claims? I want more than children who can whisper to one another across the Land, in exchange for accepting this girl and her freakish kin as comrades. I want warriors who can fight."

Jakoby rose and, so great was her natural presence, we all looked up at her. "You wish to see if she and hers can match your people in battle, Malik? Is that it? And if they could, what then? Would you accept them as allies and equals?"

"I would accept a cow if it could prove itself my equal," he snapped.

The others laughed and, though I kept my face still and calm, I seethed inwardly.

"Then there is a way to solve this matter." Jakoby turned her glowing golden eyes to me. "In Sador, we have a thing called the Battlegames. It is a series of ritual contests which run between dawn and dusk on a single day. I offer you this as a way of solving this deadlock. By it, you will learn if this girl and her people can turn their talents to winning war." She looked at me. "And your people will have the chance to prove yourselves and gain the alliance you seek. If you fail, then it is as well that this alliance does not come to pass."

"You said contests. Who would be contesting with whom?" I asked, my mind reeling at the swiftness of this new possibility.

Jakoby shrugged. "An equal number of those who would test you. His people." Her eyes flicked to Malik.

"Where would these Battlegames be held? And when?" I asked, stalling as I tried to decide what to do.

"I do not see the point of playing games," Brocade interpolated querulously.

I did not take my eyes from the Sadorian woman.

"A trial of honor is fitting at such an impasse," she said calmly, glancing at Brocade. "As to when and where, I offer Sador and the next Battlegames on behalf of my people. And whatever the conclusion of the Battlegames, the occasion may well be used to decide our own final strategy in dealing with the Council and its soldierguards."

That rendered all of them silent and thoughtful.

After a long minute Malik nodded, his eyes glittering with triumph. Perhaps he was seeing that as a victor of this mock battle, he would naturally assume leadership of the rebels. I had probably played right into his hands.

"Then it is agreed that your two peoples shall meet at the Battlegames, and that the fate of the alliance between you shall rest upon the outcome?" Jakoby asked.

"Done," Malik said savagely.

I stared at him helplessly, wanting to ask for time to think, yet knowing I must not hesitate. If I refused the contest now, Malik would win by default. Yet to agree without consulting the others went against everything that Guildmerge stood for.

I thought of Malik's eyes, filled with open hatred, and knew there would be no other way to get him to agree to an alliance. And so, truly, there was no choice after all.

"All right," I said softly.

There was a little hiatus, then a babble of talk.

"I do not think fighting among ourselves is ..." Dardelan began.

"My master would agree that this is fair, I think. . . ." Gwynedd said.

"It solves one thing, certainly," Cassell said musingly. "The need for us to meet together to plan the rebellion has been pressing for some time. Can it be organized for all of the rebel leaders to come to Sador?" Here he looked to Brydda.

Jaw clenched ominously, the big rebel nodded. "I will send birds out and the groups who have their own will have sent replies by the morrow as to whether they will journey to Sador or be guided by those who will go, and whither they will assign their vote or go with the majority on decisions."

"How long would such a journey take?" Cassell asked. "I do not like the idea of being away from the Land for too many days. Indeed, I do not like the seas at all."

"Isn't Sador very far and the road to it dangerously close to the Blacklands?" Brocade asked.

"By road it is far, but by sea it is two or three days only," Jakoby said.

"By sea!" Dardelan murmured, his eyes wide.

"We should think about this. . . ." Brydda cautioned.

"I have thought it through and it seems to me that this is a good idea," Elii said decisively. "I have no love for sea travel either, but it is a journey of two days that we talk of. If these Misfits beat Malik at this contest, it is worth whatever the bother afterward to let them stand with us. If they fail, then it does not matter. More importantly to my mind, we will be able to organize the rebellion once and for all."

The others nodded at this blunt common-sense pronouncement with varying degrees of enthusiasm.

"Well then, it seems we are to journey to Sador together—let us hope the ship does not sink, or the rebellion will be scuttled before it begins. At least this mock battle should be amusing," Cassell said, as if I had volunteered to bring a troop of clowns or tumblers to perform for them.

"What is to keep Sador from treachery when we are all in their hands?" Brocade asked querulously.

Jakoby gave him a look of scathing violence. "Were you not a barbarian, I would cut your tongue out for that insult," she hissed. "Sadorians do not betray allies."

Brocade stared up at her like a stunned rabbit.

"You do not have any honor," she said, leaning toward him like a poisonous snake about to strike. "Yet you understand fear too well, for I think you are old friends." She stared into his eyes and he grew so pale I wondered that he had not fainted.

At last she withdrew a fraction.

"You have no reason to fear, for since we of the plains desire none of your squalid little Land there would be no point in our hostaging or slaying those of you who would choose to come. My people will join you in your battle simply to keep these Herders and the like from infesting the plains. As you know, that is the price of our aid." Her eyes flicked contemptuously around the room, finally coming to settle with less fury on Brydda. Then she frowned, seeming to have some unexpected thought.

"It comes to me that I am at fault in this," she said at last. Her voice was calmer now, but colder than the sound of the Brildane howling in the icy wastes of the highest mountains. "Long have we of the tribes known that you are a people who do not know honor. Therefore I should not have expected you to recognize it. As a token of faith that you will understand, I will leave my own daughter in this city, and I shall not come for her until you are returned from Sador. Is this acceptable?"

Dardelan stepped forward and bowed to the Sador chief. "Lady, I need no proof of your good will. But I offer my father's house where your daughter may stay in fitting comfort. She will be guarded as carefully as if she were my own sister," he said earnestly.

I blinked back sudden tears; this was the sort of romantic gesture Matthew would have made under the circumstances.

The cold light in Jakoby's eyes softened. "I think you will find a daughter of Sador does not need much protecting."

Dardelan bowed. "I will speak with my father and preparations will be made at once."

"So it begins," Gwynedd said, and there was a curious finality in his voice.

"I am ready," Malik said, then he laid his head back and laughed wolfishly.

Brydda closed his eyes and sank into a chair.

XXXIII

Walking back to the safe house very late that night, the difficulties of what had been agreed to multiplied ferociously in my mind.

The worst of it was that I had to get to Obernewtyn and back within a threeday. Not such a difficult thing, except for the time it would take to convince guildmerge of the need for us to take part in the Battlegames, and I had a feeling that would be no easy matter. And if they agreed, there would be time needed to organize our team.

I would have to leave as soon as I returned to the safe house, and ride for the mountains, leaving Dragon with Kella.

Madness, Brydda had called it, and he was right. But I did not see what else I could have done. He had wanted me to impress the rebels with my normality, but right from the start it had been only too clear that most of them could not and never would see us as normal. Rushton had said as much himself in my chamber the night before I left Obernewtyn, but he had not followed that thorny notion to its logical conclusion.

Or perhaps he had, I reflected, remembering the look of fierce determination on his face when he said we would force the rebels to join us, if they would not have us as allies. But even he could not have seen how the meeting would proceed.

Whether Brydda admitted it or not, Malik had been on the verge of taking control of the rebellion. If that had happened, we would then have had to start regarding them as deadly enemies.

I had to make guildmerge see that Jakoby's Battlegames could not alienate the rebels from us further. Nothing would be lost.

I sighed.

Not quite nothing. We must lose our innocence, for to agree to the games meant literally casting aside all of our dreams of peaceful coexistence and gradual friendship. It meant accepting that we would only ever be tolerated and even that must be fought for. Well, they would have to face that unpleasant truth sooner or later. It was only too clear to me now that we had been naive and foolish to think we could win the rebels by offering our help. We had failed to take into account that the same attitude which motivated the Herders to burn Misfits, also motivated the rebels. We had wanted to believe that opposing the same enemies made us allies, but that was not so.

It was not difficult to anticipate the guildmerge response to my suggestion that we use the Battlegames to teach the rebels to respect— even to fear us—so that they would think twice before turning on us, no matter what happened in the rebellion. What other choice had we but to play by their rules?

Rushton would understand that—his whole life had been one of compromise to obtain his birthright. But I could imagine how Maryon and Roland would take it.

Under their leadership, the Healer and Futureteller guilds had violently opposed the Coercer's Talent contest when the idea was first mooted in guildmerge, claiming that competition promoted aggression. They had been narrowly outvoted and the contests had since become an important event during our mountain moon fair.

There had even been unexpected benefits. Mindmelds had increased in coordination and individual skills had been honed and strengthened with the competitions as a goad. In addition, the stress of competition occasionally revealed unsuspected secondary and even tertiary abilities.

Though there was rather more at stake than a crown of flowers, the Battlegames was still a contest.

Of course Roland would point out that what had begun as competition between guildmembers at Obernewtyn had swiftly metamorphosed into stylized displays of skill, with both competitors playing to the audience rather than trying to outdo each other; as much a team effort as anything else.

I would answer that it might be so with the Battlegames.

But that would expose the main weakness of my argument: I did not know what the Battlegames entailed, any more than Malik or Brydda did. Jakoby had refused to elaborate, saying only they were not for the faint hearted and would test our ability in battle decisively. All we knew was that each side should muster a team of ten and must reach Sador before the moon was full—within a fiveday. She would give no hint about what qualities and abilities might be needed.

I noticed a man staring at me curiously and absently coerced his attention elsewhere, wishing fiercely that I had more time. Convincing guildmerge would take time, but all the eloquence in the world would not help us if we were late, for Jakoby had explained that Battlegames were held only on full-moon days during the Days of Rain.

I had come to Sutrium galvanized by an impossible deadline and now I would leave the same way. Life seemed to resound in echoes and oblique reflections.

I made up my mind to uncover the tattoo and use it to speed the journey. If it was healed. I had not taken the wrappings off before, mindful of Maire's warning and the knowledge that, uncovered, it would demand explanations I was not yet ready to give.

But this was an emergency.

If the tattoo was still too raw or obviously new to be used, I would simply have to coerce my way past any obstacles.

I would not let myself consider the possibility that guildmerge might refuse me.

Once the discussion about the Battlegames had been concluded, Jakoby had offered any who desired it passage on the Sadorian ship *Zephyr*, which would return to her home port on the third day. She and Brydda had decided to ride up the coast with Cassell and Gwynedd to speak with some of the unaffiliated rebel groups about committing themselves to the rebellion and journeying to Sador. Those who would travel sooner, Jakoby said, might take passage on one of the many spice-trade ships which plied the short but lucrative passage between Sador and the Land. All ships for Sador docked at Templeport, for the sandy little peninsula settlement was the only accessible part of the steep, jagged Sadorian coastline. It had transpired that Jakoby's daughter had come to Sutrium with her mother, so there was no need to summon her from Sador. She would be brought to stay with Dardelan in Bodera's home as had been agreed at the meeting, and she would remain after they departed for Sador on the third day.

Alone with Brydda, I had said we would travel with them on the *Zephyr* because it would take me that long to get to Obernewtyn and back. "If we make it, I will see you the third day."

"I hope I do not see you," he had said pointedly.

Grim parting words.

I seemed to hear Malik's malicious laughter ringing in my ears, as jagged as pieces of broken glass falling through the night. He had laughed, I thought, because he imagined I had played right into his hands in agreeing to the contest. That might have been expected from Malik, but it had shocked me a little to think that Brydda felt the same.

"How can your people win against Malik and his warriors?" he had demanded just before our parting. "He is the best strategist among us. He will win these Battlegames, no matter what they involve. It was madness for you to agree, for in doing so you have made an alliance with Misfits conditional on a win. I don't know what possessed you. Jakoby was for you and Dardelan. Cassell and Elii were on side and even Tardis' man, Gwynedd, seemed disposed to speak favorably of you to his master. You threw all of that away by agreeing to this lunatic contest."

"You said there could be no rebellion without Malik," I had pointed out. "I tell you he would never have agreed to an alliance any other way than this. Nor, I suspect, would Tardis. Now at least Malik has committed himself to accepting us if we beat him and Gwynedd seems to think Tardis will agree too."

Brydda had only shaken his head and commanded me to tell Rushton that the whole matter could be dismissed as a mistake if he would send a message quickly, saying I had overstepped my authority. He had even promised to send Reuvan to the safe house with a bird which might be loosed from Obernewtyn with this message.

In honor, I must repeat Brydda's words and the doubts that fueled them.

Rushton's serious face floated into my mind, seeming at the same time accusing and deeply troubled. I wondered if he would take the rebel's advice, or mine.

Coming through the repair-yard gate absorbed by my thoughts, I was utterly unprepared to see the object of them leaning against the side of a small gypsy wagon.

I stopped dead, a fist of reaction clenching in my gut. Rushton's arms were folded across his chest and he was clearly deep in thought, a closed, brooding look on his face.

Though I had not spoken nor made a sound, he must have sensed he was no longer alone, and turned his head toward me. It seemed to me that his green eyes reached across the yard with all the force of a jet of flame.

"Elspeth."

Just that: he spoke my name flatly, almost coldly. He straightened and walked across the yard and I felt the blood rise in my cheeks. I made myself walk to meet him, to show I was not disconcerted; only to find after all, that I was too near.

Before I could prevent myself, I had stepped back. Rushton possessed no usable Talent but his face sharpened to a kind of irony at this. He stopped, and made a little bow, as if something had been agreed to between us.

"I have been waiting for you. Kella said you had gone to meet with the rebels."

I nodded, my thoughts chaotic, but on the heels of my reaction to Rushton's presence was a rising fear. "How...why are you here? What has happened?" I demanded.

"Nothing. Not yet, at least. We are here because Maryon sent us."

We? Then he was not alone.

I was about to demand to know who else had come, when it struck me, with some force, that there was only one explanation for this expedition. *Maryon had foreseen the journey to Sador.*

Could it be that need would be answered so gracefully after all the ill-fortune that had haunted our time on the coast?

Rushton nodded. "So it's true, then. She said you would understand."

"Understand?"

"Maryon futuretold us coming here, but she did not know why. She said you would."

And again that awful, swirling, helpless feeling of being a leaf borne on some impossibly strong tide. Maryon had known that I would know. It was too much.

"You just came without knowing why, because..."

"Because Maryon said it was vital for Obernewtyn. Yes." Rushton nodded, a faint challenge in his green eyes. "It would be a little late to be deciding now that we would not live our lives by the whimsical wisdoms of futuretellers, don't you think?"

"But that was..."

"Dangerous, foolhardy, rash? Of course." He spread his fingers into a gesture of acceptance. Then his expression hardened and the mockery died in it. "Why are we here, Elspeth?"

I took a deep breath. "I think because of something that happened at a meeting I had with the rebels today."

"Do you think you might manage to be a little less cryptic?"

"Brydda asked me to meet with the rebels to show them that Misfits are not monsters," I said. "You were right when you said they regard us as freaks and, in spite of Brydda's hopes, the meeting did not change that. The two main rebel leaders wanted nothing to do with us. That was why Brydda had not contacted us—he was trying to make them change their minds. He had hoped this meeting would do it...."

I told him, then, about Malik and Tardis and the other rebels, about the power struggle between them, and about Jakoby.

"The rebels liked the idea of being able to use us to communicate because they would need no overlord," I said. "All but Malik, of course, because he wants to be the overlord. But even if it were not for that, he would never, never accept us willingly. He had all but convinced the others that we were children and incapable of holding our own in a battle."

Rushton frowned. "Go on."

"He was on the verge of taking over the meeting and the rebel groups when Jakoby made a suggestion as to how we might discover if Misfits were able warriors."

I told him of the Battlegames. It was impossible to know if he was angry. He was too good at keeping his thoughts and emotions hidden.

At last he sighed. "We had better go and tell the others to prepare themselves for a sea journey."

∽

Maryon had sent seven of them, Rushton told me, naming each herself. There had been no vote in guildmerge. My heart sank when I saw whom she had sent. No wonder Rushton had sighed when I told him of the Battlegames.

The young twin Empath guilden, Miky and Angina, were sitting across from one another at the table sorting herbs. Receptive Miky intercepted my astonishment and swung around, her face creased in a welcoming smile, tinged with mischief. "I bet we are the last people you imagined seeing here."

"That is saying it mildly," I said somberly.

The stocky Coercer guilden, Miryum, was seated by the hearth with a pile of toasting forks on her knees. She had been rubbing the points over a whetstone as we entered but, hearing Miky, she threw them down and strode across the room to thump me on the back with painful enthusiasm.

"It is good to see you, guildmistress. This is a queer business, is it not?"

I was distracted from answering by the sight of a strange, plain-faced girl with yellow hair.

"Greetings, guildmistress Elspeth," she said. "I am Freya. I believe you left Obernewtyn a sevenday or so before I arrived." She gave me a slow, sweet smile that lit serene, gray eyes and I realized I had been wrong. She was not plain at all.

"Greetings," I said faintly.

The enormous, soft-spoken coercer, Hannay, was helping Kella to slice cheese and bread. "Greetings guildmistress," he rumbled, and went on slicing. I would definitely have chosen him, I thought. As much because of his deep patience as for his utter reliability. And Miryum, because of her coercive powers. But the rest?

Beside him was the teknoguilder, Fian. "Kella told us about Matthew. I am sorry," he said gently, and his highland accent hurt because it reminded me vividly of the farseeker ward.

"And Dragon," Miky murmured, her face falling. "It's so awful. Poor little Dragon. If only Maryon would have let the others come and get her."

I stared at the empath. "What do you mean, if Maryon had let the others come?"

"She foresaw Dragon following you," Rushton said briskly. "We wanted to come after you to get her—you had only been gone a few hours. But Maryon said you needed to have her with you. That it was necessary." His eyes met my growing horror and fury with bleak resignation. I remembered the words he had just said to me: *"It is a little late to be deciding now that we will not live our lives by the whimsical wisdoms of futuretellers, don't you think?"*

I shook my head, anger making my eyes burn and my head hurt. Did we have no will to exert? No choice? I remembered with a kind of sickness, that it was Maryon's futuretelling which had sent Jik with me to the lowlands, and to his death. "Did she dream of Dragon falling into a coma as well, when she stopped you bringing her back?" I snarled.

"Maryon foresaw Dragon following you, Elspeth," Rushton said wearily. "But Dragon chose to come after you of her own will. You cannot have it both ways. If you will not accept Maryon's futuretelling that saw the need for Dragon with you, then you must also erase that which saw her come after you."

I knew what he was telling me, but I didn't care about logic. If Maryon saw me walking off a cliff in time to stop it, would you not try to prevent my death? I wanted to scream at him. Might there not be moments when a futuretelling was shown as a warning? Would so much have been altered had Maryon defied her vision? What difference would it make if Dragon had not come to Sutrium, other than that she might not now be comatose?

A great deal, I realized with a queer chill. Matthew would not have rushed off in guilt to be taken by slavers, and I, having rescued Dragon from the Herders, would not have then run headlong into Swallow....

I might just as well ask how many ripples a single fallen leaf would cause in a stream, and how far might they spread.

"Dragon's not dead. She's just asleep," Angina said softly, his empath Talent swirling out to enfold me in hope and compassion.

I sat down. "I know...I know. I'm sorry."

There was a moment of silence and then the others began to talk, filling the void with words to give me time to recover myself.

"It was awful on the road, Elspeth," Miky murmured presently. "We were searched at the gate and then when they started to check our papers against a birth register I near died."

"Miryum and Hannay had to coerce us through," Angina said eagerly, taking up his sister's lead, his face a masculine echo of hers. "Even so we were lucky because the second gate guard had a natural shield. Luckily he wasn't the one checking."

"I can't believe we're really here in Sutrium!" Miky said. "When Rushton came to firstmeal an' told us that Maryon had futuretold another expedition to follow you here, we never guessed for a minute we'd be on it."

Angina took up the story without missing a beat. "We thought there would be a guildmerge and a voting, but Rushton said Maryon already knew who was to come."

Why these Misfits, Maryon? I wondered, with sudden suspicion. What are you up to now?

"She said it was vital for Obernewtyn," Miky went on.

Doesn't she always? I thought bitterly. But why choose Miky, who had great empathic Talent but no secondary ability and no physical strength; and Rushton who could not reach his powers, or this Freya who, no matter what her Talent, was a newcomer to Obernewtyn?

"She would nowt say more'n that," Fian spoke with all the disgruntlement of a thwarted teknoguilder, interrupting the dual flow of the twins' story.

"She didn't *know* any more that that," Miky said quickly.

"But Elspeth knows," Angina chimed.

The others looked at me expectantly, but I realized I did not know why they had come. Not them in particular. And there were only seven of them, yet ten were to go to Sador and take part in the Battlegames. I would fill the eighth place, of course, but there were two more places to be filled. Was Domick to come? But he had to stay at the Councilcourt. And Kella could not come, because she must stay to care for Dragon.

Then all at once, it occurred to me there might be more of them. There must be.

"Who else came?" I asked sharply with a shimmer of uneasy premonition.

Rushton gave me a queer, lopsided smile, anticipating my reaction.

"One other. Dameon."

I stared at him incredulously. Maryon had sent *Dameon*, the blind empath guildmaster, to do battle with Malik and the rebels for Obernewtyn!

XXXIV

Dameon was sitting by Dragon's bed, holding her hand. She was oblivious of his presence, though some foolish bit of me had hoped he might have reached her. But no, she was locked in a sleep that must be close to the equine's longsleep, suspended in some netherworld between life and death.

I could have wept for the sadness in his face and the bowed shape of his shoulders. I felt a rush of love at the sight of him that was nearly painful.

Of course, he sensed the surge of emotions that I could not shield quickly enough. I saw it in his sudden stillness.

"Elspeth," he murmured in his well loved voice.

Only then did he turn his face to me, the white-blind eyes gleaming in the light of a single candle guttering low in a wall sconce behind me.

"I could bear everything, if only she would wake," I murmured, coming to stand beside him.

He rose to meet me, letting go of Dragon's fingers to take mine.

"She will wake," he said. His words were a promise, but how could he know? He was no futureteller.

"Oh, Dameon," I sighed.

"There was a Beforetime story in one of the books you brought back from the underground library that told the tale of a sleeping princess," he said, drawing me to sit by him.

"A story," I said flatly.

He smiled and the compassion in his expression was like a slap, for what right did I have to expect him to comfort me? Had he not known Matthew longer?

"The story tells of a beautiful princess who may or may not have had red hair, and who, cursed, pricked her hand on a poisoned needle,"

Dameon went on. "She fell into an enchanted sleep from which none could waken her."

I looked down at Dragon, and shivered.

"She slept long, until a prince came who was her truest love, and the enchantment between them allowed him to break the spell."

"How?" I breathed, drawn into the story in spite of myself. "What did he do to waken her?"

"He woke her..." Dameon stopped in front of the bed, and took Dragon's pale hand again and lifted it to his lips, "...with a kiss."

Someone laughed. A nervous little gust of air that told me Kella had followed me, but I could only think of Matthew—the only love Dragon had ever known, and an unwilling one at that. Would that love ever return to kiss her awake?

"It is a...lovely story," I said huskily.

Dameon nodded. "It is. Miky and Angina have made it into a song, and they will sing it to you."

"Dameon..."

He shook his head and gathered me into his long arms. "I know."

He patted my back as if I were a very young child or a frightened animal, his empathic Talent wrapping me in a warm blanket of affection and reassurance. I was dimly surprised to find he had erected an empathic barrier between us. He must have sensed I would not want my emotions bared to him.

"Matthew has been taken," he said gently. "But no slaver or shackle will hold him for long. He will return, just as he swore he would. As full of gossip and wild stories as ever."

Listening to his soft accents, I felt for the first time that it might truly be so.

"Well, this is touching," Rushton said from the door. "When you have finished the tender reconciliations, perhaps you will spare us a moment."

∽

Sitting in the kitchen with the rain pattering against night-dark windows, Rushton told me for the first time what Maryon had futuretold.

"She said she saw eight of us journeying to Sutrium, and your face,

Elspeth, at the end of the journey. There was more—something about thirteen going over water." He hesitated and I sensed there was something here he had kept back. "She did not know what the futuretelling meant, but she said *you* would. She said it had something to do with Obernewtyn and figuring out what to do next." He frowned, as if this was not exactly right. "Something about finding the right road to tread."

He made a gesture indicating that I was to go on from there, and so I did. It took a long time to tell everything that had happened since I came to Sutrium, even with some small deletions. Last of all I described the meeting with the rebels.

"I do not understand why this Jakoby woman would make such an offer," Miryum said suspiciously when I had finished. "What does she get out of helping us?"

"She wouldn't see it as helping us or the rebels," I said. "There was a problem and she just offered a Sadorian solution. Sadorians are . . . are not like Landfolk, and I don't think you can judge them by our values. But honor is very important to them so I don't think they would cheat or lie."

"Are you so sure this woman's offer of the Battlegames is what Maryon's futuretelling concerned?" Dameon asked softly. "She said nothing about battles."

"It would be too much of a coincidence for it not to mean Sador," Hannay said. "Where else would we go on a journey over water? Across the Suggredoon? Maryon said Elspeth would know, and she knows about the trip to Sador and the Battlegames."

"Could it have meant something about rescuing the Farseeker ward?" Freya asked. "He has been taken over water, after all."

"Where would we search for him, and how?" Rushton asked. He shook his head regretfully. "I wish we were going to find Matthew, but my instincts say the journey foreseen by Maryon is the one offered by this Jakoby. It fits too neatly. Why else would so many of us come, if not to take part in these Battlegames and win the alliance we need?"

"But there are not enough anyway," Miky burst out. "There are only eight of us, nine counting Elspeth, and Maryon said thirteen of us would go over the water."

Rushton frowned. "Ten if we count Kella, and Dragon would make eleven—we couldn't leave her here after all. And twelve counting Domick."

"Oh," Kella said, paling a little. "Domick can't come. He was here this afternoon before you. He and two others have been sent to Morganna with some Councilmen. He won't be back for ages." Her face was serene but her eyes slanted away, full of pain. "I . . . I told him you wanted me to come back to Obernewtyn. He . . . he said he thought I should go. He left a report for . . . for guildmerge."

I did not know what to say to stop her pain, so I said nothing. The others saw the healer's anguish without understanding it.

"What about the fact that Brydda thinks it a bad idea for us to go?" Miryum said, still surprisingly opposed to the idea of going to Sador. "We should consider what that means."

"Its meaning is clear enough. He wants to discourage us because he thinks we will lose," Hannay said.

"We need this alliance," Rushton said, looking at Miryum with some puzzlement, as surprised as I that opposition should come from this quarter.

"It is possible this battle will not happen. Perhaps we must go to Sador for some other reason that has yet to be revealed." Dameon said slowly. "Maybe we will have the chance of proving to this Malik and the other rebels that we are human."

I hesitated, then shook my head, for there was no point in letting anyone have false hope.

"Why didn't you coerce him into agreeing to the alliance?" Miryum demanded.

"That is what Domick would advocate. But don't you see? We can't make them think as we wish. Not if we are to be allies. That would make us as bad as the Council. Maybe even worse."

There was a silence. A log in the fire cracked loudly, making those nearest the hearth jump.

"But would we not be using coercion against them in this competition?" Freya asked in her velvety voice.

I nodded. "But they would know what to expect, and no one will die because of what we do. They will use their skills against us without a qualm and we shall use ours."

"A sophistry," Freya said.

"Maybe, but it's a difference that makes sense to me," I snapped.

"There is no point in us going into these Battlegames imagining we can all be friends afterward. We will never be accepted by the rebels. We have to show the Maliks of the Land that we can defend ourselves from them!"

"A show of strength," Miryum said approvingly.

"If you like. Or maybe just revealing ourselves for what we are."

"And what are we?" Dameon asked, his voice threaded with sadness. "Warriors? Misfits? That is part of our trouble. We do not know what we are, and so we are constantly reacting to things, rather than taking the initiative."

"Maryon said we would find the road to tread on this journey over water," Rushton said pensively. "We have to see what happens. It might be, as Dameon said, that we will not fight these Battlegames, but we must go prepared to do so, just in case." He sighed. "Lud knows, I would not have chosen this way to force the rebels to take us seriously, but is it so bad? A contest of skills to show what we can do? Better, surely, than real battle?"

Kella shook her head.

"There is another thing you should know," I said, remembering. "After the contest, the rebels plan to meet and to decide once and for all when and how the rebellion will be staged."

Rushton's eyes flared with an unholy green fire. "Well, that puts it in a very different light. By winning, we would have gained the right to take part in their councils."

"And, of course, we will win," Miryum said, seeming to have forgotten her reservations.

"What are the games anyway?" Angina asked. "How do we play them?"

I had to admit that I did not know anymore than I had told them.

"Ritual battles this Jakoby called them," Fian mused. "It doesna' sound so bad."

"Thirteen to travel but only ten contestants," Milky said pensively. "Which ten? Dragon cannot fight, nor surely Dameon. Angina and I have never fought in our lives. I . . . am not sure I could."

"If Maryon sent us, there must be some reason for it," Rushton said stoutly. "As to battles . . . well, we must make do with those of us who can fight if it comes to it."

"I do not think we need be frightened of ten unTalents," Miryum said complacently. "Hannay, Elspeth and I can deal with them between us."

∽

It was late the following day before we stood on the deck of a ship bound for Sador.

Contrary to Maryon's futuretelling of thirteen, there were only eleven of us, counting Dragon. We could not leave without her and Kella had assured us that the journey would not hurt her.

Reuvan, calling to drop off a homing bird at Brydda's instructions, had learned we meant to travel to Sador at once. Advising that we leave it to him to organize a ship, he arranged passage for all of us with a seafaring friend and long-time secret rebel supporter.

Powyrs turned out to be a jolly, bold, brown-faced man with twinkling eyes, and a habit of winking that startled us somewhat until we were accustomed to it. He had no qualms about carrying gypsies. I had the feeling he would not have given a damn if we told him we were Misfits.

I was standing on the deck of Powyrs' sturdy little ship, *The Cutter*, waiting for the Council inspectors to come and give final clearance for us to sail, when Kella pinched my arm to get my attention. Leaning close, she whispered into my ear in an absurdly furtive way that Reuvan was coming. I was not surprised that he had come to see us off, but I was startled to see that Dardelan was with him, as well as a long-limbed, exotic girl with yellow almond-shaped eyes and a satiric smile. She could only be Jakoby's daughter. If anything, she was more beautiful than her mother, but even from a distance I could see that she lacked the older woman's powerful aura of authority.

"You are the first to leave but the rest of us will not be far behind," Reuvan said easily, as they came up to us. "Malik and his cronies are traveling tomorrow, and I will travel with Jakoby and the rest on the *Zephyr* the next day."

"Am I to be presented, or shall I stand like a nameless dolt?" the dark Sadorian girl asked haughtily.

Dardelan flushed and apologized. "This is Jakoby's daughter. Bruna, this is Elspeth."

"I am pleased to know you," I said.

"Ah. I-am-pleased-to-know-you," Bruna said, exactly mimicking my intonation.

Unnerved a little by this and by her frank scrutiny, I busied myself, introducing the others. When Dardelan and Rushton shook hands, they exchanged a measuring look and seemed satisfied by what they saw.

"You will like my land, of course," Bruna said haughtily. "*Your* people are welcome there, for like the tribes they have no need to mark the ground where they have been, like a rutting beast marking its territory. Unlike these Landfolk." Her eyes ran over our halfbreed gypsy attire approvingly, but she gave poor Dardelan a look of amused contempt.

"In Sador, there is room to run with the wind and ride the kamuli," she went on, seeming to address all of us now. Wearing little, despite the gray, chilly weather, she was as oblivious of the cold as she was to the stares of passers-by at her outlandish garments. No wonder Jakoby had looked amused when she said Sadorian women needed scant looking after.

The girl waved an imperious finger under Dardelan's nose. "And now, you will guide me to the place of many trees. The for-rest. These I do not see in my own desert and there might be some beauty in them worthy of a song."

"Of . . . of course," Dardelan stammered, and she bore him away.

"A pup watching over a bear," Reuvan said.

"A bear cub," I corrected, thinking for all her imperiousness, Bruna lacked her mother's subtlety and dangerous grace.

It began to rain lightly, as the inspectors arrived and set about searching the ship from top to bottom, seeking Landgoods which were being exported without tax being paid to the Council. When Powyrs suggested we go inside, I was glad enough to do so. The fishy smell of the ship's oiled deck and the movement of it running up and down the swelling waves were making me feel distinctly queasy.

"I will want to cast off as soon as this is over to catch the out tides. Go into the main salon," Powyrs said. He looked at Reuvan. "I will come there and warn you before we are to depart."

As we trooped along the deck, I could not help but think of Matthew, being led onto *The Calor Lady*'s gangplank in chains. Had he felt this strange, unsettling nausea? Was he somewhere out over the ocean being rained on too?

I glanced back and noticed an old beggar in filthy brown robes come up to Powyrs and speak with him. At first the seaman shook his head decisively, but then he stopped and seemed to be listening intently. I was curious enough to farseek but the queer static from whatever had tainted the sea about Sutrium's shores prevented this.

"Come on," Miky said, tugging at me.

The salon turned out to be spacious and light, despite dark wood panelling on the walls and roof, and floor-to-ceiling bookshelves. This was due to three enormous box windows along the outside wall, criss-crossed by wide-spaced metal grilles. Cushioned seats were built into the windows. Elsewhere, a table, chairs and various other pieces of furniture were fixed to the floor. The galley was adjoining this room and Kella's eyes lit up as she surveyed its miniature neatness.

Rushton dropped into a window seat and gestured to Reuvan, Miryum and Hannay to sit beside him. They talked in low serious voices while Angina and his twin began to tune their instruments. Kella came out of the galley and stood at a window. Her eyes looked out to sea, but I was sure she was seeing nothing but the face of her bondmate.

Powyrs had taken Dameon below to a cabin with Dragon. I moved to the door with the thought of going to sit with him, but Powyrs returned blocking my way.

"Casting off!" he warned in a stentorian bellow. "All who will not sail should get ashore."

Reuvan rose. "I'd better move. A seaman is ruled by the tides, and if catching the tide means an unwilling passenger or two, then so be it."

The ship lurched suddenly and all of us pitched sideways, save Reuvan, who was accustomed to walking on a shifting deck.

He smiled, somewhat wistfully. "You must learn to dance with the sea—not tread on her toes. I must go or I will be traveling to Sador with you!"

We went out on deck to farewell him. The rain had ceased and the clouds had parted to reveal the sun sinking toward the horizon.

As the ropes were cast away by Powyrs' crew and the shore began to slip away, a curious but definite feeling of loss assailed me; a feeling that I had somehow cast off from my life and was sailing toward a new one.

From the looks on the faces gathered along the edge of the deck, I was not alone. The others gazed back to the shore, their faces reflecting their unease. This was the first time any of us had left the Land. There were numerous disaster stories Landfolk told about the perils of the seas and suddenly the wildest tales seemed to gain substance.

The sun sank into the sea, becoming increasingly large and orange as it did so, staining the gray-edged clouds that framed it a livid pink. I was intrigued to feel the taint in the water fading. That meant whatever had caused it was confined to the shore area. Perhaps some Beforetime container had broken under the sea, spilling its poisons.

"That's that then," Kella said huskily, when the sun finally vanished, and Sutrium fell into purple haze that merged it with the horizon. "I feel as if I'm leaving a part of myself here."

I forebore to point out the obvious.

"To Sador," Miky sighed dreamily on the other side of me.

"I feel sick," Miryum said, and I was startled to see that she looked bright green about the face and lips.

"I do not feel so well myself," I murmured.

XXXV

Kella set about adjusting our senses to the movement of The Cutter, *but some* of us responded better to her treatment than others.

The empaths were only mildly affected by the motion of the waves and were quickly eased. I was less fortunate.

Because of the instinctive blocking ability my mind appeared to have developed as a response to intrusion, I had to hold it open to the healer. This was not easy and, when she was done, the wooden decks continued to pitch, rendering me queasy and disorientated.

Disappointed, I had asked Powyrs if there was not some seaman's remedy that would settle my stomach.

He had looked at me intently for a moment, then shaken his head. "Your illness is not physical. It is a matter of the will. You resist the ocean as if it were an opponent. You cannot defeat the sea—it is too great and too uncaring. You can only surrender to its power. While you fight, you will suffer."

I had laughed and said he talked as if the sea were alive.

He had shrugged. "Laugh, but it is true. All things that exist live, though maybe they do not measure life as we do."

I thought this absurd. The fish in the sea lived, but not the sea itself. It was just water. But seafolk were as notoriously superstitious as high-landers and I liked Powyrs too much to make fun of his beliefs.

The coercers suffered worst of us. That was not unexpected, for coercers were always disturbed by anything that altered their balance or perceptions. Roland believed this had something to do with the nature of coercing and how the deepprobe was shaped to serve their Talent. The more powerful the coercer, the more severe the response. Accordingly,

Hannay was nauseous, but Miryum violently ill. All Kella could do was to render her unconscious with a sleepseal.

Like me, Hannay resigned himself to an uncomfortable few days.

Powyrs showed us the empty chambers and we chose our beds before making our way back to the main salon. I offered to sleep in a room with Dragon, but Dameon said he would stay with her.

"There is no real need," Kella said. "She has no knowledge of the world around her, so she will not care that she is alone."

"I do not like to think of her laid out as if she were dead," Dameon answered gently. "Better to act as if she might wake at any moment and want something. Besides my blindness makes it hard for me to walk about at sea, so I might just as well remain here."

He went on to suggest that Miryum be laid to sleep in the same chamber so he could keep an eye—he smiled as he said this—on her as well.

When the hefty coercer had been shifted, we left Dameon and went to the salon where Hannay and the twins had prepared a simple nightmeal. Freya and Rushton were absent, and Fian was reading.

My stomach churned at the thought of food and I sat a little apart. The others ate a mushroom stew and regaled Kella with news from Obernewtyn.

The horses had finally decided to teach a few humans to ride—surprisingly, some chosen were not beastspeakers. Use of Brydda's finger signals enabled non-beastspeakers to commune with their mounts. Miky was elated because Avra had chosen her, though the account of her first lessons made it sound as if this was a dubious privilege.

I listened with only half an ear to their chatter. There had been some attempt to put Aras' new mindmerge into practice, as yet with no success. A skirmish had taken place between Darthnor miners and some of the coercers. Fortunately the miners had believed them to be Henry Druid's people, for it was not widely known that his camp had been destroyed, but this had also increased the likelihood of a soldierguard outpost being established in the White Valley. There was now little doubt that it would be set up in the next summerdays. More animals had come to the mountains seeking refuge.

This last bit of news made me think of the sad-faced little mare,

Faraf, who had claimed me for the beastheart. Could she have been among the recent refugees? I hoped so.

Turning away from the room, I looked through the reflection of the room and its ghostly occupants to the dark sea beyond. It was a clouded night, but a brisk wind stirred the clouds and, when they parted, moonlight gilded the waves and the occasional rock shoal that rose above the water-line. In rough seasons, the shoals would be hidden beneath the chop of the wave but Reuvan had told me there were seldom high seas during the Days of Rain.

"If it were wintertime you would have cause to fear, for sometimes the waves rise up from the ocean like mountains, and when they fall an entire ship can be crushed." He had meant to reassure me but I could not help wondering if this might not turn out to be one of the rare occasions when high seas would occur during this season?

I shook my head at the sudden melancholy that had assailed me. I had been utterly relieved to find there was no need for a mad dash to Obernewtyn; no need to turn myself inside out convincing Rushton and guildmerge to take part in the Battlegames. So why did I feel so unsettled? The sorrow I felt at Matthew's loss, and the fact that no amount of searching had located Maruman were part of it, but it was more than that.

Perhaps it was that I had grown accustomed, these last sevendays, to strife and activity and urgency. Sea travel was not like travel on land where there were always things to be done, if only to break camp and set up bedding at night. We journeyed, and yet we went nowhere.

I sighed, wishing it was not my nature to see life as if it were the reflection in a window. I could never just accept it. I had to be squinting my eyes and looking to see what was underneath it; tormenting myself with doubts and questions. And it was worse when I had nothing to distract me.

The moon penetrated the clouds for a moment, lighting up a small cluster of rock spikes. Powyrs had said these were good shoals because you could see them. But there were many more such shoals hiding just below the surface that could tear the bottom from a boat if the seamen were not vigilant. The ocean's teeth, he had named them, winking.

I was like a wary seafarer, never trusting the smooth, glimmering surface of life, for fear of the teeth hidden. Perhaps that was why I could not settle as the others had, and enjoy the enforced idleness. Even when there was no need, I watched for the teeth.

I scowled at my own face in the glass, telling myself again that I should be content. After all, Maryon's dream had solved my immediate problems.

I bit my lip, understanding that this was what lay at the root of my strange discontent. I had left Obernewtyn driven by Maryon's dreams. But once away, I had done as I chose. I made decisions and acted on them, and felt as if I owned my life. Now Maryon and her dreams had reached out to wrest control from me again. I was not the wary seaman after all. I was a ship, floating on the tides and eddies of capricious fate just as *The Cutter* was driven by the sea. But at least *it* had a captain. Who was the captain of my voyage? Atthis? Maryon? Certainly not me.

I thought of the futureteller. How did Maryon feel to know that she had only to speak of her dreams to be obeyed? It was true power. But Maryon did not control her dreams so, in a sense, the power was not hers. The dreams controlled her, pulling this way and that, demanding to be told, or acted upon. Was the self-knowledge she and all her fellow future-tellers sought worth this slavery to their dreams?

The salon door banged open and I turned to see Rushton enter.

Of us all, Rushton's body had adapted most easily to the movement of the ship. From almost his first steps on deck he had mastered the graceful rolling walk affected by Powyrs and his crew. His cheeks were red, his hair wildly tangled and his eyes bright as they swept the room. He was clearly finding his first sea journey exhilarating.

"I am ravenous," he said.

The door behind him burst open again to reveal the old beggarman who had been speaking to Powyrs at the bottom of the gangplank just before we departed.

"You can't come in here," Hannay began firmly.

The beggar threw off the hood of his brown robe to reveal a familiar tanned face in the dim candlelight.

"Daffyd!" I murmured. There were cries, as the others recognized him too.

He ignored them, eyes sweeping the room to settle on me.

I gasped, for only when he faced me properly could I see that his left eye socket was swollen to twice its size, his lip split, and bloody striations marked his cheek.

"What in Lud's name has happened to you?"

"I escaped from Ayle," he said hoarsely.

"Sit down, man," Rushton said, steering him to a window seat beside me.

"He found you out?" I asked, thinking his disappointment over failing to get to Salamander had made him reckless, and he had tried to farseek Ayle. But I was wrong.

"Ayle found nothing out. Salamander told him I was a spy."

I was confused. "He can't have returned already?" My heart rose. "Unless the slaves have only been taken to Morganna or Aborium. . . ."

Daffyd shook his head. "Salamander told Ayle, the day he came to take the slaves, that I was to be locked up until he got back." He shuddered. "Lud knows how he learned I was a spy, or what he planned to do to me when he returned. As soon as I got a chance, I broke out and fought my way free. I headed straight for the city gates, but Ayle was quicker. I spotted his people just in time. I would never have made it, and I knew if they were watching one gate, they would be watching them all."

"You went to the safe house?"

He nodded. "It was all locked up. I had no choice but to try sending out an attuned probe to you. It near killed me to hold it together when it got near the sea, but it locked onto your mind a split second before the static got the better of me. That was long enough for me to learn that you were sailing at dusk for Sador. I told your captain that I was a friend, and gave him a bit of a push with my mind to get him to take me on board. I hope you do not object to another traveling companion."

"We are glad to have you," Rushton said, but he spoke as if his mind was elsewhere.

"That's twelve of us," Miky breathed beside me.

"Elspeth believes she saw Ariel on board the Herder ship that took Matthew away," Rushton said. "Did you see him?"

Though I would not have thought it possible, Daffyd paled further. He turned to me. "Are you sure?"

"I thought I was, but I might have been mistaken."

"It seems unlikely since there is no connection between Ariel and this Salamander. . . ." Rushton said.

Daffyd stood up abruptly and stared down at him. "You are wrong." His face was clenched in misery, and he began to pace back and forward. "I said at the safe house that there was not enough time to tell my story. Now, I wish I had taken the time."

"It would be a simple matter if lives were lived by hindsight," Rushton said. "There is much we would not begin, if we could see how it would end."

Daffyd would not be consoled. "Matthew was my friend and I ought to have done something. If Ariel *was* aboard...."

"From what Elspeth said there was nothing you could have done," Rushton said firmly. He pulled Daffyd back down and motioned to Kella to wash his wounds. When the healer was settled and bathing the gashes, he asked Daffyd what connection there was between Salamander and Ariel.

"I will tell you," Daffyd said, "but I must start at the beginning. After leaving Obernewtyn with Kella and Domick last summerdays, I traveled to the White Valley and the site of the Druid encampment. My plan was to see if I could find any clue as to what direction the survivors might have taken." His eyes were distant, as if he truly gazed into the past and saw the events he described unscrolling before his eyes.

"I left the valley without any sign to give me hope, and tracked all through and around the Gelfort Ranges. I found some few scattered camping places, but there was never any way of knowing whose they had been. No convenient badges or signals had fallen by the way.

"I went about small settlements in the highlands and in the upper lowlands, talking and asking questions. I sometimes pretended to be a Councilman and at other times a Herder agent.

"Then one night at a dingy inn in a tiny settlement, I came face to face with one of the Druid armsmen from the camp!"

Daffyd's face reflected the elation he must have felt at this first breakthrough in his long search. But the smile faded at once. "He told me that shortly before the firestorm destroyed the camp—mere days—Ariel came to see the Druid."

I seemed to see that pale, impossibly fair face turning to me on the deck of *The Calor Lady*.

"As you know," Daffyd went on, "Ariel was working as an agent for the Herder Faction back then, and for the Council, while at the same time styling himself a secret friend to Henry Druid. On this last visit he told the Druid that the Council had learned the location of his secret camp, and that soldierguards were being despatched to clean it out. He advised the Druid to prepare his people for battle, and suggested sending the young, the frail and the elderly out of harm's way up into the foothills of the Gelfort Ranges. Ariel claimed he dared not remain to help drive off the soldierguards, since it would betray his identity and put an end to his usefulness as a spy. But he offered to lead those who would not fight to a safe place in the hills until it was over."

Daffyd's face twisted in a spasm of uncontrollable rage. "The Druid thanked him for his friendship and loyalty, and did as he suggested.

"When he had gone, Henry Druid decided on the spur of the moment to send out a small advance party to give warning of the soldierguards' approach. The three scouts rode out a bare hour before the firestorm razed the camp to the ground—the man who told this story to me was, of course, one of the three. He and the other two came back when it was over, to find nothing remained of their camp. They looked for Ariel and the women and children who had been led away, but there was no trace of them.

"Nor in the days that followed, did any soldierguard force materialize."

It took a moment to understand what this must mean.

"Ariel lied!" I said incredulously.

Daffyd nodded, his eyes bleak. "What other answer could there be? I suppose he true dreamed the firestorm and saw it as a natural and anonymous way to end a potentially embarrassing and no longer necessary connection with an outlawed priest. The visit was simply to ensure that everyone was *in* the camp when it burned." His voice was choked with rage and despair.

I saw that Rushton had grown pale. At first I thought he was experiencing the same shock as I, at this irrefutable evidence that Ariel had powers like ours, but then I remembered that, long ago, the Druid had befriended Rushton and treated him as a son. He had not seemed terribly affected when the firestorm destroyed the camp, but there was a difference between being killed in a firestorm from nature's random arsenal and being lured into a deadly trap. Ariel had even found a way to use nature for his perverted ends.

"What of the women and children he led out?" Kella murmured.

I could guess what was to be told next—the answer was threaded through all that had happened.

"When the three surviving armsmen could not find them they split up. Two went up the coast following some obscure lead. The third man remained, and it was he that I met. For a time we traveled together, but we found nothing to give us any clue what had become of the others. He began to fear they had all been killed and that taking them from the camp had simply been Ariel's means of getting out before the firestorm struck. A ruse, and that he had killed them after. But I could not accept they were dead. So we parted, too. Gilbert went after the other two armsmen to the west coast and I..."

"Gilbert?" I said, remembering vividly the red-haired armsman who had befriended me when I was captive in the Druid camp.

First Daffyd, then Elii, and now Gilbert. Who else would I meet out of the past, circling back to merge their lifepaths with mine? Did it mean anything or nothing?

Daffyd frowned. "You remember him? Strange that you should recall one face out of all the Druid's men. He spoke of you, but thought you were dead. Of course I did not enlighten him."

I nodded. The last time I had seen Gilbert had been on the banks of the upper Suggredoon, a look of helpless anguish on his face as my raft was swept away by flood-swollen waters into the depths of Tor. He had thought me doomed.

The armsman went on. "Well, we parted as I said. I came to Sutrium and it was here that I met another from the Druid camp; a woman. She was calling herself by another name and tried at first to pretend I was mistaken, but eventually she admitted the truth. She told me she had been a slave fleetingly, but had escaped being transported and sold with the help of a seaman who had fallen in love with her. He threw her clothes over-board and pretended she drowned herself, but warned her never to speak of it, for if the truth was known they would both be killed.

"I asked how she had been taken by the slavers in the first place. 'Taken?' she mocked me. 'I was given to the slavers. Betrayed and sold with no chance to run or fight. My bondmate saved me, but he could not save all of us. The others have gone over the waves wherever slaves are taken.'"

Kella gasped aloud. "Oh Lud. Ariel sold those he had taken from the camp to the slavers!"

Daffyd nodded. "I was a fool not to have seen it sooner. The woman told me they saw the camp burn and could do nothing. There had been men and women, hired thugs, waiting in the hills to bind them and lead them away. Ariel had sold them to a slaver called Salamander."

Daffyd ran his hands through his hair. "You know, the thing that gnaws at me is that I can have been only a little distance from their camp the day they were taken out of the mountains by the slavers. If only I had thought to farseek Gilaine as soon as the storm ended."

There was such anguish in his voice. That he had not gone looking for them at once was my fault. I had been injured terribly, and we had just found Jik's charred body. I had begged Daffyd to take Dragon to Obernewtyn for me before the pass to the mountains was closed by snow.

"I felt...helpless. Hopeless," he went on in a barely audible voice. "It had been months since they had been sold and they were long gone on the slave ships. For the first time I felt they were truly lost to me. I wanted revenge on Ariel. You cannot imagine how badly. But he had gone by then to Herder Isle.

"So I turned my mind to the slave trade with the idea that perhaps I could inveigle myself a job, and learn where they had been taken. It is madness of a kind to be so persistent, yet somehow I felt that if they lived, I must find them."

The ex-Druid's eyes burned with near-fanatical hatred; the search for Gilaine and Lidgebaby defined his existence now. Truly, he was not so far from madness.

"I suppose this woman from the camp did not actually see Salamander?" Hannay asked.

Daffyd laughed harshly. "No. No one has ever seen Salamander's face—except perhaps Ariel. It was only after the sale of the Druid's people that Salamander moved in properly on the slave trade, killing anyone who stood against him, terrorizing the rest, and streamlining the operation into one smooth, efficient monopoly. I thought Ariel's connection with him was a passing thing, but if he was aboard the ship with him, perhaps there is more to it."

"I wonder what Ariel got out of the bargain. Coin?" Rushton murmured. "He would not aid the slaver for nothing."

Daffyd's expression hardened. "Perhaps. They are as like to one another as two buds from the same plant. Both are secretive. Both love pain and desire power."

The desperation returned to his face.

I laid a hand on his arm. "What will you do now?"

"Survive," he said harshly. "If Salamander wants me dead, I will live to spite him. He will have the city scoured for me when he returns and it pleases me to think that he will be thwarted. We will have our day of reckoning. And when I am done with the slavemaster, I will find Ariel."

XXXVI

It *did not take much persuasion for Daffyd to let himself be shown to a bed.* He was clearly exhausted far beyond his endurance.

It was late but his words had given us much to consider, and the rest of us sat up talking and trying to understand what Ariel could have to do with Salamander. It was grim talk, and unsatisfying, for nothing could be resolved by it. Though no one said it out loud, we all thought Daffyd's search for Gilaine hopeless.

At last Rushton rose and stretched, saying his bed was yearning for him. Hannay got up to help the twins clear away the remnants of our meal, then all three retired. Kella went to see if Dameon wanted anything before going to her own bed.

Only Fian and I remained in the ship's salon. I felt too nauseous to sleep, and the teknoguilder was so engrossed in his studies that he had not even looked up when the others went out.

I watched him for a while, half wishing I could lose myself in books as he did. Truly it was a gift. Like the empaths he had been only slightly affected by sea, but he had refused treatment for fear it might take the edge from his thoughts.

I decided to go out on deck. Perhaps some fresh air would make me feel better.

The wind had risen and it fluttered my clothing, and snapped the sailcloth. The sea was higher too and slapped against the wooden hull in a broken rhythm. I shivered and pulled my cloak about me, trying to imagine what it would be like to do as Powyrs suggested, and give myself to the sea.

"Wet, doubtless," a voice clove into my thoughts.

I started violently for draped languidly on a mast strut right in front of me, licking one paw fastidiously, was Maruman!

"How in Lud's name did you manage to get aboard?" I demanded. "And where have you been?"

For once my questions did not rouse his ire. He stretched with slow and infuriating feline grace and jumped lightly to the deck to rub against my leg.

"There you are!" Powyrs bellowed and swooped over to scoop him up.

I froze but, instead of scratching the seaman, the bedraggled feline lay quiescent in his arms, an alarming mixture of complacence and thwarted mischief in his single gleaming eye.

"I wondered where he had been hiding," Powyrs said, pretending severity. He looked at me and winked hugely. "The fools I have working for me think he is a bad omen, but he is too smart for them to catch and throw over the edge as they would like. He torments them, the naughty thing. Darting out and scaring them. Twice he has made seamen fall overboard." He beamed at Maruman with paternal pride and I could barely stop myself laughing aloud.

I stood up and reached out to pat him. Powyrs' muscles tightened as mine had done moments before, but he relaxed as the cat allowed himself to be petted.

"Well, you are honored. Usually he will suffer no one to touch him but me," he said, sounding astonished.

"He is magnificent," I said, repressing a grin at how utterly Maruman had beguiled the burly seaman.

"Of course," Maruman sent haughtily.

"He can be savage," Powyrs warned. "You'd best leave him be, except when I'm holding him. He's used to me. Reminds me of the sea he does. My father said to me when he advised me against being a seaman: The sea is a wild beast that eats the lives of those who would try to tame it."

"You didn't listen then?" I smiled.

He shrugged. "I never liked tamish things, even as a boy. Turned out my father was right about the sea being wild, but he didn't understand that being a seaman isn't about taming the sea and controlling it. You can't *make* it do anything or get mad at it when it doesn't do what you want. It's not like people, acting out of spite or anger or desire. It just is and you have to learn its moods and let them carry you. . . ." He glanced over and noticed one of his seamen mending a sail. Snorting in derision, he set Maruman down gently before stomping over to instruct the seaman on his deficiencies.

"Well, I see *how* you managed to get yourself aboard," I sent grinning at him.

Maruman made no response. He leapt up onto a box beside me and I felt a surge of pure happiness as he climbed onto my arm and clawed his way up to my shoulders to drape himself about my neck. I breathed deeply, taking in the slightly fishy smell of his coarse fur, as if it were the scent of fresh flowers. Oddly, I no longer felt sick.

I yawned and decided I would go to bed. For the first time in many days I felt really content.

"I am glad to see/carry/smell you," I sent, repressing my usual instinct to cuddle him close and tell him I loved him.

"I am glad also," Maruman sent with rare sweetness.

∾

The tiny cabin I had chosen possessed only one bed and was no more than a closet. Its virtues were that it was situated on the main deck, which meant there was no need to grope my way down ladders in the darkness, and I would have some privacy. In a short time I was leaning down to let Maruman jump onto the narrow bed, which was fixed to the wall under a small round window looking out to sea. The moon slid out of its envelope of cloud, and the old cat sniffed suspiciously at the pillow where its silvery light fell. Then he turned to me, his eye seeming to to be filled with moonlight.

I froze in the act of taking off my sandals.

"The oldOne sent ashling to Maruman/yelloweyes. Say come. Maruman coming. Say: tell Innle. Maruman tells," he sent.

"Tell me what?" My heart pounded.

"Maruman flew the dreamtrails with the oldOnes. Saw Innle on blackdeathroad. Going to the endmost means end of barud. Obernewtyn finished and allgone for Innle."

I stared at him. Atthis had sometimes called my quest a black road.

Maruman seemed to be saying that if I completed my quest, Obernewtyn would not be there anymore. But what did that mean? That it would be abandoned? Destroyed? And why would Atthis want him to tell me this now?

I took my sandals off and climbed into the bed, shifting Maruman to make room for myself. Maybe I was misunderstanding him. After all, beastspeaking obeyed no rules. Communications were entirely idiosyncratic, dependent on how much Talent a beast possessed, their mood at the time of communication, their relationship to the human with whom they communed, and, sometimes, even on what was to be told. Beasts interchangeably used their own odd dialect, imagepictures infused with emotions and human words, enhanced by empathized emotions. This was what made beastspeaking such a complex Talent to master. And Maruman was harder than most, because of the distortions of his mind. The question was how his words about the black road and Obernewtyn might be interpreted.

The simplest reading was that if I fulfilled my quest, this would somehow prevent my returning to Obernewtyn.

The Agyllians had warned me that it would draw me away from the Land and all that I had cared about in life. *Help your friends*, Atthis had advised, but she had said nothing about my return to Obernewtyn. I had always assumed that, when my quest was over, my life would be my own, and it disheartened me to think this might not be so.

In that second, I remembered Ariel saying in my dream, "Do what you wish and you do my bidding." Was that my mind's way of warning me that free will was an illusion, and that my life would never be mine to command?

"It would be a little late now to decide that we would not live our lives by the whimsical wisdoms of futuretellers, don't you think?" Rushton had asked the previous day.

And it *was* too late. My sworn quest was the central and defining truth of my life now. Just as Daffyd's long search for Gilaine shaped him, so my quest shaped me. I could no more fight it than fight the wind that rustled the trees. If there was a black road, then I was on it already; had been all the days of my life. And I would walk it to the end—no matter where it led me. Even if it meant I could not go back to Obernewtyn.

Then it came to me. Perhaps Atthis had sent Maruman to test my resolve.

"Rest/sleep," Maruman sent insistently. "All things seem dark under the whiteface." He curled into my chest and slept.

But I could not sleep.

I turned to lie on my stomach, knowing it was not physical weariness that sapped me, so much as an endless draining of my spirit that seemed to have begun with Jik's dreadful death and, perhaps even before that, with the death of my parents and of my brother, Jes. So many, many deaths, and was not Matthew dead to me now in a way?

And, in the end, what did all of those deaths mean?

When I finally did sleep, it was to dream I was clinging to a frail raft on a wild, storm-tossed sea, paddling with leaden arms and legs toward land masses that were always illusions.

I woke at one point to find myself bathed in moonlight, but almost at once fell back into sleep and a new dream. I was on land, walking through country as Ludforsaken and desolate as the drear vista of the Blacklands I had once seen from the top of the high mountains with Gahltha by my side.

The road beneath me was black, and I saw that the darkness of it had climbed into my limbs, staining them a sickly purplish-yellow—the livid shades of advanced rotting sickness that told me the road was poisoning me.

I wondered, then, if Maruman had meant that I would not be able to return to Obernewtyn *because I would be dead*.

"I will pay the price whatever it is," I whispered.

"But what if your life is not the price," a voice whispered back. "What if the life of your friends is the price you must pay. *What if Obernewtyn is the price?*"

I woke to unexpected stillness.

It felt as if the ship were not moving at all and I wondered if at last my senses had realigned to shipboard life. There was a weight against my arm, and I opened my eyes to find Maruman sprawled alongside me, his head resting on my elbow.

I felt a burst of joy at the sight of him, for I had thought it must be a dream that he had come with us on the ship. Then I remembered his cryptic message, and my dream. But in the daylight, they did not seem so terrible.

It was an obscure interpretation of his words to think they had meant

I would not return to Obernewtyn because it had been destroyed. How could disarming the deathmachines cause the destruction of Obernewtyn? Far more likely that Maruman had been instructed to warn me that if I failed, Obernewtyn would be destroyed along with all other life.

I eased myself out from under him and turned on my side to watch him sleep. Poor, dear, muddled Maruman filling me up with his garbled thoughts and gloomy predictions.

I leaned forward and kissed him very softly, knowing he would be furious if he caught me.

Kella poked her head in the door, her face excited.

"Oh good, you're awake, Elspeth. Come and see this."

I put a hasty finger to my lips and pointed to Maruman. The healer's eyes widened at the sight of the cat asleep in the rumpled bedclothes and she backed out of the room. I climbed out of the bed, ran my fingers through my hair and laced on my sandals.

Kella was waiting for me outside. "How in Lud's name did he get here?" she demanded, pointing at the door.

"He must have had a true dream because he knew we were going to come on the ship. He just got aboard and settled himself to wait. He's the mascot old Powyrs was looking for in the salon last night! Maruman's got him twisted around his paw."

Kella's eyes shone. "I'm so glad he's all right. Oh, Elspeth, maybe it's true what Powyrs says about them being good luck. Maybe everything will be well from now on."

I stared at her, baffled. Did she mean Maruman? "Them?" Powyrs had said cats were good luck.

She beckoned, and I followed her to the edge of *The Cutter*. "Look, out there," she said, pointing.

I looked and was startled to see that the ocean was utterly still, stretching away like a mirror on all sides of us. Now I understood why my nausea had abated; why it felt as if we were on land. Not a breath of air stirred the sagging canvas sails or rippled the glass sea. We were so completely becalmed that a reflection of the ship and my face stared back with perfect clarity from the water. There was no sign of the coast, but Powyrs had explained to us the previous night that he would have to set a course directly away from land to begin with, in order to avoid the shoal beds clustered thickly in the sea between the Land and the Sadorian plains.

There were some stone spikes rising up a little distance away and, at first, I thought Kella was pointing to them.

"I don't see how rocks could be good luck," I murmured. "Seems to me, Powyrs sees luck in everything."

"Not the rocks. Beside them."

And then I saw three sleek, satiny silver-gray fish, as big as a grown men, propelling themselves high into the air, somersaulting and plunging back into the water.

I gaped, astounded at their strength and agility.

"Why are they doing that?" I whispered, struck by the queer unreality of being at the side of a ship on an ocean of glass, watching strange giant fish leap out of the water as if they were moon fair acrobats. Truly the sea was another world.

"They have been known to save the lives of humans who fall from deck," Kella murmured, riveted to the antics of the three.

"Good luck for the drowning seaman," Powyrs said, coming up behind me.

"What are they doing?" Kella repeated my question.

Powyrs winked at her. "They are jumping out of the water."

I turned back to watch the three. They must be incredibly strong to lift themselves out of the sea like that. I had never tried to communicate with fish before but some instinct told me these might be capable of beastspeaking. The sea was utterly clear of tainting and I could have tried, yet I found I did not want to, for these lovely creatures were oblivious of the humans watching them, and I was content to have it so. Humans had caused so much sorrow for the beastworld, let these remain untouched.

"They are nowt fish," Fian said, coming to stand beside me.

I jumped, for I had not heard him approach.

"Of course they are," Kella said.

"They are warm blooded an' they suckle their babes on milk after bearin' them whole as humans do. An' they need air." He held up a thick book with a mottled green cover. "This book tells all about them. They are like humans."

"Are they descended from the merpeople?" Kella asked. She had become fascinated with accounts in Beforetime books of a race of humans with gills and fishtails, who had dwelt under the sea.

Fian frowned. "I dinna know. This books says nowt of them, other than that ship fish were sometimes thought to be merpeople. It does say that Beforetimers had boats that would go under water to cities."

"Where the merpeople lived?"

Fian frowned at the healer. "I told ye, it doesn't say. Perhaps this was written after they became extinct. These books say there were ruined cities under th' sea...." His face changed abruptly and he looked across at me. "Which reminds me, Elspeth. You don't know about the city under Tor and the Reichler Clinic, do you?"

I nodded, puzzled by his forgetfulness. "Of course I do. Garth took Rushton and me there, remember, just before I came away to Sutrium? I gather Rushton has told everyone about Hannah Seraphim and Jacob Obernewtyn by now?"

Fian laughed. "It is all anyone has talked about since last guildmerge. You would be surprised what a difference it has made. Everyone feels as if we are carrying on a sacred trust now. The Teknoguild has been over-whelmed by requests for more information about Hannah and Jacob. Garth has had more applications than ever before from Misfits who have made up their minds to become teknoguilders." He looked down at the tome in his hand. "I wish he could be here. You know Powyrs has even more books in a trunk in his room an' he has told me I may look through them."

"So many books," the healer murmured.

"And all about th' sea," Fian said. "Enough for a lifetime's study and I have only a few days." He cast a final long look at the ship fish and turned to hurry back into the salon.

Kella shook her head. "Teknoguilders," she said in faint disgust. "How can he think of books when there is this to see."

But a little later she grew tired of the ship fish antics and went in.

I decided to climb up to the small upper deck, for it would give me a better view of the fish. It was piled with boxes and I sat on top of one, dangling my legs and looking out at the sea. I had never known such stillness. It seemed to accentuate the vastness of the world and, in contrast, my own insignificance, but it was not an unpleasant feeling.

What had Powyrs said? "You can't fight the sea. It's too big.... It doesn't care...."

I began to have some inkling of what he meant. In the face of this endless sea I was no more than one of the ship fish, jumping in my bit of

the ocean, making my little waves. There was a queer peace to be found
in the thought and I tried to draw the immense calmness into my heart,
to erase fear and anger and sadness.

My concentration was shattered by a muffled explosion of laughter.

"It tickles," I heard a female voice giggle. I recognized Freya's me-
lodic voice and smiled, wondering who she was with.

A moment later I saw Rushton stroll to the rail, and my amusement
evaporated.

Even as I watched, Freya stepped up beside him and shook her head,
the springing golden curls catching and diffusing the morning sunlight into
a pale halo. They had their backs to me, but I could see Rushton lean
toward her to say something.

They moved again, and I was torn between the desire for them to
come closer so that I could hear what they were saying and the fear that,
if they did, they would see me.

They stopped and faced one another.

Rushton appeared to be doing most of the speaking. Then he
grasped Freya's hands in his and stared into her face intently, as if waiting
for her response. Freya's head was sunk as if in thought.

At last she nodded.

Rushton's face suffused with joy. He flung his arms around her and
hugged her tightly.

A terrible, savage pain clawed into my chest.

"You don't know how much this means to me," I heard Rushton
saying as they moved toward the steep little stairs leading down to the
main deck. Fortunately they were on the other side of the sail, and I could
only see their shadows.

"I don't want to tell anyone just yet," Rushton said. "This is not
the time. Let it remain our secret for now...."

Their voices faded as the pain in my chest intensified, spreading
through my body like some exotic plague germ. The image of Rushton
holding Freya in his arms seemed to have seared itself onto the inside of
my eyelids so that I could see it even when my eyes were squeezed shut.
I pulled my knees up to my chest and held them tightly, making myself
into a ball.

"Rushton," I whispered.

I saw him standing on the steps to Obernewtyn with his arms folded.

And who is she? a mocking voice asked. Where did she come from, to steal him while your back was turned?

I clenched my teeth, resisting sour envy, and letting sanity leak back into me. While my back was turned? No, Freya had stolen nothing that belonged to me. What could it possibly matter that he had turned to her? There was no room for anything in my life but my quest to destroy the weaponmachines.

Perhaps that was what Maruman had been trying to say the previous night—that there would be nothing for me at Obernewtyn when my quest was over. Maybe Atthis had seen what would come, and had sent him to warn me, for fear that I would lose my resolve.

Maybe *this* was the price I must pay—not just Obernewtyn, but Rushton's love.

I took a deep, shaky breath, and made myself look into the gray calmness of the sea all around me. The ship fish had departed.

I had not wanted Rushton's affections, or encouraged them.

So why did it hurt so much to learn that they were lost to me?

It does not matter, I thought fiercely. My feet are already on the black road. It is too late to choose another and this one I must walk alone.

XXXVII

We were becalmed for two days, but by early afternoon of the third day *The Cutter* was making up lost time, running before a stiff wind.

We were sitting in the salon and Fian was describing the discovery of the Reichler Clinic in the city under Tor to Daffyd.

"You look tired," Kella said, coming to sit beside me.

I made myself smile and murmur something, but thought I could not possibly look as weary as I felt. Maruman stirred restively on my knee, but did not waken. The others had taken his appearance with some equanimity since they had only the day before learned of his loss. But I felt it was nearly miraculous to have him with me. It was Angina who pointed out that Maruman made us the thirteen that Maryon had predicted.

"Hard to believe you just stumbled on it," Daffyd was saying.

"In a city so big? No, it was more than chance. I believe we were meant to find the clinic."

"After all, Hannah Seraphim was Rushton's ancestor," Kella added, her eyes shining. "Some things are meant to be."

And some are not, I thought, and was unable to stop my eyes from going to the table at the far end of the chamber where Rushton was talking with Hannay.

Why was it so hard not to look at him all of a sudden? Before this journey, I had done anything I could to avoid his gaze and his attention. I remembered waking in the Healer hall at Obernewtyn after rescuing Iriny. Rushton had sat by my bed and I had willed Roland to make him leave.

I had refused his every overture, convinced that the force that sometimes crackled between us, arose from him; and that my own feelings were no more than reactions to it.

But in this new life of pain, the knowledge that Rushton no longer loved me, seemed to have released a tempest of conflicting emotions that had very little to do with what he was feeling. I could not believe he had endured what I now felt—this hard, painful burning in the chest, this ache in the belly and throat. How could this be love?

If it was, it was as bad as ever I had imagined it must be. I should think myself fortunate that Rushton had turned from me before what simmered between us had burst into flame.

I focused my eyes on Fian again, wondering how soon I could reasonably retreat to my chamber again. Then his words caught my attention.

"It wasn't until we had read a lot of the plasts that we realized that what we had found wasn't the Reichler Clinic after all," he said.

"But we *saw* the name carved on the wall: Reichler Clinic Reception Center," I protested.

He nodded. "We misinterpreted it. What we found was exactly what the sign said—*a reception center* for th' Reichler Clinic. Nowt th' place itself. Th' real Reichler Clinic was where Garth always thought it mun be—in th' mountains."

"At Obernewtyn?" Kella asked breathlessly.

The teknoguilder shook his head. "Obernewtyn, or th' building which stood there before our Obernewtyn, was likely th' main residence for the Misfits. Th' actual Reichler Clinic labs were almost certainly sited where the cave of the Zebkrahn now stands. We have long known some Beforetime building once stood there, but we little dreamed which building or that it . . ."

"Labs? For experimentation on the Misfits?" I interrupted with real horror, remembering Alexi and Madam Vega had called their foul experiment rooms labs.

"I dinna think the experiments run by the Reichler Clinic would have been harmful or dangerous," Fian said. "Better to call them tests, as the plasts do. Hannah Seraphim would nowt have stood fer anything wrong. Fact is, we're pretty certain she was what th' Beforetimers called telepathic. In short, a Talented Misfit."

I was surprised though, of course when you thought about it, it was the obvious answer to why she had opened the clinic in the first place.

"This were kept a deadly secret, along wi' th' names of those who came to be tested. Ye might say th' Reichler Clinic we saw under Tor were a front fer an operation very like ours or, I should say, it became so after Govamen began to stalk Talents."

"I still don't understand what they did with them," Angina grumbled.

"There are indications, as Garth explained last guildmerge, that..." Fian said.

"I know, they were trying to use them somehow for war-making. But how?" Angina interrupted again.

"As to that..." Fian began with some heat, but he stopped again and shook his head fractionally. "Well. We will know more of that when we unearth th' clinic."

"Unearth it?" I asked sharply. "Then the clinic was buried by the holocaust like the city under Tor?"

"No," Fian said. "Not buried. And nor was the city under Tor. Both were originally built *under the earth*."

He let us clamor for a moment before going on with rather a smug expression. "Th' upheavals stove in th' earth in some parts of th' city under Tor an' permitted a stream, which we suspect was originally dammed an' diverted to flood it, but in th' Beforetime th' entire city were constructed beneath th' earth."

"But why?" I asked. "Why would anyone want to build a city under the ground?"

"Because of the whiteface." Maruman's sleepy thought drifted into my mind. I looked down at him, startled. When he snored, I decided he must have been farsending in his sleep.

"I suspect the Reichler Clinic was built under th' earth so that it would be hidden. But we will know more once we have got into th' lower levels of th' buildin'." He looked at me. "We have also learned since you left that th' Reichler Clinic had a spy working with Govamen."

Kella stiffened visibly. I knew she was thinking of her estranged bondmate, but my own thoughts evoked the dream I had experienced in the bottom of Iriny's mind. The dark-skinned man and the young woman he had wanted to run away with him had clearly been Beforetimers and, from the words that had passed between them, some sort of prisoners. The man had even spoken of contacting the Reichler Clinic. Could the two in my dream have been Talented Misfits imprisoned by the sinister Govamen?

I thought of the tattoo on my arm. Perhaps Garth had learned something more of what it meant. I would ask Fian about it when I had a moment alone with him.

Freya came into the salon and I felt a wave of despair. Was this how it was to be? Every time I had begun to build a wall of calmness, it was to be shattered by the smallest thing? I half expected her to speak to Rushton, but she crossed to the galley and set about making up a tray of food. As she had been sitting with Dameon, I supposed it must be for him.

On impulse I touched Angina's arm. "What is Freya's story? How did she come to Obernewtyn?"

"She ought to tell you herself," he said and, before I could stop him, he called out to her. I forced myself to smile as she approached, wishing passionately that I had kept my mouth shut.

She was very small and dainty and, like Rushton, had adapted gracefully to the ship's movements. I felt myself to be as long and gangling as a string bean beside her.

"I have wished for the chance to speak with you, guildmistress," Freya said. "Rushton spoke of you on our journey here and, truly, your life has been one of danger and marvels. My own story is nothing to yours."

My heart bumped against my chest in a sort of frightened leap, and all my hard-won composure vanished at the thought that Rushton might have confided that he once had loved me.

"Tell her," Angina prompted Freya.

She flushed prettily. "Rushton rescued me."

Of course.

"I had come to Darthnor with my father. He is . . . was . . . a horsetrader." A fleeting unhappiness showed in her eyes. "Along with his horses, there came a day that he offered his daughter for sale. . . ." She swallowed as if her throat hurt. "Rushton offered to buy me and the horses as a lot. He seemed a great man when he rode up on his white horse and threw a fortune in coin at my father's feet."

What sort of life had she led to be flattered that a man offered to buy her as a lot with horses? If Rushton had done that to me, I would have just as likely picked the coin up and thrown it back at him! Though probably he had meant it to be a gesture of contempt for Freya's father.

"I did not know until later that Alad was with Rushton and that the horses had told him I was ... a Misfit," she went on. "But he said he would have bid whether I was Talented or not, for people should not be sold any more than beasts. He told me about Obernewtyn, though not where it was, and offered to bring me there, where I could stay and commune all I wished with horses, or I might have a bag of coin and go where I willed."

Her lashes tilted secretively and I saw that she had not needed much convincing to choose Obernewtyn. I felt a rush of savage jealousy and was astonished. Was this violent pointless rage part of love too?

"You are a beastspeaker then?" I asked, and was horrified to hear how cold I sounded.

"Not exactly," Freya laughed, obviously taking my sharpness for a joke. "I am an empath I suppose, but am not able to receive anything much."

Thank Lud!

"She may not be much good at receiving emotions," Angina said cheerfully, "but she has a unique variation of projective empathy."

"Unique," I echoed.

Angina gave me a frankly puzzled stare.

"Dameon calls her an enhancer," he said. "She can enhance another's Talent. Her ability seems to be closest to what I do when I amplify Miky's projected emotions. Only Freya can do it to whomever she chooses or switch it off altogether."

Freya's remarkably expressive eyes darkened. "I can not reach everyone. Never my father. There was a wall in him—a natural mindshield, Dameon called it. And since I saw no one but him, I scarcely knew I had a Talent before I came here. I lived in terror of my father, for he was violent and angry much of the time. He kept me with him only because I could calm even the most uncontrollable horses."

"The interesting thing is that her empathic Talent works with animals as well," Angina said eagerly.

"Sometimes it made people furious when they sold a wild horse for a few coins, only to see me riding it a little later," Freya went on, lost in her memories. "Several times we had to leave moon fairs quickly because someone claimed I had used the black arts on their horse. My father feared he would be called up by the Herders to explain.

"In Guanette, we had to leave before my father had completed his bargains. That is what made him drink and decide to sell me in Darthnor. I wonder, now that he is sober, if he thinks the price for me was fair," she added sadly.

The clear hurt in her face robbed me of bitterness. I could imagine how little joy there had been in her life, for was she not a Misfit too? Must I grudge her what I would not have? My head ached with the effort of trying to bring order to the whirl of my emotions.

"All that's over now," Fian said. "Freya's in great demand with the novices because whenever she's around they're all smarter and quicker than usual."

"Unfortunately my ability to enhance is only an illusory sort of boosting," she said diffidently. "It lets me show them what they could do, and so they strive harder."

"Which means they learn better and faster," Miky said, wandering over to join us.

"I am still learning myself," she disclaimed, flushing. "Speaking of which, Dameon is waiting to give me a lesson as soon as he has eaten." She smiled at me again, her eyes revealing of all things—the most painful to me just then—shy admiration. "Rushton told me you are a beastspeaker and might easily have led that guild instead of Alad, if you had wanted it. I wish I could speak to the horses the way you do, rather than simply feeling at them, but I am learning to use signals with them."

She turned to retrieve the tray of food and went out of the salon with it.

"She's nice, isn't she?" Miky asked artlessly.

"Yes," I said bleakly.

I looked over at Rushton and found him watching me.

I dropped my eyes quickly, feeling dizzy and heartsore.

A little later he crossed the salon to look out the window where I was seated. Flustered by his nearness I looked out too, and watched a lone seabird spend itself spiraling on the winds.

"I think I could love this life," Rushton said softly. "It is very peaceful."

Something in me trembled in fury. How easily he used the word love. I wanted to ask if his love for the sea would be more enduring than his love for me, but I bit my tongue and swallowed the salty taste of blood.

"We are very different," I said icily.

His hands tightened where they rested on the sill. They were very brown and strong and the thought came to me of how they would feel against my skin. Ruthlessly I pushed the vision away, mortified at my lack of control.

To my relief, Powyrs came in to convey a request from his men that the twins play them a few songs. They had played a great deal to while away the anxious hours as we waited for the wind.

"Out where they can hear properly," Powyrs added apologetically.

The empaths obliged and collected their instruments. Powyrs made to follow them out, but Rushton stopped him to ask when we would reach Templeport.

"We ought to have been there yesterday early, or even the day before, but because we lost time becalmed, we will arrive tomorrow. By midday if the wind holds."

"Can you tell us a little about Templeport?" Rushton asked.

Powyrs glanced wistfully at the door as the strains of music drifted in but, obligingly, he set down his jug and delivered himself of a little lecture.

"It is the only real settlement in all of Sador. The tribes are nomadic and move constantly about the desert, living in tents. They believe they should not leave any sign of their passing. The only permanent construction in all of Sador is their Earthtemple and that is in Templeport, too. They regard the port itself as a necessary evil because it is the only place along the Sador coast where boats can put in. All the rest is murderous high cliffs."

"What else is there besides a temple?" Rushton asked curiously.

Powyrs shrugged. "Tents. There are lots of people from the Land, and maybe from other places, but they are not allowed to build huts or houses. They have to set up tents, like Sadorians. Being nomadic is part of their religion and it is terribly important to them."

"What is their religion?" asked Fian, abandoning his books to listen.

"It is not easy to tell such a thing simply. Central to it is their love of the land. By that, I mean the earth itself. To a Sadorian, nothing is more important. All life rises from it and returns to it. They think humans are no more important than any other creature. They don't believe in Lud at all. They think the land is infused with an earthgoddess. They don't have priests, but some Sadorians are sent from birth to be temple guardians. It is a great honor. Everything in Sador occurs under the guidance of the Temple and its guardians."

"It sounds very different to Herder lore," Daffyd murmured.

"Truly," Powyrs said. "Where a Herder believes humans are made by Lud to rule over the world, the Sadorians believe they are important only as part of the harmonious whole. The Herders claim everybody has to think their way or Lud will send the Great White again. In Sador, belief is a matter of personal choice." He leaned forward, blue eyes twinkling sardonically. "Funny thing is, Sadorians are a lot more devout by choice than Landfolk bound by Herder lore."

"I gather you don't like the Herders," Rushton said.

Powyrs winked angrily, a peculiar combination. "What's to like? I admire the Sadorians, though I don't go for putting land before people. Now if it was the sea..."

"How can these Sadorians live off a desert?" Hannay wondered.

"Most of their needs come from the spice groves inland at the foot of the mountains. Sadorians weave cloth from a fiber they get from its bark, they get sugar and medicines from its leaves and sap, and a potent fement from its berries. Most importantly, they get spice from its flowers, and they trade that for everything else the trees cannot offer."

"What about water?" Fian asked.

"There are natural springs all around the perimeter of the desert which water the groves, and in the desert there are isis pools. The Sadorians call them the tears of the goddess."

"What of the slave trade?" Rushton asked. "Do the Sadorians involve themselves in it?"

Powyrs chuckled. "Oh, yes. The Sadorians involve themselves all right. The Sadorians send slavers and anyone proven to have dealt with them out into the desert without water. If the slavers make it to the other side, they are freed."

"Do many survive?" Kella asked.

The seaman wolfishly grinned. "One that I've heard of, and he was stark raving mad. The Temple looks after him though, just as it does anyone who is sick or aged, and who can't keep up the pace of the karavans."

"Kar-avans?" Kella echoed.

"They are what a group of Sadorians on the move call themselves. And Sadorians are always on the move."

"Have you ever heard of the Battlegames?" I asked.

Powyrs scratched his head vigorously as if to dislodge a memory that way. "You know, I believe I have. I can't recollect..." His scowl deepened. "It's some sort of ritual governed by the Temple overguardian." He shook his head and huffed in defeat. "Nope, I can't get at it. Never mind, you can ask the Sadorians yourself. They're great ones for talk." He grinned at some inner joke. The ship listed slightly, wiping the smile from his face.

"Got to watch these fools who call themselves seamen or they'll run my *Cutter* up on a shoal," he muttered, hurrying outside.

"I have to get a look at that Temple," Fian said, with all the fanatical determination of a teknoguilder on the trail of new information. "Garth will kill me if I don't."

"And I'll kill you if you start any fuss," Rushton said with perfect seriousness. "We're not here to tread on Sadorian toes. There's every likelihood that this Temple will be out of bounds to Landfolk."

Fian subsided, looking chastened.

Rushton squared his shoulders. "Powyrs told me that we will reach Sador late tonight or early tomorrow and I think it is time we spoke of these Battlegames. Fian, go and tell Miky and Angina to come in as soon as they are done. Kella, get Dameon and Freya to come to the salon."

"What about Miryum?" Hannay asked.

"She'll be no good until she gets on land again. Let her sleep," Rushton said. He got up and began to pace about the salon distractedly.

∽

In a little while, we were all in the salon.

"Tomorrow we will reach Sador. The greatest danger would be for us to forget why we are there. From what we have heard of this Malik, I am sure you will agree that we must not give him the slightest chance to use us against ourselves.

"I have no doubt we can win, but I want more than victory. I want you to become sponges from the moment we arrive in Templeport. Learn all that you can about the rebels and the Sadorians, and about their attitudes to the Herders and the Council. Listen and watch, for the information you obtain might one day stand us in good stead."

He crossed to sit in his chair again. "This is the first time we will pit ourselves against unTalents who know what we can do, and this will season us and allow us to see how we function under stress. I want you all to store up impressions about the battle, thoughts and suggestions that can be shared during guildmerge when we return to Obernewtyn.

"One warning. Under no circumstances are you to use your Talents on anyone in Sador, except during the games. No farseeking or coercing, no empathizing. Although these rebels will be our opponents in these Battlegames, we hope to fight beside them in the future as allies. We must be able to offer a code they will trust, and assure them they will not be violated by our abilities. I will give this in an undertaking when we arrive, but your restraint shall be my validation."

He glanced once about the salon to emphasize this point. The others nodded, but I thought of Malik's cold laughter and doubted anything Rushton could promise would impress him. Everything would hinge on winning.

"Daffyd has agreed to fight with us," Rushton went on. "Since Dragon cannot take part, that makes us ten if we include Dameon and myself. Needless to say Dameon will not take part in the Battlegames, and though I have no usable Talent to offer I have battle skills, and there may be need for these."

His green eyes shifted to me but I looked away quickly, afraid of what he might see in my face.

"I do not feel that I will disadvantage us," he added pointedly, and I realized he thought my refusal to meet his eyes indicated my disapproval of his inclusion. Well, what did this small misunderstanding matter?

But it seemed it did matter for, at the end of his speech, Rushton asked me coldly to see him after the nightmeal in his chamber.

XXXVIII

I *did not go.*

In time I would be able to face Rushton calmly, but not yet. I could not trust myself. What if somehow I betrayed my feelings? Perhaps I already had by speaking so stiffly to Freya. My thoughts ran wild. What if Rushton wanted to see me alone so that he could apologize for not loving me any longer? What if he tried to explain his attachment to Freya?

These were stupid thoughts, and it was the fear of making a fool of myself that made me cast about desperately after the nightmeal for some plausible excuse not to go to Rushton's chamber. I found myself plucking nervously at the bandage covering the tattoo Swallow had given me, and this produced an idea.

I would go and see Fian about the Govamen mark. He was ensconced in Powyrs' chamber and I doubted anyone would think of looking for me there. The tattoo was reason enough to have forgotten Rushton's summons. He would be angry, of course, but I would show the tattoo to him and say that I had remembered the mark and had gone off to see Fian about it without thinking of his request. That would show him how little he meant to me. I would tell him of the tattoo—and I imagined the apologetic and slightly flippant smile I would wear as I said it—and explain how it had come about. I would casually mention that the gypsy had kissed me. Just as if people were always kissing me, so that I hardly even bothered about it.

Let him dare try to pity me then!

Having worked myself into a fury, I marched off to Powyrs' cabin, taking good care to let no one see me enter.

"Elspeth," Fian said, sounding surprised. He had to flatten himself against the wall to get the door to the tiny chamber open, but there was hardly enough room even when it was closed. He waved me to the only seat that would fit, and propped himself on the corner of the rickety wooden table piled high with books.

"I'm glad ye've come. Ye know there are actually some Beforetime maps among these papers? I am tryin' to..." He stopped. "Lud, I do blather on. It is a teknoguild failing, I know, to imagine th' world revolves around them. Did ye want somethin' in particular?"

I bit my lip, suddenly unsure of how much I wanted to tell.

"I did," I said slowly. "Do you know of the mark on the Govamen plasts stolen by the Reichler Clinic people?"

Fian wagged his head impatiently. "Yes, yes. Three Guanette birds goin' around one another?"

"Was there anyone else who might have used the same mark other than Govamen?"

"Unlikely," Fian said. "It appears on every single piece of research an' plast from Govamen an' I think it was especially devised fer them. Ye remember before when I said th' Reichler Clinic was in contact wi' th' Misfits bein' held by Govamen?"

I nodded.

"Well, all of those documents wi' Govamen's special symbol have convinced us that th' Misfits' contact was nowt one of th' Misfits, but one of th' scientists—that's what th' Beforetimers called teknoguilders. Who else could have stolen th' papers an' smuggled them out, but someone who worked there?"

"You think this scientist wanted to help th' Misfits escape?" I asked curiously.

"Help them get to the Reichler Clinic, I expect—an' that would have meant first helpin' them to escape. What we're tryin' to find out now is whether or nowt they *did* escape. Why did ye ask about th' Govamen mark, anyway?"

I took a deep breath. "Did you know that our gypsies were not like the ones in the Beforetime?"

"Of course nowt. Th' real gypsies were a people called Romans an' they were swallowed up into other races long afore th' Great White. Our gypsies are just people who took on their philosophy an' nomadic habits."

"Do you have any idea what our gypsies were *before* the holocaust?"

Fian's puzzled expression deepened. "What is this all about, El-speth?"

"Have you ever heard of Twentyfamilies?"

"Some sort of council within th' gypsy fraternity?"

"Not exactly," I said, and went on to explain.

"Amazin'," Fian said. "You must tell me this again slowly, so that I can write it down. I had no idea gypsy society was so complex. A pity ye dinna have th' chance to find out more about th' ancient promises. I've nivver read or heard anythin' about them. But what have gypsies to do with th' Govamen mark?"

"The purebloods wear it on their inner forearms."

"That is odd. Why would a gypsy wear th' mark of a long dead Beforetime organization?"

"Exactly what I am wondering," I said.

"I suppose these gypsies might have adopted the Govamen sign. By all accounts, it was an enormous organization an' th' Beforetimers had a great love of flauntin' their symbols about."

"How do you explain that the gypsies regard it as a sacred mark?"

"Perhaps their mark only *looked* like th' Govamen symbol," Fian suggested.

I lost my temper a little—a thing I would not have done normally. I rolled up my sleeve to reveal the grubby bandage around my arm, and gestured for Fian to pass over a jug of water sitting on a tray.

He stared as I dipped my arm in it and let the water penetrate. "A Twentyfamilies gypsy gave the mark to me," I said. "You will see if it is exact or merely alike."

Fian listened, horrified, to my description of the tattoo procedure.

"Talk to me," I said fiercely, when the silence went on too long. "But not about this. Not yet because I haven't seen it since it was done."

Fian looked like a startled owl, but he obliged. "Tell me about Jakoby again."

I began to separate the sodden bandages. "She was wonderful, and yet terrible too in a way. You got the feeling she was capable of anything."

"An' she really offered to fight th' rebel leader of Sawlney?"

I nodded, remembering the sweaty terror of the fat Brocade. "Let's keep our fingers crossed it is healed properly," I said evenly, lifting the last layer away. We both stared.

"Is this a joke?" Fian demanded crossly.

I was mute with astonishment, for other than the crisscross reddening left by the bandage, my skin was utterly unmarked or discolored. *The triple bird tattoo had vanished!*

Leaving Fian's tiny room, I dismissed his suggestion that I had been tricked into thinking I had been given the tattoo.

No one knew better than I how it had been obtained, or exactly what it meant for Swallow to have given it. If he had intended to rook me, why would he have told me so much about himself? Besides, I had seen the needles and felt them pierce my skin.

But I could hardly blame the teknoguilder for his doubts.

I might have had the same reaction in his place, except that I *knew* I had not imagined the tattoo. Which left me wondering what had happened to it. Unfortunately, only Swallow could know the answer to that.

I sighed and decided to relieve Miky who was sitting with Dragon. Maruman was sleeping curled up at the foot of the mattress, but he woke as I entered.

When the Empath guilden had gone off yawning to her bed, I moved across to where Dragon lay and sat on the floor and took her small limp hand in mine. Maruman rose, stretched and came to curl himself into my lap. We made no attempt to communicate and I was grateful for his silent companionship. I did not want to talk anymore or think. It had been a long, confusing, painful day and I just wanted to lay my head on the bed and be still.

I put my cheek against Dragon's hand and stared out the small circular window at the sky. Almost at once I slept.

I dreamed of walking along a black road. Rushton was behind me calling. "Wait. I will come with you."

I walked faster, thinking of him holding Freya.

"Elspeth . . ."

But his voice was fading. I was crying but I walked faster still.

I fell then into a deeper dream; a chaotic tumult of images that made no sense.

There was a chair, red and bulging with carvings of grotesque faces.

One moment the faces appeared to be convulsed with mirth and, the next, they seemed to shriek with agony.

I saw a tall, beautiful woman smile.

"All the women in my family have it," she said in a soft, musical voice.

Then the same woman was slumped in the carved chair. Her hair was red like Dragon's, and her breast too, for she had been stabbed there and the knife still protruded from the gaping wound. Bending over her was a bald man with a pale, greasy face and a bloody hand. "Who will ever know it was my hand that struck the killing blow?" he whispered with feral glee.

The vision changed and I was aboard a ship going over the waves. Then I was in the sea, and the water about me was tinged with the red-haired woman's blood, for she was beside me in the water. I tried to keep her afloat, but the waves were violent and kept tearing us apart.

"My daughter," she rasped. "You are . . . You must . . ."

∾

"Templeport ho," a voice called, and I woke with a start to a blazing hot day, my head aching abominably.

The cabin door slammed open.

"We're here!" Miky announced in an elated voice.

I got up stiffly, disentangling myself from Dragon and feeling groggy. I rubbed at my stiff back, ignoring Maruman's grumbles at being disturbed.

The others were outside already when I got there, all pressed up against the side of the ship and staring out through the goldshot salt haze at Sador. I was astounded to see how high the sun was. I had slept near through to midday! The air outside was dry and hot, and breathing seemed to burn the inside of my nostrils.

The soaring sea cliffs lay before us like a black barrier, running as far as I could see in both directions. They were sheer and utterly inaccessible. But right ahead of us, the cliff was cracked as if split by a giant axe, and sand from the desert high above had trickled out to form a spit, pointing out into the dark sea like a white finger. This, Powyrs said, was Templeport.

As we came closer to the tip of the peninsula, we could see a cluster of tents fluttering white like scattered blossom, but there were no other buildings and no greenery at all. Little wonder. The spit would be barren, saturated as it was with salt from the sea, and the pitiless heat would scorch anything that tried to grow. The shore wavered and danced through shimmering waves of heat, appearing as insubstantial as an illusion.

"How could anyone live here?" Miky said. This had been directed at Angina but her twin was busy murmuring softly into Dameon's ear, describing the scene.

I kept a tight shield around my mind, for Dameon always seemed to sense my darkest moods. The image of Freya and Rushton was still fresh in my mind and I had no wish to confide my feelings to the empath, for all I loved him dearly. Some pains were not to be shared.

"It is too hot," Miryum grumbled, her voice slurred by her long sleep.

"You'd best get used to it," Hannay said. "It will get better before it gets worse. The ship will be cool compared to the land."

"Hmh," Miryum grunted. "Well, at least the ground will stand still under my feet."

"How can it be so hot? It will soon be wintertime," Kella said, visibly wilting in the strong sunlight.

"Perhaps the desert makes the sun hotter somehow," Fian said. "The lack of plant life and water..." His voice trailed off.

"There is the Earthtemple," Powyrs said, pointing. I scanned the spit for a building but could see nothing.

"Oh Lud," Daffyd murmured suddenly. "There. In the cliff. No wonder it is called an *Earth*temple."

The Temple was part of the cliff, and visible only because the cliff was carved from top to bottom. Closer, I could make out windows in the midst of the carving. From the number of them, the Temple must be enormous.

I felt someone at my side.

It was Rushton and his eyes were accusing. "I asked you to come and see me last night."

"I...I had to see Fian," I stammered. "He..."

Rushton's eyes blazed with such fury, I faltered. He turned on his heel without a word, and went to stand with Freya and Hannay.

∽

"What in Lud's name are *those*?" Angina exclaimed.

He was pointing at a group of great, shaggy, dun-colored beasts with four legs and a lump of flesh pouting up from their backs.

"They are kamuli," Powyrs said, looking over his shoulder with a grin. "The Sadorians use them rather than horses and they are not mutants, however much they might look it. They existed in the Beforetime and were called desert ships because they traverse the sands effortlessly with their soft splayed hoofs. They store water in those lumps on their backs."

"Sadorians do not use horses, then?" Freya asked curiously.

"Inland they do," the seaman said. "Where the spice groves are, the ground is hard and there is thick forestation that makes horses more suitable as transport."

I noticed Kella watching me, and made an effort to look interested.

"Act," Brydda had once advised me. "Pretend that you are clever, wise, brave, calm, courageous. Pretend, and some of the time, you can forget it is pretense."

But pretend that I did not care what Rushton thought of me?

Easier said than done.

"Since the road opened, the Sadorians have brought Landhorses in because they are very keen on breeding hardier beasts out of their own stock," Powyrs was still talking about horses. "Of course, anyone game enough to travel along the coast road uses horses or uses them to pull wagons, and everything brought for trade, including horses, must come to Templeport first to be checked for disease. In fact, all trade in Sador happens here because the only form of coin permitted here are Temple tokens."

It was incredibly noisy on the spit. Everyone seemed to shout at the top of their voice and there was a great deal of bartering that took place literally from ship decks, and a tremendous bustle as people carried boxes and bundles to and from the ships. Yet the scene was, for all its loudness, curiously colorless. The savage blaze of the sun seemed to bleach everything to a blinding bone-whiteness that made my head pound and my eyes water. More than anything else I longed to sit in a bit of shade and drink a cold mug of water.

Unfortunately the only shade available was that cast by the towering

Sadorian cliffs, looming on both sides of the sloping pass that led up to the desert, and that was a goodly step away.

"We'd better set up some sort of camp," Rushton decided. "Powyrs said Jakoby's ship might well have missed being becalmed but, if not, then we'll miss the time for the Battlegames. If that happens, we'll know we're here for some reason other than the games."

Powyrs pointed out a spot further up the spit where it widened at the base of the cliffs. "About half way to the cliffs there is a place where visitors set up their tents. You can see them? Nearby are stalls where you can purchase food, and at the very base of the cliffs there is a fresh-water spring. The water will cost you nothing, but you will have to change your coins for barter tokens at the Earthtemple if you want to buy food."

Watching us go, the plump seaman gave Maruman, who was draped around my neck, a long look of bewildered wistfulness that spoke of the strength of his attachment to his "mascot." I had coerced all memory of their brief association from his mind, and from the crew's, but clearly the impression had been deep and some residue remained, at least in Powyrs.

XXXIX

Hannay, Rushton and Miryum cleared the rough shale and set about, with the twins' aid, erecting the tents we had bought in Sutrium at Jakoby's suggestion. Daffyd and Freya were sent off to get water, and Fian and I to exchange our small store of coin for Temple barter tokens. Dameon elected to walk with us, and since the spring was on the way to the Temple, we went that far together.

I was relieved to find that Freya's presence no longer disturbed me near as much as Rushton's. Not that we did much talking. The heat beating down on our heads and thrown back as a reflection from the dazzling white sand was terrific. By the time we reached the cliffs, we were all gasping for breath.

We threw ourselves down at the edge of the icy spring and drank deeply, before retreating into the dense shade cast by the cliffs to recover.

"Incredible," croaked Daffyd in a low voice.

"Where does such heat come from?" Freya asked weakly, fanning her face with her skirts.

"Ugh," Fian groaned. "I've just realized we'll have to climb up th' rest of th' spit to change th' coins. Powyrs told me th' Temple entrance can only be got to from th' top of the cliffs."

I would have groaned, too, if I had been able to spare the energy. The first impression of coolness in the shade had begun to abate and already I was hot again. We sat a good while before I could bring myself to move.

Standing up reluctantly, I noticed two halfbreed gypsies among the throng of Sadorians. They stood out as much as we must in this land of tall, gold-skinned people in their flowing robes. Powyrs had said gypsies were treated well here. That being so, I had no doubt more would avail themselves of the coast road when the poisons had receded a little further.

Swallow's lean dark face flashed into my mind. He had seemed so sure that we would meet again, but his predictions and strange visions seemed very far away from this hot land.

"Uh-oh," Fian murmured.

He had risen, too, and was gazing back down the spit. I turned to see what had caught his attention. A number of gray-clad Landsmen stood talking, yellow cloaks fluttering at their shoulders—senior-ranking soldier-guards from the Land.

I had known there were soldierguards in Sador, yet still it was a shock to see them. Even more so the two Herders with them, clad as usual in white robes and arrogance. I was astounded to see a number of Sadorians clustered about the priests. Could these possibly be converts?

Even as I watched, the taller Herder lifted his pale haughty face to the Earthtemple, his lip curling in scorn. Letting my eyes follow the same direction, I was startled to discover that what I had thought carved patterns on the cliff were, in fact, a multitudinous swirl of faces.

"You'd better get on," Daffyd advised.

"Perhaps you should not go," Freya told Dameon, when I offered him my arm.

The Empath guildmaster smiled unerringly down at her. "I am not ill. I am only blind."

She flushed.

"I am going to have another drink before we start," Fian announced.

Daffyd caught his arm. "Don't be a fool. You will be sick if you fill your belly with water then walk in this heat. Drink when you return."

It was a steep walk up to the top of the cliffs but Fian found breath enough to describe what he was seeing to Dameon. I was glad of his monologue for it freed me of the need to speak and kept the Empath master's attention from me. Before long, though, we were all trudging along in silence again.

"The sun is like a hammer on my head," Fian panted, when we stopped to rest halfway. "It did not look so far from the camp. At this rate it will be dusk before we are back."

My own head was pounding, yet the heat in the desert running back from the cliffs must be a thousand times worse. Still the Sadorians spent their lives sailing the sea of sand on their desert ships. Strange how differently humans could live and still be human.

∾

The Earthtemple had two faces.

The grandest was the one it presented to the sea and to the spitroad. We had been sitting literally with our backs against the base of it when we were by the spring. The road from the spit had risen gradually to the height of the clifftop, where a small rocky path had peeled off to the left, running down into a deep fissure. A man had told us this would bring us to the entrance of the Earthtemple. After making our way carefully and with some relief down the shaded path running along a deep sloping cleft, we discovered the second face of the Temple. It was neither gilded nor carved, and there were no windows. A single, rough-hewn portal served as the doorway, while a great, plain slab of stone, set upon a smaller pivoting stone, served as its door. Its simplicity seemed far more in keeping with the Sadorians' philosophy as expounded by Powyrs, than the ornate carved facade of faces it presented to the sea.

The stone door was currently tilted to allow a slender opening on either side, and beyond the darkness was so complete that it was impossible to say what lay within.

There were at least thirty people lined up outside in queues. One line seemed to consist of very elderly people, worried-looking adults with sickly children or babes, and others with rough bandages or hacking coughs.

A young man with wild eyes, held tightly between two plump, distressed-looking women, lashed about babbling and shuddering. Clearly he was undergoing some sort of seizure.

This then must be the line for supplicants seeking healing.

The line next to it had more animals than people, therefore this must be where beasts were brought to be examined for disease before they could be sold. The animals were all small, so the larger beasts, such as horses, must be dealt with at some other point.

In the third line there were Sadorians carrying sacks. The acrid odor rising suggested they were the spice gatherers Powyrs had mentioned, bringing in their tribe's quota to exchange for barter tokens.

At first I wondered why the queues were not advancing, then I noticed a number of barefooted men and women clad in hooded linen tunics moving along the lines.

"The Temple guardians," Fian murmured. "Looks as if all of the ministerin' is done outside." He sounded disappointed.

I waved him back and moved closer to listen to an exchange between one of the hooded guardians and a Sadorian woman of middle years.

"What do you seek of the earth?" the Temple guardian asked. His voice and shape proclaimed him a man, but I could not see his face. Like all of the Temple guardians, this was concealed by the drooping hood.

The woman launched into a detailed litany of physical ills to which he listened with great patience. When she could find nothing more to complain about, he rummaged in a small pouch bag tied at his waist, and removed a twig. Pressing it into her hand, he bade her in a gentle voice to soak it in boiled water, then drink the fluid.

Fian poked me in the ribs, his eyes bright with suppressed laughter. "It's no more than a wee bit of relaxin' herb he's given her. A sop."

I nodded absently, wondering what the farthest line was for. People did not look sick, nor did they lead beasts, or carry spice.

A smaller guardian approached a man in this line.

"What do you seek of the earth?" asked a girl, her voice muffled slightly by the hood.

"Wisdom, Guardian. My son desires to bond, but he has yet to make his first spice gather." He seemed undaunted by the fact that the voice could not belong to a girl much older than his son.

"Is the girl he would take worthy in your eyes?" she asked.

"Yes, it is only his youth that troubles me," the man answered. "In truth it may be that he is not worthy of her."

The diminutive guardian nodded sagely. "Say to the father of the girl that he must set the boy a quest to determine his worthiness. If he fails, then he must wait another season. If he succeeds, then he shall have her."

The father nodded and went away.

"That's no more'n a bit of common sense. The' man's a fool nowt to have thought of it fer hisself," Fian muttered.

"Perhaps he had thought of it, but needed reassurance," Dameon murmured.

Another Temple guardian came out of the shadowy doorway with two clinking bags slung about her waist. She passed briskly along the farthest line, exchanging coin for tokens.

"Wait here," I said, and took my place at the end of the line. When the guardian reached me, she asked, from the depths of her hood, "What do you seek of the earth?"

"I ... We have come to pay our respects to the earthgoddess and to get some barter tokens," I said politely.

She nodded and counted the coin I offered into one bag at her waist before giving me a handful of small pale metal discs from another. She lifted her hand to my forehead and made a sign, but the words were drowned out by a scream.

I turned swiftly to find the frenzied youth had broken free of the women and was rushing toward me.

I thought he meant to attack me and flung up my hands, but to my astonishment he threw himself at my feet. "Do you bring the Moon-watcher?" he whispered fiercely.

The two women had hurried forward and pulled him away from me, apologizing profusely. "When these fits come on him, it is as if he is possessed by demons," one said.

The Temple guardian, who had been attending to me, waved the women and the now silent boy back to their place in the line, then turned to me.

"Who are you?" she asked in a strange tense voice.

My heart began to gallop. "I ... I am a visitor from the Land."

"Whom do you visit?"

I did not know what to answer, so I told the truth. "Jakoby has invited me. She is ..."

"I know of Jakoby," the woman said shortly, and now her tone was indifferent. She lifted her hand up and made the same mark on my fore-head. "May you nurture the earth and find harmony."

She moved to the man behind me, and I returned to Dameon and Fian, feeling somewhat bewildered.

"What happened?" Fian demanded.

"I'm damned if I know," I said.

∾

As Fian had predicted, the day was indeed drawing to a close by the time
we returned to the spit. The shadows were lengthening, and people were
lighting cooking fires and lamps. Already the moon had risen, and it hung
like a great coppery disc, low on the skyline; a full moon.

As we reached the trade area, Fian suggested we get some food to
take back to the camp. The atmosphere surrounding the selling tents was
as familiar as the rest of Sador was strange. In the mill and jostle there
was a similarity to markets in Sutrium and Kinraide and Morganna, that
reassured me in some deep way. Well, that was not so surprising. After
all, people had to eat and drink and trade and speak.

All about us, men and women were involved in the mundane business
of haggling with traders. Here, at least, there were almost as many Landfolk
as Sadorians.

"Got any silver to sell?" demanded a squint-eyed jack. Dameon
smiled in the direction of the voice and shook his head. The man recoiled
as if his blindness might be contagious.

"Need flints or salt?" A woman in the tent alongside him asked.

"Maybe later," I said.

She spat on the ground in disgust. "Filthy gypsies."

"Like a girl, pretty boy?" whispered a woman with lustrous painted
eyes, peering from the shadowy interior of another tent at Fian.

He shuddered and backed away with comical haste into one of the
odorous desert ships sitting with their legs folded queerly beneath them.
The creature snorted fiercely and eyed him with pouting ire.

"Greetings," I sent, wondering if its mind would accept me.

It regarded me for a long moment, but either could not or would
not understand.

"You want to buy this fine animal?" a Sadorian trader asked, appearing from nowhere at the beast's side.

"I don't think he likes the color of my eyes," I said, and walked on
leaving him to stare after me.

"How can they live in this heat?" Fian panted. "It's practically dusk.
Doesn't it ever cool down?"

"I suspect the night will be cold," Dameon said.

Fian snorted as if coolness here was something no sane person would
believe in. "They are mad, of surety, to live in such a place."

"Perhaps so," said a familiar voice.

I whirled to find myself staring at a tall woman, clad in a flowing cloak of beaten animal hides atop a thin shift of some golden material that matched her eyes, and bared the full dark muscular length of legs and arms. Her hair was woven into tight, metal-beaded braids which clinked whenever she moved.

"Jakoby," I said.

Rushton bowed. "I am pleased to greet you. Elspeth has told us so much about you. We feared you might have been becalmed, as we were."

"The winds were good to us." Jakoby smiled enigmatically, her face illuminated fitfully by the fire Miryum had kindled in the angled embrace of the tents. The others stared at the Sadorian woman in wonder. She looked about at them, taking time to examine each of the faces carefully.

"Your chosen warriors are young indeed," she said at last. "But age does not always signify, as the Landman, Elii, said. Will you come now? The two of you," Jakoby asked.

"I think Rushton..." I faltered under his green glare.

"We will be glad to accompany you," he told Jakoby tersely. "Where do we go?"

"To meet Bram. He is to judge the Battlegames. He will explain the rules of the games. They will commence tomorrow at dawn."

"Are all of the rebels here?" Rushton asked Jakoby.

"Not all, but all who will come. More, I think, than Brydda expected. The last of them came by ship with us and we moored only this evening. It was fortunate that we had a good wind at our back, since we were a day late in departing."

We were turning to leave when I heard Miryum's voice ring out angrily, and the sound of a blow.

Hurrying around to the back of one of the tents, we discovered the stolid Coercer guilden standing over a tall Sadorian man sitting in the dust, his nose running with blood.

"What happened?" Rushton demanded.

"Him," Miryum said fiercely, glaring at the man as he got to his feet.

"What did he do?" I asked.

Miryum looked over to me and promptly dissolved into confusion. "He...this fellow was making fun of me," she muttered wrathfully.

"This is not so," the man said carefully. He bowed low to her and then to Jakoby. "I am sorry if I have given offense. I spoke ravek. I did not mean to insult her. Do you wish me to kill myself?"

Miryum gaped.

"Well?" Jakoby asked her mildly. "Do you want him to kill himself for insulting you?"

"But surely you can't mean he would ... would ..." The coercer looked more disturbed than I had ever seen her. "Of course he mustn't ... kill himself. Not for a joke."

"Very well, you may leave," Jakoby told the man indifferently.

"It was not a joke I made," the man said gravely. He bowed to Miryum, and then again to Jakoby before backing away.

"What on earth did he say to you?" I asked.

Miryum reddened. "I will not say."

"Shall we go?" Jakoby murmured. "Bram is expecting us. It is only a short walk to his tent."

∽

The Sadorian walked slowly, adapting her long stride courteously to our pace.

"What is a ravek?" I asked her.

Her teeth flashed in the darkness of her face. "It is an endearment between those who are heartfasted. It means you-who-have-my-heart-beneath-your-foot. The man your friend struck offered to make her his ravek. That is a formal proposal of bonding in Sador."

In spite of everything, I smiled. Obviously Miryum had thought the poor fellow was cursing at her in his language. What would she say when I told her he wanted her for his bondmate?

Rushton began asking Jakoby questions about Sador, but I only half listened. I wondered if I should speak of the disturbed boy outside the Earthtemple that afternoon.

I felt as if the incident had meant something. Certainly the Temple guardian, who had witnessed the scene, seemed to have been worried by it.

Jakoby stopped before a large tent.

She lifted the tent flap, and the muted sounds of laughter and the clink of plates and knives spilled out into the dusk. She gestured for us to enter.

Inside, a fire burned in a ground hearth lined in stone. Three trestles were set around it in a u-shape and piled high with all manner of food and drink. Seated at the trestles were both familiar and unfamiliar faces.

At the central table on a raised dais was a wizened Sadorian man with skin the shade of old bronze and hair as white and tightcoiled as the fleece of wild mountain goats. He wore a cloak of what appeared to be animal pelts sewn together about his skinny shoulders, as Jakoby did.

It was not difficult to guess that this was Bram.

I ran my eyes swiftly around the rest of those seated.

Plump Brocade was at one end seated beside Tardis' yellow-haired emissary, Gwynedd. Brocade was wearing a jewel-encrusted vest stretched tight across his wide belly. A little further along sat a tall, fair, proud-looking woman. She wore no jewelry and her hair hung white and un-braided and perfectly straight about her shoulders like a snowy veil. Brydda sat by her, and then Dardelan. On the other side of Bram among a great number of strangers were white-haired Cassell, and Elii. It seemed Brydda's recruiting journey had borne fruit. But I had no doubt they were here first for a war council, rather than to see whether we were fit allies.

A stooped man smiled faintly in greeting when our eyes met. He was seated beside Brydda and I guessed this was Yavok, who had taken over from him in Aborium. What had the rebel called him? Unimaginative and trustworthy.

Last of all was Malik.

When our eyes met, his lips curved into a sneering smile that made me instantly conscious of my sweaty, dust-smeared face and clothes.

"It is the Misfit and its master," he told the dark-eyed man on his right, just loudly enough for us to hear.

I felt Rushton tense with anger beside me, then relax.

"As you see, this master is a stripling and barely old enough to be master of himself," Malik went on scornfully, not bothering to pretend to be speaking in an aside. Rushton's silence had made him bold, for he took it as weakness.

Jakoby said nothing and I sensed she was waiting to see how Rushton would deal with this.

The Master of Obernewtyn merely settled a long, impassive stare on the rebel, whose smirk faltered, then faded altogether.

"What are you looking at, boy?" he growled.

"I am not sure," Rushton said. "It might be a man, but then it might be a kind of performing ape. It is hard to tell in the firelight."

Malik stared at him incredulously. Then he rose with a curse, pulling out a knife.

"Enough," Jakoby said imperiously. "The Battlegames do not commence until the morrow and it is unseemly to sour our feasting with such behavior before then. All things in their right time."

Malik resumed his seat, though he was pale with fury, and Jakoby ushered us up to Bram. I was surprised to see one of the hooded Temple guardians in the seat beside him. Then I remembered that Powyrs had said the Battlegames were overseen by the overguardian of the Temple. This must be he or she. The hood gave no sign of its wearer's sex, but I thought it must be a wizened old creature, for it was very small.

"Bram, this is Elspeth Gordie of whom I have spoken," Jakoby said. "And Rushton Seraphim, who styles himself the leader of these Misfit gypsies."

"Seraphim," Bram echoed. "An old name, I think."

Rushton bowed. "I do not know if your name is old or not. I have heard only a little about the Sadorian people but it has made me curious to know more, and I am pleased at this chance to speak with you."

Bram chuckled fruitily. "Yet I think this is not an occasion for speeches. I hope you do not think to win the Battlegames with words alone."

"We are prepared to meet whatever challenge is offered," Rushton responded smoothly.

"Good." Bram's dark eyes shimmered in the firelight. "I have heard from those among my people who watched for your arrival, that your force contains warriors who are even younger than you. And though you may count yourself a man, you are too young to be seasoned properly to battle. Have you hope of winning against such men as Malik, whose prowess is legendary?"

"I would not have come otherwise."

The old man cackled. "No? But sometimes battles must be faced whether or no there is a hope of winning them. This is a truth known to men and women of honor."

"No battle is lost until it is lost. Men and women of courage know this."

Bram nodded in appreciation. "True enough! You speak well, lad. I regret that you are not yet a sworn ally and therefore have no place at this table. Yet, if your people acquit themselves well and survive the testing tomorrow, we might yet sup together and have this speech you desire."

"Survive?" Rushton echoed carefully. "Surely there is no question of not surviving since this is only a contest."

The Temple guardian stirred.

"These are the Battlegames, lad, where matters large and small may be decided without massive bloodshed. It is war in miniature. If death were not possible, there would be no true testing. Of course death is not the aim, nor is injury inevitable."

There was a silence, broken by Malik's cutting laughter. "Look. The boy is nearly unmanned with fear at the thought that death might wait for him."

"The morrow will bring what it brings," Rushton said softly. He turned his eyes back to Bram. "If it is permitted, I would like to know something more of the Battlegames."

Bram's smile died and, for a moment, he looked like a weary old man. "Are you in such a hurry for war, lad? You were more handsome when you spoke of talking and learning." He sighed weightily. "Malik asked the same question, and I told him what I now tell you. The Battlegames designed by my people are many but the earthgoddess will decide which of these may be played." He drew himself up and summoned a formal and ceremonious air. "Once among the tribes who were much sundered during the time that followed what you Landfolk call the holocaust, there were wars occasioning great bloodshed among our people and harm was done to the earth. Then came one among us who heard the voice of the earthgoddess. She commanded us to build the Earthtemple, that others might come there and learn to hear the voice of the land as well. And so it came to pass. Through her disciples, the earthgoddess forbade war forever. But still there were disputes, great and small, which needed mediation. Hence were the Battlegames devised, both to decide issues and to expiate the violent urges that are the plague of humanity.

"Each of the games is designed to test some specific quality in a competitor—courage or wit or charm or honesty or fitness—in your case the games will test fitness for battle. But the earthgoddess alone knows which of the many games will be selected, for they will be chosen at random using dice."

He clapped his hands and the overguardian uncovered a tray on the table, on which rested two small cubes with a different number of marks on each face.

"The dice," Jakoby said reverently.

"These will be thrown and, when they fall, they will show a number of marks to the sky," Bram explained. "All games included will be marked with a number. By these means will the specific battle be selected. All are different. Some games are short and others long, so there is no way of telling how many will take place at a single Battlegame. As many as ten, no less than three. The Battlegames commence at sunrise, and end at sunset for these are moments of power.

"Are all ten of a team to play each game?" Rushton asked. I guessed he was thinking of Dameon.

Bram shook his head. "Not necessarily. The number of participants for each game will again be randomly selected by a further throw of the dice, but it is up to the two leaders to choose who will fill the places. For each Battlegame completed, there will be a spoken assessment, and then when the day ends the winner shall be named."

"Do we not fight one another?" Malik demanded.

"You will contend as the earthgoddess wills," the old man said coldly. "Some of the tests require confrontation between teams and others ask a different kind of striving."

There was a stillness in the tent, and only the firelight shifted and flickered, driving the shadows before it.

"Can you tell us the sort of things the Battlegames will test?" Rushton asked.

"No," Bram said. He opened his eyes and reached for a piece of bread. This appeared to mark the end of the ceremony. All along the trestles, men and women reached for goblets or turned to whisper to one another.

"There is just one thing more," Rushton said.

"And that is?" Bram inquired through a mouthful of bread.

"I want you to understand that we intend to use all of our powers in these Battlegames, but outside this contest we would never use those abilities on allies."

Bram chewed and swallowed. "You should return to your camp now. Eat well and rest. You will be brought to the field of battle before dawn."

Jakoby escorted us outside. "If you can, forget about the Battlegames tonight. Worrying and wondering about what will come will not avail you. Rest well."

She turned and went back into the tent, leaving Rushton and me alone in the dark.

XL

"We'd better get back," Rushton said. "The others will be waiting to hear what happened."

I shivered, though it was not cold, and followed him back across the spit.

"I am . . . sorry," I said at last, with stiff formality. "I did not know there would be danger. Jakoby didn't tell me that when she offered the Battlegames."

"You think she meant to deceive you?" He did not look at me when he spoke.

I shook my head. "I do not think it would have occurred to her that it would matter there was danger."

"Then there is no blame to be laid."

Rushton's voice was remote and I knew he was still angry with me. I longed to heal the rift between us, but I kept seeing him holding Freya. The rift had become a chasm and maybe that was as it should be. I had my quest, and Rushton had Freya and Obernewtyn and that was that.

I tried to think of what Bram had said about the Battlegames, but it was impossible. I had never felt further from Rushton. I had the urge to say something that would restore even the old uneasy comradeship between us, but his silence daunted me.

We walked without speaking the rest of the way back to the camp.

Angina saw us approach as he straightened up from stirring the cooking fire, and alerted the others with a cry. In moments they were clustered around us. In swift, unemotive words, Rushton told them what had happened.

"The Battlegames are more than a contest then," Miryum said dourly, but without fear. "Is it possible that one or more of us may die?"

"Possible," Rushton said calmly. "But certainly not inevitable. We will know more when we know which games are to be played."

"I do not like the sound of this Malik," Hannay said.

"He is a hard, strong man," Rushton said. "A bitter man and a tough fighter by all accounts. I do not relish the thought of being his opponent, but if we fare well tomorrow, that strength will be at our side when we fight the Council. Wars make for strange bedfellows. We need the rebels and it seems this is the only way to win them."

"I wonder if such a victory as this will truly win us anything worth having," Dameon said, as Kella handed him a mug of mulled fement.

"It will win us the aid we need against the Council," Rushton snapped. "We cannot afford the indulgence of philosophizing about what constitutes victory. Save that for when the fighting is over."

He took a long deep breath, then shook his head. "I am sorry. I did not mean to snap, my friend. I am . . . tired." He sat down on the ground, facing the fire, and invited us all to do the same. "Let us not talk about the morrow anymore. It will come all too soon. We will nourish our bodies with food and rest, and our souls with a song."

Miky's face lit up and she went to get her gita. Freya brought us plates of stew, then settled herself beside Rushton. Watching the smile that she gave him, I found I had no appetite.

I longed to comfort Rushton, but what could I truly offer him? Even if he had loved me still, I could not say that I would never leave him because I would. I could not speak of undying love because I was not certain this bitter, painful emotion his embrace with Freya had roused in me was love.

A great sadness filled me as I stared into the red heart of the flames and listened to the lovely haunting song the Empath guilden had made from the Oldtime story of the sleeping princess wakened by a kiss. As it rippled out into the night, I could not help but think again of Dragon, locked in her secret, internal battle with her past; trapped in a fortress of her own mind's making.

Powyrs had agreed that the comatose empath might remain aboard the ship, for he was to bring us back to the Land when the Battlegames were over. He thought we were to perform at a bonding of one of the tribal chiefs. Little as we had liked leaving Dragon, she was safer on *The Cutter* than with us.

"In this long sleep, in this fortress of dreams, I live a shadow life and in it dream of one who will come...." Miky sang softly, and Angina took up the harmony in his deeper voice, at the same time elaborating the melody with tiny bells, and empathizing it delicately with his Talent.

I rose quietly and slipped away from the fire, to crawl into one of the tents. Removing only my sandals I stretched out fully clothed.

"Greetings, ElspethInnle," Maruman sent, and I looked up to see him enter the tent. I made a place for him beside me. The red glow of the fire through the tent opening made his fur appear bloody and discolored. He slept at once, but my mind was too active to let me sleep. On impulse, I shaped a probe and let it soar away from the spit and over the dunes like a nightbird.

I did not try to direct its flight, but let the music take me where it would.

Here and there, I encountered the silvery shimmer of other minds—small nocturnal creatures foraging. Once I was drawn to a brighter shimmer, and held for a moment by a deep mind which was clearly intelligent, and just as clearly non-human.

I flew until my mind was calm.

At long last I returned to my body. The fire outside had died and the music had stopped. The others had all gone to bed. I stroked Maruman's fur and wondered if the Temple guardians might not have some potion or treatment that would restore Dragon.

I fell asleep, reminding myself to ask Jakoby.

A moment later someone shook my shoulder.

"Elspeth, wake up," Miky said. "The Sadorians have come to take us to the Battlegames."

I opened my eyes, unable to believe it was morning already. I had just gone to sleep! Maruman had vanished but a warmth by my head said he had not been gone long.

"They said to hurry," Miky urged. "We have to be there before the sun comes up or the whole thing will be called off."

I sat up, pulled on boots instead of sandals and crawled out of the tent. It was still dark and the air was cool and pleasant. The moon had set, but a few stars still pricked the darkness. Wordlessly, Kella pressed some of the bread and cheese I had purchased the previous day into my hands, as Rushton announced to the two Sadorians that we were ready.

We were conducted quietly through the sleeping camp to the road where a host of shaggy kamuli and several other long-legged Sadorians waited. As we mounted the seated beasts and settled ourselves in the wooden contraptions that served as saddles, I farsensed Maruman with an attuned probe. He was prowling about the cliffs in search of eggs.

"If there is any trouble, go aboard *The Cutter* with Dragon and Powyrs," I sent. He did not deign to respond, but I knew he had heard me.

When we were all mounted, one Sadorian perched precariously behind each of us, they made a clicking noise with their tongues and the kamuli rose with a great drunken lurching. They walked with a slow, rolling lope that reminded me horribly of the pitching movement of *The Cutter*. No wonder they were called ships of the desert.

"Oh no," Fian moaned, as the kamuli made their ponderous way up the spit slope toward the cliffs. "We're headed out into th' desert."

"It was the obvious place," Hannay said mildly. "We'd better start praying to Lud for a cloudy day or the sun will fry us."

"The rebels will find it just as hard as us," Angina pointed out cheerfully.

∾

We had traveled for about an hour into the trackless desert, and the sky was empty of stars when the Sadorians pulled their beasts to a halt. I looked around, but there was nothing on all sides but featureless dunes. Were these Battlegames to take place here in the middle of nowhere where there was no shelter and no water? But if so, where were the rebels and the Sadorians? I looked up at the sky again. In the east there was a lightness that heralded the dawn.

One of the Sadorians rode up to Rushton and said something inaudible. Then he pointed.

I could see nothing but sand dunes.

"He said the place where the games will be held is there," Ruston said loudly, sounding puzzled.

The Sadorians clicked their tongues and the kamuli continued.

"I can smell flowers," Kella said, and a moment later we found ourselves riding along a long narrow crack in the ground. Through its edges, we could see that it opened up into a great cave under the earth. It was too dim to see much but I could smell greenery and flowers and, at the very bottom of the hidden chasm, the glimmer of water.

"This mun be one of their isis pools," Fian said in sudden excitement.

"So this is where their goddess weeps her tears," Kella said dreamily. "No wonder they can spend so much time out here."

"You'd never find it if you didn't know exactly how to get to it," Daffyd murmured.

Miky described the valley to Dameon as the Sadorians turned the kamuli onto a small, narrow track that wended its way downward. Powyrs had said there were a number of isis pools in the desert, and I had imagined wells. I wondered if they were all like this. Clearly the wave of earth and rock almost covering the chasm protected it from the sun, but let in enough light to allow growth. The combination of heat and water produced humidity that generated luxuriant growth of plant life. The air became increasingly moist as we descended.

By the time we reached the bottom, sunrise was only moments away. Jakoby emerged from what I had taken from a distance as a mass of greenery, but now saw were row upon row of Sadorian men and women.

We dismounted, and she brought us to Bram, who sat crosslegged on a raised dais under a gigantic drooping tree with pale, coiling, green leaves and long creamy pods. The overguardian of the Temple sat at his feet. The rebels stood in a cluster to one side, and the ranks of Sadorians were arrayed behind them.

Malik and his chosen nine stood ramrod straight in two disciplined lines facing Bram. Jakoby indicated that we were to take our place alongside them. The rebel I found myself beside was almost twice my height, his muscular arms scarred. I knew those looking at us must see the contest between us as absurdly unequal.

Jakoby took her place at Bram's side and looked expectantly at the sky. She stood that way until the sun rose in the crack where the sky was visible, casting pink and orange rays forth to stain the few straggles of cloud. I realized they had been literally waiting for sunrise to begin the Battlegames.

"Are you prepared?" Jakoby asked, and I jumped at the loudness of her voice in the still dawn.

"I am," Malik intoned.

"We are," Rushton said.

Jakoby looked to Bram, who inclined his head, then clapped her hands. The little hooded overguardian rose and offered the dice. Bram leaned forward with a grunt to take them up, and mumbled a few inaudible words, before flinging them high.

Every face turned up to watch the two gleaming cubes whirl in the air, and then down to see what number of marks they offered to the sky.

"Six," Bram said. "The Pit, then."

Wordless, the overguardian gathered the dice and passed them back to Bram. He threw them again and this time they fell showing four marks between them.

"Each leader will choose four from among their number to contend in the first Battlegame," Jakoby announced in a ringing voice.

"Choose," Bram said.

There was a momentary hiatus, then Rushton took a half step forward. "It is permitted for me to speak?"

The old Sadorian lifted straggling white brows at him. "I told you last night this is not a battle that can be won with words."

"I only wanted to ask how you expect us to choose well without knowing more about this Pit."

"I will answer your question with another. How do warriors face lack of knowledge in a battle?"

Rushton bowed and returned to face us, beckoning us to gather close.

"You must choose for diversity," Miryum advised him.

"Maybe we can take some sort of clue from the name," Dameon suggested.

"The Pit," Angina murmured.

"I suppose it will be in the ground. Another of these rifts. Therefore climbing may be needed, or lifting." Rushton swept his eyes over us. "Hannay is strongest physically."

"Powyrs told me th' Sadorians sometimes use pits to catch fangcats," Fian said. "There may be beasts, therefore."

Rushton nodded. "Freya," he said at last. He did not look at me and, hurt, I did not suggest myself.

"Maybe th' pit is worked by some mechanics," Fian continued.

Rushton frowned for a long moment. "Yes. You then, Fian. And

Miryum, because she is a powerful coercer as well as strong physically."

Neither he nor Miryum looked at me, although they both knew I also possessed coercive abilities. Neither of them knew how strong I was, because I had always tried to downplay my powers. I had no intention of using them here unless I must.

Sweat beaded Rushton's lip as the four Misfits were led away with Malik's rebels. I guessed it had been hard for him not to name himself. I felt a surge of admiration for the strength of his will. Malik had not named himself either, but it seemed to cost him nothing.

"They are permitted to choose a single implement each from the armament," Jakoby explained. She pointed as he spoke and we watched as the eight contestants vanished into a small gray tent billowing in the freshening dawn breeze that swirled through the gap in the earth and stirred the heavy air.

"How can they choose without knowing what they need?" Angina asked Rushton indignantly. "This is madness."

"Perhaps not," Miky disagreed with her twin. "After all, Malik is in the same position, as you said."

It was growing steadily hotter and I shuddered to think of what the surface temperature must be. Looking up, I saw that the roof of the cavern was moss covered, and wondered how often there were rock falls.

The eight returned. The rebels had chosen between them a double-edged sword, a huge axe, a long knife with a frill of jagged spikes about its tip, and a net. The Misfits had taken a coil of rope, a wide, flat shield, a tapered stave of wood and a knife.

Bram clapped his hands again and we were led toward another pit—almost a miniature copy of the rift we were standing in and, like the larger chasm, invisible until you were almost upon it.

"These cracks in the earth must have been left by the Great White," Daffyd murmured. I glanced at him and hoped this one was not poisonous as were many such rifts left by the Great White. I remembered the Silent Vale in the Weirwoods where orphans had been sent to collect the residue of poisonous whitestick.

When we were standing on the edge, I saw that a cage had been set into the rift, neatly dividing it. Inside the cage were two bears. The larger was lumbering slowly back and forward while the smaller sat in the corner of the cage, its paws clasped around the bars.

"Let the first Battlegame commence," Jakoby's voice rang out.

The servitors immediately lowered the Misfits into one end of the pit by rope, and the rebels into the other.

"I do not like the look of this." Miky murmured uneasily.

"Shh," Angina hissed. "Watch."

The servitors shifted to other ropes and the cage was hoisted up, removing all dividers. The bears seemed more bewildered than angry at this turn of events. They appeared not to have noticed the people at either end of the chasm.

For a long moment no one moved, then the smaller bear noticed the Misfits. It stood up and lumbered toward them, growling slightly.

Without hesitation Freya stepped forward in front of the others, her face serene.

"She is empathizing it," Miky murmured, her face absorbed as she monitored Freya's telempathic emotions. Without warning, two of the servitors at the sides of the pit lifted long, thin pipes to their lips and blew.

Both bears started violently as the darts found their mark. The larger gave a tremendous roar of fury and reared up onto its hind legs, clutching at its back.

Both Misfits and rebels in the pit froze.

I could tell from the dawning despair on Freya's face, that she had lost touch with the bear. That she could not regain a hold suggested that the darts had been drugged.

The larger bear turned to stare at Freya, its eyes red with fury. With a lowing growl it began to advance on her. The smaller bear seemed confused, staring from its companion to the girl and back.

Hannay and Fian stepped forward to stand either side of her, lifting stick and shield to fend off the beast. Freya did not move. Her eyes were fixed on the smaller bear.

"She is sending calmness and compassion," Dameon murmured.

The smaller bear stared back at her, plucking fretfully at the dart lodged in its fur, and even the larger beast seemed to hesitate.

It shook its head slightly.

"She's getting to them," Miky whispered.

On the other side of the pit, the rebel with the sword ran forward without warning and drove the blade deeply into the smaller bear's side.

I watched in impotent horror as the bear fell without a cry, and lay utterly still.

Freya shrieked horribly and fell into a faint, for her mind had been linked empathically to the bear's. If Freya had been a farseeker or a coercer, she would be dead. I reached out my mind, seeking the bear's life force, but there was nothing. Subvocal thoughts swirled out from the larger beast, revealing that the smaller bear had been its cub.

I felt Kella trembling violently at my elbow.

The female bear approached her cub's body and prodded at it. Then she put back her head and howled with such anguish that it rent my heart in two. While she was thus distracted, the four rebels began to come forward in a solid phalanx.

I poised my mind to drive them back, then realized I must not interfere.

I looked to the Misfits in the pit. Hannay had dragged the unconscious Freya to one side and Miryum had slipped past the grief-stricken bear, raising Fian's shield and the knife to the rebels.

She was trying to keep the rebels away from the bear!

The creature looked up from its cub's corpse, focusing on the coercer's back. It rose slowly, eyes blood-red, and growled with chilling hatred.

Fian ran around to its side, waving the shield to draw the bear's attention from Miryum. I wondered in horror what he was trying to do, then remembered that he possessed a weak secondary ability to beastspeak. Now that he had the bear's attention, he was trying to reach its mind.

The creature was clearly baffled and again hesitated.

All at once, it seemed to sweep the confusion from its mind. It snarled and shambled toward Fian, raising massive paws to strike. Even from a distance I could see the wicked sharpness of its talons.

Its movement opened a gap and one of the rebels crept toward Hannay, who was bending over Freya, trying to revive her.

I willed him to turn around.

There was a cry and I turned to see the bear swipe at Fian. He leapt out of her way and Miryum suddenly jumped to one side, leaving the rebels face to face with the enraged creature.

It growled again, and the rebels hastily backed away. Miryum and Fian stood perfectly still. The teknoguilder's face was set and grim. He was still trying to reach the bear.

I looked back to Hannay and saw the rebel behind him lift a knife. My mind flew back to a dark cavern and the Zebkrahn machine, and Madam Vega with her knife poised above Rushton's throat.

I felt the inimical force in the depths of my mind coalesce, and I knew that I could not sit back and watch Hannay die, to win a contest.

At that moment Freya opened her eyes. Something in her expression must have warned the big coercer because Hannay reacted instantly, spinning and using the force of the turn to drive his elbow savagely into the rebel's groin.

"Oh no!" Kella whispered beside me, and my eyes flew to where the rebel with the spiked spear and the other with the sword had driven the bear back toward Miryum. A third joined them, grinning triumphantly.

But his smile faltered and, a moment later, he flung down his weapon and began to execute a frenzied dance, slapping bare arms and legs as if they were on fire. His two companions gaped at him incredulously. Then a second rebel abandoned his sword and seemed to be trying to throttle himself. The she-bear appeared baffled and had ceased her growls.

"Miryum is coercing them," Miky murmured.

The remaining rebel, realizing that whatever ailed his companions arose from the stolid coercer, slammed his fist into her temple. She fell to the ground, leaving Fian to face the three rebels.

Again, they began to harry the bear back toward him.

Abruptly, the rebel with the axe stopped and began to claw at his eyes.

Hannay was coercing now, but he had nowhere near Miryum's strength. The rebel with the knife ran at him and he was forced to release the other man's mind to defend himself.

"Lud, if only they had nowt struck Miryum down. A little more time and she could have held 'em all in thrall!" Daffyd muttered.

All at once the bear seemed to go mad. It howled and clutched at its head, raking the air with its razor claws.

"The drug must have progressive effects," Kella murmured.

The servitors at the pit worked another set of ropes and a hidden passage appeared in the side of the rift wall. The three rebels ran for it, and the bear snarled, charging after them, but the gap was too narrow.

Thwarted, it turned.

Freya, whey-pale, was now trying to revive Miryum. Hannay and Fian positioned themselves in front of them, shield and stave raised.

The fourth rebel, now recovered, climbed stiffly to his feet. Seeing no one was watching him, he caught up his knife and rushed at Hannay, his face a mask of hatred. The motion caught the eyes of the crazed bear and it turned and charged.

Freya staggered out to set herself between Hannay and Fian and the petrified rebel. The beast stopped and its wild eyes focused their madness on her.

"No!" I whispered.

Step by step Freya approached the bear, drawing gradually within reach of the lethal claws and killing embrace. The bear made a crooning sound.

"She has it," Miky whispered.

Indeed the bear seemed mesmerized. Then it groaned, clutched at its back and keeled over.

"No!" Freya screamed, flinging herself beside the creature. It did not move, and she looked up out of the pit with a face that streamed with tears. "You bastards! It is dead."

"Poisoned," Kella breathed.

"The first game is ended," Jakoby announced.

XLI

"Interesting," Bram said.

We had returned to the side of the isis pool. In the light flooding through the crack, the water was as blue as a summerdays sky. Miryum had been laid on the grass beside Bram's dais and Kella was tending her. Jakoby had warned us that if the coercer failed to resume her position before the third game commenced, she would be disqualified, reducing our number to nine. That would not happen because, if necessary, Kella could heal her quickly. But this would drain her energy, so we had decided to wait to the last minute and hope the coercer would revive naturally.

Jakoby had not mentioned Freya's cry, and the blond girl stood beside me, pale but defiant. Malik's mocking smile said all too clearly that we had fared badly in the first Battlegame. But the day was young, I thought, gritting my teeth.

"Interesting to note what each group saw as the object of the Battlegame," Bram said. "The rebels sought to slay the bears and, if possible, to have the bears slay their opponents. Failing that, to kill the beasts and their opponents and get away alive. Would you concur?"

Jakoby nodded.

"In attempting to attain these objectives, the rebels were swift, aggressive and sure. They worked well together when it was useful, never hesitating to cut their losses at need."

Jakoby nodded again.

"The Misfits' behavior, on the other hand, appeared primarily defensive to my eye. They sought to protect both themselves and the bears. Since the female was trying to kill them, this was a confused and somewhat sentimental strategy to adopt. The Misfits' mental powers are clearly considerable, but they didn't use them in any decisive way in this instance. If they can control the bears, why not have them attack the rebels, or have the rebels turn on one another?"

Bram closed his eyes and seemed to sink into a small trance after this speech. After a moment, he roused himself and announced that the second game would begin.

The dice were thrown again, and this time their number indicated a Battlegame Jakoby called The Wall. A second casting gave two players to each team.

Rushton chose Angina, because he was agile and we thought the wall might have to be scaled, and Hannay again, because he was strong and a coercer, in case the wall had to be shifted or broken down.

We had not lost heart despite the first battle, for we were confident that we would perform better now that we had some idea of what the games might entail. The most important thing we had learned was that we must define our objectives when they were not specifically named.

When Angina and Hannay were taken off with the two rebels, Rushton frowned after them. "I hope we do better than in the first game."

Miky gave him a swift, startled look. "You can't mean you think they should have killed that bear."

"Of course not," he said. "I do not see what else they could have done. However," he looked at me, "do you think Malik instructed his men to kill us if they got the chance? Or were their attacks in the pit instinctive?"

I let him see the answer in my eyes and his frown deepened.

Angina and Hannay came back with the chosen rebels. Both were now clad in loin cloths and boots, and they seemed to be arguing furiously as were the rebel pair. None of the four contestants bore any weapons. They were ushered past Bram's dais and over to the bottom of the rift wall, where Sadorian servitors bound Angina and one of the rebels wrist and ankle.

"What on earth can they be expected to do tied up like that?" Miky said worriedly.

The servitors now turned their attention to Hannay and the second rebel, buckling them into stout leather jerkins. Their bare limbs were swathed in what appeared to be bandages, and long heavy gauntlets were pulled over their hands, and boots reaching to the knee strapped on.

"The climber must scale the rift wall to the summit," Jakoby said.

Miky frowned. "But how can Angina climb with his arms like that?"

"A strong cord will attach the climber to the burden," Jakoby went on.

We listened aghast as she explained that one in each doublet was to drag the other with them as a helpless bundle. The arms, legs and hands of the climbers were bound in cloth to protect them from the cliffs which were impregnated with streaks of holocaust poison. The burden had no such protection and must rely entirely on the skill of the climber.

"But . . . coercers can't bear heights," Miky reminded us, ashen cheeked.

"They had to let Hannay climb. Angina could never lift him," Rushton snapped.

Miky looked sick.

"At least it's not Miryum. Hannay won't be as badly affected as she would," Kella said stoutly. She did not say what she must have been thinking—what we were all thinking—that Miky's twin's life was in the hands of a man who could not bear heights.

The bout would be over, Jakoby announced, when both pairs reached the desert above.

"Climb," Bram shouted.

We watched with bated breath as the game began.

To begin with, the rebels were at an obvious disadvantage, because they were both of equal height and weight. This gave the climber an arduous task. But Hannay's fear of heights made him climb with agonizing slowness. Soon, the rebels were some distance above.

Then all at once Hannay began to climb swiftly, his hands and feet sure. Gradually he closed the gap between himself and the rebel pair.

"Angina's helping him not to be afraid," Miky said with a flare of pride.

Now the pairs were level. But the climber in the rebel team had reached a small ledge that allowed him to stand and free his hands. He began to take chunks of rock and hurl them at Hannay.

"He's trying to dislodge them!" Daffyd cried.

The big coercer paid no attention and soon had risen above the rebel climber. The rebel turned his attention to Angina and went on hurling stones and abuse.

Suddenly Hannay stopped climbing.

We stared, straining our eyes and trying to figure out what had happened.

"Angina's been knocked out by the rebel's stone," Miky said.

"Oh Lud," I whispered, knowing that, unconscious, the empath could not send courage to the big coercer. If Hannay fell now, he would kill them both. The rebel climber began to ascend again.

For a long time the coercer did not move, but at last he began to climb again, too.

"Has Angina . . . ?" I began, but incredibly Miky shook her head.

That meant Hannay was going it alone. He went very slowly, testing hand holds and creeping over the face of the cliff like an ant in a windstorm.

By contrast, the rebel climber rose with exultant speed, uncaring that his partner was being dragged and bumped against the poisoned rockwall. When he reached the top, he hauled up his trussed partner and gave a great shout of triumph.

This was echoed by the rebels below.

It was more than half an hour later that an utterly exhausted Hannay dragged himself up on the platform and pulled Angina up after him. They were brought back down on kamuli. Angina had regained consciousness, though he had a lump on his forehead the size of a hen's egg, and claimed to be seeing double. Kella drew the slight concussion out of him, and Miky went to where Hannay sat heavily on a boulder, staring at the ground.

"That was brave," she told him softly. "I know coercers hate heights. Are you all right?"

"That was the hardest thing I have ever done. But it was not bravery that moved me, Miky. It was blind terror."

"Not so blind," Miky whispered, pressing a kiss to his cheek.

A faint color rose in his face, just as Jakoby approached to summon us back to the dais. Miryum had wakened and joined us as we took our places. Bram looked closely at the stocky coercer before agreeing that she was fit to continue. Now we were ten again, but Malik had lost one player. The man who had been trussed and borne up the ridge wall had touched the walls too often and he was seriously ill. There would be no question of his returning within two games.

"The rebel climbers clearly saw the object of the game as speed," Bram said. "Having identified their objective, they lost no time in pursuing it. It is also clear that the rebels have a second objective—that is, to destroy or harm their opponents. They have been equally single minded in their efforts to fulfill this objective, but so far have failed. Oddly, this does not appear to have excited a desire to retaliate on the part of the Misfits. They have done no more than use their unusual Talents to protect themselves when they were under attack.

"Neither did they use their powers to inhibit their opponents' progress up the wall," Bram continued, tugging at the lobe of his ear. "They might have caused their opponents to jump from the cliff under some delusion. But they did not. They only appear able to use their abilities to help themselves or to defend themselves. There does not seem to be any capacity for aggression in them."

He straightened and the overguardian brought the dice again.

At the first throw, twelve marks faced up.

"The Pole," Bram intoned.

On the second throw, three marks faced the sky and we gathered around Rushton to decide which three should represent us.

"I have some skill with the pole as a weapon, but twice I have failed," Hannay said despondently. "I am not afraid, but I think you should not choose me."

"You did not fail," Angina said. "I made you brave, and when I was hurt you made yourself brave."

The coercer smiled wanly and ruffled the empath's hair. "Let us say you showed me the knack of it."

"I will do it," Miryum said stoutly. "Pole fighting is my specialty and if it is aggression they want I am the person to give it to them."

Rushton nodded. "I name myself as well to this, for I too have some skill at the pole."

"We need three," Miryum reminded him.

"I have not learned the pole but I am strong," Daffyd offered diffidently.

"Why not," Rushton agreed, sounding almost cheerful. I guessed he was glad to be involved rather than watching.

"What if they are not to fight with the poles?" Dameon murmured, but Jakoby had called for Rushton to nominate his team for the third game. Malik spoke, and the chosen six were marched off to the armoring tent.

When Jakoby explained this game, my heart sank for we had mis-judged yet again, for the game did not involve the common sport of pole fighting. The title referred instead to a long, slender piece of wood run between two high stands. Two of these constructions were erected before our eyes, to stand less than an arm's width apart.

The object, Jakoby said, was for each trio to cross the pole from end to end one at a time, without falling. The first team with all members across safely would end the bout.

Hannay groaned. "Badly as we have done already, we cannot hope to succeed now. No coercer fears heights more than Miryum."

Our only consolation was that the rebel team seemed no happier about this Battlegame. I kept my fingers crossed that at least one of their people would also be afraid of heights.

The six returned carrying short staves which were clearly to be used for balance poles. Even at a distance, I could see Miryum was white and tense as Jakoby told them each team must begin at opposite ends and proceed at their own pace.

"Begin," Bram shouted.

Rushton went first, crossing with the grace and balance that had stood him in such good stead aboard *The Cutter*, and an obvious lack of fear. The first rebel had no hope of matching him and made his own crossing slowly and carefully, sweating and swearing at every step. By the time he reached the other side, Daffyd had already taken Rushton's place and was making his careful way across the pole.

The second rebel was far more agile. He swarmed up the ladder and stepped out onto the pole with confidence. He looked across at Daffyd and smiled.

My heart began to bump uneasily as he came level with the grimly concentrating Daffyd.

He swung his stave out without warning and dealt Daffyd's a hard thump.

Panicking, the Druid armsman dropped his stave and swayed back and forward. The rebel laughed and did not see the stave fall to straddle the two poles. Still laughing, he held his own stave up and stepped forward, only to trip on Daffyd's. Taken by surprise, he had no chance at regaining his balance. He fell with a terrified scream.

"Lud help him," Miky whispered, but my eyes were riveted to Daffyd who was still swaying dangerously.

"Use your arms!" Rushton cried.

Slowly Daffyd lifted his arms and, after a long tense moment, he stepped forward again, only to misjudge.

Kella screamed as he fell but, at the last minute, he caught hold of the pole. He hung there for a long moment before beginning to make his way hand over hand to the ladder.

There was dead silence as he climbed to the ground and crossed to where the second rebel lay in the red-stained sand, motionless.

He looked up at the two rebels, who had made no move toward their fallen comrade.

"He's dead."

"Go!" snarled the first rebel to the third, shoving him. The red-haired man licked his lips, then began to mount the stand.

I looked across at Miryum.

She was trembling violently, her face paper white, her eyes fixed on the dead rebel.

Rushton cursed audibly, and set his hands on the ladder at the finishing end.

"Look at me, Miryum," he urged.

She lifted her head.

"Put your hands on the ladder. We'll climb up together. Do exactly as I do, and don't look down."

Seeming half mesmerized by his fierceness, she obeyed, putting her hands around the first rung.

And so they climbed.

The third rebel was halfway across now, but moving very slowly. The first rebel shouted and jeered at Miryum, calling her a great stupid sow, but her entire attention was focused on Rushton.

They had reached the top of the ladder and were facing one another. "Come," Rushton invited softly. "Walk across to me. Come as slowly as you wish and don't look down. Don't think. Just step out."

She did not move.

I closed my eyes, unable to bear the tension. If she managed to make it across, we would have won our first game, no matter how long it took. But how could she?

"Lud save us. She's doing it!" Hannay whispered incredulously.

I took a deep breath and opened my eyes to see Miryum had indeed taken up a balancing stave and stepped out onto the narrow pole. She walked forward, step by slow step, her eyes fixed on Rushton as if they were her lifeline. She reached the center of the pole. The exact center.

Then I saw her eyes sweep down to where the rebel lay.

She stopped.

"Come on," Rushton urged. "You've come this far."

But she was like a statue, frozen with terror.

"Come on," Daffyd shouted from below. "Reach down and swing the rest of the way like I did."

"She can't," Hannay murmured, his own brow beaded with sweat.

"I'm strong!" Miryum cried in an agonized voice. "I'm strong!"

For one dreadful moment, I thought she was going to jump.

There was a cry of anger from the rebels and I saw that Rushton had come out from the other end using his hands outstretched to balance himself. In moments, he and Miryum were facing one another. He spoke too softly for us to hear what he said, but it was clear that he was coaxing her. The third rebel had reached the end and was jeering and exorting the coercer to join the dead rebel on the ground.

Miryum shook her head at Rushton.

He reached out, talking all the while, until he was also grasping Miryum's balancing stave.

"No!" Miryum moaned, as he pulled her gently toward him.

"Yes," Rushton said calmly, firmly. "For Obernewtyn. Walk, Miryum."

And, incredibly, she did. He walked backward, leading her and feeling his way with his feet and instinct.

When they were safe, I cheered myself hoarse with the others, blinded by tears of pride. Miky and Angina were nearly crushed to death by an elated Hannay and there was not a dry eye among us.

The rebels roared too, hissing that it was a cheat.

"How so?" Jakoby inquired of Malik, who had made the charge formal.

"He helped that fat bitch. She would not have made it without him."

"That is true," Jakoby said, and for a moment her golden eyes were full of irony.

"The Misfits show great courage and great devotion to one another," Bram said. "Perhaps too much, for if the girl had fallen she would undoubtedly have taken their leader with her. A wise leader does not risk himself in this way. Not for a single of his warriors."

He went on to praise the singlemindedness of the rebels in trying to thwart their opponents, but suggested they needed to temper zeal with thought, since they had lost another player and were now down to eight.

"There must be some warriors in case a battle is only one of many in a war." He expressed regret at the dead rebel as the body was carried away, but none of the other rebels seemed overly disturbed by what had happened to their companion.

The next game to be played was called The Ride.

XLII

"I am for this," I told Rushton, for a swift probing had told me there were horses in a corral just behind a clump of trees.

For a moment our eyes met.

"Yes," he said. "But, Elspeth, we have to do more than win this with speed and grace. We won the last game, I am sure, but we have to show some aggression. It sounds as if these Sadorians value that in the rebels and we're losing because of it."

"I'll try," I said.

When Rushton named me to Bram, Malik named himself.

We were brought to the small herd of beasts I had farsensed and bade to choose our mounts. Malik immediately selected a huge gray gelding with intelligent eyes. He had clearly chosen the most powerful beast, but a race among horses sometimes had more to do with endurance than strength. I paused for a moment and swung myself into the corral to walk among the other horses.

I beastspoke at random, asking who was stronger and faster than all the rest. Suddenly I found myself face to face with the little mare, Faraf, whom I had aided at the city gate the day I arrived at Sutrium.

"Greetings ElspethInnle," she sent. "It seems our paths are twined. As you see/discover my escape did not bring me to the freerunning barud."

"You were captured?"

"Yes, and sold to these. As funaga go, they are not bad/evil. Yet I dream of the freerunning."

"Choose," Malik snarled impatiently.

Ignoring him, I explained my need to the mare.

"The other/funaga has taken the strongest among us. But you had better choose me, for I am small and not strong," she advised.

"Why? Will the strong/wise other let us win? My need is very great."

"He would if I ask it, Innle, for he knows what you are. But they will feed us a garrug/a leaf which some call prickleberry. It causes a madness that infects/burns the brain. Better still to ride a weak mad horse than a strong one."

I bit my lip to keep a smile of triumph from my mouth as I led Faraf out.

Malik looked down at the slender mare incredulously, but a servitor merely offered us a choice of saddles. The rebel chose a great solid armored thing with sharp metal spurs. On Faraf's advice, I took one that was light and deep seated. I chose the simplest bridle but removed the metal bit.

∾

When we were brought back to the isis pool, a space had been cleared, and Jakoby explained what Faraf had already told me. We would get onto the horses and they would be fed the prickleberry which would madden them temporarily. We would sit on them until the drug took effect. When one of us was unseated, the game would be ended.

"This weed will not kill the horses as it did the bear?" I asked, trying to recall what I knew of prickleberry.

Jakoby's brows lifted. "The bear did not die from the gurrug. Its heart was weak and burst under the strain of battle."

The shadows were long now, and I prayed this game would end the day. If we won, it would leave both sides equal, and perhaps that was the best way to win this fight.

"Courage," Faraf sent as I mounted her. The saddle felt stiff and hard against my backside, and the metal stirrups pressed my feet uncomfortably. A servitor brought a nosebag and, as Faraf ate, a thought came to me of how we might further impress the rebels.

"Faraf/littlesistermind, if you will let me into your thoughts/open to me, I can block the effect of this leaf so that it will not madden you."

"I will open but already it begins to affect me."

This was true, for her whole body was already twitching. I sent a probe into her mind and examined the effect of the prickleberry. It moved swiftly but I was faster, blocking nerve paths and sending it by innocent trails to the bowel to be voided. Still some of the drug remained in her system, so I took control of her nerves and immobilized her completely.

Gradually the trembling faded and she stood quiet.

Malik's horse, meanwhile, was pacing about shuddering and shying at nothing. The rebel's face was pale and he held the rein cruelly tight, ready to saw on the horse's mouth the minute it tried anything.

Without warning, the animal gave a shrill whinnying shriek and reared up.

The sound tore at me and I tried to get to Malik's horse to ease him. But the drug had taken hold and his mind was inaccessible. It plunged and bucked violently, but the rebel kept his seat. He was a superb rider.

He gave me a look of patent fury and I read his intention a moment before he kicked his horse into a maddened run—*straight at me!*

I could do nothing to move Faraf out of the way because I had shut down her nerves. As Malik thundered past the saddle spikes cut her neck and my leg deeply.

The horse bucked in a circle as Malik fought to bring him around. Then he charged again.

"Stop!" I screamed, as the metal spur this time tore open the little mare's flank. I was trying frantically to restore her motor responses but the drug was preventing me.

Again Malik fought his mount to turn it, and as he bore down on me I saw that he meant to kill me if he could, or cut my mount to pieces under me. The spikes missed but he dug the horse with his heels and it kicked out, catching Faraf on the side of her head.

Blood streamed down her face and she staggered sideways in a hideous parody of the first time I had seen her.

He turned again.

"No!" I screamed, and threw my leg over her to slide to the ground. "I forfeit!"

There was a roaring sound in my ears, and my leg felt oddly numb, but I turned to slide my arms around the mare's bloody neck.

"I am sorry, ElspethInnle. I have failed you," she sent humbly.

"Never," I whispered, looking into her eyes. I kissed her soft nose and limped with her back to the pens. I did not look at Malik, who had jumped clear of his horse.

∾

"There is nothing to be said since this game was forfeited," Bram said, when we were all assembled again.

"Ye did th' right thing," Fian whispered angrily, when I returned to them. Freya nodded and squeezed my arm. But I was not comforted. If only I had possessed the presence of mind I might have coerced Malik, but fear for Faraf had stopped me thinking clearly. I dared not look at Rushton. He had trusted me to win this game and I had forfeited. That meant we had won only a single game, while the rebels had won three. Even if we won the next game we would lose the Battlegames, for the shadows were long and the sun would soon set. I sat down, feeling as if my legs were too weak to support me.

"There is blood on your trews," Freya whispered.

Bram rose to throw again. Ironically the fifth game was named Song, and the number of players from each team was two. We could not lose, and yet it was now impossible for us to win.

"A song! This is a joke," Malik snarled.

"I told you, the Battlegames tests many qualities. Proceed, unless you would forfeit," Bram said tranquilly.

The two red-faced rebels chosen by Malik sang a bawdy battle song, probably the only one they knew.

In contrast Miky and Angina's song dealt not with the glory of war, but with the tragedy of it. It was an old song that told of two boys; brothers separated at birth and sent to war against one another. Only when one had killed the other, did they understand what had come to pass. The song was supposedly a dirge, sung by the surviving man over his brother's body.

I had heard the song before, but never like this; never with such rending sorrow. Empathized, it became something greater and deeper than a song about two brothers. It became a song about all wars. I wept for the pity of two brothers, lost to one another until it was too late. But I also wept for my own brother, Jes, and for Jik and Matthew and Dragon; for the gypsy Caldeko and for the nameless rebel who had broken his back on the pole. For all the victims of hatred and war.

And I was not alone. Kella and Freya and Dameon wept, but many of the Sadorians wept too. Even some of the rebels wiped their eyes surreptitiously as Miky sang the final words: "Will there ever be a time when war does not kill the babes and the dreams of the world?"

When the final notes faded, the sun set in a dazzling golden haze and it seemed to me that the radiant sky itself paid homage to their voices. Malik stood dry-eyed and contemptuous as Bram rose to speak, dabbing at his eyes.

"The rebel song offered humor and this is a fine thing to bolster a warrior's courage," he said. "But the Misfit song is greater, for it reaches into the very soul of a warrior and causes him to question himself."

"What does it matter that a song brings tears to the eyes of the weak and the womanish? Will it win a battle?" Malik demanded.

"A song will not wield a sword of metal, my friend," Bram said softly. "But it can put a sword into the heart that will never rust or blunt. It can cause warriors to fight when good sense bids them surrender, raise an army or quell the tears of a babe."

He rose and lifted his arms.

"The sun has gone and the Battlegames are ended."

"Who won then?" Malik demanded.

Bram cast a cool eye on the rebel.

"Impatience is not the least of your faults, Malik. It is a kind of greed and some day it may see you undone."

He cast his eyes about to take in rebels, Sadorians and Misfits alike.

"I have been asked to judge these Battlegames. I tell you now that this is not merely a matter of tallying points, but of examining how each game was played. Sometimes this makes the judging difficult, for fewer points might have been awarded to the one who wins."

My heart swelled in sudden hope. Was it possible he might decide in our favor despite the fact that we had won fewer games?

"In this case, however, the judging is a simple matter," he went on. "The games were staged to determine who were the greater warriors, and whether the Misfits and their unusual powers were worthy of alliance. The answer is that the rebels are clearly far more fitted to warfare than the Misfits. They have shaped their souls for aggression and quicken to violence as a gravid mare quickens with new life. The rebel legions, if they are truly represented by these men, are made for battle. No instinct of mercy would restrain them, no compassion stay their hand, no love of beauty keep them from destruction. The Battlegames have shown them to be swift, decisive, ruthless and resourceful. They are filled with the warrior's desire to dominate and subdue.

"As for the Misfits, if they are truly represented by these before me, they are no warriors. They care too much for life and for one another. They are not stirred by the glories of war, and the shedding of lifeblood brings them sorrow, whether it be of beast or human, friend or foe. All their instincts are for defense and so their great powers are all but useless. They are not cowardly or weak, but their minds appear incapable of allowing their great powers to serve them as weapons.

"Witness that they used the incredible ability which they call empathy to its greatest effect in a song, rather than to turn their enemies' hearts to terror.

"They will never have the rebels' singlemindedness of purpose, nor therefore their driving force, because they cannot see things in terms of simple goals."

He turned in the dead silence wrought by his powerful oratory, and faced the rebels. "We here in Sador value the earth above all life—humans and beasts alike are short lived and unimportant. This you know. We have thought that Landfolk valued their own lives too much, regarding themselves as the chosen of their Lud. But these Misfits seem to value all life and this is strange for us to contemplate. But think you this. You rebels opposed alliance with the Misfits because you thought them monsters and inhuman. Ask yourselves now which team has this day shown the keenest humanity and which has shown itself to be more monstrous."

The old man paused, then he said in a voice drained of all vitality, "I declare the rebels the victors of the Battlegames."

The rebels cheered, but there was a puzzled, halfhearted edge to the sound. Malik's face was thunderous as he moved to join the other rebel leaders and receive their congratulations.

Rushton turned to us, looking much older in that moment than I had ever seen him.

"The old man's judging was fair," he said.

I stepped forward to tell him that if I must be like Malik to be a warrior, then I would not be a warrior, but my leg buckled under me. As I fell forward, Rushton opened his arms to catch me, but I slipped through them into the abyss.

～

I dreamed I was bound to the Zebkrahn machine and my legs were on fire.

I dreamed of the Agyllian healer, Nerat, telling me she would teach my body to heal itself.

I dreamed of a red-haired woman drowning in an ocean of blood, of Swallow raising a sword to salute me, of Ariel searching for me down long tunnels.

I dreamed of Maruman telling me I would lead the beasts to freedom, and of walking on the deck of *The Cutter*, watching the ship fish dance.

I dreamed of Rushton waiting at the doors of Obernewtyn, and of Freya in his arms.

I dreamed of a shining river that called my name.

"Do not go into the stream, ElspethInnle."

"Atthis!" I thought. "At last you speak to me."

"I have spoken often through the yelloweyes and the dreamingwoman you call Maryonfuturereteller."

"Why did you never speak to *me*?"

"Because the H'rayka would hear. He flies the dreamtrails. He listens to hear what I will say so that he may thwart me/us/you."

"Can he not hear us now?"

"He would not dare come so close to the death/dreaming river for fear that it would swallow him. And so it might for you are perilously close. You must come back from the edge now. I am holding you but my strength fades."

"I like it here. There is no pain and it sings to me. If I come back, you will not speak to me again."

"It is not yet your time to hear this song."

"Then why am I here?"

"A small artery in your leg was severed during this testing called Battlegames. You bled near to death. They have stopped the blood, but you are too close to the stream. Your body has learned to heal itself, but it cannot do so when you are so close to the stream. You must draw back if you would live."

I felt a great wrenching pull to return, but I fought it. I was not sure I wanted to live.

"What you feel is the spiritcall of one who would have you live, ElspethInnle. Go back and let yourself heal, for the world has need of you. Go back, or the H'rayka wins. Go back or the beasts will never be free."

I felt the pulling again and wondered whose spirit held me so tightly. Curious, I let myself be drawn away from the stream by it.

"Who are you?" I called, but there was nothing, only a roaring sound in my ears. There was a long rushing darkness and then I opened my eyes.

A monster peered at me. I screamed and fled back to the darkness.

I opened my eyes and Kella smiled at me.

I opened my eyes and Dameon touched my cheek.

I opened my eyes.

I was lying in a bed in a dark, cold room. Beside me sat the hooded overguardian.

"You are in the Earthtemple, Elspeth Gordie," said the voice from within the hood. "You have slept long."

XLIII

"Come," the Temple guardian murmured, his voice shuddering and whispering along the damp, echo-ridden, stone tunnels that honeycombed the Sadorian cliffs.

"Where are you taking me?" I demanded, exasperated. "And when can I see my friends?"

"Soon," he answered. The same thing he had said for days in the same queer, breathy voice.

"I am no longer sick and you are keeping me prisoner!" I snapped. "I know they were in here before, so why can't I see them now?"

He did not answer.

I glared at the damp walls resentfully. Maybe Rushton and the others had not come in to see me because they had gone back to Sutrium. After all, I had been unconscious for five days and awake for three. Eight days in all since the Battlegames had ended. The Temple guardians had cared for me when I woke, weak and disorientated and I was grateful for that, but I was fully recovered now. If the place had not been such an impossible warren of tunnels, I should have long since walked out myself. As it was, I must wait until the overguardian allowed one of the underlings to escort me out.

I was about to repeat my question when we rounded a bend. Set into the side of the tunnel was a huge panel carved of wood, I had not come across in my wanderings.

I stopped and gaped at it in amazement, for there was no doubt in my mind that whoever had executed it had also carved the doors to Obernewtyn! The chisel work on the doors had possessed a precision in angling that could not be mistaken, and was as individualistic as the markings on one person's palm.

"Come," the guardian prompted.

Dazed, I did not move. "Who did this?"

He came back a few steps reluctantly. "Kasanda. Now will you come?"

I followed him. "Who is Kasanda?"

He did not answer and my temper rose again. I wrestled it down.

"When can I see the overguardian?" I asked sweetly.

Again he did not respond.

I ground my teeth and searched my mind, but before I could come up with something rude enough to fracture even a guardian's phenomenal composure, he stopped before a stone doorway.

"Go in. The overguardian will come to you here."

I stared at him incredulously. "You mean now?"

"Soon."

I opened my mouth but thought better of it and went through the door. Behind it was an enormous lantern-lit chamber. Like most of the caverns, it was devoid of furnishings. The temple was, in fact, a natural labyrinth and the guardians inhabited only a fraction of the chambers and tunnels. But unlike the other empty caverns every bit of wall space in this one was taken up with huge panels of carved stone. I could see at a glance that whoever had done them had also executed the wood carving in the hall.

"The sequence begins here," the guardian said, pointing to the panel nearest the door. "You look here and then you go that way."

I nodded absently and moved to the first panel.

It was part carved, part daubed with mud and fiber to raise up shapes, and tinted with darker and lighter tones. Little enough with which to create a world, let alone a lost world of unimaginable wonders, and yet the panel showed one of the Beforetime cities. I was reminded inevitably of the city under Tor, but the city depicted in the panel was vibrantly alive. Exaltingly magnificent, the constructions reaching to the skies embodied the greatness of their makers. The panel was a paean of praise to the Beforetimers.

I shivered, for surely such a vision could only come from one who had seen the cities of the Beforetime in all their glory?

After a long while, I tore myself from the first panel. The next also featured the towering Beforetime structures, but they were subtly different. After only a moment of admiration I noticed not the buildings, but the way they crushed and smothered the earth. I saw the caged and stunted trees devoid of sunlight. I realized that this panel spoke not of greatness, but of soaring, overweening pride and, most of all, of oppression. The Beforetimers had gouged and yoked and reshaped the very earth to their creations.

I shifted to the third panel. Here again were Beforetime structures. Above lay a pall of blackness such as rose chokingly from the smithy's forge. I did not know what purpose these buildings served, for no smith would need so much space, but the message was clear. Not content to despoil the earth, the Beforetimers had smeared the skies with their messes.

One after another panels depicted similar scenes—rivers clogged and poisoned, forests hewn down and transformed into salted deserts, mountains levelled to rubble. The Beforetimers had been masters of wanton destruction and they had built their world regardless of the cost.

I moved to the next panel and here at last were scenes of the Great White. Seen thus, it seemed to me that the holocaust had been inevitable, given the nature of the Beforetimers. How else could their story have ended, but with men and women and beasts and birds fleeing in terror from the huge fiery mushrooms that rose in the skies behind them? And when the whiteness faded, there were panels of utter desolation—sere deserts and poisoned waters: the Blacklands.

"Truly this is a place of sorrows," a boy's voice said.

I whirled to see the tiny hooded figure that had sat at Bram's feet during the Battlegames. The overguardian's hands lifted and removed the hood.

I recoiled involuntarily, for the face revealed was grossly deformed. In stark, dreadful contrast, his eyes were the color of isis pools, sad and beautiful.

"I am sorry," I said. "I did not expect..."

He smiled, a grotesque twisting of his lips. "I am the overguardian of the Earthtemple. That which poisoned the earth also poisoned my mother. It is so with all of the guardians here."

I took a deep breath, hiding my surprise at his age as much as at the fact that he was a Misfit. "I am glad to meet you. Thank you for healing me..."

"I did not heal you. Your body healed itself. We do not know how."

His words evoked a memory of my dream, and Atthis telling me my body could heal itself. Had it really been the old bird, or a feverish delusion? Yet, if it was true it would explain so many things. Perhaps even the disappearance of Swallow's tattoo.

Atthis' words sounded in my mind like the wind over a seashell: *"The world has need of you. Go back, or the H'rayka wins."*

I looked around at the carved panels and thought bitterly that it would be better if the battlemachines were activated and humanity wiped from the face of the earth once and for all. The holocaust had changed nothing. People like Malik would use anything in their hunger for victory and domination.

"There is a story," the boy said dreamily. "It tells of one who will come across the sea in search of the fifth sign of Kasanda."

I frowned, drawn from my despair by curiosity. "The same Kasanda that carved these?"

He seemed not to hear. "There are many born with Kasanda's gift here and even in your own land. But it is said when one comes in search of the signs, three companions will come also, one of whom shall be of true Kasanda blood."

"Why are you telling me this?" I demanded coldly. His talk of seeking and signs chilled me.

The boy shrugged. "Perhaps I dreamed that you would come, and that I must say these words. I have Kasanda's gift of true dreaming and so I am sometimes called a kasanda. But the first Kasanda is the one who dreamed of the Seeker."

"The . . . Seeker?"

He nodded. "After the signs. Kasanda told my people that the Seeker would bear the Moonwatcher and be borne by the Daywatcher, who is the color of shadows. You see the beauty and intricacy of the images? The Moonwatcher's daylight eye, and the Daywatcher's shadow-hue are complementary. Two sides of the spinning coin. The implication is that one may emulate the other in times of need. The interesting thing is that there is no information about the Seeker—as if that was too dangerous to be left."

I shivered, unnerved by his use of the name Atthis had given me. I thought of the disturbed youth outside the Earthtemple flinging himself at my feet. He, too, had spoken of the Moonwatcher. I shook my head angrily. This was ridiculous. The threads of my quest could not stretch this far, surely.

"It is said Kasanda took the signs from her dreams, and strewed them across the lands so that they should not be found except by the Seeker. There are rumors that they lead to the deepest treasures of the Beforetimers. Still others say they are the key to a power that is great enough to shift the stars, and even to quench them."

Power again, I thought bleakly. That was what had brought about the holocaust. "Do you know what the signs are?"

He smiled enigmatically. "I know many things. I know that the Herders come bearing lethal gifts of disease, and that they must be watched constantly to prevent them harming the earth or our people. I know that when the Seeker journeys forth with the Day and Moonwatcher, and with one of Kasanda blood, they will be looking for the final sign. Then may the kasanda, who is the overguardian, aid them."

I shook my head angrily. "This is nothing to do with me. I want to get out of here." I glanced around at the panels with loathing.

The boy sighed and resumed his hood. "Very well. Tomorrow your friends will come to the Temple for you."

He went out, but when I followed he had vanished. The guardian who had brought me from my cell rose from the step.

"I will take you back to your chamber."

∽

Left alone, I sat on the edge of the bed. My mind was filled with pictures—the Herder torturing Iriny's bondmate, my parents killed for their beliefs, Malik's eyes filled with hatred, and the dark dreadful visions in stone left by the mysterious Kasanda for the Seeker.

Well, the Seeker had seen them.

I thought of the transcendent beauty of the first panel, and tried to understand how the ability to create such wondrous beauty could have become so perverted, so destructive.

With power, my mind whispered.

I felt desperately confused and lay down, longing to be in the mountains. I closed my eyes and sent my mind out into the desert. It was night and the pale changeless dunes undulated beneath the night sky, going on as far as the eye could behold without a sign of human life. So must the world have looked *before* the Beforetime and the demon angels we named Oldtimers. The Great White now seemed the least of their evils. Perhaps not evil at all, for if it had not come, then what would they have done next? Shaken by this thought, I tried to draw the calm grace of the desert into me, but the despair was too strong.

Again I felt a fierce longing for the clean coldness of the mountains.

"*Then seek them,*" Maruman's voice whispered into my mind.

"Where are you?" I sent, trying to decide if his voice was real or imagined.

"*Maruman/yelloweyes flies the dreamtrails. Fly to the mountains if you need them.*"

I sighed. "It is too far. You know I cannot send my mind over Blacklands."

"*You can if/when you farsend you seek the dreamtrails. Come.*"

I let him take hold of me, but almost immediately I felt claws. Before I could summon the wit to struggle or fight, I had the uncanny sensation of hurtling through the air as if hurled from a catapult.

"Fly/seek!" Maruman's mindcry faded behind me.

"ElspethInnle. Come ride with me...." Gahltha's mind-voice came to me.

I opened my eyes and was amazed to find myself sitting in my turret chamber at Obernewtyn.

Dazed, I crossed to the window and looked out. The black equine was standing in the moonlit garden below. I felt a surge of joy at the sight of him.

"I'm coming," I sent, and turned from the window to drag on riding boots and a cloak.

This can't be happening, I thought, hurrying down.

"It has happened and anything that has happened can happen again. Life is filled with circlings," Gahltha sent as I mounted. He wheeled to trot down the drive. The air was cold and thin and I shivered.

"Is this real?"

"What is real? You are here and I am here, but we are also far from here. Who knows which existence is more real?"

Which was no sort of answer, but as Gahltha rode gently out of Obernewtyn's gate and along the road with its whispering green sentinels looming blackly above, it did not seem to matter very much. When the trail ran out, he broke into a wild gallop, crossing the long grassy plain like a creature possessed. His tail and mane streamed out behind as we sped through the gap in the foothills and climbed the narrow way into the valley above, and the one above that.

At last we reached the valley that lay at the feet of the highest mountains. Though it was not yet wintertime the ground was hard, and snow lay spattered on the valley floor like ash. The peaks were already white.

We rested by a hot spring and as I sat on a rock, warming myself, Gahltha grazed on the sweet grass that grew about the edge of the simmering water. "I will eat the grass and you will nourish yourself on the mountains," he sent, as if it were no more than biting into an apple.

Giving myself to the dream, I lay my mind wide open, seeking the detachment and clarity the mountains enabled. Their wild beauty always seemed to make a gentle mockery of brief human woes and lives. Had not these jutting bones of the world survived a thousand eons of human life? Could anything I or any human do really matter in the face of that?

But for once, I could not comfort myself and answer no. I had stood in the Earthtemple and I had seen the panels made by Kasanda. In my mind's eye I saw again the smothered and abused earth, the befouled waters and blackened skies. I saw again, the desolation that lay on the other side of the mountains—the endless bleared deadness of the Blacklands—and I knew that even mountains could be killed.

It seemed to me then that I felt the earth's life, the cold sweetness of its breathing winds, the deep beat of its stone heart, and I understood the Sadorians' devotion to the earth. Everything lives, Powyrs had told me, and I realized he was right.

For the first time it seemed to me that I knew the true evil of human wars and their instinct to dominate and oppress and subdue, for hadn't the Beforetimers poisoned great tracts of the earth with the holocaust? And if the Destroyer reached the hellish slumbering weaponmachines first, would not the task be finished for always? If mountains could die, and vast plains, then why not a world? Humans would perish, and perhaps it was no more than they deserved, but so would equines and bears and the brildane. Not a single blade of grass, nor a cat with one eye would survive, if the earth died.

The moon rose, a thin silver sliver now, and shone its eldritch light through a haze of cloud and onto the mountain peaks, silvering their snowy mantles, and transforming them into shimmering ghosts.

I clenched my teeth together.

My resolve, shattered and confused for so long, became, all at once, blessedly clear. When the Agyllians called, I would leave Obernewtyn as I had promised. I would obey the prophecy the birds claimed I had been born to fulfill, and all the strange strandings of fate that sent me here and there seeking signs and ways; I would follow the sinuous, difficult, puzzling manywindings of my quest, whether they led me into the deserts of Sador, or over the vast dark seas or into the very fires of hell—I would complete my quest so that what had been could not come again.

I would walk the dark road to its end and never return, for nothing was too great a price to pay for the earth and all its life. Not love or my own little life.

My quest was greater than fear or love, and it was greater than Obernewtyn and the fate of the Talented Misfits there, and nothing would ever make me question that again.

I slept then, dreamlessly, and when I woke I was in the hard little Earthtemple bed. The terrible draining tide of sorrow that seemed to have defined my whole life had ebbed, along with the fears and murky apprehensions that had haunted me for as long as I could remember.

I felt as clear and light and pure as a glass of sunlit rainwater as the guardian led me through the tunnels to the outside. It was daylight, and as I blinked into the fierce sunlight I felt as if it pierced me and filled me up.

"Elspeth!" Kella cried.

She and Dameon had come to meet me. I let them hold me, but felt a great distance had come between us. I had seen too much and flown too high.

"I am glad you are well," Dameon said gravely.

"The rebels have decided on their rebellion," Kella said, and a shadow passed over her features. "It is to be after wintertime."

I did not want to hear about rebels or rebellions.

"Is Maruman all right?"

Dameon chuckled. "He has made himself at home again on Powyrs' ship. The old man dotes on him."

"Dragon?"

The healer sighed and shook her head. "There is no change in her condition. Maybe when we get back to Obernewtyn..."

I wondered suddenly if I should go back. There was nothing there for me now. I could just as well wait to hear from Atthis in Sador. I shivered, remembering Atthis had said the H'rayka was searching for me, trying to learn what I was doing. I lifted my chin. I would not give into fear.

When we reached the tents, Miryum and the others crowded around to ask questions.

"Where is Rushton?" I asked, noticing abruptly that he was not with them.

A queer silence fell and, in spite of my new detachment, it made me uncomfortable.

"What is the matter?" I looked at Freya but she shook her head and would not meet my eyes.

I turned to Dameon and touched his arm. "Is he ... he is not hurt?"

Kella looked exasperated. "Oh, Elspeth. We lost and Rushton blames himself for our defeat. He has been odd ever since the Battlegames."

"He walks alone and hardly eats," Miryum said. "He refuses to lead us."

"He says that we ought to be led by one of our own kind," Fian added.

I stared at them. "*Our* kind? He is a Misfit, just as we are."

"A Misfit with latent Talent," Freya said, tears standing in her eyes. "He says it is not the same thing."

"We tried to tell him we had all failed, not just him," Milky said despondently.

A queer giddy feeling came over me.

Rushton had said we would learn about ourselves by taking part in the Battlegames and competing with the rebels. Well, we had learned all right. We had learned what it truly cost to be warriors. We had learned that the price was too high.

With a flash of brightness it came to me that this was why the empath's song had possessed such power. The empaths had sung it before, never knowing why the soldier sang. Now they understood. No wonder it had reached even the hardened hearts of warriors, for there was truth in it.

Bram had been right to judge us unfit warriors.

I looked around at the others. At Miryum brooding over our loss of the games; at Fian and Kella grinding leaves for herb paste; at Angina and Miky sitting side by side, practicing a new song. Angina still bore the great bruised lump on his forehead from the Battlegames, but their faces were serene.

I stared wildly about me and the icy wall that had risen around me came crashing down.

Atthis had told me once that I should go to Obernewtyn and aid the Misfits in their struggle because it was worthy. I had gone and I had worked there, but I had always felt myself to be marking time, waiting for my true quest. Now I saw that the two quests were parts of the same quest.

After seeing the carvings in the Earthtemple, I had wondered what point there was in destroying the weaponmachines when humans like Malik and the Herders would only find some other way to cause harm. But the community we had built at Obernewtyn was made up of Talented Misfits, and the Battlegames had taught us decisively that we were not made for war!

So perhaps in a world without threat of extinction from the weapons of the past, Obernewtyn would grow a new breed of humanity that would not take the same terrible path to destruction.

"What is it?" Kella asked, and I realized I had begun to grin like a fool.

I looked around and found they were all watching me. I took a deep breath. Rushton might not love me, but there was far more at stake here than my emotions. There was the future of Obernewtyn, and I understood for the first time that it was as important as my quest to find the weaponmachines, for one without the other was meaningless. I must make Rushton see that losing the Battlegames was the best thing that could have happened to us, because it had showed us our true natures.

XLIV

I *found him sitting on a rock and staring out to sea.*

"You haven't failed us," I said softly. "*We* haven't failed."

He was still for a moment. "Elspeth, I am glad you are well." His voice was dull and he did not turn. I had never heard him sound so defeated.

"Listen to me...."

"I have called myself your leader," he said. "I thought to lead you all to battle because I imagined your powers would fit you better for war; that all you needed was a leader to bind and direct you. But you are not meant for war. I did not see that because *I am not one of you*. I have no power. I failed you because I did not understand the truth of you."

"If there is any fault, it belongs equally to all of us!" I protested.

He shook his head lethargically, but still he would not turn to face me.

"What will happen to you and the others when the Council sends its soldierguards to clear out Obernewtyn, Elspeth? Or when rebels like Malik come to wipe you from the earth? I wanted to protect you."

"Us," I said firmly, gently. "Us."

Rushton shook his head. "I am not one of you. I have wanted to be and I have dreamed of it...but I know now that it will never be."

"Of course you are," I said sharply. "Aren't you descended from Hannah Seraphim? Besides, leadership has nothing to do with your being a Misfit. You began this. You freed us and gave us a place and time to grow."

"But I was wrong...."

"So were we," I cried. "I was the one who wanted to show the rebels our power and our might. If anyone is a fool, it is me. Shall I leap off the ship on the way home in remorse? Or what about Maryon, since she sent you here?"

"I am not one of you," Rushton said more strongly.

"You have Misfit powers. We have used them."

"With help," he said disparagingly.

"You think there is something wrong with needing help?"

"It is a weakness."

"Now you sound like Malik," I said hotly. "And maybe that's the point. Maybe there is a little of Malik in all of us. In spite of what Bram said, I have the feeling we could be like him if we wanted to badly enough. A Malik after all would never need help. Our need for one another is what makes us better than him!"

Now he did turn round. "*You* can say that, you who never needed anyone in your life?"

"No one could say it with greater truth," I said sadly.

"And what happens when you cannot have what you need?" he demanded angrily.

Wondering how the conversation had taken this turn, I said, "Look, I'm trying to tell you that what we learned in the Battlegames was important. We needed to know what we couldn't do, so that we could begin to think of what we can do. Remember, Maryon said this journey over sea had something to do with finding the right road? Can't you see that we've done that?"

He shook his head.

"Remember when Dameon said the trouble with us was that we didn't know what we were? Well, I think we do now."

"Will that knowledge show you how to deal with the soldierguards?" Rushton asked, apathy returning to his tone.

I held onto my temper with difficulty. "It might. Misfits are hated and persecuted because people fear us. The Herder Faction and the Council enhance that fear, just as Angina enhances Miky's songs. Maybe the answer isn't to fight and force and make, but to show. To empathize. To let them understand us so that they will see there is nothing to fear from us. I think we should try to reshape ourselves and our purposes around empathy."

"You are not an empath," Rushton said.

"No, but I can try to understand and care for the unTalents. Any one of us can learn to do that."

Rushton made a choking sound and turned away again. "You do not understand. How could you?"

A spurt of anger made me reach out and pull him back to look at me. "What do you know of how I feel? Do you think I am a machine like the ones the Beforetimers made?"

"I do not know," Rushton said with a sudden fierce bitterness. "I know nothing because you have never let me know. Because I was not like you."

I gaped at him, my anger slipping away. "Not like you? What are you talking about. I have just been telling you..."

"Then why?" he asked softly, a world of pain in his voice. "Why will you never let me come near? Why do you reject me with every look and word if not because...I cannot reach my Talent; because I am not..." His voice faded away.

"But surely Freya..." I said faintly, unable to believe I had I understood what he was saying rightly.

He nodded, misunderstanding. "She has tried to teach me to use my powers and we have had some success, though I don't know how you could know of it—but it is too little when you are...what you are."

I gazed at him, incredulous, my mind rearranging itself like the colors of a kaleidoscope. He thought I did not love him because he could not use his Talent. He and Freya had been trying to reach his powers so that he would be worthy of me! In that moment I saw that if my quest to dismantle the weaponmachines and Obernewtyn's future were bound together, so were Obernewtyn and I bound up as one in Rushton's mind. In feeling he had failed one, he now felt he had failed the other.

But he had failed at neither. And I?

I understood that this was a moment that might never come again. I had learned the hardest way of all, that beauty and happiness, like life, were ephemeral and could no more be saved up for later than a sunbeam could be hoarded. If I would have any life with Rushton, I must take it now, for now was all there ever was.

"What am I, Rushton?"

His eyes flared with a naked longing that seemed to suck the breath out of me.

He stood up suddenly, and I stepped back, almost frightened.

"You are everything," he said roughly, hopelessly. "Freya said to give you time and I tried. But you have gone further and further from me. I have been a fool to imagine that you would ever care for me...." He shook his head and the light faded from his eyes leaving them dull and sad. "I know now that I am no more fit to have you love me, than to lead Obernewtyn."

"You are a fool all right," I said tartly, half laughing.

He frowned at me, and my smile faded at the hurt in his face.

"You are a fool for thinking you failed Obernewtyn, and you will go on leading us as we strive to find some other way to make our place in the world."

He began to shake his head, but I reached out my hand and laid it against his cheek.

He stood very still and I let my hand slide around until my fingers were against his lips.

"I love you, and I have done ever since I saw you at Obernewtyn carrying that silly pig," I said simply, looking steadfastly into his eyes. "I just had to grow up enough not to be frightened of what I felt."

Rushton's face did not change and, for a moment, doubt flickered in me, but then I banished it, for surely nothing required courage so much as love, and I was equal to it.

Swallowing the fears of a lifetime, I reached out my mind, passing the barriers Rushton could not broach, and opened myself to him.

Only then did he move, and faintly, so faintly I could barely catch it, I heard his whisper inside my mind.

"Ravek, my Elspethlove."

Epilogue

Maruman gave me a jaded look. *"And what answer will that be?"*

I leaned on the tower sill and looked out into the first flurry of wintertime snow, pulling my cloak about me.

"I don't know, Maruman. But we have begun to find it, Rushton and I. The guildmerge and beasts. And whatever it is, it will be the right answer because it comes out of us and what we are."

"You will never make the funaga-li accept you," Maruman sent.

"Maybe that's the mistake we've made all along. Trying to make people accept us. I don't think making is going to be part of our answer."

I thought of Brydda. Just before we left Sador, he had come to the ship with Jakoby.

With them had been Miryum's Sadorian suitor leading little Faraf and the giant horse, Zidon, which Malik had ridden. He had gone to the Coercer guilden and held out the lead ropes to her. She had stared up at him suspiciously.

"They are a gift. . . ." Jakoby began.

Miryum interrupted, stilted and awkward. "Well, that's all right then." She took the ropes from the Sadorian's hand.

The man gave her a look of such burning intensity that her polite thanks faded. Then he turned and walked away. Miryum looked even more bewildered.

"They are his bondgift to you," Jakoby had told the astonished coercer then. "That you accepted them means you have accepted him as your ravek. When he is ready, he will come for you. That is the Sadorian way."

Miryum's mouth fell open.

Jakoby turned to Rushton, standing a little behind me.

"I ask a boon of you, Leader of the Misfits."

This was the last thing we had expected.

"What is it?" Rushton asked.

"Bram and I ask that one of your empaths remain in Sador as a guest of the Earthtemple. We would have speech with you, for there is much about your people that intrigues us. That one would be greatly honored and shown things none has seen before who was not of our people."

She and Brydda had withdrawn a little at this, so that we could discuss it among ourselves.

"I will stay," Dameon had said without preamble. "This must be my task, for there has been nothing else for me to do. This must be why I was sent here."

Miky and Angina had chorused horror, offering themselves in his place.

"You don't understand," he said. "I want to stay. I am not sacrificing myself. It is . . . a selfish desire. I can learn much of these people, and perhaps teach them something. They are such a strange mixture of barbaric instincts and true wisdom. There is much in them that calls to me. The very fact that they regard empathy so . . ."

Rushton reached out and gripped his shoulder. "Dameon, I . . . I know why you would remain here."

To my surprise, the empath flushed. "Then you must let me stay."

There was a long moment and I wondered at this strangeness between them. Rushton expelled a breath of air. "Very well. One season. When wintertime is over and the pass is thawed, we will come for you. The two horses will stay here as well for, in any case, they would not like the sea journey."

I shivered. So already there was talk of returning. I seemed to see the ruined face of the overguardian of the Earthtemple.

"When the Seeker returns in search of the fifth sign with one of the Kasanda blood . . ."

"You cannot stay alone," Rushton was saying to Dameon. "Someone must stay with you to be your eyes and guard you."

"I will stay," Fian offered eagerly. "I will protect Dameon with my life and soul. And I can research this region for Garth."

"I can protect him best," Hannay said, flexing his muscles.

There was some more talk and more offers to accompany the Empath guildmaster, but in the end Dameon and Fian stayed because it was felt there would be no need for guards. The Sadorians had too much honor to let anyone harm a guest.

∽

Saying goodbye to Dameon had been harder than I could have imagined. I would have opened my mind and heart to him, but he had set a wall between us. Perhaps, so that he would not be hurt by our sorrow at this parting; perhaps, because he still felt Matthew's loss.

"It will not be the same without you," I had whispered, holding him tightly.

"Ever was Obernewtyn empty when you were not there," he had said. "Yet I survived and you will survive."

"Rushton needs you, especially now."

"He does not need me, especially now," the empath said. "He has what he has long desired."

I felt the blood surge in my face.

He smiled, his blind eyes turned to me. He reached up and touched my hair and face, running his fingers over me lightly. Seeing. I made myself smile so that he would think of me that way. His fingers had reached my lips and seemed to tremble before he took them away.

He had embraced a tearful Miky and a pale Angina then, reminding them that they would rule the Empath guild in his stead.

"Only until you come back," Miky choked.

Dameon kissed her cheek and then farewelled Freya, who had not known him long and yet wept too.

"I am ready now," he said. Smiling farewell, Fian had offered his arm to the empath. As they departed, Rushton put his arm around my shoulders and held me tightly. "He will be well, Elspeth. He . . . he needs to do this. It is but a season."

Then Brydda had come to bid us farewell. "I wish things might have been different."

"Perhaps this is for the best." Rushton clasped the big rebel's wrist.

"I thought an alliance was the answer, but we would want such different things after it was over and we will always be Misfits to them. We must be what we are."

Rushton's eyes had shifted to me fleetingly, and this time I had not flinched from the desire in them. If there was a loss in loving, I was learning that there was a finding in it too.

Brydda had looked from one of us to the other, and then had leaned across to embrace me. "Goodbye, little sad eyes, though they are not so sad now."

"You will always have our friendship, Brydda. No matter what," I said.

He had crushed my hand then. "Friends. Always," he said gruffly. "No matter what."

And so we had gone our separate ways. He to his rebellion, and we, first by sea to Sutrium, only to find that Domick had not yet returned, and then home to Obernewtyn. Where I belonged; where Dragon lay in her endless coma; where Matthew might one day return; my home, which I must someday leave forever to take up the dark burden of my destiny.

"What if the oldOne calls before this answer is found?" Maruman asked. "Will you obey? Will you walk the dark road?"

I shivered as the bitter wind changed direction slightly, pressing its icy fingers through the folds of my cloak. The snow was falling more heavily now, blurring the jagged darkness of the mountains; making them seem far away. "All roads are the one road. I gave my promise," I said soberly. Then I smiled. "But there are five secrets to be uncovered and I must go to Sador, and I must meet a gypsy whose life is bound to mine and who will stand with me in battle. These things will not happen in a moment, and so there is time in the midst of this for me to live.

"Atthis has not summoned me yet and perhaps the call to walk the dark road will not come until I am old and gray. I have promised to go, but I have not sworn to live out my life in the dark shadow of that vow. I have learned that happiness is like the sun. It must be enjoyed when it comes and while it shines."

∽

But Maruman was not listening. He was looking up, searching for the moon's cold face.

Glossary

Beast guild: A Council of animals at Obernewtyn led by the mountain pony, Avra.

Beasting guild: Beastspeaking is the ability in animals to produce an idiosyncratic combination of images, human words and feeling impulses on a level of the mind which may be reached by Talented humans. There is far greater ease of communication between humans and creatures who have lived among them than with wild beasts who have had little contact with humans. Common to all beasts are dialect words which appear to derive from a rich cycle of myths and legends, whose origin is a mystery.

Beasting-guilders possess a particular combination of limited empathy and farseeking Talent, that enables them to receive and project their thoughts in beast-speech. They can also communicate at a basic level with non-beastspeaking animals. Beasts who have developed beastspeaking abilities do not appear to have coercive powers, but many more beasts than humans possess futuretelling ability, though again this is often largely idiosyncratic. The guild charter of the beastspeakers is to promote the harmony and true equality of all creatures. It administers the extensive farms and orchards that produce Obernewtyn's vital wintertime stores.

Coercer guild: Coercing is the ability to enter and manipulate other minds. Coercers use the same root ability to deep probe as many of the other Talents, but it is honed for use as a manipulative tool to alter and control both Talented and unTalented minds. Members tone their bodies and train with weapons, for they regard themselves as the physical protectors of

Obernewtyn. They vigilantly patrol the highlands and the mountain valley, gathering intelligence.

Empath guild: Empathy is the ability to read or project emotions rather than conscious thought. Empath guild-members strive for emotional and ethical harmony. Many use music to enhance their concentration, particularly when projecting emotion.

Farseekers guild: Farseeking is the power to communicate mind to mind, even over long distances. The prime charter of this guild is to find and organize rescues of other Talented Misfits.

Futuretellers guild: Again using the root ability to deep probe, futuretellers turn their powers on themselves, sinking into their own minds so deeply in their search for self-knowledge that at the deepest level where all minds merge, and close to mind death, they are able to see fragments of the future. Any tedious or monotonous job is welcomed by them, because it aids the continuation of their inner cogitations. They manage the household at Obernewtyn.

Guildmerge: The decision-making body made up of guildmaster or guildmistress, guilden and ward of all guilds at Obernewtyn, and chaired by Rushton Seraphim, Master of Obernewtyn.

Healerguild: Healers use the ability to deep probe, shaping it into thin tendrils which are used as conduits into the molecules of mind or body to repair and heal. Deep probing is the ability to go beneath the conscious levels of the mind, and healers are also able to use it in reverse, to siphon off pain and heal it within their own bodies. Their charter forbids the opposing of nature. They are skilled in the use of herb lore.

Teknoguild: The Teknoguilders are the researchers and chroniclers of the Misfit community. Members of this guild have slight psychokinetic powers allied with a machine empathy, which enables them to manipulate the workings of the forbidden machines of the Beforetime without understanding the technology that produced them.